THE SWORD
THE STAR

THE SWORD & THE STAR

TEMPLE MOUNT

Daymon Andrews

TATE PUBLISHING & *Enterprises*

Published by Tate Publishing & Enterprises, LLC
127 E. Trade Center Terrace | Mustang, Oklahoma 73064 USA
1.888.361.9473 | www.tatepublishing.com

Tate Publishing is committed to excellence in the publishing industry. The company reflects the philosophy established by the founders, based on Psalms 68:11,
"The Lord gave the word and great was the company of those who published it."

Book design copyright © 2007 by Tate Publishing, LLC. All rights reserved.
Cover design by Jennifer L. Fisher
Interior design by Lynly D. Taylor

Published in the United States of America

ISBN: 978-1-6024729-7-6

1.Fiction: Political   2. Espionage and Intrigue

08.02.25

This book is dedicated to my lovely wife who has believed and supported me throughout this endeavor. I couldn't have done this without you. To family and friends who have been there for numerous readings and consultations, I thank you. I also want to extend my sincere thanks to my friends at Tate Publishing. Without your help this dream would not have been realized. Most importantly, I want to thank my Father in Heaven for helping me find my purpose in life.

AAA Anti-Aircraft Artillery
AEW Airborne Early Warning
AMRAAM Advanced Medium Range Air-to-Air Missile, aka AIM-120
APC Armored Personnel Carrier
AWACS Airborne Warning and Control System
CAG Commander Air Group
CAP Combat Air Patrol
CDC Combat Direction Center
CENTCOM Central Command
CFFC Commander, Fleet Forces Command
CIA Central Intelligence Agency
CIWS Close-In Weapon System a.k.a "sea whiz"
COG Continuity of Government
CONUS Continental United States
CSG Carrier Strike Group
DMZ Demilitarized Zone
DNIS Department of National Intelligence and Security
DOW Dow Jones Industrial Average
ECM European Common Market; also Electronic Counter Measures
EU European Union
FLIR Forward Looking Infrared
GDP Gross Domestic Product
GPS Global Positioning System
HARM High Speed Anti-Radiation Missile
HOTAS Hands-On Throttle and Stick
IAF Israel Air Force
ICBM Intercontinental Ballistic Missile
IDF Israel Defense Force
IFDL Inter/Intra-Flight Data Link
JDAM Joint Direct Attack Munition
LZ Landing Zone
MEU Marine Expeditionary Unit
MIRV Multiple Independently targetable Re-entry Vehicle

NATO	North Atlantic Treaty Organization
NORAD	North American Aerospace Defense Command
PLO	Palestine Liberation Organization
PPBL	Price per Barrel of Oil
SAM	Surface-to-Air Missile
SATCOM	Satellite Communication
SIGINT	Signal Intelligence
SIOP	Single Integrated Operational Plan
SLBM	Submarine Launched Ballistic Missile
SSBN	Ballistic Missile Submarine-Nuclear Powered
UN	United Nations
VIP	Very Important Person
V/STOL	Vertical/Short Take Off/Landing
WMD	Weapons of Mass Destruction
XO	Executive Officer

...To those neighbors and allies who share our freedom, we will strengthen our historic ties and assure them of our support and firm commitment. We will match loyalty with loyalty. We will strive for mutually beneficial relations. We will not use our friendship to impose on their sovereignty, for our own sovereignty is not for sale.

As for the enemies of freedom, those who are potential adversaries, they will be reminded that peace is the highest aspiration of the American people. We will negotiate for it, sacrifice for it; we will not surrender for it, now or ever.

Our forbearance should never be misunderstood. Our reluctance for conflict should not be misjudged as a failure of will. When action is required to preserve our national security, we will act. We will maintain sufficient strength to prevail if need be, knowing that if we do so we have the best chance of never having to use that strength.

Above all, we must realize that no arsenal or no weapon in the arsenals of the world is so formidable as the will and moral courage of free men and women. It is a weapon our adversaries in today's world do not have. It is a weapon that we as Americans do have. Let that be understood by those who practice terrorism and prey upon their neighbors...

Ronald Reagan, 1st Inaugural Address, 1981

THE FUTURE IS NOW

HOTEL INTERNATIONAL

BERLIN, GERMANY

November 20th

8:38 a.m.

The black S600 Mercedes parked at the entrance of the grand old hotel. The Hotel International was one of Berlin's most luxurious. Renovated after the fall of the Berlin Wall, it had become the lodging of choice for the discerning business traveler. The hotel boasted of every conceivable amenity one could need. However, it was not the award-winning culinary skills of the chef in the restaurant *Das Speciale* or the luxurious services offered by the Mediterranean spa the visitor was in need of. No, it was none of the physical amenities the hotel offered this visitor needed, but one that was esoteric in nature. On this particular visit it was discretion; the need for privacy in certain matters. This resulted in a capable staff that understood the needs of the guests of the hotel. It was for this reason the Hotel International had been selected for their meeting. They entered the lobby bypassing the usual check-in required of other guests. His advance team had already paid for the room and secured the keys. In fact, each suite on the floor where his room was located had been secured, albeit all under separate names.

Much of what he did was for image. One aspect of that image was that of a ladies' man. The brunette that was on his arm was to further enhance this reputation. She would also act as a cover for his being there at this time of the day. He was not concerned about public scrutiny of his private life regarding the pending election. Europeans did not hold their elected officials to the degree of scrutiny their American counterparts did. Affairs were common among the ruling class in Europe and had always been so.

Why the Americans held their elected officials, especially their President, accountable to such antiquated Puritan ideals he would never know. Her leopard print dress, with a slit starting from just below the hip, was a perfect compliment to her brunette hair. Sunglasses hid her ebony eyes from prying eyes. She leaned over and gave him a deep kiss as they crossed the lobby toward the waiting elevator. The heads that turned to see the couple did not give any indication of approval or disapproval. Some thought they recognized the man but they were unsure as he was wearing sunglasses. As the couple entered the elevator it was clear to everyone in the lobby this was not the usual business trip.

The elevator stopped at the top floor where the suites were located. An exchange of euros along with a good-bye kiss signaled that her job had been well completed. This was the easiest money she would earn all month and without having to actually work. She was a little disappointed though. *It would have been fun*, she thought. After all, he was a striking man. Beneath his snow-white hair were two piercing blue eyes and a radiant smile that conveyed warmth and understanding. Not the typical lonely businessman, and she had known many, passing through who required her services. No, he knew what he wanted. She could tell by his movements. Every action he took indicated purpose. He bid her farewell as she made her way to the suite he had rented for their rendezvous. He told her an account had been set up with enough euros for dinner and breakfast. Just because the suite would not be used for the original purpose there was no reason she should not avail herself to the amenities of the hotel he had told her.

As he watched her walk down the deserted hallway he wondered if he should not allow himself this pleasure. If all went well, he would not have time for such distractions in the future. No, it was time for business he reminded himself. Plus, his host would not appreciate being delayed for this reason. He proceeded to suite 903 where his contact awaited him. The meeting, if all went according to plan, would usher in a new age of world politics and would shift the global balance of power. Approaching the suite, he noticed two men on either side of the door as previously arranged. On the left was one of his bodyguards and on the right the bodyguard of his host. His man opened the door for him. Entering the room he found the lights low and the curtains drawn. The smell of

French Roast coffee wafted in the room. Seeing no one he took a few steps further into the room. Off to the right in the master bedroom of the suite he heard a voice. One individual was kneeling on the floor facing toward the window. It was early morning and the rising sun was peaking through the curtains though they were drawn. Gerhard moved away from the door and waited quietly for the old man to finish. After a few moments the man completed his activity and moved to the great room where his guest was awaiting him.

"I am honored for your time," the older man said as he bowed slightly toward Gerhard.

"No, the honor is mine. I am thankful you were able to meet with me. Please forgive my intrusion. I was not aware you were occupied," replied Gerhard. His guest returned the bow and stretched out his hand. They shook hands, each testing the other man's grip for a moment before relaxing. No need to end the meeting before it began. The true test of strength would come later.

"Please, let us make ourselves comfortable," said Gerhard's host as he gestured to the pillows arranged on the floor. "Perhaps some coffee?" he offered Gerhard as he poured himself a cup.

"Yes, thank you."

He filled another cup and handed it to Gerhard. Gerhard took a small sip of the hot liquid as he waited for his host to join him. The flavor was excellent. His host joined him on the pillows sitting across from him.

"We have much to discuss. I have done as you requested. Our people will support you in your elections this week. Are you prepared to support us in our cause?"

"Yes. There are many who feel as you and I that we have a common enemy who needs to be eliminated," Gerhard observed taking another drink of the coffee.

"They have powerful friends in the world. One in particular," the other man noted.

"They do. But we can control them. They will be isolated. You will find the elections will bear this out. But are your people prepared to make the sacrifices necessary? More will be asked of them than has ever been before or will again."

"They will be ready. Allah will speak to them and they will listen," he said with a nod of his head.

"Good then. We understand each other. We will continue contact through our usual channels. I will contact you when all has been readied," Gerhard concluded.

Their business being concluded, he rose and turned to the door, and knocked once. The door opened and he exited. As he was leaving he glanced at his assistant. The man understood. He reached into his jacket and pulled the integrally suppressed HK 9mm from his shoulder holster as he made his way to the suite where the brunette was. There would be no eyewitnesses to place him on this particular floor at this time of the day.

FLIGHT OF THE SURGEON

AMIR AIR BASE

NEGEV DESERT

November 30th

4:37 p.m.

D arkness was beginning to overcome the daylight again as it had been doing for thousands of years. The deep orange of the setting sun would soon surrender to the stars and moonlight. However, if the weather forecasters were correct there would be neither stars nor moonlight at takeoff. Colonel Sharon Goldman had just stepped out of flight control as his aide pulled the Humvee to a stop.

"Good evening, Colonel," said Corporal Joseph Zimmerman as he snapped a sharp salute.

"Good evening, Joseph," replied the Colonel returning the salute. "To the flight line."

Colonel Goldman took his seat in the back and began to review his notes again as the Humvee pulled away. He noted the corporal did not bother with the usual banter this evening. One could sense a change in the mood of the base. There was something different about tonight. Everyone seemed to be sharper. Even the cooks in the mess hall had served up their best meal in weeks. There was something different about the real thing that all of the simulations you ran could not duplicate. His American friends called this change in mind set *Game Day*. This was good. His men were ready.

Approaching the flight line, Goldman could see the thirty F-22C(I)s of Zero Squadron lined up in their hardened concrete revetments. Their crews were swarming around them making final preparations for the pending mission. The Lockheed Martin F-22C was the latest evolution in fighter plane technology and was the preeminent air superiority fighter in the world. The Americans had initially been reluctant to authorize their sale but strong lobbying of selected U.S. Congressmen provided the key votes needed to approve the sale. The F-22C(I) was a further development of the F-22A Raptor. The "I" stood for the export version to Israel. The C model's combat radius had been improved sufficiently enough to reach targets twelve hundred miles away.

Two GBU-32 GPS guided bombs, each fitted with the Boosted Unitary Penetrator warhead, would be the primary weapon. This weapon's ability to penetrate hardened structures or those buried underground at depths of more than six feet made it the prime choice for this mission. The GPS targeting system would allow the bombs to strike within three meters of the selected target enabling its one thousand pound warhead sufficient accuracy to wreak havoc on any target. Twelve planes would each carry two of these deadly and accurate weapons. Their primary mission would be to destroy the nuclear reactors at Esfahan and Natanz. The remaining planes would carry the AGM-154A, which would be armed with the CBU-87B Combined Effects Munitions. This weapon would inflict maximum damage upon buildings and other soft targets by detonating munitions over a wide area.

The initial scenario called for a strike by F-15Is and F-16Is. To stand a reasonable chance of success these planes would have required radar suppression assets as well as multiple refuelings. It was estimated that less than half of the aircraft employed would survive the mission. There had been much debate as to whether Israel could afford to lose half, or possibly more, of these aircraft and be in a position to respond to the expected counterattack.

The acquisition of the Raptor had changed all that. The greatest asset the Raptor added to the battlefield was its unique stealth characteristics. The radar cross section of this plane was reported to be that of a bee or a very small bird. In other words, it would be practically invisible to all known types of radar. Not only was it virtually undetectable to radar, but its detectability in the infrared spectrum was minimal as well. In essence, the plane was invisible to almost all man-made detection systems except the naked eye. And by flying at night, even that remote chance of detection was nullified for all practical purposes.

The pilots were conducting their final walk around: kicking tires, checking the weapons load out and running their hands along the skin of the plane. It was almost as if they were doing final grooming before a night on the town. Everything had to be in perfect order. There would be no second chances. And to the credit of the ground crews all was perfect.

The ground crews were nothing short of perfection. Goldman had handpicked each man for this assignment. They were the best his country could offer, as were the pilots. They had been on the flight line since 0600 checking and double-checking the systems and engines on each plane. Nothing was left to chance. Each man took special pride in his duties knowing that the slightest omission or error could cost a pilot his life.

The pilots returned this respect. While they had been sleeping during the day and had later enjoyed a sumptuous meal, their ground crews had been servicing their planes. As a small way of repayment, the aircrews had pooled their pay and had purchased dinner for the ground crews at their favorite restaurant. It was being delivered for their enjoyment after the planes departed. Such was the bond that was forged between men facing combat and potential death.

Possible scenarios were racing through Goldman's mind as he contemplated the mission ahead of him and his squadron. They had been practicing and running simulations for four months. Every detail of the mission had been committed to memory, but it was the unknown variables that troubled him. Had the Raptor's stealth capabilities been compromised? Would the Iranians be able to mount an effective response to the attack? What if there had been a leak in their security measures and they were flying into a trap? He had to dismiss those thoughts as his mind turned back to the mission.

The refueling would be the trickiest aspect of the mission as this called for a rendezvous over the ocean at night. For this purpose they had been practicing refueling over the Mediterranean and Red Sea.

This was to be the deepest strike carried out away from Israel since the raid on PLO headquarters in Tunisia in 1985. Yet, the plan was fairly straightforward. The squadron would depart Amir, then dash down the Red Sea and cross over into Saudi air space south of Medina. Flying below radar contact, the squadron would cross the largely uninhabited peninsula and exit off the coast of Oman. At the designated coordinates over the Arabian Sea they would rendezvous with the recently acquired

KC-10 tanker/transport planes from the United States. Upon refueling they would drop to attack altitude of one hundred feet and proceed to their targets: the Iranian nuclear facilities at Esfahan, Arak, and Natanz. Esfahan was the most crucial target as intelligence indicated it was the primary location of Iran's nuclear weapons program.

Upon destruction of the targets, the squadron would turn to a southeasterly course that would carry them to the Arabian Sea off the coast of Oman. At the designated coordinates they would rendezvous with the second flight of KC-10 tanker/transport planes. Once refueling was completed they would return to Israel by again flying over Oman and then into Saudi airspace. Crossing the great desert in the southern part of the peninsula, they would exit Saudi air space three hundred miles south of Mecca and fly the remainder of the way back to Israel in international airspace over the Red Sea. It was felt this course diversion was needed to avoid the expected response by the Iranian Air Force. Once the attack had occurred, the planners anticipated Iran would marshal its aircraft and air defenses in the western part of the country in an attempt to shoot down the returning Israelis. It was estimated the entire mission would take ten hours if all went according to plan.

In 2008, the Iranians had agreed to halt research on their nuclear weapons program. International Atomic Energy Inspectors had been allowed on the premises and were convinced all research had been terminated. Six years later, a new wave of Islamic Fundamentalism swept Iran as it had all of the Middle East save Iraq, Saudi Arabia, Kuwait, and the Gulf States. A constant theme of the Fundamentalists called for the destruction of Israel and her ally the Great Satan: the United States.

The Mossad had obtained hard intelligence that research was to be restarted at Esfahan along with Iran's other nuclear facilities in the next two months. High-level meetings were held within the Israeli government to discuss the possibility of destroying Iran's nuclear program, as Israel had done in 1981 during OPERATION OPERA, when she destroyed Iraq's Osiarq nuclear facility. The difference then was that the other Arab countries feared a nuclear-armed Saddam and had turned a blind eye to Israel's action. After the raid, the usual condemnations were made from her neighboring Arab states. However, what was not known was that Saudi AWACS, staffed with American and Saudi crewmembers, had detected the attack but chose not to disclose any details. Saudi officials, along with those of the Gulf States, did not want a nuclear-armed

Saddam. They secretly feared his overall intentions in the Mideast and did not want him to become too powerful. It indeed was a rare moment in Middle East relations when Jew and Arab cooperated, albeit unknown, for the benefit of all.

As Colonel Goldman exited the Humvee, his aide leaned out of the window.

"Good luck tonight, sir. May Jehovah bless you on this mission. All of Israel would be praying if they knew."

"Thank you, Joseph," replied the Colonel. He was not a particularly religious man. His faith was in the *Hayl Ha'avir*—the Israeli Air Force. "We will need every advantage we can have."

No need to offend the young man's beliefs. Besides, he had seen things in Israel's history that logic could not explain. Maybe higher forces were indeed at work.

As he walked toward the flight line, one of his senior pilots, Lt. Caleb Solomon, called out, "ten, hut." Both air and ground crews quickly fell into formation and awaited their final instructions. Goldman stood before his men for a moment before beginning his briefing. He looked at the face of each man and liked what he saw.

"Gentlemen, I want to congratulate you on the training and prepara-tion for this mission. You were selected because you are the best Israel has to offer...the best the *Hayl Ha'avir* has to offer. There are no other pilots or crews in the world today that compare to your excellence. As our fathers did in 1981 against Iraq's Osiraq facility, we shall tonight do to Iran's nuclear program. The Mossad informs us they are preparing to reactivate their nuclear program if they have not already. Well, tonight we are going to deactivate it," he said to the nodding faces lined up before him.

"Our mission tonight is straightforward. This strike will be a signal to the Fundamentalists that Israel will not tolerate nuclear weapons that would one day be used against our cities...our homes...our families."

He watched the faces of the men as these last words sunk in before he continued. He could see the backs stiffen and hands clinch in the crews. This was good. Most of the men had wives and children. Each had family that had been lost in combat for Israel. It was this motiva-tion he was addressing—the almost primal instinct in a man to defend his family without regard for his own safety. He knew men had accom-plished the unbelievable because of this instinct during the Yom Kippur

War when Israel's right to exist was threatened. He believed it was what willed those pilots to fly seven, sometimes ten missions a day. The Arab pilots managed at best three flights a day. Due to the number of sorties the IAF was able to fly, the tide of battle slowly, methodically, turned to Israel's favor causing what appeared to be apparent defeat to be turned into surprising victory. He knew his men were ready.

"Gentlemen, man your planes and may Jehovah bless you." *The blessing couldn't hurt*, he thought.

He climbed the steps to his plane as he had done on hundreds of prior sorties. Settling into the cockpit, he adjusted his helmet and fastened his safety harness. He began the usual series of final checks before starting the engines. Looking outside of the cockpit he could see the other pilots performing the same tasks. Satisfied all systems were functioning he started the engines. He felt a familiar rumble as the Pratt and Whitney 119–100 engines ignited to life.

"Tower to Surgeon leader. Updated weather for takeoff. Winds from the southwest at five knots. Ceiling at twenty-eight hundred meters. Visibility six kilometers. Clear for takeoff at your discretion on runway eleven-niner."

"Copy that tower," replied Surgeon leader.

"Surgeon leader to surgeons. Prepare for taxi and takeoff. Follow my lead. Out," ordered Goldman.

A round of "yes, sirs" crackled through his headset. He eased the throttle forward and felt the instant response from his plane as he began to taxi to the runway.

"Surgeon leader to tower. Commencing takeoff. Leader to surgeons. Here we go."

With that he pushed the throttle forward and felt the plane lurch forward as it quickly accelerated to speed. At one hundred seventy knots, he pulled the throttle back and felt the plane practically leap off the runway. He had once again achieved mankind's oldest dream: the ability to soar above the earth. A quick scan of his radar indicated that all of his surgeons were airborne as well. Communication would be handled through the Inter/Intra Flight Data Link. This piece of technology on board the Raptor allowed each member of the flight to "see" what his fellow pilots saw on their cockpit display. In essence, they would be communicating without using their radios, further minimizing their chance of detection. He set the altitude at thirty-one meters and eased back off the throttle.

This would be a long flight and fuel economy would be paramount even with the super cruise capability of the Raptor.

As he looked up through the canopy he only saw the darkness of the night. He was glad he could not pick out the individual constellations. Every extra bit of cover was a blessing. Had they been visible he would have been able to navigate using the constellations. He had learned this basic navigation skill as a boy from his father by looking at the stars as they fished in the Red Sea. His father always told him they would lead him to wherever he wanted to go. He hoped these skills would not be needed tonight.

Looking down he saw the darkness of the Red Sea. They were flying outside of the normal shipping channels and were low enough to avoid any ship's radar. The whole success of this mission lay in the element of surprise. He was not worried about detection by a ship but why take chances. Only the sound of their engines disturbed the night air and that he could not help.

Back at Amir, Lt. General Kohn, Commander of the IAF, was following the plot of the mission on the tracking board. He checked his watch again.

"General, they should be crossing over into Saudi airspace now. No AWAC activity is being detected in the Persian Gulf area or over the Kingdom. Unless the Saudis have moved additional radar assets into the desert they should be clear."

"Thank you, Colonel Epstein," Lt. General Kohn said as he sipped on his coffee. "We shall see if the Raptors are as stealthy to Saudi radar as we hope. Time to refuel?"

"Two hours, sir. The tankers, code named Capable, left on schedule. So far so good. The Raptors will be practically invisible to Arab radar unless they've made a substantial breakthrough we're unaware of. I seriously doubt their radar is better than ours. Even we couldn't detect any of the squadron on their training flights," Epstein said with a hint of confidence in his voice.

The two KC-10s were on flights to India to deliver earthquake relief supplies to the largest democracy in the world. It was fortuitous that a 7.8 earthquake had struck along the border of India and Pakistan two days earlier destroying several towns. The Israeli government felt it would be good public relations to extend their assistance to these countries in their time of need. It also provided the perfect cover for the tankers to be in the air. A second flight of two additional KC-10s was scheduled to leave Israel for India in time to rendezvous with the squadron on their return flight.

Colonel Goldman checked his instruments. They were now two hundred miles off the coast of Oman over the Indian Ocean and climbing to seventy six hundred meters. These coordinates had been chosen to avoid the international air routes. His navigation had been perfect. They were at the exact rendezvous coordinates. He hoped the navigation of the tankers was equally as good. His radar alert began chirping in his ear. Contacts were approaching from the east and northeast. The sound of birds soon filled his ears as the pre-arranged signal was broadcast from the tankers.

"Surgeon, this is Capable One. Your men ready? Over."

"Capable One, this is Surgeon. We have some thirsty birds. Ready to receive fuel."

He could make out the silhouettes of the KC-10s in the night sky and began to maneuver his plane into position for refueling. Three other planes of his flight were beginning the refueling process. After forty minutes all planes were refueled.

"Capable One. Drinks on us when we return. Surgeon out."

"Copy, Surgeon. May Jehovah bless you tonight. For Israel!" Goldman descended to ninety meters and turned his plane on a northwesterly course toward the Iranian coastline.

Goldman checked the IFDL for the status of the squadron's weapons. Two hours to weapons release and all reported weapons ready. They had so far been able to avoid the main shipping and air lanes, but it was not going to be possible to do so on this leg of the mission. The Gulf of Oman was one of the busiest waterways in the world. Every day hundreds of tankers, freighters, and fishing boats plied their way in and out of the Persian Gulf. He would actually feel safer once they entered Iranian airspace. Their course had been plotted to avoid the five Iranian air bases in the southeastern part of the country. Intelligence had detected a pattern to the Iranian's air patrols. If the Iranians followed their usual routine, and most militaries did, Goldman and his squadron would catch them at the moment they were standing down for a shift change. Iran's Air Force would be on the ground when Zero Squadron entered Iranian airspace.

"Colonel Epstein, was the refueling successful?" inquired Kohn.

"Affirmative, sir. Word is that all came off without a hitch. Second flight of tankers is on goal to rendezvous with Surgeon on their return. Surgeon should be here," as he indicated on the tracking board, "assuming no headwinds, navigation errors, etc. They are within one hour of weapons release."

"Colonel, I am not sure which is the greater strain. Waiting here and tracking the mission over which we have no control, or being in the cockpit where you have every bit of control. This reminds me of when my Julia delivered our first child. Nothing I could do but wait. They wouldn't let you in the delivery room back then like they do now. How I wish I could have been there."

"I understand, sir. The greatest thrill of my life was being there when my Daniel was born. My relatives did not think I had the stomach for it. As I told them, I was there when he was conceived and I would be there when he arrived."

Both men grinned at the implied innuendo, as did the others in the control room within earshot. They were not surprised to hear their commanders speak in this manner. They knew they were strong family men and felt the pride of having fathered children. They also knew they cared immensely for the aircrews now flying over Iranian airspace.

"All right, everyone listen up," Kohn said as he addressed the control room. "Surgeon is fast approaching weapons release. To the best of our knowledge they have not been detected. It appears we have achieved strategic surprise. Our recon satellite, as well as everyone else's, will be able to detect the detonations. Fifty thousand pounds of ordnance simultaneously exploding will resemble a tactical nuclear warhead's signature. Communications, I want you to be monitoring the news channels in Europe and the United States. *Al-Jazeera* will probably be the first to report. Lt. Greene, is satellite link secure?"

"Yes, sir. Our recon satellite is scheduled to pass over Iran fifteen minutes after Surgeon's strike. We should have a nice picture. No cloud cover over the target tonight."

"Very good. All we can do now is wait," Kohn said as he reached for his coffee. It had been a long night.

"Surgeons, Surgeon leader. Check weapons and prepare for release. Assume attack coordinates." So far everything had gone according to plan. His section of the squadron was detailed to strike Esfahan. The two other sections had altered their course and speed to place them on station for the strikes on Arak and Natanz. The plan called for simultaneous weapons release by all three sections of the squadron. Goldman checked his radar again. No sign of the Iranian Air Force though their 8th Tactical Air Base was in the vicinity. The F-14B Tomcats based there were not airborne. Iranian radar had not detected them. The stealth characteristics of the Raptor were as good as advertised. They had achieved strategic surprise. The Iranians would never know what hit them and if they did it was too late for them to react.

Out of his cockpit glass he could see Esfahan looming in the distance. The cloud cover had cleared and the facility was bathed in the light of a full moon. Of course, he realized his plane was too. The HUD display indicated he was within twenty miles of the target and fast approaching the range of his weapon. He climbed to altitude to release the weapon. Using the HOTAS to bring up the weapons loadout, he selected the GBU-32. He then ordered the squadron to release weapons and execute evasive maneuvers via the IFDL.

Fifteen miles from the target he pressed the firing button on the joystick twice and felt the plane rise, as it suddenly became two thousand pounds lighter. His radar indicated the GBU-32s were tracking toward the target. The GPS system would guide the bombs the rest of the way.

He banked his plane to the left and set his course on the egress route. All pilots had reported weapons release and were executing their turns. They would still be in Iranian airspace when the weapons struck the nuclear facilities at Esfahan and the other two targets. If the pre-flight intelligence was correct the Iranian planes would not rise fast enough for interception. In the event it was not correct, each plane carried two AIM-120 missiles for defense. He checked his radar again for enemy contacts and saw none.

The two GBU-32 bombs from Goldman's plane were gliding toward their target from their launch altitude of six thousand meters. This would enable them to strike from the top and burrow into the target prior to detonation causing greater damage. Inside the JDAM guidance system a tiny brain was receiving course corrections from GPS satellites orbiting the earth. As the bombs were released from the Raptors they were immediately detected by the Russian supplied Raduga radars guarding the facility. Alarm claxons instantaneously sounded throughout the facility. Weapon control officers stirred in their chairs struggling to make sense of the blips moving rapidly across their radar screens.

"All units fire! Do you have missile lock yet?" asked the Colonel in charge of air defense.

"No, sir," replied the enlisted man. "There is nothing for the missiles to lock onto. Radar is not detecting anything!"

"That can't be," screamed the Colonel as the blips on the radar continued their approach.

Air raid drills had been conducted on a regular basis, but the surprise of the real thing was overwhelming to the men, as it was to most soldiers who have never experienced combat. One AAA battery was able to fire off an initial salvo but to no effect. At the airbase, Iranian pilots were scrambling to their awaiting planes but to no avail as the intruders were now one hundred miles away. The Colonel in charge had already sent the code red warning to headquarters alerting them of the raid. He now stared angrily at the seemingly useless radar-tracking screen as he attempted to ascertain the direction of the retreating intruders. All it displayed were the incoming tracks of what he knew to be missiles. The absence of any outbound tracks mockingly stared back at him.

Each missile obediently followed its programming. The primary targets at Esfahan were the three reactors, the Fuel Manufacturing Plant, and the Uranium Conversion Facility. The first GBU-32 targeted the structure housing the Heavy Water Zero Power reactor. Despite the hardened concrete and steel shell designed to protect the reactor, the BUP warhead penetrated the structure and erupted in a spectacular fireball. This was followed by two additional GBU-32s, effectively destroying the reactor. Six missiles struck the Light Water and Miniature Neutron Source Reactors with similar results. Two additional missiles zeroed in on the Uranium Conversion Facility. Two AGM-154A missiles armed with the CBU-87B were targeted for an area of housing suspected to be used by Iran's leading nuclear scientists.

The remaining AGM-154A missiles were targeted on the research and control facilities. As these weapons detonated, secondary explosions were ignited causing further destruction of the facility. Similar results were occurring at Arak and Natanz as the other two sections of the squadron were making their attack runs. As soon as it began it was over. In less than two minutes, over fifty thousand pounds of ordnance had reduced three of Iran's principal nuclear research facilities to fiery ruins.

Amir Air Base

Inside the control room Lt. General Kohn and his staff huddled anxiously around the satellite desk. They were rewarded with a thermal image indicating a large blast had occurred in the Esfahan region. Additional images were being received indicating explosions at Arak and Natanz. The room erupted in cheers at the prospect of having destroyed Iran's primary nuclear facility along with two other facilities. They continued to study the images for another twenty minutes when the officer manning the communication desk signaled.

"General, *BBC* is reporting a large explosion has occurred near the nuclear facility at Esfahan. They're reporting the explosion may have occurred from an accident at the facility. *Fox* and *CNN* are not confirming this. Nothing from *Al-Jazeera* yet. Nothing on Arak or Natanz."

"Word is out, sir. That place is going to be the biggest news story of the decade. I wonder how our men are?" Colonel Epstein said to Lt. General Kohn.

"We will find out shortly. Meanwhile, contact the Prime Minister. He'll want to inform the Cabinet." Lt. General Kohn headed to his office to make his initial report to the Prime Minister. He would perform a more detailed briefing once the crews returned and additional images from the satellites were available. He was relieved the target had been hit, but his worries now turned to his aircrews. What was the reaction of the Iranian Air Force? Had there been any casualties? How he wished he were in the cockpit.

Surgeon Flight

The return flight was proceeding to plan. They had departed Iranian airspace undetected and had refueled for the flight home. The squadron was now over the Red Sea on course for Israel. Colonel Goldman was reviewing the mission in his head. Everything had worked according to plan. He would have to brief the General Staff and Cabinet on this raid.

A red indicator light on his left engine was about the only thing that had not gone according to plan. The engine was overheating slightly but was nothing to worry about.

"Surgeon leader to Operating Room…making final approach. Requesting clearance for landing. We have some folks who are ready to be back on mother terra."

"Surgeon leader, you are cleared for landing. Welcome home. Jehovah has blessed you tonight. All of Israel rejoices with you."

Yes He has thought Colonel Goldman. *He has blessed all of Israel.* A great terror had been removed from his country. The runway lights were now visible in the distance. Lowering the landing gear and flaps he eased the stick downward as he began his descent. It would not take long as they were flying at ninety meters. The runway was fast approaching. Another adjustment of the flaps and he was down.

The wheels screeched with a puff of blue smoke as the rubber made contact with the runway. As his speed slowed, Goldman taxied his plane toward the hangers. He could see the ground crews running toward the planes. They knew there had been success, but they did not know to what degree. Their main concern was that all thirty planes had returned safely. As his plane rolled to a stop, Goldman raised the cockpit and lifted his arms in victory in spite of his fatigue. A Humvee with general's markings was approaching the flight line. Lt. General Kohn stepped out of the vehicle when it stopped.

"Colonel, you and your men are to be congratulated! Preliminary intelligence indicates all targets were effectively destroyed. Here is a picture of your handiwork tonight," he said handing him the satellite photos of the destroyed facilities. "The nuclear threat from Iran is neutralized for now. Reports from the international media are attributing the explosion at Esfahan to a malfunction at the reactor for now. We do not think that will last for long though. A well executed mission. You and your men go get something to eat. We will debrief in one hour."

"Yes, sir, and thank you. We were successful tonight and have bought ourselves time. But, General, will we ever see peace in this region?"

"Probably not in our lifetime, Colonel. Let's get you and your men to the mess-hall."

Ein Volk, Ein Kontinent, Ein Euro!

Paris, EU

December 1st

10:30 a.m.

The cheer of the crowds was exhilarating...almost like a narcotic. Hans Gerhard, newly elected President of the European Union, was completing his tour of the European province of what was formerly the free and sovereign state of France. Throngs of people were lining the streets of Paris in hopes of gaining a glimpse of Gerhard as his motorcade made its way through the historic city.

France, along with twenty-one other nations (Germany, Italy, Denmark, Belgium, Luxembourg, Spain, Portugal, Greece, Great Britain, Ireland, Finland, Austria, The Netherlands, Sweden, Malta, Poland, Czech Republic, Estonia, Cyprus, Latvia, and Lithuania) had forsaken their national sovereignty for the unity, economic benefits, and security of the new European Union. Twenty-two countries, now recognized as provinces without borders and with one official currency and language. Ironically, it had been agreed that English would be the language as the majority of the population spoke English as a second language. Twenty-two countries, whose economic and military might as individual sovereign states were inconsequential in world affairs, but as united provinces now reached the status of superpower.

Yes, Gerhard knew there had been previous attempts to unify Europe in the past. Many would-be rulers had tried and failed in this daunting task. But these had been attempted by the sword. As his motorcade passed by the Arc d' Triumph he was reminded that Napoleon was one of the first to try and subdue Europe. However, his armies were ground down on the Russian steppes in the brutally cold Russian winter. He was finally defeated by the British at Waterloo ending his challenge for domination of the continent.

Hitler was the next to attempt the feat. He came the closest to conquering all of Europe through the Third Reich. Hitler proclaimed The Third Reich would last a thousand years. But Hitler was ultimately defeated in the twelfth year of his quest. The flag of the Third Reich had flown atop the Arc for four years before Paris was liberated by the victorious Allies. Gerhard knew the Americans had primarily been responsible for the liberation. Some American politicians had used this point to remind the French on more than one occasion of their defeat in the Second World War, and as such, an obligation to support American foreign policy. Needless to say, it was a point that all Frenchmen cared not to be reminded of.

The Russians were next in the attempt to dominate Europe. The Soviet Union had become the master of Eastern Europe after the Second World War and attempted to subjugate Western Europe under its sphere of influence. But NATO, led by the United States, had blunted the Russian bid for dominance on the continent in the early fifties and sixties. United States' foreign policy and will to resist Soviet expansion then appeared to languish in the morass of Vietnam and the malaise of the Carter years in the 1970s. With American power waning, it appeared the Soviets would be able to coerce Western Europe into submission as a result. However, the re-arming of the United States under the Reagan administration in the 1980s, and the strong anti-communist foreign policy advocated by his administration reversed this trend. Two events stand out from the 1980s and this shift in foreign policy. Reagan did not hesitate to condemn the Soviet Union, at one time calling it an evil empire. Then later in his administration, with one line in a speech delivered in Berlin, Reagan set in motion events that further accelerated the downfall of the Soviet Empire. Speaking before the Brandenburg Gate at the Berlin Wall, he delivered perhaps the most audacious statement of his administration when he delivered that unforgettable challenge, "Mr. Gorbechev, tear down this wall!"

The Solidarity movement in Poland had been energized by this strong surge of anti-Communism and began the loosening of the Soviet hold on Eastern Europe. The Berlin Wall, symbol of all which divided East from West, was torn down reuniting Germany and signaling the end of Soviet rule in Eastern Europe. With the collapse of the Soviet Union, their grip on Eastern Europe, and any claim to Western Europe dissolved.

Now a new empire was being forged. Replacing the Tricolor above the Arc d' Triumph was the flag of the grandest empire to grace the continent. The EU flag, whose design incorporated twelve gold stars in circular formation against a blue background, was now fluttering in the winds above the historic landmark. As with all national flags, symbolism was very apparent in the design of the EU flag. A prime example was the number of stars in the flag. A common misperception among many outside the EU was that the stars represented the member states. To the contrary, the twelve stars had nothing to do with the number of members. Rather, the number twelve traditionally has been associated with perfection. And without a doubt the EU was perfect. The circle had been chosen as a symbol of unity and perpetuity among the European peoples. Thus the flag was a symbol of perfection, unity, and perpetuity.

Nothing like this new unity among the European states had been accomplished in modern times. The rise of the Europe First party had been meteoric. And the credit belonged to one man and one man alone—Hans Gerhard. It was upon the platform of a strong and united Europe that Gerhard had waged his successful campaign soundly defeating his opponent from England. He could easily recall his campaign speech's conclusion.

"...Europe will be the world's next superpower. In terms of economic and military strength we will no longer have to cower under the threat of communism...we will no longer have to worry about the threat of nuclear war on our territory...we will no longer see our products taxed and tariffed out of competition with others...our citizens will enjoy the highest standard of living, along with health care, the world has ever seen...and last, but most importantly...as a united continent, we will no longer allow the United States to dictate when and where our strategic interests are in the world! We will end their unilateralist foreign policy and restore peace to the world! Join me as we form *ein volk, ein kontinent, ein euro!*"

It was this last line that he enjoyed delivering the most. It was also the one that solicited the most response from the crowd. It had been exhilarating watching thousands of individuals hang on his every word. His campaign stops had been very picturesque and well orchestrated.

European Union flags were ever present fluttering in the gentle winds. He would often tease the crowds before delivering what political pundits had come to call "the line." The teeming crowds that gathered before him could sense his cadence as the pitch of his voice rose at the end of the speech, approaching the line they loved to hear. Often they would join in with him and then rupture into thunderous applause. He could picture what it must have been like in his native Deutschland during the thirties when another leader arose to inspire a nation. Gerhard had set his sights on loftier goals. Now he was attempting to inspire a continent…and possibly a world.

Gerhard knew the elections had been monitored all around the world. The results had been decisive. His opponent, Malcolm Cunningham of the Conservative party from England, never stood a chance. Gerhard had won by a substantial margin of victory in each province except England, Poland, Estonia, Latvia, and Lithuania. More importantly, ninety-three percent of the burgeoning Muslim population in the EU had supported him. Al-Saim had made good on his promise of Muslim support in the election. Now Gerhard would have to make good on his promises to Al-Saim.

The election results made it clear to the world that under his leadership Europe would no longer accept treatment as a junior partner from the United States: especially in foreign policy. Why should they? Europe's history was much longer than that of the United States. Had not European adventurism colonized the world? It was only after the Second World War that the United States could lay claim to power. Yes, it was Europe that had stood the test of time. And it was Europe that would lead the future—under his direction.

The seven-vehicle motorcade continued its progress down the Champs-Élysées, crossed the Seine River at Pont Neuf to the Île de la Cité and finally arrived at the Justice Palace where the Council was meeting. The Justice Palace had been chosen because it was situated on the Île de la Cité in the middle of the Seine River, thereby allowing controlled access to the facilities. River traffic had been halted for the duration of their meeting.

Located just to the southeast of the Justice Palace was Notre Dame, perhaps the most famous church in the world. Though majestic in its construction and rich in history, it was, after all, just a building to him.

That religion should play a part in a progressive society was an anathema to him. The EU constitution had not bothered to include any reference to the influence of Christianity in Europe's history. Why should it? The overwhelming majority of the Union did not even attend church. Many had come to have a distrust of organized religion. Was it not in the name of God that many of Europe's wars had been conducted?

However, Gerhard realized that appearances were everything. Not wanting to totally alienate the continent's church officials he thought it wise to visit the grand church.

Gerhard entered Notre Dame through the Portal of St. Anne as any regular tourist would. Making his way into the dark, towering interior he gazed around at the various saints depicted on the walls. The most interesting was the one that was said to depict Judgment Day. *Interesting and ironic*, thought Gerhard. Some might say the results of his meeting with the Council could result in Judgment Day. He took a seat and bowed his head in feigned prayer. After a few moments he rose and went toward the altar to greet the priest. The priest offered Gerhard the sacrament, which he took to the astonishment of his aides who had remained within a discreet distance.

As he departed the church for the Justice Palace he looked at his aides and with a slight shrug of the shoulders merely said, "When in Rome."

Entering the Justice Palace, Gerhard and his party made their way to the main conference room. As he entered the room the members of the Council rose in his honor.

"Thank you for coming today," said Gerhard. "Please be seated. We have much to discuss so let us dispense with the pleasantries. Ladies and gentlemen, it is time to cut the ties that bind us. As promised in my campaign, I propose that we immediately disengage ourselves from the NATO alliance. We no longer have need of the United States. As I see it, our Union will be a counter to the ever-growing hostility of the United States within the world. We cannot allow the Americans to continue to invade country after country and topple any government not friendly to them, or more importantly, that may be friendly to us. I would imagine that if some in their government had their way, some of our countries might have undergone regime change instead of Iraq!"

This last statement drew a round of laughter and applause from the Council, especially the French and German delegates. A motion was made to act on Gerhard's proposal. Normally, a unanimous vote was required for any action to be taken by the Council. One of Gerhard's first moves as President had been to dispense with that provision and substitute approval by a simple majority. His foresight was wise in this manner for a vote of the Council showed seventeen in favor of withdrawal from NATO with five opposed. Gerhard noted these five were the same countries where he did not win at least half of the vote.

"Thank you for your support. I know this is a difficult vote to make in light of our history with the United States. But I believe that we have to continue to look toward the future. Our future. A future that is secure and that means a world where the United States is held in check. Which brings us to the second item on our agenda."

"Herr President, we have read your proposal and we have concerns with some of the operational aspects of this endeavor," voiced Antonio Gerabaldi of the Italian province. Details of Item Two, as it was simply titled on the agenda, had only been distributed to the Council two hours before his arrival. The nature of the topic had not availed Gerhard the luxury of an earlier distribution.

"I expected there would be questions and concerns," agreed Gerhard. "This is the single most ambitious plan ever attempted by man. If, and I repeat if, we are successful, then we will be able to answer two of the greatest concerns within our borders: the safety of our citizens and guaranteed economic prosperity. More importantly, on an international level we will have achieved the status of a true superpower," he said leaning forward as he extended his right arm toward the council with a clenched fist. "Able to wield political and military influence outside of the continent at our discretion. We have watched for decades as the United States and the former Soviet Union attempted to do what we are proposing. They were not able to. They were too close to the problem. We are not."

"Herr Gerhard, have you seriously considered how the Americans will respond? They have invested much political and economic capital in the operational area, and may not be content to stand by and watch these be eroded away. And they will be eroded away if your plan, excuse me, this plan, is successful," said Malcolm Cunningham of the English province. He, along with the ministers who had voted against withdrawal from NATO, was alarmed over the proposal. "But more importantly, Herr Gerhard, have you considered the consequences of such an undertaking? There will be serious political and military fallout throughout the world. I am sure Her Majesty's Government will not approve of any of these measures."

The other representatives at the table eyed the two men. Gerhard felt his jaw muscles tighten at this attack. All plans, great or small, had the potential for success or failure. One calculated the odds and decided if you made your play. He and the English representative had not agreed on many issues facing the Union prior to the election. It was Cunningham who had opposed him in the election. One of the primary issues on which they disagreed was the potential withdrawal from NATO. Cunningham disagreed with the sentiment that withdrawal from NATO was in the best interest of Europe. After all, the United States had been a friend of Europe delivering them from Communism after the Second World War. The Americans had saved Western Europe through the Marshall Plan and had been a strong ally through the decades following. She had asked for nothing in return other than to resist the Red Menace. It was American leadership that had been responsible for the defeat of Communism. Many English, and indeed many Europeans, could trace family to America. The bond of a common people was there and there was no need to shatter it. A united America and Europe would be able to control world affairs and work for the betterment of mankind.

"Whose government, my dear, Cunningham?" Gerhard asked with the voice a parent uses to address a small child. "We are all one here I remind you." The others at the table noted the coolness of Gerhard's voice. "However, I do agree with you. There are potential consequences if we fail. But we will not."

"Don't you realize the Americans will intervene? Israel is the oldest democracy in the region. Surely they will not abandon her," Cunningham continued with his objections.

"I understand the Americans. They are weary of fighting after their war in Iraq. Their continued presence there cost the Republicans the Presidency and their House of Representatives after Bush. They barely maintained control of their Senate," Gerhard countered.

"You seem to have forgotten the most recent American election," Cunningham quickly responded. "The political pendulum has swung back in favor of the conservatives. Sullivan is a conservative. Failure to recognize that is foolish."

By now Gerhard had heard enough. He understood American politics better than Americans did and certainly much better than Cunningham.

He knew they would not fight. He had grown weary of the exchange with Cunningham and moved to terminate the debate.

"And you seem to have forgotten the most recent European election. That is what is foolish," Gerhard said as he spat the words at Cunningham. "Failure to act is the greater concern. Time is of the essence. Our window of opportunity is very narrow. Ladies and gentlemen, I need to know if I have your approval. There are other parties we need to initiate discussions with."

The call to vote was taken. Seventeen in favor with five opposed. Gerhard looked around the table at each of the representatives. His eyes met Cunningham's and locked for a moment. He would deal with him and the others later. A small man with limited vision like Cunningham would not stop him.

"I want to thank you for your support. I know there are risks but the rewards will be well worth our efforts. We will implement Operation Rosh at the earliest convenient moment."

THE BELTWAY

Washington, D.C.
December 1st
6:15 a.m.

Alex Stanton, Special Assistant to the President of the United States, was not a happy soul. He was stuck in traffic. He had been appointed to this position at the request of his former employer, William T. Sullivan, when the latter was elected President of the United States. The two had met while Alex was employed at CFA Consulting, a crisis management consulting and think tank firm. Though Alex was fifteen years Sullivan's junior, Sullivan had been impressed by the young man's ability to see the global picture and articulate the appropriate policy to their clients on short notice. It was a gift to be able to deliver the goods under pressure, and Alex was the best Sullivan had seen at CFA.

Alex had somewhat anticipated Sullivan's call after the election was certified. The geo-political balance of power was shifting in fundamental ways. The President needed people who could work in the atmosphere of Washington and not become swept away by the politics of the town. As Sullivan explained, he needed someone who was not there for a career.

His exact quote as Alex recalled was, "Alex, I need someone who isn't kissing my back side all the time to shoot it to me straight and to give me a swift kick in the rear if needed. I can't get all my advice from folks who are trying to be on *Fox News* or *CNN*."

Alex had been very adept at just that while they were at CFA. Sometimes he wondered if a pink slip would be in his next paycheck after some of their discussions. Fortunately for him it never was.

"Looks like it is going to be about a thirty minute delay, Mr. Stanton," advised his driver, Special Agent Filipe Juarez. "Sorry to hear about the Cats, sir. Tough game. Could have gone either way." He was referring to Kentucky's 87–86 loss to Michigan State.

He knew his boss had a lot more important things on his mind than the game but thought some light banter would be good for him. It was good to remind people at Stanton's level they were people first, and indentured servants to the state second.

"Yeah, it was a good game though. Still very early in the season. Coach knows his game and will have'em ready come March. Hope they get to play your Spartans again. Should be a good re-match."

"Yes it should," Juarez agreed.

Traffic was moving slowly. Up ahead, Alex could see one of D.C.'s finest directing traffic into one lane.

"The one thing I really hate about D.C. more than the politics is the traffic. Kills your productivity. I don't know what we did before cell phones and XM radio. Course, I used to say I never wanted a job where I had to have a cell phone. And here I am today," he said as he checked his phone again hoping he would not see the number from the White House.

"Good things to have on a day like today, sir," countered Juarez as he merged the Crown Victoria into the single open lane of traffic.

"Yes it is. Gotta call the Boss and let him know I will be delayed. Best guess on time?"

"Will have you there in thirty minutes, sir, in spite of this Code Orange traffic," said Juarez, referring to the extra problems the increased security alert was causing in addition to the accident. "Crossing the bridge now and from there we'll take the short cuts."

Alex really appreciated Juarez's approach to traffic. Neutralize the enemy and advance. He had a knack for identifying the slow downs and knew D.C. like the back of his hand. Alex pulled out his cell phone and spoke into the unit, "White House." The phone automatically dialed Tom O'Hara, the President's Chief of Staff.

"Tom, this is Stanton. Traffic is all screwed up. Crossing the Potomac and should be there in thirty if Juarez knows what he is doing. Let the Boss know for me."

"You know how he hates folks who are late," came Tom's reply. "Even on days like today. Much less former business partners who are late. Better have your ducks in a row, Stanton. The agenda is full today."

"Yeah, they are quacking up a storm. Meeting place the same?"

"Yes on the meeting place. Today should be a lively discussion day. We will hold breakfast for you. Hurry your tail up. Oh, and tell Juarez my grandmother can drive better than he can and she is blind in one eye," Tom said as he hung up.

"I will do that," Alex noted with sarcasm.

Juarez was as good as his word. Twenty-nine minutes later they were at the first security checkpoint at the White House. The White House had become a small fortress after 9/11. Any increase in the Terror Alert level prompted an increased level of security at the People's House as one former President had described the residence. Practically all roads around the White House had been blocked to traffic since that fateful day. Stanton noticed extra concrete barricades had been installed along the streets since word of the explosions at Esfahan and Natanz. He knew there were snipers and men armed with surface-to-air missiles on the rooftop. The good thing was that he could not see them and he knew where to look. It would be almost impossible for a potential adversary to spot them. He had no doubt that one of the snipers had a scope centered on his car in the unlikely event it veered off in an attempt to car bomb the White House. If the snipers were unable to stop such an attack there were shoulder-fired anti-tank missiles, which could stop an Abrams tank if needed. If a terrorist group wanted to make the White House a target for invasion, it would take a lot of them just to penetrate the layers of external security. The survivors, if any, and that was a huge if, that actually made it into the White House, would then have to fight their way past a small army of Secret Service agents and Marines. These men and women had received the finest training and equipment their country could offer. Invasion scenarios of the White House were rehearsed on a routine basis to keep their skills honed to a sharp edge. The President, along with the First Family, would often participate. Nothing was left to chance in the event of another terrorist attack. This was one case where Alex thought the taxpayers received their money's worth.

"Good morning, sir. I will need to see both of your IDs please," a young Marine corporal said as Stanton pulled out his identification and handed his along with Juarez's to the young soldier. "This will take just a moment, sir," the corporal said as he took the IDs to perform the security check. Stanton raised the window to keep out the December cold.

Lance Corporal Michael Williams stepped back inside his guardhouse and checked Stanton and Juarez's IDs against the White House security database. As he was doing this, two other Marines with dogs were inspecting the car. The ID numbers and thumbprints matched those on record in the database. The license plate on the car was also a match. Corporal Williams stepped back out into the cold for one final check. As Stanton lowered the window, the Marine leaned in to visually ID both occupants of the vehicle. Satisfied they were who their IDs indicated, he checked with his detachment that had completed the inspection of the car. Two thumbs up were given.

"Sir, you are clear to proceed. Welcome to the White House," Corporal Williams said as he offered a stiff salute and waved them through.

"Thank you, Corporal. You and your men keep up the good work," Stanton said as he returned the salute. As a former Air Force Captain, he still respected military protocol. How could he not after their drill instructor ran their class halfway around the world if they did not salute in the correct manner.

Stanton could feel a small knot forming in his stomach as they drove forward. This happened every time he came here. There was a certain awe that was inspired by this building in spite of the simple, yet elegant design of the White House. The snow-covered grounds were immaculately groomed as he had come to expect. Ground crews had been up early clearing the snow and removing any patches of ice. Even decorated for Christmas the building conveyed a sense of purpose and power.

He reminded himself it might have been destroyed on that historic day in September had it not been for the brave actions of the passengers of United Flight 93 over Pennsylvania. He often imagined what he would have done if he had been on board when the call came, "Let's roll."

"Here we are, sir. Call me when you are ready and good luck today," Juarez said as he stopped the car at the entranceway to the East Wing.

"Thank you, Juarez. This promises to be a long day. Stay warm and out of trouble," Alex said exiting the car.

"Will do, sir," Juarez said as he drove away.

As Alex made his way up the steps and to the door he was greeted with another security check. There would be an additional one as he made his way to the West Wing and then finally the Oval Office. At each stop he had to present his ID and be confirmed again through the database. As he approached the Oval Office he stopped by Jeanette Brown's desk. She was the President's personal secretary.

"How is the Boss today?"

"He is not a happy camper, as my kids would say. He has been waiting on a valuable, yet easily replaceable member of his administration to come to work," she said with a wolf's grin.

"What, Secretary of Defense not here yet?" he countered with an innocent look as he straightened his tie while checking his appearance in the mirror on her desk. In the great tradition of Ronald Reagan, coat and ties were always neatly worn in the Oval Office.

Jeanette lifted the phone on her desk. "Mr. President, Mr. Alex Stanton to see you."

"Tell him it is about time, Jeanette, and send him on in." His voice projected enough that Alex could hear the reply.

Jeanette looked at him and grinned. The Boss was not happy his day was starting behind schedule and time was something he did not have an abundance of. The President of the United States of America was the single most powerful man in the world. But not even he and all the vast resources at his command could alter time.

"Good morning, sir, and my apologies for being late," Alex offered as he entered the Oval Office and took his seat. He could see he was the last to arrive. President Sullivan was seated just in front of his desk. Beginning on his left and going clockwise were seated Secretary of Defense James Clairmont, Secretary of State Kathryn Stanfield, and Department of National Intelligence and Security (DNIS) Secretary Christopher Sheffield. This was the President's inner circle of his national security team.

"Morn'n, Alex. Come on in and grab some danish and coffee. This is going to be a working breakfast. Ladies and gentlemen, we have a lot to discuss. First off, Iran," Sullivan said, nodding to his DNIS Secretary as he selected a danish and a Coke. He was not a coffee man.

"Mr. President," began Secretary Sheffield, "our recon birds detected explosions at the Iranian nuclear facility located at Esfahan at 12:24 a.m. local time. Subsequent recon has confirmed the destruction of the reactors and adjacent facilities," he continued as he distributed satellite pictures of the destroyed facilities. They were marked EYES ONLY. "As you can see, the housing area was hit pretty hard. Casualties estimated to be at four hundred plus. It is believed their top nuclear scientists were present but we cannot confirm this. We also have confirmed explosions at Arak and Natanz. Satellite imagery will be available within the next hour."

"News sources are still reporting this as a potential accidental explosion at the facility. The reactor the French sold them and helped develop did have a reputation for problems," offered Secretary Defense Clairmont. "Nothing on Arak and Natanz yet."

"There is more, sir," Sheffield added as he opened his laptop and placed it on the table for all to see. "DNIS had reports that our Iranian friends were preparing to restart their nuclear research program. As noted, we had our birds tasked to monitor Esfahan and other facilities in Iran. This was downloaded from the satellite monitoring Esfahan last night. Ladies and gentlemen, please observe carefully."

The screen was showing thermal images of the reactor facility. Various images of red, orange, and purple indicated activity at the various structures. After a moment, multiple white-hot images emerged from the right side of the screen and headed to the facility. The color enhanced thermal images flared as the streaks made impact. The screen erupted in brilliant flashes of white light from the resulting explosions. The light was so intense it temporarily washed out the images until the satellite's camera adjusted for the intensity. Alex looked around at the faces of those watching the screen as the reality of the moment sunk in. No doubt there would be similar images of Arak and Natanz.

"It would appear that someone has done the world a favor and has eliminated, or at the least curtailed, Iran's nuclear research program for now," Stanfield noted.

"Radiation levels?" inquired Sullivan as he continued to review the photos.

"Nothing to be alarmed about. We were fortunate they had not restarted their research," Clairmont noted.

"Two questions. How long before they figure out this was not an explosion?" Sullivan asked. "After that, who has the ability to mount this type of coordinated strike besides ourselves?"

"Sir," Clairmont offered, "not counting ourselves, there are only a handful of countries capable of this type of activity in the area. Let's assume it was someone from the local neighborhood. That gives us three candidates—India, Russia, and Israel. Of those three, which one has the motivation to attempt this? That Iranian defenses were caught flat-footed suggests stealth aircraft were involved. The Russians have been working on a stealth aircraft but it has not been deployed as of yet. I think only one obvious answer is on each of our minds—Israel. They had to have used the Raptors we sold them last year."

"So it appears our Israeli friends may have done the world a favor," Sullivan observed, breaking the silence in the room. Each person present knew the implications of what they had just seen.

"It would not be outside the realm of possibility," said Secretary of State Stanfield. "There is precedence in their history for preemptive action when their national security is at stake. They took out Iraq's nuclear facility at Osiraq in '81 if I recall. In '67, Israel preemptively attacked her Arab neighbors destroying their air forces in a matter of hours launching the Six-Day War. They have both the ability and motivation. The rise in Fundamentalism in the Mideast is a concern not only for Israel, but for us as well. Antagonisms between old rivals in the Islamic world are being swept away overnight behind a common call for the destruction of Israel and the end of our involvement in the area.

"The rhetoric against Israel is the most vitriolic we have heard dating back to the days of Nassar just before the '67 war," Stanfield continued. "The long-standing peace treaty with Egypt has been abrogated by the new Fundamentalist government in Cairo. Jordan fell to the Fundamentalists after the Hussein family was forced to abdicate the throne for alleged sympathies to us. Syria has reemerged as a sponsor of terrorism after laying low since Iraq went democratic. Libya, Tunisia, and Algeria have also seen governments sympathetic to the Fundamentalists come into power in the last year. It goes without saying that the current Iranian government wants to see Israel destroyed."

"There is the formation of what is being called the Islamic Alliance," Sheffield interjected. "It is an attempt to unite the military and political aspirations of those countries. Both Mossad and DNIS agree that Al-Saim is behind this movement. Incidentally, the whereabouts of his location cannot be confirmed. He hides like a chameleon. If they are successful, this Alliance will easily surpass that of the former Arab League in terms of cohesion and purpose."

"It sounds like an attempt to revive the first Arab Empire, circa 750 AD. It ruled Spain, North Africa, and the entire Middle East including Iran and parts of India," commented Alex, who had a minor in history.

"Yes, the motivation is there for that possibility. Saudi Arabia is battling internal attempts to displace their government," Stanfield continued. "Their oil production has dropped off by a quarter. The Saudis, Iraq, Kuwait, United Arab Emirates, Qatar, Bahrain, and Oman have escaped the Fundamentalist tide so far, but their positions are tenuous at best. Their pledge to maintain the oil supply has kept the price from skyrocketing even higher. It is currently at $119 a barrel. The whole place is a powder keg just waiting for a spark," Stanfield concluded with her assessment.

"Playing havoc with our economy along with the rest of the world's also," commented Sullivan. He, like all Presidents past and future, had to worry about economics. A sagging or growing economy could be the difference between a one or two term presidency. "If the Fundamentalists gain control of the world's oil supply, they could strangle our economy on a whim. If they are unable to gain control, every tanker that transits the Gulf becomes a potential target."

"It is understandable why our Israeli friends would have cause for concern," said Clairmont. "Mr. President, only Iran had the immediate potential for nuclear weapons in the Middle East. The chemical and biological threat is still there with many of these countries. As we found in Iraq, these programs are easier to conceal, but they cannot be concealed forever as many have discovered."

He was referring to the Iraqi chemical and biological weapons discovered in the western desert of that country. Their discovery revealed the depth of the elaborate deception plans Saddam Hussein and his regime had undertaken to conceal these weapons. More damaging though was the revelation of the extent to which the French and Germans had been aiding Hussein in the development of those weapons and their concealment. This had led to a further deterioration in relations between the United States, and what then Secretary of Defense Rumsfeld, had defined as Old Europe, that had started with the Iraqi War in 2003.

"Status of armed forces in the region?" Sullivan inquired.

"Signal Intelligence has detected an increase in the alert levels of all countries in the region. Increased air activity mostly. Most surprising is the fact that the Iranians have not launched any counterattack. Probably because they are like us and not sure who did this. Would be a bear to strike back at the wrong folks. The expected anti-Israeli rhetoric is being broadcasted through the region. Indian, Pakistani, Russian, and Chinese nuclear forces have increased their readiness. All very understandable in light of several unknown explosions at critical nuclear facilities," noted

Clairmont. "Just look at our own response. We are at Code Orange and Combat Air Patrol assets are patrolling our major cities."

"Suggested posture we take when this breaks?" Sullivan asked.

"Mr. President, we should recognize Israel's right to self-defense. After all, we have essentially exercised this right since 9/11 in Iraq and Afghanistan, and rightfully so," emphasized Secretary Stanfield. "She is a long standing ally and deserves all the support we can provide. The UN will of course vote to condemn their attack. Though I rather doubt they would have condemned Iran if she were to have used nukes on Tel-Aviv. We need to send the message that this class of weapon will not be tolerated in nations that are considered to be outside of the community of nations."

"I agree," said Sullivan. "We cannot leave Israel hanging on this one. If we do she will be torn to shreds. As would Kuwait, Saudi Arabia, and the Gulf States. Iraq's fledgling democracy would also be a prime target. Whether these countries like it, or would even admit it, Israel's survival is in their best interest." The others in the room all nodded their heads in support of this posture.

Alex was continually amazed at the new breed of diplomat that had emerged in the post 9/11 era of foreign policy. Kathryn Stanfield had come to epitomize the new hawk. She made no bones about defending United States' interests either at home or abroad and the exercising of preemptive foreign policy to fulfill these goals.

Old Europe bristled at this shift in foreign policy, which they had come to label as "cowboy diplomacy." It harkened back to the American West where shoot first and ask questions later had prevailed. So far though, this tact had served the United States well. American led intervention in Iraq had enabled that country to develop into the second democracy in the region after Israel. Though the regime still faced sporadic terrorist attacks, her armed forces had acquired enough experience and training to assume defense of the country, allowing the withdrawal of all Allied forces. It was fortunate the democratic experiment was holding in Iraq in light of the rebirth of Islamic Fundamentalism in the Mideast. And more importantly, no terrorist attacks on American interests either at home or abroad had occurred since Sullivan was elected President. Iran, Syria, and North Korea still remained on the Axis of Evil list. There was much discussion in Sullivan's administration if preemptive action was necessary in these countries. But they had not come to a consensus regarding these countries.

It was this concern of another preemptive strike that had led European leaders to perceive the United States as a destabilizing force in the world. Gerhard's campaign had vowed to oppose this foreign policy initiative by the United States. Especially in regions where European Union economic interests were involved. Gerhard and others in Europe had been embarrassed and outraged at the disclosure of their activity in Saddam's Iraq. Saddam's capture and subsequent confession of French and German support for his regime had put a chill on relations between the Old and New World so deep many were not sure they could be restored.

Further complicating the matter was the role of the UN in the Oil for Food program. This had been a debacle from the beginning. The initial plan was sound on paper. However, its implementation was a dismal failure. Under the plan, Iraq was allowed to trade oil for food, medicine, and other humanitarian needs. Instead, much of the food found its way into Saddam's palaces and to the tables of the Republican Guard. The money Iraq had been allowed to earn for medicines and other humanitarian aid had been funneled to Saddam's private bank accounts and research for his weapons of mass destruction. That officials from France and Germany had overseen this program was not lost on the Sullivan administration. Investigations by a Congressional investigative committee were able to trace money that had been transferred from Saddam's accounts to the private bank accounts of several European and United Nations leaders. Gerhard was one of these leaders.

"Ok, moving to the European elections. How much was the pool?" Sullivan asked referring to their bets on the elections. He had nominated himself to be the holder of the money. As he noted, he was the only elected official in the room and U.S. currency was official government property. And it was, after all, his sworn duty as President to safeguard American property.

"One hundred bucks," recalled Stanfield with a very disappointed look on her face.

"Let's see," Sullivan said as he said checked the pool. "Alex, you won the pool on this one. Congratulations!" he said as he reached into his wallet and gave Alex the money. "Your man, Hans Gerhard, won the election in rather stunning fashion. Gathered sixty-five percent of the votes in all but five countries. With returns like that, I want his campaign director for the next run!" he said to the laughter of everyone in the room. "Not bad prognosticating for a rookie. This Gerhard fellow makes our liberals look like Sunday school teachers. Assessments?" Sullivan directed.

"Yes, congratulations to Alex on his political prowess," said Stanfield with a smirk on her face. "Now, if you can do that with this year's Superbowl, we can all retire rich and get out of this town." The joke was an old one but nonetheless still solicited a few chuckles and here, heres from everyone.

"Mr. President," began Stanfield, "I anticipate our already strained relations with the European Union will probably be pushed over the edge. Gerhard is the leader of the Europe First Party. They are ultra Europeanist and view us as the problem in the world today. Amazing as that is. Fundamentalists are wanting to nuke Israel, North Korea threatens to nuke us, and Gerhard thinks we are the problem! He made that abundantly clear during his campaign. I would not be surprised if we hear notice from across the Atlantic they are withdrawing from NATO."

"Secretary Clairmont, what would be the impact of this on our military posture?" inquired Sullivan.

"Sir, if that does occur, and I agree with Stanfield that it will," observed Clairmont, "our defense capabilities will be minimally impacted. With the collapse of the Soviet Union, the strategic value of our bases in Germany and Italy had diminished. Our focus on terrorism shifted our base structure to one of portability. The bases in Europe were becoming unnecessary financial burdens so we closed them. The Germans hollered the loudest, but only for economic reasons, as the local folks realized our troops and logistic contracts were going away. Put a dent in their local economy for a while. They may hate us but they love our dollars.

"We still have reciprocal agreements throughout Europe for use of air and naval facilities if needed, but I would not rely too heavily on those. That leaves us with our carriers. With the firepower of our carrier strike groups there are not many folks who can play with us today," he said with his voice echoing the pride he felt for the American military. "Incidentally, the strike fleet is available. *Kittyhawk* and *Vinson* are undergoing maintenance and will not be available for eight months. *Kennedy* is receiving an upgrade to her Combat Direction Center and should be ready for sea in three weeks. Good thing we reactivated her earlier this year. She wasn't ready to retire in '07. She still has a lot of kick left. *Stennis* is completing exercises with the Japanese and Taiwanese navies. *Bush* and *Reagan* have just completed their training and are available. Mr. President, these carrier strike groups still carry a lot of weight in the world today."

"Yes they do," commented Sullivan. "Hard to believe folks are still trying to say we don't need as many of them as we have. What is the status of *Ford* and *Halsey?*"

The *Ford* class of aircraft carriers was the next step in the evolution of carrier design. Though the new carriers would be roughly the same size as a *Nimitz* class carrier, their overall efficiency was enhanced by roughly twenty percent.

"On schedule, Mr. President. *Ford* and her sister ships will offer a twenty-five percent faster launch and recovery capability than the *Nimitz* carriers with a ten percent increase in aircraft. *Bush* and *Reagan* had many of the features incorporated into their design as they were prototypes for the new technology," Clairmont observed. "We can only hope Congress has the wisdom to authorize the next four ships in this class. Fifteen carriers will enable us to continue operations in the event of hostilities in either the Pacific or Atlantic."

"We just may need every one of the carriers. The most serious impact of Europe leaving NATO would be a loss of prestige around the world. It may give some of our enemies the impression we are alone which may tempt them to try some rather unpleasant activities," added Sheffield.

"You thinking about North Korea?" Sullivan asked reaching for another danish with nuts. His wife would give him grief if she saw this breakfast. Of course, he knew he could not hide it forever. His waistline continued to betray him. What did he always tell her? There was more of him to love? "I am scheduled to address the Foreign Policy Institute in California on the North Korean situation. How worried should we be?"

"Yes, sir, I am definitely thinking about North Korea. And let's not forget about China," Clairmont said emphatically. "It does concern me that the dissolution of NATO would send the wrong signal to both the North Koreans and Chinese. China still has designs on Taiwan and makes no secret of that fact. She is modernizing her armed forces at a disconcerting rate with an emphasis on sea and air assets. If we were drawn into a conflict in the Middle East, we might not have much left to counter any potential actions from either party short of nukes. Can you imagine if either of them aligned themselves with the Fundamentalists? They could provide the Alliance with the WMDs they have long sought after. A very nasty prospect. It is one thing to be involved in a war against terrorism. But a ground war in Asia, especially with a nuclear-armed North Korea or China, is another matter."

"Prospects for victory if conflict occurred?" Sullivan asked.

"Probability of victory is rated at good. But it would be better to have some friends around with some firepower. It wouldn't hurt to have our British allies. It would even be beneficial to have the French. For all the rhetoric the talking heads did about needing France in the coalition to show the Iraqi's how to surrender, they did acquit themselves rather well in OPERATION DESERT STORM."

"Are we having any progress with our assets on the ground over there? I know it's taken time to rebuild our human intelligence operations that were gutted in the nineties," inquired Sullivan.

"We are having some success, Mr. President, but not to the degree we would like. As you noted, it is taking time to reacquire that capability. I am glad we finally realized you can't do everything with satellites and remotely piloted vehicles. Successful intel operations need the personal touch," Sheffield said with frustration in his voice.

"Alex, you've been sitting over there like a school boy on the first day of class. What do you make of all this?" Sullivan said with a sly grin on his face. He had enjoyed putting Alex on the spot in the boardroom at CFA. What he liked in those meetings were Alex's comebacks. He did not back down at his boss's or anyone else's jabs.

"Mr. President," Alex reminded himself he was in the Oval office and not the boardroom at CFA, "to be quite honest, it's going to be a challenge. Israel will be a sitting duck when this breaks. If she is not attacked within forty-eight hours, I will be truly amazed. We need to do some serious thinking and determine how much support we lend, if, and when she is attacked. Her enemies will bring everything they have. This time Israel does not have the Sinai as a buffer. Egypt and Syria have been rearming like Armageddon is just around the corner. Which it could be if war broke out. Our French, German, and Russians friends are making up for what they lost in arm sales to Iraq to the other countries in the Mideast. The qualitative edge Israel has always enjoyed is disappearing. Israel cannot afford to give ground to gain time for mobilization. It could be Yom Kippur all over again. My biggest fear is that the situation would go nuclear and there would be precious little we could do to stop it."

"Mr. President," interrupted Secretary Clairmont, "we have war-gamed an updated version of the '73 Yom Kippur War from several perspectives. Scenario name is Yom Kippur-2, or YK-2. The prime determinant of success for Israel is how quickly she can mobilize. They train like there is no tomorrow. I surmise they feel there may not be one if they didn't. Bottom line is they need seventy-two hours to mobilize for a fifty-nine percent chance of success."

"Does the scenario envision nukes?" asked Sullivan.

"No, sir, YK-2 is purely conventional and is confined to theatre only combatants from the Yom Kippur War of '73."

"Mr. Secretary," though they sometimes addressed each other in an informal manner, except of course the President, Alex still could not bring himself to address anyone in the room in any way other than their official title, "does YK-2 contemplate our involvement? We were pretty close back in '73 if I remember my history."

"Good question, Alex. You are right. We were close to involvement. YK-2 does make provision for a scenario variant that anticipates American intervention. The results are somewhat more decisive. If I recall, 6th Fleet and Air Force involvement turns the tide to Israel's side. The mobilization time is reduced to forty-eight hours, and the probability of success increases to seventy-two percent."

"Pretty good odds in a combat situation if you ask me," noted Stanfield.

"Better than what you had in the pool," Sullivan joked as he winked at Alex. Stanfield continued to wear her poker face, pretending to ignore the remark. She hated to lose and would not give anyone the pleasure of seeing her frustration at having lost the pool.

"Problem with this variant, though, is that it envisions the utilization of NATO airfields and it presupposes that the political climate will signal that the chance of war is imminent. We will upgrade the parameters and see how the loss of NATO bases would impact the outcome," Clairmont said making notes on the scenario changes.

"All right, Alex, continue with your observations," directed Sullivan.

"Yes, sir. With regard to Europe, we've seen this coming for a while. It should not be a surprise to anyone if and when they withdraw from NATO. That's all their press has been talking about. I think the alliances we have with our other allies will not suffer. The North Koreans would be crazy to attempt anything, but I would not put it past them. They have too much to lose by fighting. They would be better served coming to the negotiating table but that stubborn pride won't let 'em. It's an even money bet on China and Taiwan, Mr. President," Alex concluded.

"I appreciate all of your discussion this morning as always," Sullivan said as his steely grey eyes met each one of theirs. "I want position papers and options for Esfahan with emphasis on our support for Israel. Be sure we are ready for the UN debates. Secretary Clairmont, let's review our strategic situation if Europe does withdraw from NATO. We are in bed with 'em on a lot of sensitive issues. Let's know what we will lose if they do break. Might be a good idea to step up recon activities over the peninsula to see what our Korean friends are up to as well. Any questions?"

The staff shook their heads. "Good. Now I'm off to see the queen of the Cranberry Festival. If you will excuse me." Political debts were the hardest.

REVIVAL

SOMEWHERE ALONG THE PAKISTANI/AFGHAN BORDER...

Al-Saim looked around the cave where his men had gathered. He could see the worry and questions in their eyes. The cold winds and snow of Afghanistan did not lend much comfort to their worries. Those worries had been present ever since their revered leader, Usama bin Laden, had been killed by the Americans a year ago. His death, though expected at some point, had sent shockwaves through al-Qaeda. His invincibility had become almost mythic. He had survived the Soviet occupation in the 1980s and had participated in the campaign to drive them out of Afghanistan. Afterwards, he relocated to the Sudan but their government eventually forced him to leave in 1996. He returned to Afghanistan where he became involved in the plans for the 2001 attack on the World Trade Center. There had been talk of the possibility of such an attack in Western intelligence circles, but the likelihood of such an attack occurring was considered marginal. There were too many obstacles to overcome. Too many details. The timing and coordination were too difficult. They were all proven wrong on that glorious morning in September. Bin Laden's position as enemy number one of the United States was cemented on that day.

The Americans had hunted him down like a common dog. In the end, he was betrayed by a local farmer for American money and a promise to move his family to America.

Over two hundred U.S. Special Forces had mounted a search and capture mission based on the information from the old farmer. With directions from the traitor, they cornered the elusive al-Qaeda leader in a cave. The Americans were close to capturing him alive. He knew he would be paraded around and his picture shown like Saddam's if captured. He had given orders this must not happen. As the Americans were entering the cave one of his lieutenants pulled out his sword. Bin Laden knelt to the ground facing Mecca. Eternal glory was awaiting him. His lieutenant, with tears in his eyes, understood and completed his mission. He then pulled out his pistol and joined bin Laden denying the Americans their triumph.

Al-Saim was an excellent reader of men. They never publicly questioned his authority. Instead, their eyes asked all of the questions. He knew and understood their concerns. He also knew al-Qaeda was in trouble as an organization. The establishment of a democratic government in Iraq and subsequent defeat of the insurgency there had been a key blow against the organization. The Americans had killed or captured much of the leadership. Major attacks had been thwarted due to the cooperation of the United States and European authorities. Funding had all but ceased as a result of the Americans' stranglehold on their finances. There was talk al-Qaeda was finished as a major terrorist threat.

However, as winter gives to spring, events in the world had occurred to inspire hope for the future. His Islamic brothers had found their calling again in the Mideast. Regimes loyal to Fundamentalism from Algeria to Syria had spread like wildfire in a drought. For indeed they were in a drought. The long-sought goal of a nuclear device was delayed with the destruction of Esfahan and the other facilities, but they would acquire one in due time. He knew it was Israel that had conducted the attack. He had no need of intelligence briefings. Only the swine from the stolen lands were arrogant enough to attempt to deny them their weapons while they continued with their own nuclear program.

More importantly, the recent election in Europe had confirmed Al-Saim's inspiration of a plan that was greater than 9/11. He had approached the nominee of the Europe First Party on the prospect of his vision and had gained his support. The grandeur and daring of the plan was almost unbelievable in its scope. If successful, his name would replace bin Laden's around the world. It might add weight to his claim of Caliph, Ruler of the Islamic world. His closest followers had mentioned that possibility to him but he dismissed them for now. Surely though, his place in Heaven would be guaranteed.

"Great followers of Allah and bin Laden…lift your spirits today," he began with raised arms. "Allah has indeed smiled on his followers. He has given me a vision that will lift the hearts of our brethren everywhere. The magnitude of this vision will require the sacrifice of many…but the price is justified for we will see the destruction of our common enemy and the return of the stolen lands will be our reward!"

His men were somewhat skeptical of the words they had heard, for they had heard them many times before. Still, an excitement filled the cold damp cave. Eyes that were previously downcast began to burn bright with fire and zeal. Surely it meant one thing.

"Jihad, Jihad, Jihad," they all cried in unison, rising to their feet.

Al-Saim stood before his men as they continued to chant. He knew their hearts and their passions had been stirred. He motioned them to return to their seats.

"Yes, indeed Jihad. But in time," he said with a raised hand. "First, and this is where the sacrifice will be paid by many of our brothers. There must be peace."

Stunned silence now filled the cave. *Peace?* He could see the questions in their eyes. Peace had never served their cause. Israel still occupied land taken in the 1967 war. Peace had seen Israel further settle the stolen lands. Peace had seen Iraq turn to democracy. Peace was not their friend.

"Yes, my brothers, peace. We cannot have victory without peace first. But when the peace comes, trust me, as Allah has trusted me with the vision, we will see victory. There is much to do. We must contact our brothers in America for their help is needed. I will call for the Council of the Alliance to convene and meet with our brothers to secure their help. But remember, we must exercise the diligence of the mongoose closing in on its prey. Too apparent and we die. Too slow and we die."

There was much to do but he knew he had struck a cord. There was new warmth in the cave. The fire had been lit.

Esfahan, Iran

December 1st

10:35 a.m.

General Kahlid's helicopter arrived at the site of the destroyed facility. He was not pleased with what he saw. He had been awakened by his aide with word that the main reactor had exploded damaging the facility. As his pilot circled two hundred feet above the inferno, he knew the damage had not been caused by an explosion. At least not one that occurred within the reactor. There was too much damage. Most of the buildings had been destroyed at the complex. The reactors had been reduced to a pile of rubble. Emergency crews were struggling to contain the fires that were blazing into the morning sky. The smoke from the fires was obscuring the sun that was continuing its rise in the east. No, this was not an accident. This was deliberate.

"Land this thing," Kahlid ordered.

His pilot maneuvered the Mi-24 to the landing strip. Kahlid was on his feet at the hatch before the machine landed. As the landing gear touched down, he opened the door and bolted out to what was once a key component of Iran's nuclear weapons program. He stood for a moment with his feet wide and hands on his hips as he surveyed the damage from ground level. Emergency crews continued to arrive but he knew all was lost here. The main concern now was containment of the main reactor itself. He did not need another Chernobyl. He did not think this would be the case, as the reactor itself had not been activated. But what of the nuclear material? It was paramount that it be secured and recovered.

More tragic than the loss of the reactor was the loss of the scientists. He could see the area where they had been housed. Only ruble remained. Buildings could be replaced quickly. The trained scientists, several of whom were Russians, were irreplaceable. Rescue teams with dogs were in route, but he knew it was a futile effort. Any doubts this had been an accident had long been eroded away.

Kahlid now made his way to one of the three remaining structures of the facility. These had survived only because they were constructed behind an outcrop of rock. The building he was concerned with was the Air Defense building.

"Where is the dog that is responsible for this mess?" Kahild demanded as he burst through the door. His drawn pistol signaled the intensity of his demand.

"Sir, I am Colonel Parphez. I am in charge of defenses," a shaken man announced as he entered from an office in the back of the room.

"Colonel, I want an explanation as to how this happened!" Kahlid demanded.

"Yes, sir! Please step over to this monitor. This will answer all of your questions."

Kahlid stared at the man as he approached the monitor. The technician nervously pressed the replay button with trembling hands bringing the monitor to life. The images showed incoming streaks from the east. AAA fire was shown reaching for the streaks. The monitor went bright from the impact of the streaks with the complex and then went blank.

"Who? Who are the dogs that did this?!" Kahlid demanded. "Were there no images of the planes?"

"No, sir. Our radar has a one hundred mile range. It sits atop the highest point in this area. We have a clear view in all directions. I alerted Air Defense headquarters immediately after the alarm went off. None of our radar sites detected any intruders." He hoped that the General would be pleased with his efforts to alert headquarters and stop the intruders.

Kahlid glared at the man. How could this incompetent rise to the rank of Colonel? No wonder his country had not been able to defeat Iraq in the eighties if this were the caliber of men in service. He had no doubt achieved his rank through family connections. Kahlid did not care. He would deal with his incompetence later.

Kahild thought for a moment as he went through the nations with inventories of aircraft capable of such a strike. Stealth aircraft had to have been involved. That meant three countries. The Russian dogs were eliminated as they were providing technical assistance for the reactor. That left only two: Israel and the United States. In his heart he knew it was Israel with assistance from the Americans. They had a history of this type of treachery. They benefited the most.

It was possible that fragments of the missiles might exist. If he could find these, he could prove to the world the hostile action of this rogue nation. He needed proof, though. The weak-minded United Nations would not condemn Israel without it. However, he was not worried about the United Nations. They were a puppet organization of the United States anyway. The goal he sought was to ignite the Jihad against the common enemy once and for all. He would need help with this. But first things first.

"Colonel, your incompetence has resulted in the destruction of this facility and has made us weak in the eyes of our enemies. I hope that you defend your home with more diligence. I hold you responsible." The Colonel moved to speak, but was cut short as Kahlid raised his pistol and fired. The control room personnel stood in stunned silence as the Colonel's body fell to the floor.

"Remove this swine," Kahlid ordered as he left the building and made his way to his helicopter. His pilot already had the chopper warmed up and ready for takeoff.

"Back to headquarters. I have work to do," Kahlid said as he settled into his seat. There would be retribution for this.

SIGNS

Naval Station Mayport
Jacksonville, Florida
December 2^(nd)
5:05 p.m.

Javier Abukar was completing a sale of beer and cigarettes to yet another group of sailors leaving Naval Station Mayport. He and his brothers worked at the Quik-Mart located three blocks away from the base. They had chosen this location for a reason. Located along the North Florida coast, Mayport was the homeport of the *John F. Kennedy*. What better place to gain intelligence on the day-to-day occurrences at the base than by its front door? As the base civilian personnel left at five every day on the dot, many stopped in for gas or munchies for their commute home. The sailors who had liberty often made this store their first stop on the weekend for the essentials of beer, ice, and cigarettes. Akubar made it a point to be friendly to the customers. He knew many by sight and many more by name by simply paying close attention to their credit cards or checks. He found that most Americans responded in a friendly manner if you addressed them by name. Yes, they had chosen their location wisely. What better way to infiltrate a naval base than to have the base come to you?

He had been employed there before 9/11 as a member of one of the hundreds of terror cells posted across America. His employment was merely a cover story. His cell, like many others, had not been activated for that attack. In fact, he had not known of the impending attack until the reports began filtering in over the television behind the counter. He was as surprised as his American customers at the audacity of the attack.

He had learned much about the base and its operations after the attack from just listening to the customers coming in. Their biggest gripe had been the increase in security. For the civilian personnel employed there, longer security checks to enter the base were the norm meaning they had to get up earlier to be at work on time. That civilians were employed on a military base was a foreign concept to Abukar. He thought of the training camps in Afghanistan. Only soldiers were present, as it should be.

The greatest benefit of his employment was being able to report when the *Kennedy* would be departing for missions. He would see a noticeable drop in store sales just before the carrier deployed as the crew began pre-deployment activities. The long looks on the faces of the female customers were also a telltale sign. Many had boyfriends in the Navy and they would often come in with their girlfriends talking about the need for their man. He had taken advantage of this need several times. Abukar was a striking man and he had learned the right phrases to say to his female customers from listening to the sailors.

He had also learned more about Mayport from listening to those who worked on the base than all of the American spy satellites would ever know about his cell. Yes, much could be learned if one just listened. It amazed him that the CIA, now DNIS, had neglected this aspect of intelligence. He had watched the news reports during the recent Presidential race; national security was the dominant issue. Charges flew that both sides had neglected the intelligence community, in particular the human side of intelligence gathering. As a result, more money flowed in the new Department of National Intelligence and Security than did the Department of Homeland Security after 9/11. An increased emphasis on human intel was the focus of the new Secretary of DNIS. That organization was now beginning to see the dividends on their reinvestment in the human side of intelligence. Three weeks earlier in Chicago, two cells had been arrested in connection with al-Qaeda. The members of those cells had grown careless, which resulted in their arrest. He knew he and his brothers would have to be extra careful.

"Thought you boys would be heading out to sea pretty soon. You have been here for a while," Abukar said to the sailors as they handed him the money for their purchases.

"Not for a while. Ship is receiving upgrades to the computer software. Supposed to help radar interceptions, fire control, junk like that.

Biggest mess I've ever seen," said one of the young men. "Glad I'm in search and rescue. No problems there."

"Computers. I hate 'em. This one at the store crashes all the time," Abukar said as he empathized with the young men. *Be friendly and get them talking and they would tell you anything. Just listen,* he reminded himself, *and let them talk.*

"Junk if you ask me," chimed in the other sailor. "Ain't nothing ever loaded right the first time. We couldn't shoot or see spit right now if we had to. Ain't nothing working on board right now. Feel bad for the dudes stuck on board this weekend! Too pretty out to be on ship."

"Yeah, me and Tom here got some hot dates for the weekend. Well, mine is, but yours..." he said to his friend. "Let's just say it must have been lonely on the last cruise. Distance is the only thing help'n her!" he said as he and Abukar enjoyed a laugh at the expense of the other man.

"Come on, jerk, let's get outta here," said the friend as he reached for the beer.

"You have a good time this weekend with the babes. Save one for me!" Abukar said to the sailors as they were departing. They hoisted their already opened beers in his direction.

"No chance for that," they replied exiting the store.

As he was closing the cash register the phone rang.

"The sun rises in the east," said the voice on the phone.

"And sinks in the west," he replied.

He gazed through the store window as he returned the phone to the cradle. The sun was beginning to slide into the St. John's River. He knew this day would come. He had prayed it would and now his prayers had been answered.

Esfahan, Iran

December 3rd

6:35 a.m.

General Kahlid's helicopter stirred the early morning air as it again descended and landed at the former nuclear facility. By now the fires had been contained and were almost all extinguished. Several fires were still smoldering around the reactor as crews continued to work in that area. Three other helicopters also landed. Packed into these machines were men equipped with some of the most sophisticated search equipment on the planet. In fact, many would say the most sophisticated.

"Colonel, have your men search the site. You know what we are looking for. We must find evidence of who launched this attack. When we have this, I will personally lead the retaliatory strike. I will be in the Air Defense building awaiting your findings," ordered Kahlid.

"Yes, sir," replied Colonel Shavaz as he turned to his men. "Sergeant, deploy your search crews. Report to me with any findings."

The sergeant snapped off a smart salute and turned to face his search crews with their orders. The search crews were equipped with Golden Labs. The dogs had been trained in Russia and acquired by the Iranians to search for explosives in sensitive areas. Kahlid knew the dogs were good. He had seen them in their initial demonstrations by their Russian handlers.

The nine search crews began to fan out across the grounds of the facility. The dogs were straining at their leashes as they moved through the ruins. They would stop and sniff an area for a moment before moving on. Their handlers were concentrating on the housing areas in hope of finding remnants of any explosives. They did not want to risk the dogs at the reactor for fear of potential radiation. The monitoring equipment placed around the reactors had not yet detected any radiation leaks. The work crews had done a tremendous job in sealing off the reactor from potential leaks.

It was getting late in the day. Colonel Shavaz was beginning to think his dogs were not going to have any success. He knew they would have to soon stop the search and give the animals a break. Like their human handlers they got tired and hungry and needed a rest from their jobs. He was preparing to signal his teams to end their search for the day when Team Four's dog began to paw at one pile of rubble. That was the sign she had found something. The sergeant in charge of the team excitedly called for Shavaz who sprinted to the site.

"Sergeant, what do you have?" he asked somewhat winded.

"Sir, she appears to have detected explosive residue. Allow me one minute to look a little closer. I think I see something."

The sergeant and his men knelt down and began to carefully remove the rocks and broken cement. Their search was soon rewarded. Within the debris was a piece of metal that was charred on one end but relatively clean on the other. It was on this end he saw what he was hoping for.

"Colonel, I have found what we are searching for," shouted the sergeant exuberantly as he proudly held up the missile fragment.

Colonel Shavaz climbed up the mound of debris to where the sergeant was. He took the charred fragment and examined it for himself. He had to be sure it was what he was looking for before he presented this to Kahlid. Shavaz had seen how the General rewarded incompetence. Carefully, he turned the metal fragment over in his hands. The lettering was unmistakable: English and Hebrew. He knew the Americans would not add Hebrew to their weapons.

"Get the General," he said to one of the privates.

AL JAZEERA HEADQUARTERS

DOHA, QATAR

6:45 p.m.

The lights were burning bright on the set as the newscasters were making last minute changes to their scripts before airtime. Final preparations were being made for the evening news that was broadcast worldwide. The producer was speaking to them through their earpieces.

"Get ready. We are fifteen minutes from airtime."

The light above the green phone on his control panel began to flash red. This was his version of the hotline. He had given this number to many of his sources in the event of breaking news so they could contact him. Like his newsmen counterparts around the world, he knew the value of being first to report a story.

"Yes," he said as he continued his preparations for the pending broadcast.

He almost dropped the phone with the news from the caller as he listened to the details.

"Are you sure?" he inquired. His hands began to sweat as he hurriedly reached for a pen and began taking notes. "One hundred percent positive? There can be no error." The caller assured him of the accuracy of the information. Satisfied with the credibility of his source, he hung up the phone and sat for just a second to compose his thoughts. Turning to his computer he anxiously rewrote the lead story.

He finished typing and printed a copy to review what he had written. He waved over the editor to review the new lead story. The editor's eyes went wide as she read the story. She had to reread it again as the enormity of it began to sink in. She handed the draft back to him.

"Get this out there. I am printing you additional copies. No time for the teleprompter."

He keyed the mike to his newscasters as the editor left the control room to deliver the story to the anchors. "I am sending you a story that is earth-shattering in its content. I am counting on your professionalism to deliver this. I do not want to see your passions. The story will serve that purpose. One minute to airtime."

On his monitor he watched the faces of the newscasters as they read the updated lead story. They both looked up at the control booth in disbelief. In their earpieces they could hear their producer count down: "Three, two, one."

"Good evening. Our lead story tonight," boomed the voice of the lead anchor. His voice was steady and calm as he read the words on the paper in his hands though inside his heart was racing. Juxtaposed over his right shoulder were pictures of the destroyed facility of Esfahan. "*Al-Jazeera* news has just learned that the Israeli Air Force is responsible for the recent attack on the peaceful civilian nuclear research centers at Esfahan, Arak, and Natanz in Iran. Iranian military officials have recovered residual remains of the missiles employed in this unprecedented and unprovoked attack on Iran's peaceful nuclear research program. The missile fragments were inscribed with Hebrew and English lettering. It is estimated that over three hundred innocent individuals were killed in this attack. We will bring more on this story as it continues to unfold. Again, repeating our lead story…"

THE OFFER

EUROPEAN UNION HEADQUARTERS

BRUSSELS

December 4th

8:27 a.m.

The pressroom was filled to capacity with the world's media. All were anticipating the interview with the new European Union President, Hans Gerhard. There had been much speculation as to the comments he would make in his first formal press conference since being sworn in as President of the European Union. Gerhard entered the pressroom from a side door. The European press corps rose to their feet with thunderous applause. News crews from the rest of the world joined them in standing and offered their applause. Their attention and cameras were more focused on the reaction of their European counterparts than Gerhard. Flashes from the cameras transformed the room into a small fireworks display. Gerhard, relishing the applause, took the podium while pretending to quiet the room. He allowed the applause to continue for a few minutes and then began to speak. The applause died down as the press corps quickly began taking notes.

"Ladies and gentlemen of the press, thank you for that very warm welcome. I am glad you could be here to join me as we begin our journey. For indeed these are historic days for the peoples of Europe."

He spent the next few minutes thanking all who had supported him in the election and making the usual platitudes toward his opponents. He fielded typical questions on his reaction to the election along with trade and employment issues. He could sense the room was waiting for the real purpose of the press conference. Unlike other press conferences the media was accustomed to, this one had an agenda. A specific order of topics had been distributed to the press members with strict instructions that the order would be followed.

"Now let me turn to international affairs," began Gerhard. "You will recall that I campaigned on the premise that Europe was strong enough to stand on her own in terms of political and military affairs in the world. I intend to make good on that promise. To that end, after consultations with and support from representatives of the Union, I am announcing our withdrawal from the North Atlantic Treaty Organization effective immediately."

A brief outbreak of applause was heard from the European press, but the remainder of the room was instantly firing follow up questions. However, Gerhard was not finished. He motioned the room to quiet down so he could continue.

"We live in a world that is fraught with danger. We are particularly concerned with one part of the world more so than any other and that is the Middle East. You have seen the report from *Al-Jazeera* regarding the unprovoked Israeli strike on the peaceful civilian research facilities at Esfahan and other locations in Iran. Tragically, many innocent Iranians have died as a result of the imprudent course of action taken by Israel.

"The Middle East has been a powder keg for far too long. The world has seen eight major conflicts in this area since World War II alone. The Yom Kippur War almost involved a nuclear exchange between the United States and the Soviet Union. This underlies the potential for war in this area and it would be a war that would most likely involve the world.

"To this end I am calling for a summit meeting between all parties involved to discuss peace in this area. As a purely neutral party, the European Union is willing to assume the lead role of peacekeeper. To support this I am pledging the military forces of the Union to stand in the gap to insure peace. I have ordered EU peacekeeping forces to prepare for immediate deployment to the area pending agreement from the involved parties. These will include air, land, and naval forces.

"I am asking all parties to remain calm and to not take retaliatory action. I have been in contact with General Kahlid of the Iranian government. In a remarkable display of statesmanship, he has assured me the Iranian government will not be exacting what would be justified retaliation in light of the tragic loss of life involved with this attack, and violation of Iranian sovereignty. We are grateful at their measured response to this unprovoked attack on their peaceful nuclear research facilities. Iranian forces, in addition to other Alliance forces, are understandably remaining on high alert. We are thankful they are restraining from taking military action. Together, we can work through this."

"Mr. President, when and where will the summit be conducted?" asked the *BBC* representative.

"I should like to convene the meeting in Geneva within three weeks. We cannot allow a further destabilization of this area to occur. Time, ladies and gentlemen, is of the essence."

"Mr. President, will the Americans be invited to the summit in light of their support of Israel?" asked the reporter from the Associated Press.

"Not at this time and for the very reason you mentioned," replied Gerhard to the still stunned press corps. "For this summit to be successful it must be free from potential antagonisms. I mean no disrespect to our American friends, but their long-term support of Israel would be too much of a distraction at this time. Due to the surprise nature of the attack some have speculated that American-supplied stealth aircraft were employed in the raid. You may recall it was American-supplied aircraft that were employed in Israel's unjustified attack on Iraq's peaceful nuclear program in 1981—back when Iraq was actually pursuing weapons of mass destruction. Unlike what the Americans told us leading up to their illegal invasion of Iraq in 2003," Gerhard said with a devilish smile. The European press broke out in boisterous laughter at this last statement. Gerhard pretended to quiet them down before continuing.

"America's recent imperialist interventions in the Middle East would cast further dispersions on their objectivity. It is time for a fresh approach."

"Herr Gerhard, do you really think the world's sole superpower should be left out of this peace process?" asked the representative from *Fox News.*

"You mean the world's *other* superpower?" Gerhard fired back at the American reporter.

The room noted the tone and manner in which Gerhard replied to this question. It was clear there was a new power in the world, at least in the mind of the new European President. His scathing attack on American involvement in the Middle East and support of Israel was intended to signal the world of this change in the geo-political balance. The questions continued regarding the details of the summit and the likelihood of success. What demands would be placed upon the parties? Was this a realistic attempt at peace or just grandstanding on Gerhard's part? There were some questions involving the dissolution of the NATO alliance, but all had been overshadowed by the proposed Mideast peace talks as Gerhard had calculated.

AIR FORCE HEADQUARTERS
DAMASCUS, SYRIA
December 4th
6:45 a.m.

Al-Saim had risen for morning prayers after a long night's sleep. The journey from his base in Afghanistan had been hard and the extra rest was needed. His two-vehicle caravan, consisting of captured Land Rover Defenders, had driven non-stop to Damascus. He was aware the Americans were attempting to do to him as they had done to members of al-Qaeda's leadership. But he had taken steps to prevent that. For travel at night, his men had equipped themselves with Newcom Optic night vision goggles to search for the Predator drones operated by the United States. He was pleased with the diligence of his men as they twice spotted the Predators while crossing through Afghanistan enabling them to take evasive action. He had no doubt that the Americans would have fired if he had been spotted. To help confuse the spy drones, they would frequently stop and change the camouflage on the vehicles. Many blankets and pieces of canvas had been packed in anticipation of this. Also packed in the vehicles were two shoulder fired Russian SA-18 Grouse SAMs in case a Predator, or any other aircraft, approached too close.

His accommodations were the guest quarters of the commanding officer. He reasoned that the guests who occupied this room on a frequent basis were more of the female persuasion than visiting dignitaries. Even among the faithful there were some who struggled with earthly pleasures. Perhaps the commander's service to Allah would enable him to see his reward in the next life. The room was lavishly appointed even by the decadent standards of the West. Every amenity had been thought of, including plenty of fresh fruit. He was not tempted by the movies or other entertainment that was available through a phone call. The fruit and a long hot shower were the only luxuries in which he allowed himself to indulge. The staff had seen to his every need. Indeed, when they recognized whom their guest was their attention to detail increased dramatically. *It was as they should*, he thought. He would be thoughtful and commend their superiors. He checked the clock beside the bed. It was time to meet his guests.

Al-Saim exited his quarters and made his way across the compound. An armed guard accompanied him along with his aide. He was careful to keep his head down to avoid having his face photographed by American spy satellites. All members of the Islamic Alliance were here for this meeting as he had been promised. The call for a Mideast peace summit that did not involve the United States had been the catalyst that was needed. So far, the infidel Gerhard had been faithful to his word. Now, he would have to be faithful to his.

He entered the spacious banquet room of the headquarters building. It was as he had been promised. Representatives from Hamas, Intafada, Islamic Jihad, PLO, Hezzbollah, and Al-Fatah were milling around the room with many others. Representatives from Egypt, Iran, Jordan, Libya, Algeria, Tunisia, Morocco, and of course, Syria were there. His aides had been dutiful in their mission of gathering leaders from every country and sect in the region that were enemies of Israel and the United States. He could not recall when all had been present in one room and for one purpose. In fact, this assembly of brothers had never been attempted. If the Mossad or DNIS had intelligence on this meeting they could eliminate the leadership of the Islamic Fundamentalist world in one strike. The removal of so many key leaders in the movement would have dealt the Alliance a serious blow. Had the Mossad or DNIS detected anything? Had any aspect of security been overlooked? Every foreseeable precaution had been taken in contacting these brethren. All had been contacted in person. None had flown to minimize the chance detection of a name on a passport even though they traveled under false passports. There was no electronic trail for the DNIS to follow as no phones or emails were employed. Nothing had been left to chance. Granted, it had taken extra time, but the security was worth the delay. He could not worry about such things as that now. He had to trust Allah.

His entrance caused a stir among the faithful that were gathered there. All came to him and greeted him with the traditional kiss. His reputation as leader of the faith had been cemented with the death of bin Laden and now he was going to exercise that role to bring glory to all believers.

"Brothers, thank you for coming. I bid you to be seated." Once they had taken their respective places, Al-Saim stood before them.

"I know you have many questions regarding our meeting today. But I have good news. I have received a vision. Yes, Allah has spoken to me. He has given me a vision on how to regain the stolen lands of our ancestors. This is the message I bring you today. This task will not be easy but it will eliminate our enemies.

"The recent changes in Europe have opened a window of opportunity for us and on this we must act. The United States stands alone in the world today. Her allies have deserted her. The European Union has separated itself from the United States. NATO is no more. The new European President has signaled that Europe is willing to act as an intermediary between us and the Israelis in peace negotiations. To be successful, we must be prepared to offer things in negotiations that we have never considered before, and will never have to consider again. Sacrifices will be required. We will be required to turn the other cheek. We must show the world that it is not the Muslim, but the Israeli, who is opposed to peace."

The room stirred with the buzz of muffled conversation as each man conferred with aides and neighbors. Questions were aired to Al-Saim. Did they really hear what they thought they heard? Sacrifices to be made? What more could be offered? How much more of their innocent blood must be shed by their enemy? What guarantees was Europe offering? What would be the reaction of the United States?

"My, brothers," Al-Saim said as he stood with outstretched arms, "I understand your concerns for they are my concerns also. I know our enemy has shed much of our people's blood while they continue to occupy the stolen lands. My heart weighs heavy on the sacrifices our people have endured since our land was stolen in 1948. But a new day is here. The United States will not be in a position to influence these negotiations. The Europeans are going to be neutral in these affairs, for they have no Jewish lobby to distort the truth regarding whom the rightful owners of the sacred lands are. Nor do they have any elected officials to be bribed by the Jewish lobby as in America. My friends, they are willing to guarantee peace in this area. But there is more. A matter of greatest importance that I must speak of only to you without the presence of your aides. Bid them farewell until our business here is concluded."

Another stir swept across the room. What could not be spoken among brothers? Reluctantly each man bid their aides to leave the room. Each was somewhat apprehensive as their bodyguards were among their aides. Though they were united in their desire to rid the world of Israel there were still factions within their circle. Old scores had not been settled between some. Trust was not a luxury they could afford. One did not reach their position in life by trusting unless it was backed by the sword. Each had their vision of how best to solve their common goal of eliminating Israel, but to date none had been able to gather all present as Al-Saim had. The room grew quiet as the aides gradually exited closing the doors behind them.

"Trust," Al-Saim said as he walked among the room looking into each man's eyes. "It is not an easy thing. Yes, there are old scores to settle and differences within this room among us. I know this. But, my brothers, the first step has been taken on our journey and you have made it. Look around. We are gathered here united as one, for one purpose. To regain the stolen lands from our common enemy. To regain Palestine." He allowed that thought to play in their minds before continuing. "But before we move forward, I must ask for your complete trust and that what we speak of will not be shared with anyone outside of this room. If this trust is broken we must ask for the life of that individual. What I am asking requires you to place your life into the hands of your brother."

Al-Saim walked over to the first man and gazed intensely in his face as he stood before him awaiting his agreement. Al-Saim deliberately chose him for he was the representative from the PLO.

Of all the groups present, notwithstanding the Iranians, the PLO representative had the most significant right to reject Al-Saim's proposal. His people had perhaps suffered the most politically and spiritually since the creation of Israel as a nation-state. It was his people who had lost their land to the Israelis. Their demise originated with the Balfour Declaration of 1917, which provided for a Jewish "national home" within the borders of what was then Palestine. The call for a home for the Jews was further accelerated after World War II and the Holocaust. Israeli control over what was Palestine was further solidified in 1948 with the formation of Israel as a nation-state. The subsequent wars between Israel and her Arab neighbors only cemented Israel's ownership of the land and her claim to her ancestral homeland, diminishing any prospect for the return of the land to the Palestinians. No other country in the Middle East had been forced to give up any land to Israel as Palestine had. To this end, the PLO was created in 1964 with the stated goal of liberating the land currently occupied by Israel.

An attempt had been made between Israel and the PLO to return control of the Gaza Strip and West Bank to PLO control in 2005 via the Disengagement Implementation Law, or Gaza Pull Out Plan. Israel did withdraw from these areas as agreed, but increasing terrorist activities launched from these areas forced the Israeli government to reoccupy the lands in 2009. Once again, the Palestinians were without a homeland.

He nodded to Al-Saim. Al-Saim repeated this until he had stood before each representative and received their approval. All in the room now followed his every move. This was a meeting unlike any had ever attended or would attend again.

"Brothers, I thank you for your trust in each other. For that is who you are trusting from this moment forward. I will now share with you the vision Allah has given to me. We are going to enter into peace negotiations with the Israelis. These meetings are going to be brokered by the European President. We are going to give the Israelis more than they could ever dream of at the peace table. They want us to recognize their right to exist—we shall recognize it. They want a cessation of what they call terrorist attacks—they shall have it. Brothers, please understand—this includes the *al-Haram al-Qudsi al-Sharif*," Al-Saim said watching the expressions on their faces.

Al-Saim paused for just a moment to allow these words to register. A stir rippled through the room. Each man understood the significance of this statement. Al-Saim was offering the third most sacred site in all of Islam, after Mecca and Medina, as a sacrifice. He further explained the sacrifice would require allowing Israel the right to rebuild her Temple alongside the Qubbat Al-Sakhrah.

The Qubbat Al-Sakhrah, or Dome of the Rock, was the key obstacle to peace in the area. It is actually one component of the structure more commonly known as the Noble Sanctuary (*al-Haram al-Qudsi al-Sharif*: Arabic) or Temple Mount (*Har ha-Bayit*: Jewish) depending on one's perspective. There are three main components of the area known as the Temple Mount. The most prominent and famous is the Dome of the Rock. Located in the middle of the Temple Mount, the golden Dome dominates the Jerusalem skyline and is a symbol of all things Muslim in the Jewish city. The second, though not as well known in the western world, component of the Temple Mount is The Al-Aqsa Mosque, or the Furthest Mosque. Third is the Western Wall. Jews consider this to be the remaining part of an outer courtyard wall of the Second Temple.

Resting atop Mount Moriah and located in the walled part of the Old City of Jerusalem, this piece of real estate is the most contested land in the world. The Temple Mount plays a key role in the history and future of Christianity, Islam, and Judaism—three of the world's greatest religions. Both Jew and Arab have claimed ownership to the sacred site. The history of the Temple Mount area is a long one beginning around 2000 BC.

For the Jewish believer, this land, specifically the part upon which the Dome of the Rock is constructed, is where Abraham, father of Israel, offered his son Isaac as a sacrifice before the goodness of Jehovah stopped him from completing the sacrifice. Later in Israeli history, it was on this sight that King Solomon completed construction of the first Temple in 950 BC as commanded by Jehovah. King Nebuchadnezzar subsequently destroyed the Temple in 586 BC during the Babylonian invasion of Israel. The Temple was then rebuilt by Israel through the leadership of Zachariah and Haggai in 515 BC.

Herod the Great, of the Roman Empire, ordered that the Temple Mount area be renovated around 20 BC. His plans called for the destruction of the existing Temple and a new, enlarged Temple to be built. To accommodate the structure, he doubled the size of the Temple Mount area by erecting four massive retaining walls. The Western Wall is the remaining portion of this structure. The Romans, under General Titus, laid siege to Jerusalem in 66 AD in response to the Jewish Rebellion, ultimately destroying the Temple in 70 AD a final time as punishment for their rebellion.

It was at the Temple that Jesus taught the masses. He later threw the moneychangers out declaring that His Father's house would not be turned into a den of thieves. His own prophecy predicted the destruction of the Temple. Christian prophecy states it will one day be rebuilt again. Standing in the way of this prophecy being fulfilled is the Dome of the Rock.

For the Muslim believer, this is the site of the Prophet Muhammad's Night Journey. During the ninth year of the Prophet's mission, Muhammad arose in the middle of the night to visit the sacred Mosque in Mecca. He fell asleep near the Ka'aba after a time of worship. The angel Gabriel appeared and awoke him. Upon mounting the wings of al-Buraq, the Prophet and Gabriel sped northwards from Mecca to the Furthest Mosque, Al-Aqsa, in Jerusalem. Upon reaching Jerusalem, the Prophet dismounted and prayed near the Rock of Moriah. He then embarked on the ascension in which he received the command to pray five times a day and the revelation of the beliefs of Islam.

Al-Saim's ancestors captured Jerusalem and this Holy Site in 638 AD, some six years after the death of the prophet Muhammad. Caliph Abd al-Malik commenced work on the great Dome of the Rock beginning in 688 AD and completed construction in 691. Constructed atop the remnants of the former Israeli Temple where the Holy of Holies stood, the Dome of the Rock remained under Muslim control for 1276 years until the Israelis captured East Jerusalem and the Temple Mount in the Six Day War of 1967.

With Jerusalem reunited, recognition of that city as Israel's capital was now absolute amongst Israelis. However, not wanting to further infuriate the Arab world after their victory, the Israelis placed control of the Temple Mount under Arab authority with the stipulation that Israelis would have access to the Western Wall.

It was a compromise, and with most compromises, both parties felt they had given up too much. But, with the Israeli Air Force in command of the air and Israeli tanks encircling Jerusalem, there was little Al-Saim's ancestors could do but agree to the compromise. The agreement to share the sacred site had been made to avoid further bloodshed and placate Arab pride in light of Israel's stunning victory.

"In return," he continued, "the Israelis will make concessions to us that will be trivial in comparison. We will seize world public opinion and prove that our negotiations are serious. This noble gesture will prove that it is the Israelis, and not Muslims, that stand in the way of peace if they refuse. Europe in turn will provide peacekeeping forces in the border areas. And this is where additional sacrifice must be made. If any of our brothers attempt to sow discord we must deal with them." He paused to garner their attention again. "Through death. We cannot allow the passions of a few to undo our quest.

"This next part is why your pledge of secrecy is so vital. If broken, it must be redeemed by your life." He paused again. "After a period of time, during which it appears the peace is legitimate and all are living in harmony, a sword will come out of the night. Then we, in conjunction with our European allies, will swoop down on the unsuspecting Israelis. The Europeans will close the Mediterranean and prevent the United States from reinforcing Israel as they did in 1973. This will leave us with local superiority and the opportunity to eliminate Israel once and for all. We are prepared to continue even if they employ their nuclear weapons. If they do, we will retaliate with the chemical and biological weapons we smuggled out of Iraq before their betrayal.

"We were close in 1973 to destroying Israel. If we had pushed harder we would have had victory. A handful of Israeli tanks on the Golan Heights prevented us from driving into Israel. This time we will stop at nothing. *We will succeed*," he concluded his eyes burning bright with excitement.

The room was quiet in astonishment. They could hardly believe the words they had just heard. The plan was grandiose beyond belief. Was this the voice of a madman or the voice of Allah? One had heard enough.

"This is preposterous!" yelled Shariff Abdul-Yumar from Iran. "You are asking us to believe that Allah would have us give the Dome of the Rock to the Jewish pigs, and that the infidel Europeans would join us in battle against the Americans and Israelis? The Americans sold them the Raptors used in the attack. They will not sit by idle if Israel is attacked. You believe in fairy tales old man. We have proof that the Israelis were the ones who bombed our nuclear facilities. You have seen it. We need no more evidence. We should be discussing plans to attack instead of these foolish peace talks. Our people will not understand! I do not understand. You have been in the mountains too long old man. I will hear no more of this nonsense."

Abdul-Yumar rose from his seat and demanded, "Brothers, will you follow this old fool or me? I will lead you to victory. Not useless words as this one would." He then began to make his way to the front where Al-Saim stood impassively. Before he could make it, one man arose and drew a sword that he planted in the back of Abdul-Yumar. He withdrew the weapon as Yumar spun around to meet his aggressor, but it was too late as the sword again made contact and cut across Yumar's abdomen. Abdul-Yumar's eyes went wide as he gasped for breath and fell to the floor. With life rapidly departing he lifted a hand toward Al-Saim.

"Forgive me, brother," he said as life left him.

All in the room were stunned at the sudden turn of events. All now redirected their attention to the old man from the mountains. Each man nervously eyed his neighbor. Would there be others to fall by the sword? Al-Saim knew what needed to be done next. But did the men gathered before him? Had his message been understood regarding sacrifices?

"Call for his aides," said Rasheef Jallud, the one who had drawn the sword, as he looked at Al-Saim. He motioned to three others who joined him at the doors. Jallud's gaze was fixed squarely on Al-Saim as he placed his hand on the handle to the door. Al-Saim nodded slightly toward Jallud. He opened the door and called for Yumar's aides. There was no hint of excitement or stress in his voice. Jallud was no stranger to the sword. On several occasions he had employed it to defend himself from zealots who thought they could usurp his leadership. He had dispatched those individuals with the same cold efficiency as he had Yumar. Al-Saim noted the poise displayed by Jallud. He had found one who understood. Would the others follow?

General Kahlid and two others entered the room feeling honored to have been the first called into the meeting. Surely their master was calling them in to announce plans for the attack on Israel. Kahlid relished the prospect of leading the counterattack. As they entered the room they noticed all were standing before the table. Curiously they did not see their master among them. Kahlid began to feel uneasy as he saw the anger in the eyes of those in the room. His aides had seen the same anger in his eyes previously. Before they could inquire about their master, those standing parted to reveal Yumar's crumpled body in a pool of blood on the floor. The sight of blood and their master's body on the floor deflected their attention from the three men with drawn swords approaching from behind. Kahlid recovered first from the shock but was too late in moving to defend himself. The swords cut into the men dispatching them as easily as their master.

"Brothers," Al-Saim addressed the room, "my blood boils at what happened at Esfahan. No one would question if we retaliated. But we will not. Not yet. That is a small sacrifice for now. We will use this as a catalyst to bring Israel to the table. The world will immediately condemn them. They will be seen as the pariah. Our patience and self-restraint will be admired around the world. You now understand the sacrifices that must be made. There will be greater ones than Esfahan that we will have to make in the future. Our journey will not be easy. Many will not understand. It will be up to you to provide the leadership necessary for our success. Because of his faith, I appoint Jallud to lead us in our negotiations with the Europeans and Israelis. You have seen by his example the sacrifices we must all make. In addition, I appoint him to be the general that leads us into battle against the infidel Americans and Jews. Allah was right in choosing you for your leadership and faith. I will inform our European friends that we are prepared to begin the negotiations."

EXPECTATIONS

WASHINGTON, D.C.

December 4th

6:32 a.m.

A lex was sleeping soundly after another long day in Washington politics. The alarm started chirping at six o'clock. After hitting the snooze button twice he roused himself from his warm bed. He looked and saw that his wife of ten years had already left for the day. Her job as comptroller of the accounting firm where she worked kept her almost as busy as his job. On his nightstand was a card with a little note she had scribbled inside. She was the thoughtful one. Alex knew he needed to do more of those little romantic things for his wife. A very striking woman, she still turned heads when she walked down the street or entered a restaurant. He did not want some smooth-talking Lothario to come sweep her away. He was not too worried about this as they were still very much in love. But he knew one should never take things like the love of a great woman for granted. He made a mental note to stop and get some roses on the way home.

As with his usual routine, he headed down to the basement to begin his morning workout. Alex had always been a physical fitness fanatic. The gym, as Michelle derisively called the basement, had a treadmill, a free weight bench, and a dip bar. The room had been wired for cable so they could watch television while working out. Beginning his three-mile run, he turned on the 42-inch Sony flat screen television that was mounted on the wall. The television was tuned to the popular morning show *Fox and Friends* but he had the volume down. He was reading the crawler that continuously displayed on-going news when the alert icon flashed on the screen. Reaching for the remote he turned up the volume. The announcer was saying the newly elected European President had conducted his press conference and they were preparing to show the videotape.

The screen changed to the pressroom of the European Union head-quarters. Alex could see the usual milling around of reporters waiting on President Gerhard to make his official entry. He heard the applause as Gerhard entered. The usual pleasantries were given as in all press conferences and then Gerhard got to the heart of the meeting. Alex was not totally caught off guard when the announcement came concerning Europe's withdrawal from NATO. That was expected. It was what Gerhard had waged his campaign on. *Well, he did not waste time in making that announcement* Alex thought to himself.

The bombshell involved Esfahan and the Mideast peace talks. Alex stopped the treadmill and increased the volume. The cat was out of the bag now. Alex paid particular attention to the exchange between the *Fox News* reporter and Gerhard regarding peace talks involving the world's most volatile region. He knew Gerhard had a high opinion of himself, but how could you have peace talks and not have the world's lone super-power involved after an Israeli attack on an Islamic country? Gerhard's answer about Europe being the other superpower summed up everything Alex had surmised about the new European President: he was witnessing the birth of America's next rival.

The phone rang. He knew what this meant. "Yes, sir. One o'clock. I will be there," Alex confirmed with the President's Chief of Staff. He knew he better finish his workout as this might be the last one for a while. He would not have time for weights today. He resumed his run but upped his pace to a six-minute mile and began to analyze the events of the day in his mind. Gerhard's tone did not lend itself to that of a peacemaker. Could war be around the corner? The President would be demanding a course of action.

AMIR AIR BASE

9:35 a.m.

A hard knock sounded on Colonel Goldman's door as his aide entered. "Sorry to interrupt, sir, but I think there is something on television you need to see." Goldman rubbed his eyes as he reached for the remote and turned on the television in his office. He was working on two hours sleep having spent most of the night in the Command Center monitoring Arab military movements. Amir had remained on constant alert since the raid on Esfahan. The TV was tuned to the *BBC*. He recognized the newly elected President of the European Union. He listened intently as Gerhard made his announcements. *A peace conference involving all parties in the Mideast except America?* he thought.

"Joseph, what do you make of this?" asked Goldman.

"Sir, my honest opinion?" he asked somewhat hesitantly.

Goldman nodded to the young man. "You may speak freely."

"Sir, there are many who are tired of the homicide bombings. They are tired of seeing family members lost in these attacks. And there are not many families in Israel today who can say they have not been either the victim of these attacks or know someone who has." He hesitated for a moment not sure if he should continue.

"Go on, Joseph. Say what's on your mind," Goldman prodded his reluctant aide.

"Sir, I...well. It's hard to say as a soldier. It feels almost treasonous..." he said as his voice drifted off.

Seeing how uncomfortable Joseph was, Goldman encouraged him again to finish his thoughts. "Go on, Joseph."

"Sir, I feel almost treasonous for saying this. But many of us, that is the men I speak with, are tired of war. They long for a day when they can live in peace. When their families can be safe, sir. It is not that they won't fight if needed. They are just tired. Tired of worrying for their families."

Goldman was alarmed at Joseph's reply. Not realizing it he fired off several questions at the young man. "Do you think we could ever trust the Alliance to abide by words on a piece of paper in light of the news on Esfahan? Can we trust Europe to enforce the treaty given their history of anti-Semitism? Do you think it would be good to have peace talks without the U.S. involved?" Seeing the look on Joseph's face he regretted jumping on the young man as he did, but he did not understand what he was hearing.

"Sir, I do not know," Joseph said, not sure if he had spoken too freely. But he continued. "Egypt honored the Camp David Accords. Jordan honored our Peace Treaty. Of course all that has changed with the Fundamentalists. It would take a strong leader in the Muslim world to make peace happen. With the news out on Esfahan, peace seems like the last thing that will happen anytime in the future. As for a peace conference without the United States? Well, they do have strong ties with not only us, but the whole region. There is still a huge amount of resentment in the hearts of many Arabs for the Americans' overthrowing Saddam. Europe could be seen as a neutral party. That Gerhard fellow seems pretty focused if you ask me. Maybe it could work."

"You may be right, Joseph. I still prefer to trust in the IDF though. You are dismissed."

As the young man exited, Goldman leaned back in his chair contemplating their discussion. Joseph could be right. He was a sharp and observant soldier. Goldman had previously sought his opinions and had found them to be insightful. He was also aware there was an age gap between them. Perhaps it was Joseph's youth that was speaking. The young were always more optimistic than their elders. He remembered what it was like to be young and entering training with the IAF. The world was at his feet and he was going to tame it. Bulletproof was the term he and his friends used to describe their perceived invincibility. He would never be shot down. Many mistook their confidence for arrogance. In reality, it was a shield that all combat pilots around the world wore. One could not doubt oneself in the cockpit during combat. The slightest hesitation could cost you your life or that of your fellow pilots. Perhaps the reality of combat had curbed his optimism and turned him into a realist. Perhaps the death of his friends had removed part of that shield. Perhaps it was simply maturity.

Goldman had heard his own crews discussing a desire for peace. And these were the elite of the IAF. There had been more defections in the IDF this past year than at any time in Israel's history. If this feeling was widespread, the ground could be right to plant the seed of peace. He hoped the ground would be cleared of any weeds before anyone made any commitments. There was a time for everything. With the news on the strike on Esfahan, he knew the time for peace was not near. The time for war, however, seemed right around the corner.

He reached for the phone on his desk. "Joseph, alert the squadron. Have them meet me in the ready room in fifteen minutes. Alert the ground crews. I want to be in the air within half an hour."

"Ladies and gentlemen, the world continues to be an amazing place," the President began. Sullivan was not in a good mood and for just cause. "I can handle Europe withdrawing from NATO. We anticipated that. I can even handle someone thinking their country, or Union, is a superpower. But what I cannot handle is that anyone would have the audacity to snub the United States of America when it comes to peace negotiations in the Mideast. To insinuate that we are the cause of global instability…well, we will let history make that determination. Do you know what the Jewish lobby on the Hill is saying? They are hopping mad about the whole thing. Ok, what do we have?"

"Mr. President," began Alex. He had seen Sullivan like this before at CFA. Normally he was a very cool executive, except when he personally had been insulted, and Alex knew his former boss took Gerhard's comments personally. As President of the United States you embodied the spirit of the country. It was one thing for Democrats and Republicans to bicker amongst themselves. That was family and expected. But when strangers began meddling in the family's affairs one took it personally. Sullivan had been growing more and more frustrated with the cynical attitude coming from across the Atlantic. "*CNN* is reporting widespread protests throughout all capitals in the Middle East and North Africa. They are calling for Jihad against Israel. Preliminary polls in Europe show support for Gerhard and the proposed peace talks at over ninety percent."

"They got those results out pretty quick, didn't they? And I thought our polling folks were fast," observed Sullivan.

"The most recent opinion polls in Israel, and these are a week old, continue to indicate support for Weissman's coalition is at an all time low. His government is in trouble," noted Stanfield.

"Our SIGINT and recon birds show a continued increase in Alliance military activity beyond the norm. That is to be expected in light of recent events. Russian and Chinese forces are maintaining their alert level. Nothing happening on the Korean peninsula for now," noted DNIS Secretary Sheffield.

"It would seem that only European forces are deploying at this time," observed Stanfield.

"Yes, and in quite an amazing number," noted Clairmont as he distributed a sheet of paper with a projected order of battle to each one present. "Six squadrons of fighters, four armored and four infantry divisions, plus components of their Mediterranean fleet have been detailed for deployment. They will be taking up positions in the Sinai, Golan Heights, and Jerusalem. Their mission is being reported as manning the observation posts along the borders. They are supposed to be keeping an eye on everyone. Estimated deployment date for their ground troops is three weeks. That is moving pretty fast. The air components are beginning to deploy as of 12:00 local time."

"What is our status?" inquired Sullivan.

"Currently our forces are at DEFCON-4," Clairmont noted. "That is an automatic transition in the event of certain specified events. Terror alert level remains at Orange in light of the attack on Esfahan and the other facilities. *George Washington* is currently off the east coast and *Enterprise* is in the Persian Gulf. *GW* has been alerted for possible deployment to the Med pending your approval, Mr. President."

"Tell them to get going. It would be good to have a friendly face over there for Israel at the moment. Now, the United States cannot be left out of these talks. I want a seat at those peace talks. Options?"

"I doubt we will be able to have anyone present with official status. However, it might be possible to have an observer in attendance. This would be a good time to have some of Israel's friends on the Hill contact Tel-Aviv. They could make having an observer from the U.S. part of their requirements for the negotiations," said Stanfield.

"I like that idea. I think I know just who I want that observer to be," Sullivan said as he looked straight at Alex.

"He would be an excellent choice, Mr. President," agreed Stanfield. "He doesn't hold any official diplomatic credentials. The title of Special Assistant can be conferred on almost anyone and does not require the approval of Congress. He is not operating within the official capacity of the United States government. If diplomatic protocol still means anything, and I believe it does, he should be accepted. Plus, if we are reading Gerhard right, his ego is as big as the world. By allowing Alex as an observer he will probably view this as a gesture of goodwill on his part to the 'other superpower.' I will contact Minister of Foreign Affairs Jeremiah Levine. He knows the game."

"Alex, what do you say?" his old boss asked. "Stanfield is right. Officially you are not part of this government. No way Gerhard could refuse this. It would shift the blame to him if the talks broke down over such a small request as this. No way he is going to let that happen. Alex, I need, your country needs, someone there to be our eyes and ears."

Alex suddenly felt the whole room staring at him. He could see Stanfield give a quick wink to the others in the room. He was not sure he liked what he was hearing. It was one thing to come to the White House and give advice to his former boss. He had become adept at that while in the boardroom at CFA. But this was not the boardroom. The cold reality of that was sinking in like a lead weight. If mistakes were made in business they could be overcome. In those situations the only people who might suffer injury would be the stockholders. At worse, they would lose their investment. But this was the White House. Decisions made here had the potential to impact the lives of every person on the planet. The prospect of representing the United States at a meeting where the decisions made could impact the entire world was another matter.

"Mr. President, I am honored you and the Secretary have the confidence in me. However, I'm not sure I am the man for the job. I don't have the diplomatic training or background. Surely there are others more qualified. This isn't the boardroom at CFA. We are talking about possible peace in the Middle East. Not exactly the most politically stable place in the world. They have been fighting over there since way back," Alex said as he shifted in his seat rather uncomfortably.

"Alex, do you know what diplomacy is all about?" Stanfield inquired with her best poker face.

"No, Madam Secretary, I don't think I do."

"I'll explain Diplomacy 101 in less than one minute. You walk into a room, put on your best smile and shake hands with everyone you see regardless of whether you like them or not. You say a lot of high-sounding platitudes and try not to tick anyone off. Agree to nothing and say you'll have to study any proposal made. But be sure they understand you think it is a wonderful concept that has merit. Remember, everyone likes to think their ideas are the best. In most cases, they want someone to listen to them and appear to agree with them so they can give a good sound bite on the news. After all is done, you talk with the press and say much progress was made. Smile, wave and leave. Plain and simple."

Sullivan and Clairmont were attempting to suppress their amusement at Stanfield's version of Diplomacy 101. Alex was not quite sure if she was serious or kidding. In reality, it was probably a little of both.

"Well, if it is as easy as the Secretary says, and I guess it must be as I've seen her in action, I think I can handle it," Alex said as he attempted to counter the Secretary's review of diplomatic training. He was again reminded of why Sullivan liked her so much. She was a straight shooter by nature, but could play the political game with the most seasoned politician.

"Very good, Alex. You will do fine." Sullivan felt like he was talking to his son. "I have confidence in you for this. The Secretary will have some higher level briefings to bring you up to speed on all of the issues. Unless anyone has any objections, I am starved. Let's grab some dinner. I have a feeling this is going to be the first of many long nights."

"Well, be sure we have plenty of coffee," Alex said as they rose to go eat. "And not that vile stuff you liked back at CFA. That stuff could take paint off the wall."

Sullivan enjoyed the ribbing from Alex. He knew his Special Assistant was the right man for the job.

E

USS ENTERPRISE
PERSIAN GULF
December 4th
11:00 a.m.

The *Big E*, as she was affectionately known to the crews who sailed her, was plowing the waters of the Persian Gulf. The *Enterprise* was America's oldest nuclear-powered carrier; not that she knew that. For an old lady she was kicking up a lot of spray, as her eight nuclear reactors propelled the massive steel gray hull at twenty-two knots through the choppy waters of the Gulf. The remainder of the strike group was deployed in the classic battle circle with *Enterprise* riding center.

Seventy-five miles to the northwest, an E-2C Hawkeye of the Bear Aces, call sign Goldeneye, was maintaining electronic surveillance of an area two hundred fifty miles square. To the southeast, another E-2C, Focus One, was performing a similar task. Eight F/A-18F Super Hornets were at their assigned CAP stations.

Rear Admiral Mark O'Brien was a concerned man in spite of the impressive array of firepower at his disposal. He had ordered General Quarters since the explosion at Esfahan and the other nuclear facilities in Iran. He did not need twenty-five years of navy experience to know that nuclear facilities do not explode without cause—at least not in the Middle East. To further complicate the situation, *Al-Jazeera* was giving round the clock coverage of Israel's attack on Esfahan. The network had obtained interviews with some of the surviving family members from victims of the attack. The images of now fatherless children and babies were having a strong emotional impact.

His task force was cruising one hundred miles north of Bahrain. From this vantage point the *Enterprise* was best positioned to strike at targets in Iran or move to aid America's Saudi allies. The disadvantage was that they were cruising in a body of water with only one way out; through the Straights of Hormuz. If hostilities did break out, reinforcements for his strike group would have to fight their way into the Gulf. Or, he might be faced with the prospect of fighting his way out.

The *Enterprise's* Hawkeyes were monitoring the communications in the region. Anti-Israeli and American rhetoric, with increasing tenor, was being heard on all channels. The Fundamentalists were boasting of the day when the world would be rid of the Great Satan and her ally. Of course, as O'Brien noted, they had been saying the same thing since 1979, but this time the words were more vitriolic than before. And their actions more than symbolic. Pictures of O'Brien and his family at the World Trade Center from a vacation in the eighties reminded him of that salient fact.

"Admiral, all ships are maintaining General Quarters," reported Commander Tom McLaskey.

"Let's have a rundown on our tactical situation," ordered O'Brien.

"Iranian air units are maintaining patrols within their own airspace. Goldeneye continues to track two *Hudong* class missile boats. They're maintaining their position forty miles to our northwest on course three-two-zero. They are equipped with Exocet anti-ship missiles. Nasty suckers those Exocets. Brits learned a hard lesson about them during the Falklands War. The *Sheffield* took a couple of hits from the Exocets. Put her on the bottom of the Atlantic. To be sure that doesn't happen to us, we've two Hornets orbiting the *Hudongs* if things start to get nasty.

"CFFC has ordered *George Washington* to take up position Eastern Med. She is making thirty-four knots. Getting there in a hurry. Looks like the Boss is giving Israel some public backing in light of Esfahan," observed McLaskey. Gunboat diplomacy still had a place on the world stage. And there was no better instrument to exercise this than a *Nimitz* class aircraft carrier.

O'Brien's steely blue eyes were transfixed on the tactical display. The light from the display was casting an eerie pale blue glow on the faces of those in the CDC. "Tom, any word out of Riyadh?"

"No, sir. Their last contact was 0630 hours. At that time they reported all quiet in the city. Streets appeared to be calm."

"I want to be ready if they call or if we are attacked," O'Brien ordered as he continued to concentrate on the tactical display. To some in the CDC, it appeared the Admiral was trying to read the very thoughts of those in Tehran and Riyadh.

"Yes, sir," echoed McLaskey.

"With news out that Israel was responsible for Esfahan, the whole Mideast is a tinderbox right now. Gotta admire them though. They see a problem; they deal with it. No political correctness there. The proposed peace talks might resolve the crisis, though I have serious doubts. Lots of bad history in this part of the world." O'Brien continued to analyze the tactical display. He took another sip of his coffee. "Tom, alert CAG. Let's get some additional assets up for CAP. Maintain General Quarters. I will be on the bridge. Contact me if the situation changes."

"Aye, sir." McLaskey reached for his headset to make the necessary orders.

TEN KINGS

GEORGETOWN

WASHINGTON, D.C.

December 7th

7:38 p.m.

Alex had invited Will Thompson, his college roommate, over for dinner and to watch a key basketball game. Kentucky was playing UCLA in what was supposed to be a closely contested game between the two basketball powerhouses. The two schools were ranked 2nd and 1st respectively in the latest AP poll.

The two had remained close friends since graduating from college. Alex's wife had given them free reign of the home for the evening. As she put it, she did not want to hear the wailing and gnashing of teeth if Kentucky lost nor the inevitable gloating in the event of a Kentucky victory. She also knew Alex would provide her with a play-by-play account when she returned home whether the Cats won or lost.

The doorbell rang. "About time you got here," Alex chastised his buddy as he opened the door. "Come on in. They're about to tip off. I'll get the pizza."

"Hey, you know how hard it is to get a cab this time of the day? Plus, coming over from the Farm isn't exactly like walking 'round the corner," retorted Will.

Will had joined, what was then, the Central Intelligence Agency after graduation. Even though DNIS had replaced the CIA, career intelligence people still referred to where they worked as the Farm. He was currently working as a Political Analyst in the Directorate of Intelligence. His current assignment there was to assist in providing an analysis of the recent events in Europe and the Middle East.

"One large, deep dish supreme," Alex said as he took out a slice of the pizza and passed the box to his friend.

The game was all that it was promised to be. UCLA surged out to a quick ten-point lead. The first half ended with Kentucky down by five points. Alex and Will knew the UK coaching staff would be providing a very inspiring half-time talk as all coaches did when their teams were behind. As former athletes in high school they had been on the receiving end of such talks. Invariably, all of these motivational talks included some threat of running for the rest of your natural life if play did not improve. Alex again experienced that same philosophy when in the Air Force. It seemed that the appropriate amount of running was useful for curing everything from poor free throw shooting to a squad's performance on the rifle range. One day he half expected Sullivan to order Congress to run the Capitol steps if they could not approve his Tax and Social Security Reform legislation. Judging from the waistlines of some members of Congress that would not be an altogether bad idea.

The second half began with Kentucky employing a trapping full court pressure defense. The halftime speech was apparently paying off. The UK players seemed to have an extra bounce in their step. Their passes were much sharper and the shot selection improved. UCLA began to wilt under the intensity. Spurred by a couple of three point baskets and several UCLA turnovers caused by the pressure defense, Kentucky went on a 15-2 run in the opening five minutes of the second half. UCLA never recovered and Kentucky cruised to an 86–60 win regaining the number one ranking for another week.

"Man, what a game. UK looks good," Alex said, high-fiving Will as the game ended.

"They keep playing like that and prospects in March look good. Time will tell though. Time will tell. The season is still young."

"Yes, it will." Shifting the conversation from the game, Alex inquired, "They keeping you busy at DNIS? What's the thinking over there with all of this mess in Europe and Esfahan?"

"Yeah. Esfahan, Europe's withdrawal from NATO. The world is changing very fast. And I thought we were busy after 9/11. It's enough to make a fellow wanna drink. The mood is pretty intense as you can imagine. We are all dumbfounded the place hasn't blown up yet in light of Esfahan. If you had bet me a peace conference would be what we are talking about and not a call for a ceasefire after what Israel pulled off, I would have given you any odds or points you wanted. By all accounts, the Mideast should be a war zone by now. Gerhard is the whole key to this thing. He is a talented and astute politician. In fact, I am working up an analysis of our future relationship with Europe. If there is one," Will added thoughtfully.

"Things have definitely changed, haven't they?" Alex noted in agreement. "Makes me miss the Cold War. At least then we had a pretty good idea what the Russians were up to. They were so predictable. It's still surprising to find us at odds with Europe, though I guess we have seen it coming. Relations on both sides of the Atlantic have been deteriorating over the past five years. Gerhard is a shrewd politician. He played his cards right and won big."

"Yes, he did," Will agreed. Will sat back in his chair and closed his eyes. Alex could tell something was bothering his old friend—the two could read each other like a book.

"What's on your mind, Will? You've got that worried look on your face again. Just like you always got around finals."

Will opened his eyes and gazed at his old buddy. "Speaking of worried looks, how is life at the White House, Mr. Special Assistant to the President? Keeping the coffee cups filled?"

It was apparent Will was not ready to share whatever was on his mind.

"Yeah. That's all I do. Get coffee. Carry luggage. Don't I wish! Been working like a dog since Esfahan. This is my first night at the house since."

"And Michelle let you hang out with me and watch some hoops?" Will asked with raised eyebrows.

"What can I say? I married one of the good ones. Besides, she is off shopping with her girlfriends," Alex noted with a shrug of his shoulders.

"Word is that you are heading off to a little peace conference across the pond," offered Will with a hint of satisfaction that he knew more about his friend's plans than his friend wanted him to know.

"What makes you say that?" Alex asked in an attempt to deflect Will's assertion.

"Come on now. Think for a moment. Where do I work? You know.

We know all, see all, tell all," Will said with a widening grin. "It's a little thing we like to call intelligence."

"Yeah, you and your crystal ball. Well, Swami, if you can read the future, how about some picks for the NCAA champ? Or better, come up with winning numbers for Powerball and we'll all retire early."

"That would be very sweet indeed. I do believe we have some folks in cryptology working on that last one by the way. Ok, here's the deal," Will began now ready to talk. "We were asked to prepare an analysis of the political impact in the Mideast if the peace talks were to actually occur and be successful. It could change the fundamental structure of the balance of power as we know it today. I believe you will be seeing the analysis on Monday," Will said as he reached for another piece of pizza.

"Did you write it?"

"Not all of it," Will said wiping pizza sauce off his chin. "Just the intro. Better study up, Alex boy. You're playing in the big leagues now."

"Is this what's bugging you? A shift in world politics?"

"No. It's something more than that. Potentially much bigger. Gerhard's election started me thinking about it again. Been thinking about presenting something I wrote while we were in college, but I am not sure how it would be perceived at the Farm. It is one of those out of the box theory papers. It is pretty interesting in light of current events though."

"All right, Sherlock. Seeing how you know so much, tell me about this out of the box paper if you can. It might help me with this trip across the pond. If nothing else, it might make you feel better," Alex said trying to get Will to talk.

"Are you serious?"

"Yes!" Alex said in exasperation.

"Ok, hang on to your hat. It goes something like this. I call this the "Ten Kings" theory. What was the name of that class we had? Oh yeah, *Religion in Political Studies*. Covered religions and their impact on politics if I remember."

"The professor had some way out theories if I remember," Alex recalled. "Interesting class though. Took a B in that one. Professor did not like my final paper."

"Yeah, I remember. You were pretty fired up about that. You shouldn't have told him the class was dull."

"Well, it was at the time. It had so much potential that I thought he didn't capitalize on. Though in hindsight, it probably was not a wise thing to tick off your prof before finals."

"I am glad you are finally admitting it after all of these years. By the way, I received an A+ on mine," Will reminded his friend as he gloated. "Anyway, the premise of the paper is based on Revelation."

"Revelation? As in end of the world? Armageddon? Antichrist?" Alex said with raised eyebrows. He knew his friend had a penchant for eschatology and sometimes the dramatic.

"Yeah, very apocalyptic stuff. Brought over a copy for you to read," Will said, reaching into his briefcase. He passed the paper to Alex who began to thumb through the work as his friend began to explain. "The theory is that Europe is united by a strong, charismatic leader who establishes a ten nation confederation along the lines of the former Roman Empire. Negotiations are entered into and a peace settlement will be made between the Arabs and Israel. Now here is the kicker: the leader of the ten nation confederation proctors the negotiations. Sounding familiar?"

Alex nodded as his friend continued.

"Then, at a future point when Israel is at peace with her enemies, the Arabs, led by the ten nations, turn on Israel. The conflict ends with a nuclear exchange and Israel emerging victorious. Barely though."

Alex could not believe his ears. He almost laughed as he asked his friend, "Are you saying that Gerhard is the Antichrist? And that the EU is the ten nation confederation?"

"Not necessarily. It is what we like to call in the intelligence business, an estimate. But what if they are the beginning of the End Times? Some things appear to be falling into place. The EU is real. Europe is united for the first time in history. I can't recall a time in history when sovereign nations have sacrificed their identity to morph into another political entity. Again, this is all an estimate."

"That's one heck of an estimate!" Alex noted.

"Alex, that's exactly what intelligence has been and always will be: an estimate. People forget that. They think we can predict the future actions of a nation or person with regularity. Any intelligence analyst will tell you, if they are honest, that you look for trends, facts. What is within the norm and what is outside of the norm? You look at all the pieces and attempt to draw an educated conclusion. Sometimes we are right and sometimes we are wrong."

"That's true, but couldn't your theory, or estimate, just be the natural course of politics? A vacuum was left when the Soviet Union collapsed. Politics, like nature, abhors a vacuum. Besides, the EU has more than ten members," Alex countered.

"That's true, but don't let the number of members in the EU fool you. There are really ten countries that form the core of the EU. Plus, there is the possibility some will splinter off. There is a fair amount of discontentment within the western, or old NATO countries, with the drain on the overall economy from the members from the old Warsaw Pact. Our analysts think it will become an issue Gerhard will have to deal with eventually."

"That might explain some of the trade policies we are seeing from the EU," Alex said.

"And that's not all. There are other things all this talk of the EU has made me think about. Nothing to do with the paper, but interesting events are occurring that are more than coincidence or random chance."

"Such as?" Alex said reaching for more pizza.

"For instance, we are seeing an increase in the use of biometrics in the U.S. You know, using fingerprint or retina scans for security on a national basis. Europe already has a national ID card that contains the essential financial, social, and medical data of a person. To purchase anything over there you are now being required to use the card. Euros are being phased out next year. They are going cashless. There is also a move to integrate this information onto your body with biochips. Possibly on the forearm or somewhere else. Think about the practicality of that. You go to a store for a purchase. Instead of plunking down your euros, a scan of your arm over the computer deducts the money from your account."

"The Mark of the Beast. Introduced as safe and practical," Alex commented as he recalled Revelation.

"You hit upon the magic words. Safe and practical."

"You mean Mark of the Beast aren't the magic words?" Alex said half jesting. "Just kidding, Will. In what way is it safe and practical?"

"Think about it. Think of the savings realized by not having to print money. You would never have to worry about leaving your wallet again or it being stolen! Identify theft becomes a thing of the past."

"No banks to rob. No lost money. Those would be huge selling points," Alex added.

"Yes, it would. Now let's look at the safety aspect. Say you want to be able to monitor criminals or other persons of questionable repute. How could you do it?" Will asked, seeing that Alex was now intrigued with their discussion.

"We do that now with GPS devices to a degree."

"That's right. But what if a government wanted to know more about *all* of its citizens? Possibly their whereabouts? Their spending habits? Think about how easy it is to track people now. And it is all being conducted under the premise of safety or security."

"What do you mean?" Alex asked, obviously intrigued by the topic.

"Alex, we are in the information age. Anything you do on the Internet leaves a trace. All of your credit and debit card purchases are recorded. Companies buy that information and use it to tailor their marketing efforts. All cell phones are now GPS enabled. Every time you use your cell phone it can be monitored, or it is being monitored. If your car has Onstar, GM, or possibly others, can track your every movement on the road. What's preventing all cars, or people for that matter, from being GPS enabled? Here's another one to consider. Remember the London bombings in 2005?"

"What about 'em?"

"How did they catch the terrorists?"

Alex thought a moment and then remembered. "Security cameras. London had them everywhere."

"And there was a big push here in the States to install cameras in public areas to guard against a possible attack right after that. Now you can't walk down Broadway without your picture being taken. Also, think about the traffic cams here in D.C."

"Yeah, we ticket drivers for running red lights if they trip the camera. Why couldn't they be used for other purposes?" Alex said as he thought about the implications.

"Exactly my point, Alex. We are fast approaching the point where unfettered and untracked movement by the individual is coming to an end. The Mark of the Beast."

"Will, that is all fascinating. You're making my head hurt."

"Sorry, I got off topic. But I love that stuff. It makes me think. You can't deny the coincidence of current events. Why are these things happening?"

"I don't know, but some people would say you are bordering on paranoia."

"That could be true. Maybe I am. But these things are happening. Anyway, back to the paper. My professor thought I might be on to something, though, from a foreign policy perspective. Keep in mind this was written over twenty years ago when all of this was still speculation."

"Come on! You're pulling my leg!" Alex cried.

"Wish I were, buddy. Check out the date. Also, check out the comments at the end of the paper. I asked our professor to review it just for kicks."

Alex eyed his former roommate for a moment. He opened the paper again and turned to the back page. If his friend were kidding he was up for an Oscar on his performance. Their professor always provided his comments at the end of their papers. Alex glanced at Will before turning to the last page. Will was as good as his word. Their former professor's comments were indeed there.

"Will, this is incredible."

"Didn't believe your ol' roomie, did you?" Will said obviously pleased with himself as he leaned back on the couch and downed the last piece of pizza. After finishing the pizza he reached for his cell phone and called a cab.

"Ok if I hang on to this?" Alex said as he scanned the table of contents.

"Sure. That's why I brought it over. Anything to help out a buddy. Besides, you just might be holding the key to our future foreign policy if I am right."

Alex switched the channel to *ESPN* to catch the highlights of the game as they waited on Will's taxi. *Sportscenter* was halfway over by the time the cab arrived. As they were walking to the door, Alex stopped his friend. "You're not gonna get fired or anything over this are you? No breaches of security?"

"No way. Not even been discussed at the Farm. Though I may bring it up. Hey, thanks for the pizza. Glad we could pull the Cats through. I'll give you a holler."

"Later on, buddy. Stay in touch. I just may need that crystal ball in the future," Alex said as he watched his friend climb into his cab. Just as

Will was closing the door another taxi pulled to the curb and stopped. His lovely wife exited and ran up the steps to their door.

"Hey, babe, how was your night?" Alex said as he greeted her with a kiss. "You should've seen the Cats."

"Why don't you tell me about it in the morning," she said as she showed him the Victoria's Secret bag and headed up the stairs.

FEARS ABOUND

The economic reports confirmed the fears of the government officials gathered in the People's Great Hall. The Democratic People's
Republic of Korea was starving and had been for the past twelve years.
The findings being presented to the Cabinet cast a somber atmosphere
in the room. For one man in particular, the results were especially disconcerting. More than his fears of the poor results were his fears for his
life.

Hu Park had been appointed Cabinet head of the Agricultural Committee. The leader had looked to him to reform food production. As
with any newly-appointed leader he had an agenda for how best to gen-
erate results. Part of that agenda entailed visiting the collective farms in
an attempt to inspire the workers. It was during these visits that he had
become acquainted with the desperate situation of the farms. He had
heard rumors of the conditions, but he was overwhelmed at the actual
reality. The machinery that was available was either antiquated or inop-
erable, leaving much of the work to be performed manually. Rusting
hulks of tractors and other farm implements that had long since out-
lived their usefulness were commonplace scenes of the landscape on the
farms.

He had requested new equipment for the farms but found his requests
were blocked or denied. Park soon began to understand that it was
pointless to request new equipment. Any available money was spent on
the military as that was the Leader's priority. North Korea could boast

about one of the world's best-equipped armies, but she could not feed her people.

He realized early in his new position that he would fail as had the Chairman before him. More importantly, he knew failure was not tolerated within the regime. Excuses were not tolerated either and there was no way to falsify the findings. One could not make food appear where there was none. Adhering to the atheist beliefs of the party, he did not believe in the miracle of the five loaves and two fishes.

There were many reasons for the failure in food production. The lack of equipment and inefficiencies of collective farming could be overcome. But there were two events that dominated all the others for which there was no answer. Floods had again ravaged the crops. What could one do to stop the onslaught of the rains? Far worse, a new breed of insect had found its way into the rice fields. The little creature had a voracious appetite and was immune to the few existing insecticides. Those rice fields not devastated by floods were besieged by the insect with devastating effect. The military insisted the insect was bred in South Korea and loosed to ravage their northern neighbor's crops. They could not comprehend it was their activities, not the South's, that were ruining their country.

The yield from the crops would not be enough to meet the minimal nutritional needs of the people. Very little fresh fruit was available. Meat was even scarcer. The effects were apparent as one looked at the people. Obesity was a concern in the Western countries but not in North Korea. The majority of the people were existing on 1000 calories a day or less. Over eighty thousand had succumbed to death through starvation in the past two years. It was estimated that fifty thousand would die this way in the coming year. Within three years it was estimated that the death rate from starvation would increase by thirty percent and would only continue to worsen. The Great War of Unification would not have to be fought at this rate. The South only had to be patient and wait for the North's population to perish. Then reunification would occur, for there would not be enough people to prevent the South's armies from marching into the North unless something occurred to reverse this trend.

There had been some outbreaks of riots in the previous year when the government warehouses ran empty. These had been confined mostly to the rural areas. In its usual efficient manner, the Army had quelled the riots. The price paid were the lives of those rioting.

The military was an exception to the lack of food, as were the men in the Cabinet and other government agencies. The Leader understood the importance of keeping his armed forces well fed. Hungry troops would be prone to revolt and that was a dangerous situation that could not be allowed to develop. In a dictatorship, power was enforced through those who controlled the weapons. In effect, the Leader was buying the allegiance of the military through an abundant supply of food. For many of the peasants in the Army, the three meals a day they received were far more than they would receive as a worker. In fact, duty along the DMZ was often volunteered for as the troops deployed in this area were the best fed in all of North Korea. Only the tallest of the volunteers, those over six feet in height, were selected. The logic behind this was sound. A soldier would not present an intimidating presence if he measured any less.

It was, of course, all part of the calculated propaganda effort of the government as were all things in North Korea. It was designed to show the people of the South, and that of the world, that the North could afford to feed her people. What was not known to the outside world was that these soldiers were placed on a 10,000 calorie a day diet for two months before deploying to the DMZ to fatten them up. It was one of the cruelest ironies Park had seen. It was also a tribute to the insanity of the ruler of North Korea. The world knew their country was starving; yet the Leader was attempting to portray the image of a well-fed nation through a fat army.

"We cannot continue to survive under these conditions. The youths being inducted into the Army look like skeletons. They are useless until they are fattened up!" reported General Kim Sun-Jing. "The trade embargo headed by the United States and Japan is crushing us. We need not worry about war with them. They are defeating us far more efficiently than a war would. We cannot import the food we need so they leave our cities and industries intact for their use until our people die from hunger. And there is no sacrifice on their part. Plus there have been additional riots in the rural areas. The arrogant Americans must be made to pay."

"General Sun-Jing, you offer excellent criticisms, but do you offer any solutions?" asked the great Leader.

"Sir, please forgive my passion," Sun-Jing said as he bowed at the waist toward the Leader, realizing he may have exhausted his favored status. "Like you, I do not like to be dictated to by the Americans. I do believe there is an opportunity to reverse our misfortune. The Americans are now alone in the world. Europe and America have split. NATO is no more. The time is right to demonstrate to the Americans the true power we possess. We must show our unwillingness to bow to their pressure before they do to us as Israel did to Iran. We must create our own pressure."

"What do you propose?" asked the exalted Leader.

"To demonstrate our desire for respect, I propose we launch a Taep'o-dong 5 missile. Recommended trajectory will be over South Korea and Japan with detonation in the Pacific. Warhead yield will be one hundred kilotons. This will force the Americans and the Japanese to realize we are determined to end this tortuous death through starvation. They will end their food embargo and recognize our right to possess the weapons necessary for our defense. They will force the South to enter into peace talks. In either case, we will emerge victorious."

The other Cabinet members looked toward the Leader for his reaction. Several were alarmed at the expression he wore, though they did not express this outwardly. There was genuine interest in the Leader's face. This was not the course their nation needed to take. The people were dying. But none voiced any concern or gave any indication of their fears. They had seen the punishment vetted to the victims who spoke out. A few moments passed while the Leader contemplated this course of action.

"General Sun-Jing is correct. We have been dictated and lied to. We have waited far too long to show the world, especially the Americans, our power. It is time that we demonstrate we will not be intimidated by anyone! How long before you are ready, General?"

"Three weeks, sir!" Sun-Jing replied with an air of confidence.

"Very well. We will make one last offer of negotiations with the Americans. They will naturally, reject our offer. Then the world will realize that it is they, and not us, that are the roadblock to peace. General, prepare the plans and may the glory of our revolution be seen across the Pacific."

THE LAMB AND THE LION LIE TOGETHER

December 20th

10:39 a.m.

Alex flew to Geneva on one of the C-20H Gulfstream IV aircraft maintained by the 89th Airlift Wing at Andrews Air Force base. These exceptional aircraft are part of a fleet used for conveying VIPs on behalf of the United States government. He had flown similar aircraft while working at CFA. The only significant difference he could ascertain was in the amenities. The C-20H was not as richly appointed as the CFA jets. However, Alex did admire the amenities aboard the aircraft. Everything on board was what one would expect for conveying VIPs. Even the finest first class accommodations on the major airlines did not compare to the C-20H. He had to admit that it was not bad for government work.

Stanfield had been right. Israeli Foreign Minister Levine had contacted Gerhard regarding attendance for a guest of Israel from the United States as an observer. Gerhard had practically gushed at the prospect of granting such a small favor to Israel and the United States. Stanton was not a trained diplomat or intelligence agent so what threat could he pose? Plus, he would not have a seat at the main table. He would be relegated to the third row of seats where the assistants were. Barely window dressing for the United States.

His flight over the Atlantic was a smooth one for which he was again thankful. He had been fortunate once again. In all of his years of flying, including the Air Force, he had yet to encounter the gut wrenching turbulence he heard his friends describe. For this reason his buddies did not consider him a real airman. Everyone eventually lost it they noted. His time would come they advised.

He made good use of the time. After reading the briefing material again for what seemed the umpteenth time, he reclined his seat to the bed position. He thought some sleep would be in order to help offset the inevitable jet lag. One of the benefits of this mission was that he was flying solo. Other than himself, there was the pilot, co-pilot, and one steward. As an unofficial representative of the United States, he could not be seen deplaning with the usual diplomatic entourage.

Colonel Davidson eased the Gulfstream IV down to a smooth three-point touchdown at Geneva International Airport. So smooth was the landing that Alex was not disturbed from his sleep. Only when the steward came forward and awoke him did he realize they had landed. Colonel Davidson taxied the Gulfstream toward the main, and only, terminal.

Geneva International Airport is unique among airports. The terminal is located in Switzerland along the EU/Swiss border. Because of the proximity to the EU province of France, part of the terminal had been designated a French, or EU sector. This enabled a traveler to bypass either Swiss or EU customs, depending upon destination.

Colonel Davidson stopped the plane at a designated section on the tarmac. As the turbine engines began to wind down, Alex unbuckled his seatbelt and stretched his legs. One day someone was going to install a treadmill on overseas flights. A nice two-mile run would work the kinks out of his back and legs. Maybe there would be time for a run after he arrived at the Center.

As he looked out of the window he could see a black limousine with two individuals waiting outside the car. Two other black vehicles flanked the limo. Obviously a security detachment was being provided. This would be his Swiss escort to the Geneva International Conference Center where the meetings would be conducted. Fortunately, the ride to the Center would not be a long one as it was less than a ten-minute drive from the airport. He was greeted by one of the two individuals after he had deplaned. Alex noted the other individual had moved to gather his luggage and open the car door. He could get used to this kind of traveling.

"Bonjour, Mr. Stanton," he said with an outstretched hand. "Welcome to *Suisse*. My name is Jean Bartier. I am the Charge d' affairs and I will be your contact while in Switzerland. I trust your flight was a smooth one."

"Merci, Monsieur Bartier," replied Alex, firmly shaking the offered hand. "*Oui, c'etait un bon vol.*" ("Yes, it was a good flight.") He was glad he had continued his French since college.

"You speak French very well, Monsieur Stanton," he said as he stood aside to allow Alex to enter the car. "The ride to the Center will take just a few minutes."

"Merci. Your English is excellent also," Alex said as the car speed off the tarmac toward Geneva. Was this how the diplomatic game was played?

USS Kennedy

Naval Station Mayport, Florida

December 20ᵗʰ

7:35 p.m.

Captain Harmon Spivey was in a foul mood. He was currently staring at blank monitors in the CDC that should be showing signs of life. Only the whir of the fans in the room dared to make any noise.

"Ok, let's try this again," Spivey said into the phone. "Tell the consultants from Advanced Applied Technologies this is beginning to get real old. We couldn't shoot spit out of a straw right now if we had to! I want this ship combat ready, Mister. Is that understood?!"

"Understood, Captain," came the reply on the other end of the phone. Specialist Ramon Sanchez hung up the phone and gazed at the two consultants as they huddled over the mainframe. It was hard to believe that one machine the size of a refrigerator was capable of handling the complex computer demands of the *Kennedy* and her battle group. But now the refrigerator was on the blink and these guys did not appear to be the Maytag man.

"I know, I know," said the senior consultant with an exasperated look on his face. "It should be working. I don't know what is causing the blasted system to crash. Was that the captain?"

"Yeah it was. Guys, I know you are under pressure to make this work, but the captain ain't a happy man. When the captain's upset, the ship is upset. See what I'm saying?" Sanchez said trying to describe the level of frustration he was feeling. "Now, are you guys sure the software is not in conflict with what is already on board?"

The two consultants looked at each other. That thought had not occurred to them. Sanchez could see that from the look on their faces. *College boys. What did they know?* It was going to be a long night.

THE JOURNEY BEGINS...

GENEVA INTERNATIONAL CONFERENCE CENTER

December 21ˢᵗ

8:30 a.m.

Alex was reviewing his notes one last time. The peace talks were going to begin in twenty minutes. Alex was thankful he did not have to drive, or be driven, to the meetings. It had been decided that all of the delegates would stay at the Center. That way, everyone would be afforded the same accommodations and service. The stakes in this version of the Arab-Israeli peace negotiations were too high to be undermined by something as inane as who had a view of the sunrise or the sunset.

Another benefit of having the meeting in one place was that it eased the job of providing security. Alex had noted it was everywhere in and around the Conference Center. In addition to the regular Swiss security forces, EU security forces were omnipresent. Overhead, Combat Air Patrols of Jaguar fighters, augmented by Mangusta A129 helicopters, maintained a constant vigil over the Conference Center. On the rooftop were snipers and men armed with surface-to-air and anti-tank missiles. A brigade of soldiers was deployed on the premises. Soldiers permeated each floor. If an attacker were successful in gaining access to the interior of the hotel, they would face additional armed guards of the European Union.

Just to move about the facility required an exercise in patience due to the layers of security. Identification cards were required to enter the Center. To move from one floor required another security check and inspection of the ID card. Each delegation had been color-coded to help ease initial identification for the guards. Individual ID cards had been electronically encoded with information about each delegate that had been provided by their respective nation. Another component of the ID card was a small GPS transmitter that would allow for each delegate to be accounted for at all times. As an extra degree of security, the EU had offered subcutaneous GPS implants for each delegate in the event someone forgot or lost his or her ID card. The Israelis had politely turned down this offer as had Alex. The rumor was that the Islamic delegation had accepted the implants. It went without saying that EU personnel had the implants.

Each country had, of course, brought its own contingent of security. Alex was no exception, though his paled in comparison to those of the other parties. He had been assigned four security officers from the U.S. Embassy. There still was the issue of trust that permeated the thinking of all leaders of the world. You wanted to have security on premises that was loyal to you. No nation would chance the safety of its leadership to another nation. Alex was glad that political correctness did appear to have some boundaries.

Alex checked his watch. It was time to go. Reaching over, he picked up his ID card from the night table. As he looked at the card, his mind flashed back to his conversation with Will. Though the ID card contained only basic information about him, the security officer had informed him there was plenty of room to store more information if needed. Swinging his legs off the bed, he stood and pondered the piece of plastic in his hand. He would be mindful to leave the card on the table when he went to the bathroom. There were some things the EU didn't need to know. He slipped on his jacket and gathered his notes. His unofficial representation of the United States of America was about to begin.

One question kept coming back to him as he walked down the hall. What price would each side pay to have peace in the region? How far would they be willing to go? That had always been the question for which no one could formulate an answer. How would you erase centuries of hatred between two sides that even refused to acknowledge the other's right to exist? Add to that equation the recent Israeli attack on Esfahan and the other locations. He theorized this set of peace talks, like so many others before, would attempt to answer the questions on everyone's mind. And would most likely fail for the very reasons the previous talks had broken down.

There were four heavily armed EU guards and one civilian at the elevator. As he approached them, he put on his best diplomatic smile.

"Good morning, Mr. Stanton," said the civilian. "May I check your ID please?"

Alex thought this was a little overkill as he was the only one staying on this floor. But diplomacy was diplomacy. "Certainly. Here it is." He handed his card to the civilian. The man checked the front and back of the card, and then scanned it through a device that reminded Alex of a supermarket checkout lane. Of course, the function being provided by this device was of greater importance than the ones in the supermarket. The display on the security computer confirmed he was indeed Alex Stanton. The whole process took about ten seconds to complete.

"Mr. Stanton, you are cleared to pass," the civilian said as he handed his card back to him. "You will find the meeting in the main conference area on the fourth floor. I trust your talks will be productive," he said as Alex boarded the elevator.

"Merci. History is waiting for us to do the right thing for a change," Alex said as the doors closed.

The doors opened again to another contingent of security guards. Alex noted there were around thirty uniformed guards that stood between the elevators and the doors leading to the main conference room. It was impossible to distinguish the security personnel in civilian clothes, but Alex knew they were present. Another check of his ID confirmed he was whom the badge purported him to be. He made his way past the security checks, which he had to admit had been rather thorough. Metal detectors and guard dogs, along with two separate body checks, had confirmed he was not carrying any weapons.

Alex opened the door to the conference room. Inside there were perhaps forty people already present. The total number of attendees was to be fifty. By international standards this was a small number of delegates. He scanned the room to see who was not yet there. The Israeli delegation was present as was the delegation representing the Islamic Alliance. Based on the disposition of the two delegations not much progress had been achieved so far. Neither side was talking to the other. They had segregated themselves on opposite sides of the room. It reminded Alex of parties he attended in junior high where the boys and girls stood huddled in separate camps until someone was brave enough to break ranks and talk with the other. Hopefully this meeting would produce better results than those parties.

Some members of the EU delegation were present but not all. The key player missing was Hans Gerhard. Alex looked at his watch. There were about ten minutes to go before the meeting began. He quickly recognized the power play that was about to unfold. He made a bet with himself that Gerhard would stride through the doors with one minute to spare drawing all attention to himself. As he was preparing to get a cup of coffee, a member of the Israeli delegation moved his way.

"Mr. Stanton, please allow me to introduce myself. I am Colonel Goldman, Israeli military attaché. We are pleased to have you here. Your President has told us much about you."

"Colonel," Alex acknowledged as he shook Goldman's hand. "May I pour you a cup of coffee?" replied Alex wondering what the President had told the Prime Minister.

"Yes, please. Just black. I understand you are a former Air Force pilot. I too am a pilot. We will have to talk more after today's session. We would be honored to have you as our dinner guest tonight."

Alex was a little taken back over this invitation. How could he be seen as a neutral party and be having dinner with the Israeli delegation? He would try to equal the playing field and arrange for dinner with the other parties.

"The pleasure would be all mine," replied Alex as he handed Goldman his coffee.

Before any other conversation could take place the room burst into flashes of light. Alex turned to see the leader of the European Union enter the room. Alex had seen grandstanding before, but Gerhard had elevated the form to a new level. He glanced at his watch. Hans had made it with thirty seconds to spare. Photographers and other media were pushing their way into the room as they preceded Gerhard's entry while recording every moment. He knew what the lead story on the six o'clock news, or whatever the local equivalent was, would be tonight.

"Good morning, ladies and gentlemen. Please forgive my tardiness. Pressing matters delayed my departure. I trust everyone had a good night and an enjoyable breakfast."

The delegates in the room nodded and a general chorus of yeses were heard. Gerhard began to work the room like the seasoned politician he was. What was interesting to Alex was not so much the time that Gerhard spent with each person, for it was not more than fifteen seconds, but the manner in which Gerhard interacted with them. Gerhard made some form of physical contact with each person that seemed to draw them into him. Whether it was a handshake or a touch of the arm, each person responded in much the same manner; a broad grin on their face and a nod of appreciation.

It was like watching a movie star enter the room. Everyone wanted to be around that individual. The recognition given by the star was validation of the fan's life. Gerhard was displaying the same charisma. Everyone was waiting for Gerhard to come to them and validate his or her existence. It was a rare gift indeed. He could see how Gerhard was able to sweep the European election. Alex recalled his granddaddy's description of such an individual; he was a snake charmer.

Alex decided on a different approach. He moved to greet Gerhard while his back was to him. "Mr. President," he said placing his left hand on Gerhard's right shoulder, turning him just enough so Alex could shake his right hand. "Alex Stanton, special observer from the United States."

"Mr. Stanton," Gerhard said somewhat taken aback as Alex shook his hand. Recovering quickly, Gerhard now turned to fully face Alex. "I am pleased to have you here. It is so important to have the United States represented in these meetings. I only wish it could be in an official capacity."

"As do I, Mr. President. I wish you success in the negotiations. Oh, and congratulations on your election. That was a remarkable campaign," Alex said as he slightly tightened his handshake and then let go. "Now, if you will excuse me, sir." *So much for diplomacy* he thought.

"Thank you," replied Gerhard. He glanced at Alex for a second and then moved off to another delegate.

After Gerhard had greeted everyone the meeting began. The Israeli and Alliance delegations took their positions on opposite sides of the table. Gerhard assumed the seat at the head of the table. Alex found his seat in the third tier of seats behind the Israeli delegation. The room had stadium-style seating so the delegates not at the table were able to view the main negotiation table. The table itself was a rather unusual design. It was not much larger than a picnic table. There was room for four, maybe five, individuals on the long side and two on the short side. The dimensions of the table had been chosen so the delegates would sit in close proximity to each other. The justification was apparent. If the two sides could not at least sit close together for a couple of hours, how could they be expected to live close together?

Alex also noted the room was conspicuously bare of decorations aside from some paintings that appeared to be from the Impressionist period. Then he noticed what was missing. There were no flags from Israel or the Alliance. However, the flag of the European Union was behind Gerhard. The symbolism could not be missed. The angle from which the news reporters were allowed to film the opening meetings clearly captured the EU flag and only the EU flag. The European Union was exerting its newly found prominence in world affairs.

Opening statements were read by all three sides. The statements were very similar in their content. All expressed a sincere desire for peace this time. Each indicated a willingness to negotiate on any topic and pledged an open-minded approach to the meetings. What was notably lacking were accusations and reminders of past atrocities committed by both sides. Very vanilla and generic, Alex noted. He thought most of the prepared statements were for the benefit of the press. The press was excused after these statements were read. Now the real negotiations would begin.

With the press removed, the mood of the room took on a more serious feel. It was as Alex's high school basketball coach used to say, "about to get real."

It had been agreed that the Oslo Peace Accords would be the initial framework upon which their discussions would be based. The thrust of the Accords was over land control within the West Bank, Gaza, and East Jerusalem, as well as Israel's right to exist. The initial failure of these talks had led to the second round of Camp David talks in 2000. These too had failed for essentially the same reasons: common ground could not be reached on control of these disputed areas. This was just the starting point. Both sides had issues they felt had to be addressed in order for the talks to be successful. It had been intimated that Israel would have to apologize for the attack on Iran for any real negotiations to occur. Another feeler that was sent out was recognition of Israel's right to exist from all Islamic countries in return for possible negotiations to occur over control of the disputed territories.

"Gentlemen, as previously agreed upon, the Israeli delegation will begin our dialogue today. Prime Minister Weissman," Gerhard said gesturing to the Prime Minister.

Esfahan, which had become symbolic of the Israeli strike on Iran's nuclear facilities, was the key topic that would determine success or failure of this current round of talks. Israel's sole justification for the attack was for self-preservation. Prime Minister Abraham Weissman had been watching the Fundamentalists gain control of every country in the region. The rhetoric from Islamic media calling for the destruction of Israel had become too shrill to ignore. After consulting with the Knesset he had given approval for the raid. It had been an avowed policy of his government that no enemy of Israel would be allowed to develop nuclear weapons. This raid, coupled with the ongoing violence in the disputed territories, had seriously weakened his party's political standing in Israel. Momentum for peace, even if that meant returning some sovereignty over the disputed lands, was gaining support among a majority of the population. In order for his coalition government to remain in power, he knew he would have to make concessions regarding the disputed lands.

As Weissman looked around the table, he opened his diplomatic folder and withdrew a sheet of paper. He began to read Israel's formal apology for the attack on Esfahan. It was diplomatic, yet very eloquent at the same time, for it touched on the lives that were lost and offered Israel's and, more importantly, his own personal apology for the lives lost. Weissman accepted full responsibility for the attack. There was no mention of the justification for the raid. Upon concluding he returned the paper to the folder.

Gerhard glanced at the representatives of the Alliance. Their faces had remained impassive during Weissman's apology. Gerhard moved to speak.

"Gentlemen, we have embarked upon a unique journey. History is calling us today to act for the future. Mr. Prime Minister, thank you for your statesmanship today. You have set the tone for our work. Any success we have will be credited to you and your humanity."

Alex had also observed the reactions from those around the room. From his vantage point behind the Israeli delegation, he noticed Colonel Goldman's shoulders stiffen ever so slightly during Weissman's statement. It was clear he was not in agreement with this course of action. Alex could understand why as DNIS had reports that it was his squadron that had led the strike on Esfahan. What Alex could not understand was the reaction of the Islamic Alliance. Not a head had moved, not a whisper or passing of notes among any of the delegates. Had they been paying attention? He was even more dumbfounded at their reply.

"Mr. Prime Minister," it was Jallud speaking for the Council, "your words today have touched our hearts. We too, offer our apologies for past transgressions committed against your people. I dare say that if I were in your position, I would have made the same decision. Your apology is fully accepted without reservation."

Alex could not believe his hears. History's oldest antagonists, Israel and her Muslim neighbors, had just offered apologies to each other. Further, there were no accusations or reminders of past, or current, atrocities from either side. The magnitude of these statements sent a chill down his spine. If the rest of the negotiations went this well, a dream that was previously thought unobtainable by scholars and politicians since Israel's restoration as a nation could be within reach—peace in the Mideast. Truly, this had the potential to be the historic meeting of the ages. The true test would come when disposition of the disputed lands was discussed.

Gerhard made the next statement. "Gentlemen, I know what you have done here today has not been easy. It has been significant for there is much history between your two peoples. When we are finished with our talks, and we have achieved our common goal of peace, your names will be recorded as history's greatest statesmen." Gerhard now stood before the table and addressed the entire room. "We have now embarked upon the historic journey. Your leadership has determined our course. I have been honored to have the privilege to be present at today's discussions. Tomorrow, we will begin our dialogue on the disputed lands. Until then, may peace go with us all."

As Gerhard began to make his way out he warmly embraced Weissman and then Jallud. He said something to each one but Alex could not make out what it was. Maybe he could find out from Colonel Goldman at dinner. He was anxious to discuss the meeting with him. Before he left the room, Alex made his way over to one of Jallud's assistants. He intended to invite himself to dinner with the Islamic Alliance. He wanted to avoid any potential diplomatic *faux pas* by dining only with the Israeli delegation. Plus, what better way to possibly obtain some insight into their mindset regarding the talks. It was one thing to offer platitudes at a meeting but what were the real motives? Maybe breaking bread would help.

GUARDIANS

USS GEORGE WASHINGTON

MEDITERRANEAN

December 21st

11:43 a.m.

Upon receiving orders from CFFC, Admiral Ramond Alvarez had ordered the *Washington* strike group to take up position one hundred miles off the coast of Israel. The nine ships of the task force had plied their way across the Atlantic and through the Mediterranean at flank speed and arrived on station within five days. As they made their way through the Mediterranean they encountered only routine air patrols from the air forces of Tunisia and Libya. Alvarez was somewhat surprised the patrols had not attempted closer inspections of his task force. The relatively narrow waters between Sicily and Tunisia offered an ideal opportunity for just such an attempt. Perhaps the memory of the Libyans was tempered by their encounters with American naval airpower in the 1980s when F-14s on more than one occasion dispatched Libyan planes that ventured too close.

After arriving at their assigned patrol station, Alvarez ordered a figure eight course for the task force. From this vantage point, Alvarez would be able to provide both air-to-air and air-to-ground support for Israeli forces if needed. The Hawkeyes would also be able to monitor air and ground movements, in addition to SIGINT traffic, in the region effectively serving as an additional airborne early warning asset for Israel.

Though they had broadcast a warning to maintain a clear radius of fifty miles from the task force, several ships chose to ignore the warning. According to international maritime law they were within their legal right to do so. They did not have to honor the warning being transmitted from the *George Washington*. Alvarez's concern was that you could not determine which ships had been modified with anti-ship missiles. Some of the traffic passed to within fifteen miles of his task force. At this range there was precious little that could be done to stop an attack if any of these ships carried the Exocet, or any other variety of anti-ship missile. Even the advanced Aegis II Battle Management System aboard the cruisers and destroyers would be hard pressed to respond.

Alvarez was not taking any chances. He had ordered the SH-60N Seahawks to track each ship as they passed. According to the rules of engagement, he had also determined a justifiable defensive zone of three miles around each ship of the task force. Warnings were broadcast that any ship entering this zone would be fired upon. Orders had been given to target the propulsion areas to disable the ships if possible; not to sink them. Extra Combat Air Patrols had been launched in the event any unwelcome aircraft approached the fleet.

The area *GW* was patrolling was transited by many ships as they made their way toward ports in Syria, Lebanon, and Israel. Most of the captains understood the message, especially after being buzzed by the Seahawks and Hornets, and steered clear of the *GW.*

One ship, identified by the code name Tango 39, had altered course and appeared to be ignoring the defensive zone. Mystic One, the call sign for the E-2D Hawkeye, reported the change to the cruiser *Vella Gulf* as the two ships were on an intercept course.

"Captain, Mystic One is reporting contact Tango 39 altering course. Puts her on an intercept course with us. Visual ID confirms she is a Libyan flagged cargo ship. Range ten miles and closing. Speed fifteen knots," reported the deck officer of the *Vella Gulf.*

"Transmit warnings to that ship. Tell him to change course or we will have to take action," ordered Captain Tom Halsey.

"Aye, Captain. Sir, incoming message from *GW.*"

Halsey reached for his command phone. It was Alvarez aboard the *GW.*

"Halsey, you are authorized to take appropriate defensive measures against that ship if she continues her course. Warning shots first. If that doesn't make the captain change his mind, then aim for the engines."

"Aye, aye, Admiral. We have been attempting to contact the captain, but no luck."

"Probably some drunk fool at the helm. We are not taking any chances, Tom," replied the Admiral.

"Very good, Admiral," Halsey said as he returned the phone to its cradle.

On board the bridge, Halsey continued to observe the approaching ship through his binoculars. The SH-60 helicopter was approaching the Libyan ship.

"What is that idiot thinking?" he asked no one in particular. "Range?"

"Eight thousand yards and closing, sir," replied the radar watch.

"Very well. If that is how he wants to play this. CIC, this is the Captain. Weapons release is authorized. Aim the five-inch for fire across the bow. Say again, aim the five-inch for fire across the bow. Await my command to fire."

"Confirmed, Captain. Five-inch is aimed for fire across the bow. Awaiting orders to fire," replied the Tactical Action Officer in the CIC.

Halsey trained his binoculars on the ship again. She was still closing.

"Captain, range is now seventy-five hundred yards," noted the radar watch.

"CIC, this is the Captain. Fire warning shots across the bow. Repeat, fire warning shots across the bow."

A flash erupted from the forward five-inch gun of the *Vella Gulf* that was followed by a second as she fired in anger. The first shot landed fifty yards across the starboard bow of the Libyan vessel while the second landed thirty yards away. Halsey was watching the entire scenario through his binoculars. On board the Libyan ship he saw the crewmen hit the deck as the shots sailed overhead and detonated in the water. The last shot was close enough to throw water up on the deck. The captain of the ship apparently understood the meaning of the shots and began to alter course. The SH-60 reported that she was indeed changing course away from the task force. The pilot radioed that crewmembers could be seen waving white flags. Teddy Roosevelt's idea of foreign policy was still effective: speak softly and carry a big stick.

Alex was seated at the table with Prime Minister Weissman. Flanking his left side was Colonel Goldman. Other members of the Israeli delegation were also present. The table before him was a sumptuous presentation of the best foods and wines Europe had to offer. This meal would definitely require a couple of extra miles on the treadmill. The conversation had so far been very informal, covering topics ranging from bird watching, a surprisingly favorite pastime of the Prime Minister, to ancient world history. Alex mostly sat and listened. However, he knew the light banter would not continue. After dessert, the Prime Minster excused all in the room except for Alex and Colonel Goldman. The three men retired to an ante-room. Numerous lounge chairs were present of which they availed themselves. Weissman reached into his coat and pulled out two *Cohiba SigloVI* Cuban cigars to Alex's surprise. He did not picture the Prime Minister as a connoisseur of cigars. He offered Alex one but he politely declined. "So, Alex," said Weissman as he lit his cigar, "what do you think of diplomacy so far?"

"An interesting beginning to this most auspicious occasion," Alex said as he carefully chose his words.

Weissman broke out into laughter at his guarded reply. Goldman cracked a sly smile in recognition of Alex's predicament.

"You are as your President said you would be. Observant and smart. I see why he chose you for this mission."

"Thank you for your kindness, Mr. Prime Minister. I think President Sullivan has a most unusual sense of humor at times, especially for having chosen me for this mission."

Weissman again erupted in laughter. "Alex, you are as humble as the President said you would be. Now, let's get down to business. Alex, do you believe I am serious about a negotiated peace with our Arab neighbors?" he asked reclining back in his chair while rolling the cigar back and forth with his thumb and middle finger.

Alex carefully thought over his answer. "Yes, Mr. Prime Minister, I do. Or else I do not think you would be here today."

"But why do you think we are doing this?"

"Honestly, Mr. Prime Minister?"

"Yes, honestly," Weissman said eyeing Alex.

"The strike on Esfahan, albeit a brilliant tactical move, and one that the world should appreciate, has altered the strategic situation in the Middle East."

"In what way?" asked Goldman.

"Israel has removed the possibility of quick and virtual elimination via nuclear attack for now; but in doing so has galvanized support among your natural enemies," Alex replied rather surprised at Goldman's question. Perhaps he was fishing for the official American position. "Of a greater concern, if I may be so bold, Mr. Prime Minister, is that your coalition government is in deep trouble as a result of this strike. There are many in Israel calling for peace at almost any cost. This appears to include the possible return of the Gaza settlements and West Bank and dismantling of the security wall in Jerusalem, which some have called the *Berliner Mauer.*"

"The Berlin Wall," observed Goldman. "Yes, we have heard that," he said as he caught Weissman's eye.

"You seem to have a grasp of the situation, Alex. But there are other factors involved," Weissman said as he leaned forward with a concerned look on his face. The twinkle in his eye that was present earlier had now disappeared.

"May I ask what those are, Mr. Prime Minister?" Alex boldly inquired.

"Economics are coming into play. The massive expenditures on our military, even with your generous foreign military assistance, are becoming a burden on our economy. Trade with our European markets has been slowing ever since the rise of Gerhard and the Europe First party."

"DNIS estimates military spending is approaching eleven percent of your GDP," noted Alex.

"Your DNIS is good but they are underestimating the amount. Suffice to say, it is becoming a burden. We have to cut our defense spending. This peace treaty will enable us to do so." Weissman continued, "There are political factors to consider as well. Certain members in the Knesset are threatening to withdraw support for my coalition. They also suggest they continue to hear alarming comments from a couple members of your Congress."

"For instance?" asked Alex feigning surprise. He knew the comments by several Congressional members Weissman was referring to, but diplomacy required he play the game. Alex had considered the comments by the Congressmen irresponsible at the time they were made. To insinuate that Israel was responsible for 9/11 was beyond the pale. What logic was there for Israel to attack its primary supporter in the world?

These Congressmen had continued their attacks on Israel to the present day. That they were made again during the recent U.S. Presidential election caused further dispersions to be cast upon them. Nonetheless, the press picked up the comments and ran multiple stories on them. Fortunately, the American public saw through the foolishness of the comments and voted out one of the representatives. The other representative was re-elected very narrowly. However, the damage was done and the enemies of Israel had their story.

"Certain comments have been made by some of your Congressional officials suggesting Israel is the cause of the War on Terror. Some news reports from your country have even suggested we were responsible for 9/11, as outlandish as that sounds. If we were removed, or neutralized, as I believe the Congressman put it, the War on Terror would be over."

"Mr. Prime Minister, I assure you, it is the position of President Sullivan to support Israel's right to defend herself. Upon hearing Gerhard's announcement in the press conference regarding Israeli activity involving Esfahan, he ordered the *George Washington* to the Eastern Med as a show of support."

LISTENING POST

7TH FLOOR GENEVA CENTER

The technician pressed the headset closer to his ears in another vain attempt to hear. His efforts were again rewarded with static. About the only thing he could hear with clarity was the beating of his heart. He adjusted another setting on his equipment but without any positive results. With an exasperated look he turned to the man standing behind him.

"Sir, I am getting nothing. Whatever he is using is masking our devices most effectively."

"Blast it! I have to know what he is saying," Gerhard exclaimed.

"I am sorry, sir. I cannot break this interference."

"Yes, she is cruising off our coast as we speak. We are grateful for his support. And that leads me to why I asked you here tonight. Alex, we are prepared to make significant concessions for this peace treaty. I mean very significant. I am not prepared to discuss these with you at this time. Some things are best kept secret," Weissman said his grey eyes narrowing as he gestured to the walls. Though the room had been swept for monitoring devices by Israeli intelligence, Weissman was electing to keep his cards close to his vest. *It was a prudent move* Alex thought. Weissman now clasped his hands together. "But, we must have assurances from your President that America will not abandon Israel if, for some reason, the peace treaty were violated. We are not naïve. There are many out there who never will accept our presence on this planet. Words on paper are one thing; but the barrel of a Merkava tank is another."

Alex knew what he was being asked. To make a commitment that the United States would guarantee the right of Israel to exist and would come to her aid if attacked. He knew what the Prime Minister wanted to hear, but he did not have the authority to make such a pledge. It was true that America had been Israel's closest friend and had assisted her in the past. He felt Sullivan would continue to do so but he could not guarantee that. Alex tried one more angle.

"President Gerhard has promised deployment of EU forces to enforce the observance of the treaty. Are you not confident of his promise?"

"Alex, I remind you that some of these forces are coming from the very country that tried to eliminate us as a race while others on the continent stood by," Weissman said referring to Nazi atrocities against his people. "And this was before Germany began the war. It was American influence that helped restore our land to us, and it has been America that has aided us since then."

"Mr. Prime Minister, I can only say this. It has been, and continues to be, the policy of the United States to support the right of all democracies to exist. This most definitely includes Israel."

"Is that a guarantee?" asked Weissman.

"No, sir. However it is the policy of this administration. I cannot promise anything further without consulting with President Sullivan."

"I see," said Weissman who sat with his arms folded for a moment before he spoke again. "Alex, I have enjoyed this time. We shall dine again before this is all over." Weissman extinguished his cigar, stood, and extended his hand to Alex. Alex knew he was being shown the door. "Colonel Goldman will escort you through security. Good night, Alex."

"The pleasure has been all mine, sir," Alex said as he rose and shook his hand. "I look forward to that next meal."

OVAL OFFICE

6:35 p.m.

"Kind of late for government work isn't it, Alex?" inquired Sullivan noting that it was close to one o'clock in Geneva. Alex had contacted President Sullivan via the secure phone he had been provided. The phone was equipped with a dampening field that would render any listening devices useless. The remarkable thing about the phone was that it was not much larger than a standard cell phone. Alex had been briefed very carefully by DNIS officials on the protocols for secure communications in an unsecured environment.

"Yes, sir, sorry to call so late but I felt it was significant."

"All right, Alex. Everyone is patched in. Go ahead," Sullivan advised after a moment.

"Mr. President, at dinner tonight, Prime Minister Weissman advised they were prepared to make major concessions to bring about this peace treaty. They are being pressed by severe economic and political domestic pressures. More than we have estimated. He hinted there is also pressure being exerted from certain sectors of our own government. He didn't give specifics on that, but we know who he is talking about. The Prime Minister sounded very worried about the future of his coalition government."

"Even after the opening statements by both sides? They have caused quite a stir in the world. What does he want?" inquired Stanfield.

"Yes, the statements were rather stunning in their content. But as we know, words are just words until acted upon. What does he want? In a nutshell? He wants a pledge from us that we will support Israel and guarantee her right to exist and support that right militarily if the peace treaty were violated. For historical reasons, he is ambivalent in his faith of the EU forces' reliability to enforce the treaty," replied Alex.

"What did you tell him?" It was Sheffield.

"I told him it was the position of the United States to support the right of all democracies to exist. I did not address the EU peacekeepers."

There was a long pause on the other end of the phone. Finally, the President spoke. "Sounds like he put you in a tight spot, Alex, but your answer was dead on. You're getting pretty good at this diplomacy. I will keep you in mind if I need another Secretary of State. Alex, we're having a Security Council meeting first thing in the morning to discuss this issue. I'll get back with you on what you can tell Weissman. You get some sleep."

"Thank you, Mr. President. Tell the Secretary her job is secure. Not enough money for me."

Alex looked at the clock as he closed the phone and reclined on his bed. It had been a long day.

SESSION THREE

GENEVA

December 24th

7:58 a.m.

Alex was downing his third cup of coffee. Dinner the night before with Jallud and his entourage had been quite different than with the Israelis. It was well past two when Alex returned to his room. The meal started off very pleasantly, but as Alex feared, had turned into a rather heated debate afterwards.

The fundamental issue Jallud kept addressing centered on who was the rightful owner of the land that currently comprised Israel. The debate centered on which son of Abraham God established His covenant with: Isaac or Ishmael. For the covenant, including the Promised Land, would pass to that son. Jews and Christians believe Isaac was that son. Muslims believe Ishmael was that son. He and Jallud cited the Bible and Koran to justify their respective positions as to who was the rightful owner of the land. It was a debate Alex had prepared for in his briefings with Stanfield should it come up. To be honest, he was surprised it had not come up during his talk with Weissman, but perhaps the secrets Weissman did not reveal to Alex involved land. After several hours of discussion, Alex noted to Jallud that perhaps the topic of land ownership was one on which they had best agree to disagree. Surprisingly the topic of Esfahan did not even come up. Alex was thankful it had not when he bid his hosts good night.

He continued to sip on the coffee as Gerhard opened the meeting with a review of sessions one and two. He had been, as Alex observed, characteristically late. Alex could not help but feel that the meetings were really about Gerhard. He knew Gerhard would, and perhaps justifiably so, take credit for any success in the peace talks. If the results were unsuccessful though, Alex knew he would blame outside forces that conspired to derail the meetings. However, it was those very outside forces that brought about a quickened pace in the negotiations. And it was under circumstances no one could have envisioned.

OBSERVATION POST 36, SECURITY FENCE

JERUSALEM, ISRAEL

December 23rd (the night before)

12:14 a.m.

Along the Security Fence, two Palestinian boys had been playing in the remains of a building long abandoned by its former Israeli owners. There were many such buildings along the Security Fence. Palestinians had occupied some, while others had been destroyed by fighting between Israeli and Palestinian forces. This building was in the latter category.

It was midnight as the two boys emerged from the building. The two ten-year-old lads had left their homes early that morning for a day of exploration. Despite clear instructions from their mothers to avoid them, they disregarded their admonitions, as did many boys their age, and headed for the ruined buildings. Each carried a backpack that contained some food and water for their day's adventure. They had removed their backpacks and were carrying them as they came running out of the shadows of the building.

Observation Post 36 was located across the road from the area in which the boys were playing. The two IDF soldiers manning the post were at the end of their watch. They had been on duty since six o'clock that morning and were feeling the effects of their eighteen-hour day. To further complicate matters, their relief was late again for the third day in a row.

Tensions had been high all along the fence since the news of Israel's strike on Esfahan. The soldiers had endured daily insults, accompanied by rocks, and sometimes broken glass hurtled in their direction. The soldiers had been ordered not to fire back even if hit with the debris.

Perhaps it was fatigue. Or maybe that part of the human psyche that reaches its limit and has to strike back. Whatever the cause, the soldiers had reached their limit.

Private Greene noticed movement out of the corner of his eye. The full moon had cast an eerie glow over the landscape. He could not readily identify what was causing the movement. He signaled to his partner who switched on the searchlight. Private Bernstein swung the light to the building where the movement was occurring. The boys had now fully emerged from the building.

The sudden brightness of the light destroyed the night vision of the boys. In an instinctive move to shield their eyes from the intensity of the light, they raised their hands to their eyes. In doing so they raised their backpacks.

To Greene, the backpacks looked like the satchel charges they had seen in basic training. The movement of the boys raising their arms looked like a throwing motion. Greene had already raised his rifle. In an instant, his training took over. Acquire the target. Aim. Fire. Acquire the second target. Aim. Fire. It was over in less than five seconds. His aim was dead on and the two boys fell to the ground. No second shots were required. The shots were heard throughout the neighborhood. The shots were also heard in Washington and Geneva.

SESSION THREE (CONTINUED)

GENEVA

It was understandable to Alex that the mood of the conference room was less amicable than the previous meetings. There had been some attempt at small talk, but both camps were fairly entrenched as a result of the shootings. One positive was that neither side had abandoned the peace talks. So many prospects for peace had previously been destroyed by similar events in world history. Alex wondered if the talks could be salvaged. Gerhard spoke first.

"Gentlemen, we are all saddened at the events along the Security Fence. This morning, I issued a statement on behalf of this conference condemning the shootings. I also stressed that this event, tragic as it is, would not deter us from our efforts. The world is watching and waiting to see how we respond."

Jallud now arose and addressed the conference. "Brothers, we have come here for peace. Prime Minister Weissman, I understand the activities of your soldiers. We train our men the same way. In the shadows of the night the eye can play tricks on the mind. The boys should not have been where they were; especially at that hour. Their blood is on the hands of their parents. We are still desirous of peace," he concluded returning to his seat.

It was now Weissman who addressed the meeting. "We have contacted the commanding officers of the two soldiers involved. They violated standing orders and will be duly punished. On this I give you my word. Our sympathies are extended to the families. Losing a loved one, especially a child, is the most devastating of all losses. A parent should never have to bury a child. Neither punishment of our soldiers or any other action can restore the life of the two boys. I realize these are mere words. Perhaps our actions taken, will in some small measure, atone for those of our soldiers."

"Punishment of the soldiers is not necessary," Jallud noted. "Their punishment will be the knowledge they mistakenly took innocent life. That is punishment enough."

With these statements the tone of the meeting shifted. Alex could feel a renewed sense of commitment stirring within the room. As each had spoken, their opposite sides had nodded in approval. It was nothing short of incredible, Alex thought. A shooting incident, coupled with the bombing of a nuclear facility that should have derailed, or at least delayed, the peace talks was being condemned by both sides. More importantly, each side had assumed responsibility for the incident. No accusations, no blame.

Gerhard now spoke. He noted the Security Fence represented the best place to begin negotiations as it symbolized the central issues of their talks: land and security. UN Resolution 242 had called for a return to the 1967 pre-war boundaries. Both Jallud and Weissman agreed that while this was ideal, it was not practical in light of the position of Jerusalem. Great historical significance was associated with the city for both Jew and Arab. Israel had declared the ancient city to be its capital. Many Arabs lived within the city. Both sides had strong religious claims to the city. It appeared the talks would again bog down on the same issue that had foiled previous attempts at peace. There seemed to be no way to resolve the land issue.

Sensing the time was right Jallud spoke, "Brothers, there is a way. Our respective religions are very important to us are they not? They are sometimes what have separated us. Perhaps there is a way we can overcome this."

He paused for a moment before continuing.

"The House of Israel has been without a place of worship for far too long. As a gesture of our sincerity for peace, we are prepared to offer the right to rebuild the Temple alongside the Dome of the Rock. There is sufficient land there for both to exist. We additionally propose to recognize Jerusalem as the true capital of Israel. Further, we pledge to support Israel's right to exist and henceforth insure her security. And this we pledge..." pausing a moment for effect, "if we can worship together, we can live together."

Alex and the rest of the delegates were stunned. The reality of the offer struck him with a realization that this was the central issue. Why anyone had not seen this before was unclear. It was more than just land. The Temple Mount represented the heart and soul of both Jew and Muslim, not only in the region, but worldwide. Jallud had taken the negotiations into an entirely different arena. Perhaps peace was now indeed at hand.

Weissman was overcome with emotion. Tears were streaming down the faces of many of the Israeli delegation. A few were openly weeping. Only Goldman appeared unmoved. The faces of the members of the Islamic Alliance were practically beaming though they were trying to conceal their true feelings. Alex realized they had played their trump card. The question now remained whether Weissman would meet or exceed the offer.

Gerhard called for a recess to allow both sides to evaluate the events that had just unfolded. He reminded the delegates that private facilities were available for just such a contingency. All parties now adjourned from the main conference room. The Israeli party availed themselves of one of the rooms. Gerhard and Jallud met each other in the main hallway. Both men were nodding as they spoke. They shook hands and retired to their respective delegations. Two hours later, Weissman indicated they were ready to continue the discussions.

Gerhard reconvened the conference. Weissman, who was still visibly overcome by the emotional appeal at the prospect of having the Temple rebuilt, was first to address the room.

"Today is indeed an historic day in the life of Israel. Never would we have entertained the notion of rebuilding the Temple as proposed today. Indeed, many in Israel have foregone the possibility of the Temple ever being rebuilt. We graciously accept your magnanimous offer," he said with a slight bow in the direction of Jallud. "To show our sincerity and commitment to the peace process, we are prepared to renounce all claims to the settlements in Gaza and recognize Palestinian claims along the West Bank. We will make provisions for returning the land. The dismantlement of the Security Fence will also begin to allow access for all residents. We have but one issue to resolve. Security."

"Very understandable and prudent, Mr. Prime Minister. I believe I can address that issue," interjected Gerhard. "The European Union is prepared to act as intermediary on behalf of all parties. Deployed EU forces will act as peacekeepers. We will draft language that will provide a means of addressing violations of the treaty. Lastly, terms of the treaty will clearly outline Israel's right to exist, including recognition of Jerusalem as Israel's capital, from all of her neighbors as noted by Jallud. All will sign a formal treaty. The nation of Israel will be at peace with her neighbors for the first time in her history."

The parties continued negotiations to hammer out the fine points of their historic agreement. After six hours of deliberation all was finished. Gerhard had their notes quickly transcribed to parchment for all to review. All parties read the document and were satisfied. He checked his watch. It read 12:03 a.m. It was now December 25th. Gerhard looked at Weissman and Jallud.

"Gentlemen, I believe we have an agreement that is more than satisfactory to all. If you will check the time you will find it is now Christmas Day. I can think of no better gift to give the world. Shall we announce our gift of peace to the world?" Gerhard reached out his hands to both Weissman and Jallud who reciprocated. All three men moved to the end of the table where they hugged each other to the applause of the room. Gerhard then suggested they move to the media room where they could announce their good news.

It took close to an hour for the press and respective parties to make their way to the room for the press conference. Weissman and Jallud stood by each other on the platform to the right of Gerhard. Members of the media were finishing setting up their cameras and lights. Gerhard, clearly relishing the role of peacemaker, took the podium and signaled for the press to quiet down. He began his opening statement regarding the agreement that had just been reached.

"Ladies and gentlemen, today is a momentous day in the history of not only the Middle East, but also the world. For on this Christmas Day, which shall long be remembered for generations to come, we offer the world the gift of peace, which has come to this most troubled part of our world. Long time adversaries have today reached across the divide to build a bridge for peace. Others around the world need now only to look to the Middle East as the symbol of hope for peace in our world. The Prime Minister, Representative Jallud, and I will now sign the treaty to be known henceforth as The Jerusalem Accord."

Each signed the Accord. When they completed their signatures, the three stood together on the platform before the press. Gerhard stood in the middle flanked by Weissman and Jallud. The three reached out to shake hands with each other. As they did, they held the handshake as a symbol of solidarity with each other to the applause of those gathered in the room. Gerhard then moved to the podium.

"I am thankful that the European Union was able to play a small part in this historic event. It is certainly remarkable what we can accomplish when we remove those things that divide us and focus on those things that unite us. I would like now to invite Prime Minister Weissman and Representative Jallud to join me at the podium for your questions."

The press began their onslaught of questions as Alex knew they would. He was standing off to the left of the platform taking in the moment. It was indeed an historic day for all. The press was already dubbing the event a Christmas Day miracle. Alex was still overwhelmed at the sudden turn of events. In just four days, ancient enemies had turned swords into plowshares. Perhaps, the lion and the lamb were indeed prepared to lie together. If diplomacy were this easy he might consider a career change. Then it struck him. This had been an easy negotiation. Maybe it had been too easy.

MISSTEPS AND WARNINGS

SHINK-U LAN LAUNCH COMPLEX

NORTH KOREA

December 29th

5:15 a.m.

It was a marvel of engineering that rivaled the construction of the American NORAD complex. The fundamental difference was that this site had remained undetected in spite of the enormity of the project. Total secrecy was one of the benefits of a closed society. The launch complex was yet another component of North Korea's clandestine nuclear program. From all accounts Western intelligence had no inkling of its existence. If they had, it was certain the Americans and their puppets in the South would have included the facility in the recent disarmament negotiations.

Ten missile silos had been carved out of the mountain. Their launch doors had been camouflaged so as to remain undetected by American spy satellites. To avoid possible damage or destruction of the complex during launches, the Taep'o-dong 5 missiles were forcefully ejected from their silos by gas pressure. This cold launch technique, perfected by the former Soviet Union, preserved the silo for future launches.

Currently four of the silos contained missiles. This represented the total nuclear arsenal of North Korea. Missiles for the remaining six silos were under construction. Warheads would be available within six months. The current yield of the warheads was in the one hundred kiloton range. The scientists had not yet mastered the techniques to produce larger yields, but these would be sufficient to ensure victory on the battlefield or in the political arena. Japan would soon learn of her neighbor's newfound strength. The Leader had planned to move with final reunification of the South when all ten missiles were operational.

"Colonel Kim, are we prepared for launch?"

"Yes, General Sun-Jing. All is ready. Trajectory and payload have been configured for optimum impact. Impact area is one thousand miles east of Japan. Nothing but open sea. The most damage inflicted will be several thousand fish killed."

"Very good, Colonel. The Leader will be pleased. With the Americans preoccupied by the peace talks in Geneva they will be unable to respond. This demonstration will give us the upper hand in our reunification efforts. Colonel, begin the countdown and launch when ready."

MARRIOT HOTEL

LOS ANGELES

December 28th

1:00 p.m.

"Alex, I have been monitoring the press coverage of The Jerusalem Accord. This is an unprecedented turn of events. No one here ever envisioned this scenario unfolding. Certainly not in this time span."

"Yes, sir, Mr. President, I agree. I think the whole key to this was your guarantee to the Prime Minister that the United States would stand behind Israel in the event the Accord collapsed. The additional economic aid package you promised was a very positive gesture also. Weissman is a good poker player, but he understands each deal gives you a new set of cards. Right now he is holding a strong hand."

"Yes, I would say a royal flush. Alex, you sound a little uncertain about this. What's on your mind?"

"Probably nothing, sir. As you noted, it is an unprecedented turn of events. Almost too remarkable in some aspects. But I guess that is when great events occur. I remember all of the pundits said Reagan was crazy when he went to Berlin and told Gorbachev to tear down the wall."

"Yes, that did shake things up a bit, but Reagan was right. The wall did come down and so did Communism. Perhaps the Accord will have the same impact in the Middle East. Alex, you have done a great job of keeping me informed during the talks. Stanfield wants to know when you are coming to work for her. In fact, she is a little worried about her job!"

"If they would all be this easy I would take her up on the offer. However, I think I will keep my day job. She need not worry about me."

"I understand," acknowledged Sullivan. "I am due to deliver my speech pretty soon. Now don't forget to do some shopping for your bride. You missed Christmas, so you better not come back from Europe empty-handed. That would indeed be an international crisis!"

Both men laughed at the implications of Sullivan's last statement as they knew it was true. "Yes, sir, Mr. President. That's one order I will fulfill to the letter. I'll see you in a couple of days. Good luck with your speech, sir."

SPACE EARLY WARNING SYSTEM

EARTH ORBIT

The satellite was parked in geo-stationary orbit over the mainland of Asia. The cold quiet vacuum of space was lost on this sentry. This sentry, like the ones before it and the ones that would follow, dutifully performed its responsibility without complaint. Its infrared eye searched the blue ball beneath looking for heat signatures that indicated the launch of a missile. The satellite had been tasked by its masters of the 1st Space Operations Squadron, 50th Space Wing, to pay particular attention to the peninsula of land that jutted off the eastern coastline of the continent of Asia. The rogue nation was rumored to have nuclear weapons. The disarmament negotiations had broken down again and rumor was a demonstration was to be performed.

The infrared eye detected a rise in thermal energy emanating north of the 38th parallel. Microprocessors on-board the spacecraft began to process the information and within seconds communicated its conclusion to its masters in the Cheyenne Mountains.

Staff Sergeant Manuel Vasquez was about to complete his shift at the Missile Warning Center. A warning indicator that should have remained dark unexpectedly turned red. He studied his monitor for a moment to be sure of the information the satellite was transmitting before he made his phone call. Once sure, he lifted the red phone at his desk.

"General, I have a launch and confirmation at longitude 128' 32" 55'" east, latitude 40', 50", 60'"north," said Staff Sgt. Manuel Vasquez. His voice was calm and reasoned. No hint of panic. "North Korea, sir."

"Confidence?" inquired General Larry Bryant as he laid aside the performance report he was reading.

"Confidence is high, sir. Signature is that of a Taep'o-dong 5, sir," Vasquez replied.

"Trajectory?" Bryant demanded as he switched his monitor to reflect Vasquez's.

"Sir, projected course puts it heading toward CONUS. If it is a Taep'o-dong 5, the range is sufficient to bring the west coast in as a target."

General Bryant checked a monitor at his desk. It showed the President was in Los Angeles. He immediately lifted the red phone on his desk. "Get me the President. We have an Urgent Tango. Repeat, Urgent Tango. I am declaring an Air Defense Emergency. The base is being sealed."

MARRIOT HOTEL

LOS ANGELES

2:30 p.m.

President Sullivan had just concluded his speech to the Foreign Policy Institute. It had been a stinging indictment of the North Korean leadership. In the speech he called for North Korea to allow access by International Atomic Energy Association inspectors to their nuclear facilities. Only by doing so could talks resume regarding normalizing relations and providing much needed assistance.

He was returning to his seat when six Secret Service officers burst onto the stage with weapons drawn. Sullivan was momentarily stunned by their sudden appearance, but quickly regained his composure. He knew why they were there. One of the responsibilities of the office was to be familiar with the National Crisis Emergency Evacuation Procedures. Unlike some of his predecessors, he frequently participated in the drills. He moved to rise from his chair but the Secret Service men were faster. Two men circled behind him grabbing the world's most powerful man under the arms while the other four formed a shield around him. He was practically carried off the stage to the stunned gasps of the audience.

"What the devil is happening?" Sullivan asked as he ran with the Secret Service men toward the elevator leaving the audience to wonder what was happening.

"Urgent Tango was received from NORAD, sir. Marine One is warming up. Air Force One is rolling to taxi. We have eighteen minutes to make this happen, Mr. President."

He could see the whirling blades of Marine One as they exited the door to the helipad atop the hotel. Normally he traveled via motorcade, but given the disruption to local traffic, and consideration that they were voters and had voted for him in the last election, he had chosen to fly to this speaking engagement. It did not have the fanfare of the motorcade, but it was more efficient and placed less stress on the Secret Service.

The Secret Service moved to form a perimeter around the helicopter even though they were thirty stories above the ground. The Secret Service men practically threw Sullivan on board and strapped him into his seat. They had barely closed the hatch on the VH-60 when the pilot gunned Marine One's engine and performed an emergency takeoff for Los Angeles International Airport. Sullivan looked out of the window as they cleared the landing area. He could see swarms of emergency and military personnel and vehicles beginning to encircle the hotel.

Lt. Colonel Davidson was opening the Football. The rather innocuous looking suitcase contained the nuclear options and launch codes of America's nuclear forces, if needed. Sullivan reached for his wallet and retrieved his copy of the Gold Codes he would need if a launch were to be authorized. Davidson handed Sullivan a small plastic card known as the *biscuit*. "Mr. President, this is your authentication card. General Stowe is on duty aboard NIGHTWATCH. General Bryant is on duty at NORAD. You are patched through to both." He also handed the President the SATCOM phone.

"Gentlemen, this is the President of the United States, William T. Sullivan. My authentication is Able, Zulu, Tango, Foxtrot, Delta One. What the devil is happening, General Stowe?"

On board NIGHTWATCH, the E-4B that serves as one of four National Airborne Operations Centers, the codes were verified and confirmed. "Authentication confirmed, Mr. President. At 1430 hours local time we detected an ICBM launch from North Korea. Trajectory is projected for CONUS. Probability of impact area is Los Angeles. General Bryant at NORAD has issued an Air Defense Emergency. All air traffic within a one hundred mile radius is being cleared for your departure. Fighter escort has been scrambled and will rendezvous with EAGLE-

ONE at predetermined coordinates. Ballistic Missile Command has been notified. We are holding at DEFCON-3."

"General Bryant, what is the range of that missile?" Sullivan asked anxiously.

"Sir, if it is the Taep'o-dong 5, it is capable of reaching Kansas. Los Angeles is well within range. Warhead yield is estimated at 80 kilotons."

"Recommended action, General?" asked Sullivan as he looked over the list of retaliatory options Colonel Davidson had handed him.

"Mr. President, our missile defense system will engage the target within one hundred miles of CONUS. If intercept is not successful, recommend SIOP option X-Ray 5. It provides the fastest retaliation and is a measured response involving our missile subs and carriers. It will target the launch area, key communication, command, and control targets. USS *Florida* is in position. Captain Ben Richardson in command."

Sullivan had reviewed similar scenarios over in his head and asked himself the same question that every President in the nuclear age had asked. What is the appropriate response to a nuclear attack on the United States that resulted in the murder of millions of Americans? He knew the advice he was receiving was reasoned and had been war-gamed in a thousand scenarios. The people giving him counsel were professionals who had no desire to escalate what could theoretically be a mistake, into a nuclear nightmare. However, this was not a mistake. There had been no communication with the North Koreans. No call warning of a mistaken missile launch. This had the trappings of a sneak attack.

Marine One was approaching LAX. Air Force One was waiting at the end of the runway. He had to make a decision now. To wait until he boarded the plane would be wasted time and time was the one luxury he did not have at this point.

"Generals Stowe and Bryant, as President of the United States of America, and by the powers granted by the Constitution, I authorize you to execute X-Ray 5 in the event of unsuccessful missile intercept and subsequent detonation on U.S. territory. Authorization code is Mike, Hotel, Alpha, Omega, Three. Say again, you are authorized to execute X-Ray 5 in the event of unsuccessful missile intercept and detonation on U.S. territory. Authorization code is Mike, Hotel, Alpha, Omega, Three. Move us to DEFCON-2. May God be with us. We are transferring to Air Force One."

"Orders received and confirmed, sir. I am wearing out some carpet as we speak. Good luck, Mr. President," replied General Stowe.

Marine One had barely touched down as the hatch opened and Sullivan was literally lifted out of his seat by the Secret Service. He and the occupants exited the helicopter and sprinted up the boarding steps into the great airliner whose engines were now being brought up to full power. The boarding steps were rolled back just in time as Air Force One began rolling for takeoff. Forty-five seconds later they were airborne.

The pilot of Air Force One began a steep bank to the east as the massive plane continued to gain altitude. After two minutes, a flight of four F-15Hs took up escort stations around the airliner. Sullivan could see them outside of his window. These would escort the plane to its recovery destination. For now though, Air Force One was headed toward the Rockies and would remain so until the incoming missile was shot down, or worse, had detonated.

"Status of the missile?" Sullivan asked. He could now see a crystal clear image of the generals via satellite uplink. The communications team on board had already established satellite links with five other command sites throughout the United States in addition to the Pentagon and White House. These were currently displayed on the monitors at his desk. The communications onboard Air Force One had been greatly enhanced after 9/11 when they had been found lacking. At one point during that fateful morning, then-President Bush was unable to communicate with his staff as effectively as Sullivan was now.

"Sir, missile is maintaining course," General Bryant reported.

"What are those fools thinking? Have they gone berserk? Why weren't we warned about this?" Sullivan demanded from Clairmont as he fired his questions like an automatic rifle.

"Mr. President, I am at a loss…" Clairmont began.

"That isn't good enough, Jim," Sullivan began but was interrupted.

"Mr. President." It was General Stowe. "We're detecting a change in missile trajectory. It is now describing a descent. Looks like the impact area will be mid-Pacific. Approximate impact point is Longitude 150' east, Latitude 32' north. Impact in three minutes. We may have bugged you out for nothing, sir."

"Nonsense, General. The Urgent Tango alert was the right thing to do. Though I am afraid this does not answer the 'why' of what just happened."

"Mr. President, if I may?" Clairmont said recovering from the initial questions. "The North Koreans have been threatening this very scenario in an attempt to force our hand at the negotiation table. It may also signal a prelude to war. This would suggest they are getting desperate. They have also tipped their hand, as we now know where at least one of their launch complexes is located. We may want to address that issue as our Israeli friends did. Recommend we surge two carrier strike groups to lend some support to our friends in the South and Japan. I bet they are as shaken as we are."

"Mr. President, we are now confirming detonation of a sixty-four kiloton warhead in the Pacific at the previous coordinates," reported General Stowe.

"Thank you, General. Secretary Clairmont. Recommendations?"

"Maintain X-Ray 5, Mr. President," Clairmont noted from deep under the Pentagon in the Emergency Conference Room. "Surge the carriers. Also recommend deploying a squadron of Nighthawks to South Korea. This will send the right message and enhance our options. Remain at DEFCON-2 until we have clarification of their intentions, or else."

"General?"

"Mr. President, I concur with the Secretary."

"Very well. Maintain X-Ray 5. Surge the carriers and the Nighthawks. Maintain DEFCON-2. Gentlemen, thank you for your work today. The worst may be over. But there are a lot of questions I want answered!" Sullivan pressed a button on his desk.

"Communications, put a call through to the North Korean embassy. I want them to be in our State Department in three hours and be ready to talk. Notify Stanfield they are coming. Tell them the President of the United States looks forward to their presence and will not accept excuses."

SPELUNKING

Temple Mount
Jerusalem
December 28th

The two men moved with caution in the tunnel. Their helmet lights were casting shadows on the walls. The tunnel was one of several that ran deep under the Temple Mount. The original purpose of the tunnel was to mask the movement of soldiers during the time of the Crusades. This tunnel, along with the others, had been sealed for over a thousand years and had almost been forgotten. Only the local Waqf knew of their actual existence. It was a secret passed from one generation to another.

The particular tunnel they were working in ran parallel to the Eastern Wall and then turned to run along the Southern Wall. It was thirty meters below the area known as Solomon's Stables. This tunnel had been chosen for a particular reason. Construction activities, along with the occasional earthquake tremor, had destabilized the area along the Southern Wall. In fact, a section of the wall had begun to bulge when work was halted five years earlier. The damaged area had been reinforced, but archeological estimates indicated that no additional work could continue in this area without further damage to the wall and possibly the Temple Mount area itself. As the Waqf was responsible for this sacred site, it had been agreed that all future construction would be halted and the damage repaired. It was for this reason that Al-Saim had chosen this particular tunnel.

The men were still unsure their task was sacred. However, Al-Saim had convinced them that Allah had bestowed this mission upon them and that they had been chosen as His instruments. Without success in this area, Jihad would not be successful.

They removed their equipment and began their work. The drilling was slow due to the hardness of the rock. A slight tremor occurred causing some rocks to fall raising even more dust. The men knew such tremors were not uncommon in the area. They had often felt them as they lay in the comfort and safety of their beds. However, neither had been underground when one occurred. The lights from their helmets played on each other's faces as the dust drifted through the lights. Neither would admit the fear that registered in the eyes of each man and neither could hide it though they tried. They had heard the stories of how the Crusaders had moved through other tunnels and were buried alive as Allah's judgment came upon them.

Though it was cool in the tunnel, the two men were sweating as much from their fear as work. They wiped the sweat from their faces. One reached into his workbag and produced a canteen. They each shared a drink of water as they waited a minute or two before resuming their work.

They knew their drilling was not of sufficient strength to damage the walls or even trigger additional tremors. Still, they did not want to take any chances as they proceeded with caution. They had discussed just leaving the explosives in the tunnel instead of burying them in the wall. However, it was eventually decided there was a chance, though remote, as access to the Temple area was off limits to anyone but devout Muslims, that someone could stumble upon them. For that reason, the equipment and materials had been purchased from Jewish-owned businesses. Anything found would have Hebrew lettering. Believability was the key to the success of their mission Al-Saim had told them.

Sweat poured off of their brows as they continued their work. The explosives were packed into the freshly drilled holes just as they had been trained. The holes were sealed with a plaster-like material that upon hardening would resemble rock. At least it would pass for rock in the darkness of the tunnel. The only indication anything was in the wall were the razor thin antennae attached to the explosives. They checked their work as they sealed the last hole. With a nod of approval to each other, they gathered their tools and began to work their way back through the tunnel. They had not taken five steps when another tremor, this one much stronger than the previous one, shook the tunnel. Though it lasted only fifteen seconds, the tremor was strong enough to shake the rock loose above their heads. A piece of rock struck the first man on the temple instantly killing him. This caused his partner to stumble and fall. As he did his helmet and light fell off. The lens struck one of the fallen rocks breaking it and extinguishing the light. He was now in total darkness. Perhaps it was fortunate, for he was unable to see that the tunnel had collapsed twenty meters ahead. He called out for his partner. Nothing was heard but his own breathing, which was becoming rapid and shallow as panic began to set in on the man. He crawled a few feet forward before he felt the warm body of his partner. He burst into tears as he shook the man calling his name, but there was no reply. Hakim now felt for the wrist of his fallen friend. Checking for the pulse he found none. His sweat had now turned clammy as the coldness of the tunnel was making its impact. Hakim sat for a moment. Then it struck him in overwhelming fashion. Panic. The type a man feels when his life is in jeopardy. Adrenaline began to flow through his body so much so that he began to shake. He felt around for his fallen partner's helmet but to no avail. "No! No!" He was screaming now. He would not die this way. He attempted to run in his panic. He had run all of fifteen meters when he struck his head on an outcrop of rock that rendered him unconscious. No one could hear his screams for help when he regained consciousness two hours later. Hakim would join the ghosts of the Crusaders.

They had long passed their estimated time of completion. But there would be no one coming to help. The tremors had been felt. It was assumed the worst had befallen the two men. That they could not reach the explosives was of little consequence. They were to be detonated by cell phone. The strength of the signal would be weakened but it would still be sufficient for the task. The tremor had been a blessing in disguise. The far end of the tunnel was sealed so there was no chance of escape for the two. There would be no breach of security. The two men from the Waqf finished resealing the entrance to the tunnel and departed. They would report the event to Al-Saim who would be pleased.

The North Korean ambassador was sitting impassively across from Stanfield's desk. So far their discussion had not been fruitful.

"Mr. Ambassador, you realize the actions of your government could be interpreted as an act of war."

"As could your deployment of stealth aircraft and your aircraft carriers," countered the ambassador referring to the announced deployment of these forces.

"They are a measured response to what may or may not have been the first salvo in another Korean War. A war, I might add, that your country can ill afford," Stanfield shot back.

"Madam Secretary, with all due respect. The missile was not intended for the United States. The target area was intended to be in China. We had an agreement with the Chinese that would allow us to fire our missile there for testing purposes. A malfunction of the guidance system caused the missile to regrettably veer off course on an unintended trajectory toward your country."

"Mr. Ambassador, let me see if I have this straight. Your country launches a missile with a nuclear warhead, which you have been claiming does not exist. Its initial target is supposed to be China, but its course targets the United States, which you would have us believe was a malfunction of the missile's guidance system. Now honestly, Mr. Ambassador, would you believe this if our positions were reversed?"

The Ambassador moved to speak, but Stanfield did not give him a chance to respond as she continued on.

"No, you would not. The President is expecting a formal apology for this incident and a pledge to return to the negotiating table. Let's not take this to the next level for which the President is prepared to do if necessary," Stanfield emphatically stated.

"We will not be dictated to by you or anyone else, Madam Secretary. We have the right to self-defense and peaceful nuclear research," the North Korean Ambassador replied tersely. Inwardly he agreed with the Secretary but he was acting under direct orders from the Leader.

"Agreed, Mr. Ambassador, but not when nukes are being lobbed across the Pacific which pretty much negates your position on *peaceful* nuclear research. The ball is in your court, Mr. Ambassador. Good day, sir," she concluded while coolly eyeing the Ambassador.

Stanfield rose, signaling the meeting was over. As the door closed behind the North Korean she lifted the phone. "The President, please." A moment passed as contact was established with Air Force One.

"Yes, Madame Secretary, how did it go?" inquired an anxious Sullivan.

"They are a stubborn lot, Mr. President. We'll have to wait for their reply. I wouldn't count on a Hallmark card though."

"Any explanation for what happened?"

"The Ambassador is saying a malfunction in the guidance system threw the missile off course."

"Do you believe him?"

"I am not sure, Mr. President. He did seem rather shaken by the event. I felt sorry for him in a way. Poor devil can't say what he wants without approval from Pyongyang."

"*You* felt sorry for him? Now I am worried," Sullivan said dryly. "Overall though, pretty much what we expected?"

"Yes, sir. We are of course keeping the usual channels open. I will contact you if any further developments occur. Mr. President, one more question. Are you ok, sir? Is there anything we can do? Your family, anything?"

For all of her exterior toughness, Stanfield was a different person when it came to personal relationships with people with whom she worked. There was a softer side she rarely allowed folks to see. Sullivan knew her exterior toughness came from the loss of her husband and children in a heartbreaking airplane accident. They had been on a skiing trip to Colorado during spring break. On the return flight home their chartered plane ran into heavy cloud cover. The pilot lost his bearings and crashed into the side of the Rocky Mountains.

Afterwards she plunged herself into her work. Still stunning in appearance at age fifty, she had refused any attempt at a social life. Sullivan respected her privacy and never mentioned the possibility of remarrying.

"Thank you, Kathryn, I appreciate that. I am fine. The family has been moved to secure locations until we are confident this thing was really an accident. Secret Service has me as safe as a babe in her momma's arms. It was quite an interesting situation there for a while. Let's pray we don't have to do it again."

"But what if it wasn't an accident?"

Sullivan could see the concern in her face.

"Then we have a potentially bigger problem on our hands than we thought. Thank the Good Lord there is peace in the Middle East tonight."

"Amen to that, Mr. President."

AIR FORCE ONE

SOMEWHERE OVER THE U.S.

7:30 p.m.

President Sullivan was sitting in his executive chair reviewing the steady stream of information that was being reported. "Mr. President, as per your orders, *Truman* and *Eisenhower* are deploying to take up station in the Sea of Japan. *Stennis* will be first on station as she is currently forward deployed at Guam. Nighthawks are deploying to Kadena Air Base on Okinawa. *Florida* is holding her launch position. Japanese are pretty nervous that a nuke-armed missile was launched over their country. Their press is hollering to high heaven about this. Japanese Self-Defense Forces are on full alert. South Korea has begun mobilization of their armed forces. They believe this is prelude to an invasion," reported General Stowe aboard KNIGHTWATCH. "Chinese have increased their air activity in anticipation of hostilities. They have increased the readiness of their nuclear forces. Russians have increased their air activity around Vladivostok. Plus they have increased the readiness of their nuclear forces. No statements have been issued by Beijing or Moscow on the explosion."

Sullivan adjusted the angle of the monitor on which he was watching General Stowe. The picture he was receiving was flawless.

"Sounds as if X-Ray 5 is proceeding according to plan. My compliments to your staff, General. I hope we don't need the options under the plan."

"Agreed, sir. By the way, how did things go with the Ambassador?"

"Not very well. All Stanfield got was a lot of denial and blaming us for their problems. Poor devils. I really didn't expect that much from them given the system they work under."

"Any comments on the weapons they had so vigorously been denying?" asked Stowe.

"No. Stanfield concluded none were needed in light of the launch. We know they have a nuclear program and we know where one of their bases is located."

"Not very good poker players are they, Mr. President? Showing their hand like that."

"I am not sure, General. They sent a message by sacrificing one of their nukes. That tells us they have more than one. Or at least that's the message they want us to have. Pretty expensive message either way. Next time the target might not be the Pacific. Maintain X-Ray 5 until further notice. I am returning to Washington in two hours." Sullivan switched off the monitor and leaned back in his chair. What a day. The only bright spot in the world seemed to be the Mideast. At least there was peace in that region of the world for a change. A passage from the New Testament came to mind: *And on earth peace, good will toward men.* If only it could be.

BOYS AND THEIR TOYS

COASTAL BOATS

JACKSONVILLE, FLORIDA

December 28th

9:46 a.m.

I t was another sunny day in Jacksonville. Abukar figured this was the best time to buy a boat. He hoped many people would be taking advantage of the post-Christmas discounts being offered by the dealership. As he parked his car in the crowded parking lot of the dealership, he knew he had guessed right. In fact, this particular dealership was the busiest of the ones he had driven by that day, and it was for that reason he picked this one. He had shaved off his beard in an effort to blend in with the crowd. His training had paid particular attention to blending in with the local community. His clothing was what one would expect of a person looking to buy a boat. Attired in khakis and a polo shirt with a baseball hat that sported the logo of the local football team, he appeared to be as American as they came. There was nothing particular about him that a salesman would remember.

He stopped to look at one boat and then another to give the appearance of the typical buyer. He had often visited car dealerships to observe the shopping habits of people. One thing he noted was that most people arrived at a dealership without a clear idea of what they wanted to buy. They would mill around until the salesperson arrived and began the buying process. In fact, he had gone on several practice-buying missions at car and boat dealerships to get a feel for the real experience. Now he would put those experiences to the test.

"She's a real beauty and handles great in the water." Abukar turned and saw the salesman. "Bert Jenkins, how can I help you today, sir?" said the salesman with an outstretched hand.

Abukar shook his hand and said, "Bill Fernandez. I am looking for a boat. Something with room and speed. I plan to be traveling the intracoastal this spring with some buddies and do some fishing." He had used his fake name that he used on all purchases. All information about him had been created fictitiously prior to coming to the United States. After crossing the porous Mexican border in Arizona he quickly obtained his fake identification. It had been all too easy to do this. That a major country like the United States would not secure its borders was unfathomable to him. If his brothers could obtain the coveted nuclear warhead they long sought, they would be able to easily transport it into the United States the same way he entered the country. There were always plenty of willing couriers who would transport people or property across the border for the right price and no questions asked.

"Mr. Fernandez, I have just the boat for you. Please follow me." The two headed toward another row of boats. The boat the salesman was showing him was exactly what Abukar was looking for. It was a sport yacht. At thirty-four feet in length it was a sleek design. The specs indicated it was capable of forty mph. It would sleep five and had all the amenities of a small home. Not that it would matter. The passengers he would be carrying would not care about the amenities on board. The cabin capacity and speed were the primary needs he had today.

"Would you like to take a spin in one?" asked the salesman.

Abukar thought for a second. He could really care less to do this but appearances were priority. "Yes, that would be nice. Would hate to spend this much money and not like her," replied Abukar with a smile.

"Excellent. You won't be disappointed, sir. We have an exact model tied up at the slip. If you will come with me please, we'll take her out." Jenkins led him to the slip area of the dealership. An exact model of the boat Abukar was considering was tied up along the dock. Abukar helped Jenkins clear the mooring ropes. They made their way to the bridge of the boat.

"Let me back this baby out and I will turn her over to you," said Jenkins. "Ever do much boating?"

"Yes, my family owns a place on the river. Been on the water all of my life," replied Abukar.

Upon clearing the docks, Jenkins quickly explained the controls and stepped aside, turning the helm over to Abukar. Two hours later they were back in the salesman's office completing the transaction. "She really did handle well. She will be perfect," said Abukar.

"I know you and your friends will have many enjoyable hours aboard this boat. Mr. Fernandez, how would you like to finance this? We offer several payment plans."

Abukar listened as the salesman explained the different options. He decided upon the one with a sixty-month payment plan and one percent down at closing. No need in giving the money away. The salesman began checking Abukar's credit for the financing.

"Mr. Fernandez," Jenkins said with a pained look on his face. It was the look of someone who knew he had just lost a sale and possibly something worse. "We have a serious problem."

Abukar's heart fluttered for just a moment. The identity of Bill Fernandez was not stolen. He knew that. The one credit card he had was always paid off. In fact, Abukar had checked his credit rating before coming to the dealership just to be sure there were no problems. What had he found?

"What seems to be the concern?" he asked.

"Mr. Fernandez, we don't have a name for your boat? What are you going to call her? Some folks say the name gives the boat good luck. Any ideas?"

Abukar thought for a moment. Then his eyes brightened and he flashed a grin to Jenkins.

"How about *Mayport Majesty?*"

Jenkins sat back in his chair and put on his best salesman's face. "A perfect name. She will be a lucky boat for you." Just then, his computer began to print out the credit approval information. "See look, good luck already. With your credit rating we are able to offer you our Premier Finance Plan. No money down except the first payment which is only $424.00."

"That will be excellent," Abukar said handing his credit card to Jenkins to make the payment.

They completed the transaction. Upon giving Abukar the receipt he told him the boat would be ready for pickup in two days. Jenkins told him the dealership wanted to prep the boat by cleaning and waxing it. Abukar shook the salesman's hand thanking him for his kind service and then proceeded to his car. Allah had again blessed him.

Alex fell asleep in the car on the ride back from Andrews Air Force Base. His return to the United States had been a quiet one, which was fine with Alex. It gave him time to reflect upon what had just transpired. He had been a part of a landmark event in human history. He was fairly exhausted after the peace conference and was content to avail himself of the amenities of the Gulfstream on the return flight. One of these was the satellite feed of the news media.

The news agencies in Europe had been very in-depth in their coverage of the North Korean missile launch and the President's evacuation from Los Angeles. But what had rankled him was the depiction of the President running for cover as if he were a coward. They had taken the footage of him being escorted out of the conference and splashed the headline "President Runs for Cover" as their lead story. Alex wondered what the reaction would have been in Paris or Berlin if Gerhard were ever thrust into a similar situation. *No doubt heroic stoicism*, he thought.

He awoke as the car pulled in front of his house. "Here we are, sir. Home, sweet home," noted Juarez with a grin as he placed the car in park.

"Juarez, that's the best time you have ever made. You get your real license yet?" Alex enjoyed chiding Juarez's navigation around the city. The two men shared a laugh as Juarez helped Alex unload his luggage from the trunk.

"I've got it from here," said Alex as he reached for the bag Juarez was holding. "You want to come in for some grub? I know Michelle probably has something we can put in the m-wave."

"Thanks chief, but I better head on back. Your better half just might want to see you instead of me. That is, if you know what is good for you," Juarez noted with a wink in his eye. "Don't forget, *it is* New Year's Eve."

"Yeah, you're right. See you next week. You have a safe and happy New Year's," Alex told his friend.

Alex watched as Juarez drove off. He turned to go up the stairs. After fumbling for his keys he stumbled into the house and exclaimed, "Honey,

I'm home." He stood there for a moment figuring she was going to surprise him by running down the steps. Then he looked down at the table in the foyer. There was a note: "Gone to the market. Back soon. Happy New Year! XOXO." His wife still left him notes that sounded like they were junior high sweethearts. It was one of the many endearing qualities he appreciated about her.

He grabbed the mail, climbed the steps to their guestroom, and dumped his luggage there. He began to unpack and sort his clothes for the laundry. Doing this chore struck him as rather funny. He laughed out loud and said to no one in particular, "A week ago I was involved in the greatest peace talks in the history of man, and today I am doing laundry."

After starting a load of laundry he went into their bedroom and sat down at the computer to begin sorting the mail his wife had left. Bills, junk mail, more bills, and more junk mail. At the bottom of the stack was a small brown box. The EU postage markings caught his attention. He pulled it out for a closer look. It was specifically addressed to him. He was curious about who would send him a package from Europe. He shook the box. Hearing nothing he grabbed the letter opener and slit the top of the package open. Inside was the usual packing material. He reached his hand into the box and felt around. Taped to the bottom he felt a DVD jewel case. Removing the case from the box, he turned it over to see if there was anything on the back. No markings were on the case or the DVD. Alex thought that maybe Gerhard had sent a video of his press conferences as a souvenir of the peace talks. It would not have surprised him if he had. He opened the case, inserted the disc into the DVD drive of the computer and clicked the play button.

The disc whirred as the image began to play on the monitor. The black and white image was from a security camera. In the upper left hand corner of the video was the date and time. The scene appeared to be that of a hotel lobby. One could see the check-in desk and the elevators. The angle of the camera provided a clear shot of everyone who entered the elevator. No doubt for security measures. A few minutes passed by with not much activity. Alex was preparing to turn the DVD off when three men walked across the lobby. They walked differently than the rest of the clientele. One man walked ahead while the other two flanked him. Their dress also appeared to be of Middle Eastern design. As they entered the elevator, Alex thought he recognized the lead man but he was not sure.

The images on the security tape then began to move in fast-forward manner. Whoever had made the tape was advancing it for a purpose. When it resumed normal speed another individual with a small entourage was preparing to enter the elevator. This man had a woman with him who gave him a deep kiss as they boarded the elevator. The leopard print outfit she was wearing indicated she was there for business, but not the kind conducted on Wall Street. Alex instantly recognized the man she was kissing: Hans Gerhard. Alex looked at the time on the tape. Was this tape for blackmail?

The images on the video were again fast-forwarded. Alex wondered if the next scene would be that of Gerhard and his mistress in a compromising position. It was not. The video showed Gerhard's entourage emerging from the elevator. But this time there was something different about Gerhard's group. Someone was missing, but who? After a few seconds Alex realized it was the woman. *What happened to her?* he wondered. The video was fast forwarded again this time showing the first man and his two aides leaving.

The screen went dark for a couple of seconds and then displayed another image. It was a newspaper article. Alex recognized it as the obituary section. Every newspaper had them. He never understood what the appeal was about reading about the death of others. The article was not very long, mentioning only a name and residence. The picture however, was that of the girl. Well, that answered the question about what happened to her, but not who did it to her. But the implications were obvious.

Then the monitor went blank as the images ended. Alex clicked the fast forward button on the DVD player to be sure he did not miss any additional images. Next, he performed a search on the DVD to see if anything else was there. Nothing else was on the disc. He played the DVD three more times to be sure he had not missed anything. He picked up the box the disc had arrived in and dumped the packing material on the floor. He spread it out to be sure all of the contents had been emptied. He found nothing. Satisfied he had seen everything he leaned back in the leather chair with his hands behind his head. What had he just been shown?

He reached for the phone on the desk and pressed speed dial six. "Will, this is Alex. You busy right now?"

"No. What's up?"

"Good. I've got something important I need to show you."

"Just email it to me."

"Don't think so, buddy. Too sensitive for that. I need for you to be here to see this."

"Dude, it's New Year's Eve. Don't you ever take a day off? Besides, I have a party to go to in about three hours," Will replied somewhat annoyed at Alex's request.

"Will, you *will* want to see this. I promise. Better than any party you're headed to. Besides, whoever she is will just have to understand national security comes first. Right?"

"Oh, that is so wrong to play that angle," Will replied attempting to counter Alex's argument. But he knew Alex was right. "All right. On my way."

His curiosity peaked, Will arrived within the hour. He reviewed the video twice just to be sure, though he was very confident after the first viewing.

"How did you say you got this?" he asked with a hint of disbelief in his voice as he looked at his buddy.

"It came in the mail when I was in Europe. Truth is, it was mailed from Europe," he said handing Will the package. "I recognize Gerhard but who is the other guy?"

"You wouldn't believe it if I told you," Will said shaking his head. "Heck, I am not sure if I do and I am seeing this. That 'other guy' is none other than Al-Saim—leader of the Revolutionary Council of the Islamic Alliance. Their whole reason for existence is for the eradication of Israel. And if they could take us out of the picture that would be gravy. He is the most wanted terrorist in the world. Rumor was that he was recently in the Mideast with the leaders of the Revolutionary Council, but nothing we could confirm. Alex, this is huge. This is the first sighting of him in four years. Can you burn me a copy of this?"

"No problem," Alex said as he slipped a blank DVD into the E drive of his computer and clicked the appropriate buttons. As the computer made the copy Alex asked, "Will, what were Gerhard and Al-Saim doing in a Berlin hotel at the same time?"

"That is a good question. Too bad we can't ask the chick who was with Gerhard."

"Yeah, too bad on that…especially for her. I am sure she would like to be able to talk with us. Don't you guys get sensitivity training over at the Farm?" he chided his friend.

BARRIERS TO PEACE

OBSERVATION POST 36

ISRAELI SECURITY FENCE

December 31st

10:00 a.m.

The Jerusalem Accord called for the dismantlement of the Security Fence in areas deemed to segregate the local Palestinian population. The first area to be removed was in the vicinity where the two boys had been shot by Israeli security forces. Though the Accord was in force, it was apparent that not all of the citizenry was in full support just yet. The crowds that had gathered remained on their respective sides of the fence. On the Israeli side some were waving Israeli flags on which olive branches had been painted. Others carried placards that denounced the Accord as treason. On the Palestinian side of the fence similar scenes were repeated. However, there were more people present who supported the Accord, or at least appeared to, than those who were in opposition. Standing in front of the crowd on the Palestinian side were the families of the two boys who had been shot. They were waving Palestinian flags that had also been adorned with olive branches. In fact, the olive branch had become the universal symbol of support for the Accord. Local merchants had begun to sell T-shirts with the olive branch superimposed over both the Israeli and Palestinian flags. These shirts were especially popular with the young people who were attending the demolition.

Atop the concrete wall a platform had been constructed. A single microphone was present. Speakers had been strategically placed along the fence so all present could hear. At noon, a solitary individual climbed the steps leading to the platform. He also was wearing one of the T-shirts with the olive branch. He approached the microphone and began to speak.

"A week ago our leaders signed into place the most significant peace treaty in the history of mankind. Today, we put those words into action so that we may begin to live as civilized neighbors."

Upon concluding his brief remarks he signaled to two men on opposite sides of the fence. They acknowledged his signal and climbed into their respective wrecking cranes. The diesel engines roared to life as they started the machines. They looked to the man again who made one additional comment, "Let the removal of oppression begin!" to the roar of the crowd. The cranes began to swing their wrecking balls to gain momentum for their task. One crane had gained enough momentum and its operator swung the huge wrecking ball against the concrete fence. It struck the fence producing a crack. Almost immediately the second crane's ball struck and part of the fence collapsed to the cheering of the crowd.

Several more hits from the wrecking cranes tore a sufficient part of the fence down so that bulldozers could finish the rest. These moved in and began clearing the remaining debris. The crowds on both sides of the fence continued to cheer as each pile of concrete and rebar was pushed aside to create a hole in the once formidable wall. One family had stopped cheering however. It was the parents of one of the boys who had been killed. They had been holding hands and crying as the fence was being torn down. Now they knew what must be done next. Boldly, they began to walk toward the fence, carefully negotiating the debris of the fence that once separated Jew from Arab. As they began to move, the crowds quieted down. The couple paused for a moment and then crossed over to the Israeli side of the fence with open arms. At first, no one on the Israeli side moved as they stood in bewilderment. Here were the parents of the slain boy standing on Israeli territory, with arms outstretched and waiting. The news cameras were capturing every moment.

The first to move on the Israeli side was an elderly couple. They walked toward the parents and stopped. The husband removed his jacket and began to roll up one of the sleeves of his shirt revealing his forearm. The Palestinian couple watched him with inquisitive eyes. When he had finished, he raised his arm for all to see. The couple realized what he was showing them. On his arm were numbers that had been permanently etched into his skin. The numbers were somewhat faded but were still legible.

"At one time I was kept behind a fence," he said with a voice that was still strong in spite of his advanced years. "May our children never have to live behind fences again."

Tears welled up in the eyes of both couples as they embraced. They remained for a moment talking and holding hands. Unbeknownst to them, others began crossing the now destroyed Security Fence and embracing their former enemies.

MORE TOYS

GEORGETOWN

WASHINGTON, D.C.

December 31st

7:00 pm

Alex said goodbye to his friend. He figured Will was heading to
Langley to begin another review of the DVD. He went into the
kitchen to prepare a sandwich. Before he opened the refrigerator for the
turkey and mayo, he turned on the television on the kitchen counter. It
was tuned to *Fox News* as usual. His wife was almost as much of a news
junkie as he was. He grabbed a knife from the drawer and opened the
mayonnaise. As he did a *Fox News* Alert sounded. He was spreading the
mayo as he listened to the announcer.

"…this dramatic footage of the initial dismantlement of the Security
Fence highlights the beginning of the new peace in the Mideast. Many
distracters said this could not happen. In a related story, Palestinian
police forces killed four Palestinians as they were attempting to attack
an Israeli family preparing to leave their home in Gaza…"

Alex finished preparing his sandwich as the newscast continued. The
video of the Palestinian family embracing the Jewish family was remarkable. It was fascinating to be watching history unfold before his very
eyes. He never would have dreamed Palestinian would fight Palestinian
to protect an Israeli. He knew that would be the lead story on every
newscast around the world. The newscaster went on to discuss the time-
line for the construction of the Israeli Temple. The camera was showing
images of the Dome of the Rock and the preparations being made for
the ceremonial groundbreaking. As the images were playing on the TV

screen, his mind kept going back to the DVD of Gerhard and Al-Saim. The more he dwelled on the DVD the more it began to bother him. Something was not right. Why, after all of the long, rancorous history between Israel and her Arab neighbors, had peace suddenly come to the region?

He looked at his watch. His wife would be home in another hour or so. He went upstairs to their bedroom and began looking for the paper Will had previously brought by. Finding it, he walked over to the computer desk, sat down, and began to read the paper again. The *Ten Kings* paper was also subtitled: *Europa: Rise of an Empire*. Alex was so engrossed in the paper that he did not hear his wife come in to the room. He almost jumped out of the chair when she slipped her arms around him.

"You scared the life out of me!" he said as he picked her up and tossed her on the bed.

"You just need to pay more attention or maybe I need a better perfume," she said with a smile. "I am glad you're home from hopping around the world. I've missed you."

"Me too, sweetie," he said as he looked into her hazel eyes. How he had ever talked this beautiful woman into marrying him was one of the great mysteries of the world. He had definitely married up as his friends reminded him. He leaned forward to kiss her and forgot about the world.

Four hours later he awoke to the sound of rain. He looked over at his sleeping wife and then the alarm clock. It was two in the morning. He quietly climbed out of bed and slipped on a robe. On his way out of the room he picked up the *Ten Kings* paper and went downstairs to finish reading. He stopped by the kitchen and poured a Coke. Moving into the den, he settled into his leather recliner and opened the paper. Will had postulated an interesting theory. It predicted the rise of Europe, specifically ten nations as a confederation, into a world power. The leader was of such great persuasive powers that he led the confederation to negotiate a peace treaty between Israel and her neighbors. The neighbors subsequently turned on Israel. The fact that Will had written this while they were in college was remarkable. Current events were unfolding in such a similar way that it was rather unsettling. Will had included maps in his paper that detailed a two-pronged attack against Israel. He had even included hypothetical orders of battle. The conclusion of the paper suggested an Israeli victory after the use of nuclear weapons. Ironically there was no mention of the Temple or the Dome of the Rock.

Alex closed the paper and thought for a moment. There were too many similar trends occurring. He made his decision. He would call President Sullivan and request a meeting. *After all, what was the worse thing that could happen?* he asked himself. *I could be fired or ridiculed.*

OVAL OFFICE

January 2nd

7:15 a.m.

"Son, you've got a lot to learn about government work. Meeting like this on a Sunday morning best not become a habit," Secretary Defense Clairmont said to Alex as he sipped his coffee. "People might come to expect this all the time."

"Now you see why I hired Alex at CFA. He was one I could count on to speak his mind. Saved us on a couple of deals, right, Alex?" said President Sullivan with a grin. He had been ribbing Clairmont for having to get out of bed so early on a Sunday. He knew his Secretary of Defense did work on the weekends, just not at 7:00 a.m. "Now what's on your mind, Alex? Your call said it was of the utmost importance."

Alex took a deep breath before he spoke. "Mr. President, Mr. Secretary, I apologize for the earliness of this meeting, but I think I have uncovered a threat to Israel."

"Threat to Israel?" Clairmont scoffed. "What threat? They just signed an Accord with over one hundred million Muslims who have wanted to eliminate them since 1948. Jerusalem is being recognized as Israel's capital by every Muslim nation on the planet. They are being allowed to rebuild their temple. Now what could be the threat?"

"Precisely, sir, the Accord is the threat," countered Alex as he shifted in his seat.

"How so, Alex?" asked Sullivan.

"Well, Mr. President, it's nothing that would stand up in court. It is more of a gut feeling. The whole Accord seems to have come about rather easily. Too easily in my humble opinion. Long-standing enemies are now sitting at the same table or as my preacher used to say, 'the lion and lamb are lying together.' Persian and Arab are united behind a solid political and religious front as never before in history. There is an undercurrent of anti-Semitism in Europe and the head of the EU brokered the Accord. The EU has deployed troops to the region, replacing the UN observers along the Golan Heights and Sinai, with the French taking responsibility for Golan and the Germans Sinai. Israeli forces have withdrawn four miles from the Ridge Line. By withdrawing from this strategic site they have blinded themselves in the Golan Heights. And there is an absence of American influence in this process. Gentlemen, I have prepared this position paper for your review," Alex said as he handed Sullivan and Clairmont copies of his summary of the *Ten Kings* paper and events involving the Accord.

Alex sat back in his chair as they read the paper. He was careful to watch their body language as an initial measure of their reaction. Clairmont's eyebrows arched in a way that indicated extreme skepticism. He looked up at Alex midway through reading the paper as if to say, "son, where did you get this fairy tale?" Sullivan on the other hand remained impassive while he read. He was displaying the cool detachment he showed during intense business dealings at CFA. When the two men had finished reading Alex's assessments, Clairmont fired first.

"Pretty bold assertions, young man. Don't you think Israeli defense forces have considered all of this? Is this *all* you have?" Clairmont scoffed.

"Yes, sir, they are bold," Alex acknowledged to the Secretary. "But I am not sure that Israel's leadership is thinking clearly now. There is one more thing you need to see. Gentlemen, if I may." He reached into his briefcase and opened his laptop. He placed it on the table in front of Sullivan and Clairmont and started the DVD.

Clairmont leaned in closer as the image of Al-Saim played on the screen and exclaimed, "Mr. President, that is Al-Saim! The most wanted terrorist in the world and head of the Islamic Alliance. This is the first public sighting of him in over four years." The two men intensely watched the remainder of the DVD. Alex pressed the stop button when the DVD ended. Clairmont asked Alex to play the DVD again. Sullivan shot a glance at Clairmont when the DVD ended and again winked at Alex.

Clairmont removed his reading glasses and leaned forward in his chair, now obviously interested. "How did you say you got this video?"

"It was mailed to my house from Europe, Mr. Secretary. It was waiting for me when I returned home," said Alex.

"Does anyone else know about this?"

"I have a contact at DNIS who has a copy. I gave it to him Friday night. I needed him to confirm who Al-Saim was before I came to present this information."

"*You did what?* Alex, that was a serious breach of security..." Clairmont began to rip Alex but Sullivan intervened.

"Hold on, James. If Alex felt he needed to contact his friend to confirm the identity of Al-Saim, I am ok with that. If he hadn't, he might not have had the confidence to come in this morning. Alex, call your friend about the tape."

"Yes, Mr. President. Right away."

"Hopefully your friend kept his mouth shut or *The New York Times* will have it as headline news tomorrow. We don't need the whole world knowing we have this until we have something more solid to go on. I want the original so our folks can review it further. Also, if you still have the original package we can check it for fingerprints. Alex, do you really think the EU and the Alliance are in bed on this?" Clairmont asked now more enthusiastically.

Alex reached into his briefcase again and handed Clairmont the package. "Yes, sir. In some way this is all connected, and I believe it started with this meeting between Gerhard and Al-Saim."

"How do you know they were not there because of the girl? Or any other hundred reasons Gerhard could explain away if this story hit the news." Clairmont turned to look at Sullivan.

"Mr. President, I hope you are not thinking of acting on this. We have three carriers off the coast of South Korea because the North Koreans just detonated a nuclear-armed missile in the Pacific that may or may not have been fired at the United States. That should be our primary focus at this point."

He continued, "What Alex has presented is circumstantial evidence at best. It might make a good novel but to base policy on this? I would hate to know I was going to the court of world opinion with this as my case. It would be dismissed as paranoid delusion."

"James, what would you have said if someone told you on September 10, 2001 that terrorists would be crashing planes into the World Trade Center and the Pentagon the next day?" responded Sullivan as he eyed his Secretary. "We had video of the terrorists as they entered the airports. We even stopped and searched some of them and let them pass after they set off the metal detectors. The clues were there but we failed to put the pieces together. Granted this sounds even more incredible in its scope, but 9/11 was incredible at the time. Yes, Korea is real and this is well, I'm not sure. But in the world we live in today I don't think we can leave anything to chance.

"I do think Alex may be on to something here for a couple of reasons," continued Sullivan. "First, from what he conveyed regarding his meetings with Weissman in Geneva we know there is extreme political pressure at home to secure peace. We've been seeing the intelligence briefings on what is happening in Israel's internal politics. The peace movement is very strong. Apparently stronger than we realized. The stability of his coalition government is tenuous at the moment. Not only have all Islamic states now formally recognized Israel's right to exist, they have also agreed to recognize Jerusalem as the capital. They are even preparing to send diplomats. Plus, let's not discount the opportunity to rebuild the Temple as a prime motivator.

"Besides, James, you might be willing to believe in the hope of peace after all the years of fighting and terrorism Israel has endured. Especially if outside parties are guaranteeing the enforcement of the terms of the Accord," concluded Sullivan. "The specter of another Holocaust resonates with Israelis and Jews everywhere. And there is one more thing. If Gerhard and Al-Saim showing up at the same hotel is not a coincidence, our European friend has yet to share any of the details of their meeting. That would be an abrogation of our agreement to share intelligence on terrorists. If there is nothing to hide, why not pass along the info?"

"Mr. President, you may be right. Alex may be right. It's just that the magnitude of the idea of a conspiracy between the EU and the Alliance is…well it boggles the mind to say the least," Clairmont said shaking his head still in disbelief at the discussion they were having. "It is the stuff the conspiracy crowd thrives on. If the media got wind we were considering this we would be run out of town in the next election."

"If we made it to the next election. You're right, Mr. Secretary," acknowledged Sullivan. "This is something we cannot go public with. We can't even leak it." He thought for a moment. "Alex, I need your services again. I want you to take point on this. You're going to go to Israel and meet with Weissman and share this…" he paused looking for the right word.

"Intelligence estimate?" offered Clairmont.

"Good. I like that," said Sullivan. "Share this intelligence estimate. Maybe it will keep them from getting complacent. After all, we made a pledge to support them if the Accord was ever broken. We owe it to them to share any information we receive regardless of its nature."

"Mr. President…," Alex began. But Sullivan cut him off.

Sullivan held up a hand. "I know what you are going to say and forget it. Weissman knows and trusts you. You are the only one who has been involved with this from day one. All of the arrangements will be made. Get your bags packed. Convey to your wife my apologies for pulling you away again so soon."

Alex placed the laptop back in his briefcase and closed it. He rose and shook hands with Clairmont and Sullivan and began his way out of the Oval Office. Turning the door handle he stopped and turned. "Mr. President, one last thing."

"Yes, Alex?"

"Does the government offer frequent flyer miles?" he asked with a grin on his way out.

EUROPEAN UNION AIR DEFENSE STATION

ROTA, SPAIN

January 3rd

7:18 p.m.

The technician adjusted the radar image on her monitor. The Air Defense Station was formerly a part of NATO's air defense system. The European Union had merely adopted the air defense network across Europe for its own defense. It was said it was as easy as changing the flag that flew above the facility. In addition to providing for air defense in the event of an attack, it also served as an intelligence listening post. Each aircraft that traversed through European airspace was required to file a flight plan. Any deviation from this plan was reported to the normal air traffic control stations. Individual aircraft of interest could be monitored for destination, course change, or communication. One aircraft did warrant such individual attention.

"Sir," the technician spoke into her microphone, "I have an American Gulfstream entering the Cadiz air traffic sector."

"Destination?" asked the Section Supervisor.

The technician checked her monitor and replied, "Flight plan indicates Tel Aviv, sir."

"What is the flight number of that plane?" asked the supervisor as he walked over to look at the radar display. He had received orders to monitor and report on any American planes with a destination of Israel. As this included commercial aircraft, he had been rather busy filing these reports.

"U.S. Air Force 91963, sir."

"Run a cross-check on that aircraft for prior flights to Europe or the Middle East," he ordered.

The technician entered the flight number into her computer. She was surprised at the information she was supplied with. "Sir, a cross-check of that aircraft indicates the most recent European destination was Geneva. The dates correspond to that of the peace conference."

"Very well. Continue to monitor the flight. Inform me if there are any changes," the supervisor said as he headed back to his control desk. He reached for the phone as he sat down. He pressed the button for European Union Air Defense Command.

"This is Rota Sector. I am monitoring the transit of an American Gulfstream with a trip destination of Tel Aviv. The flight ID corresponds to that of the plane that attended the peace talks in Geneva."

"Very good. Continue to monitor and report any deviations," came the reply on the other end of the phone.

Charles de Gaulle

Eastern Mediterranean

The flight deck of the *de Gaulle*, like that of the *Nimitz* class carriers, resembles a small airport. While at forty thousand tons she is not as large as the American *Nimitz* class aircraft carriers, she nonetheless boasts the ability to carry forty planes including the Rafale fighter, Super Etentard, and Hawkeye AEW. Along with her sister ship, *Francis*, which was nearing completion, they are the most powerful aircraft carriers in the world outside of the United States Navy.

From the bridge, Captain Morganeau could see the flight deck crew was preparing to launch two Rafale fighters. His pilots were conducting touch-and-go landings. Steam from the catapults was rising from the deck as the planes awaited launch. Massive blast doors protected the crews and awaiting planes from the engines of the planes being launched. Elevators were lifting additional Rafael fighters from the hanger for launch. The *de Gaulle* boasted the ability to launch one aircraft every thirty seconds. Satisfied everything was going smoothly on the flight deck, he sat in his Captain's chair and began to review communications received from EU headquarters. As he read the messages his command phone rang. Reaching forward he lifted it and spoke. "*Oui.*" He listened intently as the voice on the other end explained the mission. "*Oui,* the orders will be carried out," he said and returned the phone to the cradle. He rose from his chair and walked over to the window where he could see the operations on the flight deck. He returned to his chair.

"Flight operations," he ordered as he picked up his phone. "I want the following pilots ready for flight in thirty minutes." He listed the names of the pilots and continued, "Have them meet me in the pilots' briefing room. These pilots only. Understand?" He returned the phone to the cradle.

He looked at his XO. "You have the bridge," he said as he departed for the briefing room.

C-20H Gulfstream

Eastern Mediterranean

Alex had completed another review of the information he was to use in his presentation to the Israeli Cabinet. Satisfied he was as prepared as one could be for such an event, he decided to stretch his legs. Unbuckling his seat belt he stood and stretched a couple of times to loosen the kinks. He made his way to the cockpit and knocked on the door as he opened it.

"E'vning, Colonel. How are things up here? Getting pretty dull back there," Alex noted restlessly.

"Pretty routine, Mr. Stanton. We have good air the rest of the way to Tel Aviv. Normal air traffic," replied Colonel Davidson with a grin. He knew Alex was a former F-15 Eagle driver. The only thing worse for a pilot not to be flying was to be flying with someone else at the controls.

"Ivey, you look tired," Davidson said to his co-pilot. "Why don't you stretch your legs?"

Ivey looked over his left shoulder at Alex and then back to Davidson.

"Yes, sir, I understand. Enjoy the drive," he said to Alex as he unbuckled the four-point harness and vacated the co-pilot's seat.

"Thanks, Lieutenant," Alex said and patted Ivey on the back as he exited the cockpit.

"Try not to hit anything," Ivey chided Alex as he made his way back to the cabin.

Alex slid into the co-pilot's chair and buckled the harness. He took a moment to orient himself with the flight instruments before taking the stick. The basic instruments found in all planes were there, though positioned somewhat differently. That commonality of instruments was one of the things that made flying relatively easy. As a former Air Force pilot he recognized the other instruments on the panel and above his head.

"Looks like we have a pretty good ECM package on board," he commented. It had long been rumored that the planes of the Executive Fleet of the 89th Air Wing had been fitted with advanced ECM and defensive countermeasures. It was one of those military secrets that had actually remained a secret. There was relatively little public knowledge available on this issue. It was known, however, that after 9/11 every plane in the fleet received upgrades to their defensive capabilities.

"I can't share the details with you but let me put it this way. You're as safe as a baby in her mother's arms," replied Davidson. "Of course, this electronic stuff is only as good as the pilot," he added with the bravado characteristic of all military pilots.

Alex looked at Davidson and flashed a grin. "Amen, Colonel. Wouldn't it be great if you could go back in time to the early days of dogfighting? None of this electronic stuff. Just hop in your Sopwith Camel or P-51. Only you and the other guy dueling in the sky. Best man wins."

"Yeah, that would be a dream come true. Autopilots and radars have almost taken the fun out of flying. Seems like the only time we do any real flying now is takeoff and landing. I reckon one day that will be automated as well. You comfortable with the controls?"

"Yes, Colonel. She's a smooth flying plane."

"Ok, hotshot. I'm going to join Ivey for a moment," Davidson said as he slid out of the pilot's seat. As he turned to exit the cockpit he looked at Alex and said sarcastically, "Try not to hit anything."

EU Fighters

Eastern Mediterranean

The two Rafale fighters were cruising at forty-five thousand feet. They were flying under radio silence with their search radars off. They were receiving updates on the course and speed of the Gulfstream over their helmet speakers. They were as invisible as non-stealth aircraft could be. The Gulfstream was maintaining a constant altitude of thirty-eight thousand feet and was on course for Tel Aviv. The pilots of the Rafales had taken up positions eighty miles north of the course of the Gulfstream and two hundred miles west of the *de Gaulle*. Their intent was to approach from behind and assume the classic six o'clock firing position.

The radar signal being received from *de Gaulle* was now tracking the Gulfstream. It had passed their position and was maintaining course. Using prearranged signals with their wing lights the pilots adjusted their course and began to close on the Gulfstream.

C-20H Gulfstream

Eastern Mediterranean

A red light on the instrument panel began to flash, accompanied by an audible alert that Alex recognized. It meant someone was tracking them with radar designed for air-to-air missiles and had obtained radar lock. All they had to do was shoot and the Gulfstream would disappear in the explosion. A scan of the radar screen indicated two bandits approaching very fast from the stern of the plane.

His pilot training instinctively took over as he pushed the stick down and increased throttle. Hoping he would be able to shake whomever it was behind him he began to bank the Gulfstream. He had to be careful to remember he was not in his F-15 Eagle. The Gulfstream was a good plane but it was not designed for aerial combat. He did not want to snap the wings off. Alex turned and shouted toward the cabin. "Colonel, get up here now!"

Davidson had been thrown out of his seat and was struggling to recover his balance. Looking around, he saw Ivey had been knocked unconscious when his head struck the bulkhead. Blood was oozing from his right temple. The cabin attendant was moving to tend to Ivey. She grabbed the onboard medical kit and began to apply a dressing to Ivey's wound. Reaching for the seat to pull himself up, Davidson's left arm seared in pain. He attempted to raise it only to find that it was broken at the elbow. Davidson made his way down the aisle and entered the cockpit quickly taking his seat. "What in the world are you doing!" he yelled. Then he saw the red light and heard the alert.

"I was trying not to hit anything," Alex replied dryly.

"You're gonna have to handle the controls. Ivey is out and my left arm is broken. I will work the ECM," ordered Davidson as he slipped on his headset. "Mayday, Mayday, Mayday. This is United States Air Force, niner-one-niner-six three under attack. Say again, Mayday, Mayday, Mayday. This is United States Air Force, niner-one-niner-six three under attack." He was giving position coordinates as he continued the call.

Davidson leaned forward and pressed several buttons on the instrument panel as the warning alert's blare continued. Alex attempted to try evasive maneuvers with the Gulfstream in an effort to shake the intruders. He was not having much success.

"Any idea who they are?" Alex asked.

"No. They've turned their transponders off. Nothing on IFF. Looks like someone doesn't want you to make your meeting."

"Colonel, there is no way we are going to outrun these folks. We can't outmaneuver them either. I'm going to put her on the deck to shake their radar."

"Tell me something I don't know. Do it!" confirmed Davidson.

Alex pushed the stick down sending the plane into a steeper dive. He eased off the throttle as the plane picked up speed during the descent. A quick glance of the radar showed the bandits were following. He knew he was going to have to go low. Just how low he was not sure.

Patriot Six

Combat Air Patrol

The two F-18F Super Hornets of Patriot Six were flying Combat Air Patrol west of the *George Washington* when the pilots heard the Mayday call.

"Captain, did you hear that Mayday? One of ours is under attack by an unknown hostile," Lt. Hanson said as he checked his radar. He could see the contacts on his radar screen.

"Yeah, now stow it for a second," came the gruff reply from Captain

Jeff Beckham. "Patriot Base, this is Patriot Six. We have a Mayday call from a U.S. Air Force plane. They report they are under attack. We are responding, over."

The message was received in the CDC. The duty officer, Ensign Jeanette Jennings, immediately took action. "Acknowledged, Patriot Six. Mystic One has reported the Mayday as well. Call sign indicates this is a VIP. Light the fires and get your tail over there. Be advised the rules of engagement are in effect. Confirm coordinates with Mystic. Patriot Base over."

Mystic One was the E-2D Hawkeye. Jennings did not want to start a shooting war over a possible misunderstanding, but she was also not going to let a VIP be harassed or even worse, shot down on her watch.

Her next call was the bridge. "Admiral, this is Duty Officer Ensign Jennings. We have received a Mayday from a VIP. Patriot Six is moving to intercept the bandits."

"Launch the ready five. Repeat, launch the ready five," Alvarez ordered. "Vector Patriot Four to their coordinates. Signal *Wasp* to send one of the Osprey's so they can tank. The Gulfstream can't tank from the Hornet. They are going to burn some fuel getting there and will need it on the way home. How many bandits, Jennings?"

"Admiral, VIP indicates two."

"Who is fool enough to screw around with an Air Force plane? Who is the VIP?" he inquired.

"Sir, call sign indicates passenger is Special Assistant to the President, Alex Stanton. I believe he was our rep in the recent peace negotiations."

"Looks like he didn't get enough of the Mideast on the first trip over. I'm on my way."

C-20H Gulfstream

The Gulfstream was now flying about one hundred feet above the Mediterranean. Any lower, Alex thought, and he could grab a surfboard and catch some waves. The radar continued to show the bandits on their tail, but they were maintaining an altitude of six thousand feet. It was apparent their attackers were content to play a cat and mouse game. He checked the instrument panel and focused on one indicator. He did a quick calculation in his head. At their present rate of fuel consumption they would not be able to make Tel Aviv. That left two equally unattractive alternatives. Either ditch the plane in the Med or land in Libya or Egypt.

The good news was that the radar lock indicator was no longer sounding. At this altitude the wave action of the Med was serving as a jamming device. Whatever the radar was aboard their attackers it could not lock onto the Gulfstream at this altitude. In essence they were in a stalemate but were destined to lose unless someone responded to the Mayday.

"Colonel, we are running out of options," Alex noted.

"We're going to have to ditch. We can't afford to land in Libya or Egypt. They would impound the plane, its contents, *and* personnel. Whatever you are carrying would fall into their hands. Can you swim?"

"Yeah, but I'd rather not," Alex acknowledged.

Alex did not like the sound of that. Davidson pressed a button on his mike and said, "Prepare the cabin for ditching. Say again, prepare to ditch. I'll get the chutes."

Davidson unbuckled his harness and moved to get the two chutes in the bin. He handed Alex one and slipped on the other. He checked the cabin for the status of the others. The attendant signaled all ready. She was finishing securing Ivey's chute. He was groggy but was now able to sit.

"All ready, Colonel," noted Alex.

"Very well. I don't think they are going to shoot us down. If they had wanted to they would have blasted us on their first radar lock. More likely they are trying to tick us off. It's working too. Take us up to a thousand feet. Then we'll jump."

PATRIOT SIX

The F/A-18s had kicked in their afterburners and rapidly closed the distance between them and the bandits. However, in doing so they had expended their fuel past the bingo point. Without tanking, they would run out of fuel on the way back to the carrier. To ward off the attackers, Beckham and Hanson had activated their radars. They were hoping the electronic emissions would be detected by the bandits and scare them away.

"I have missile lock on bandit one, Captain," reported Lt. Hanson.

"I have lock on two. Let's see what these guys are up to," said Beckham. "To unidentified aircraft, this is Captain Jeff Beckham of the United States Navy. You are engaging an aircraft of the United States. You are ordered to break away or you will be fired upon. You have ten seconds to disengage."

Suddenly, the IFF signal came on. It identified the two planes as EU Rafale fighters based on board the *de Gaulle*.

"Captain, are you believing this?" radioed Hanson.

C-20H GULFSTREAM

"EU planes!" Davidson exploded. "They're gonna have a lot of explaining to do." He looked at Alex, who was thinking the same thing.

PATRIOT SIX

"Captain Beckham, this is Captain Monclair of the EU Navy. We did not realize the aircraft we were tracking was one of yours. Our radars indicated an unidentified plane approaching *de Gaulle*. With the current tensions in the area we were attempting to identify and ascertain its intentions. We offer our sincerest apologies. Is there any way we may be of assistance to aid your aircraft to its destination?"

Beckham could not believe his ears. He pondered his reply before replying.

"Captain, I find it hard to believe that a civilian aircraft with its transponder on could not be identified by your most capable aircraft. I suggest you have your plane's electronics checked out when you return aboard *de Gaulle*. It would have been most unfortunate if we'd had to press the issue. It is a good thing the *apparent malfunction* of your IFF cleared up when it did. You had about five seconds remaining before I blew your plane out of the air. I am sure your captain would not have wanted to write your loved ones."

"Your measured response is greatly appreciated, Captain Beckham. I will take your suggestion under advisement. We are returning to *de Gaulle. Au revoir, mon Capitaine.*"

The two Rafael fighters peeled away and altered course for the *de Gaulle*. Their afterburners were glowing brightly as they sped off into the distance.

"VIP, this is Captain Beckham. We are prepared to escort you to your final destination. Do you need assistance?"

C-20H GULFSTREAM

"Captain, this is Colonel Davidson. Affirmative. We're on fumes over here. You got a tanker somewhere close?"

"That is a roger, Colonel. Gas Hound 21 is in route. ETA ten minutes."

"Confirmed, Captain. Tell 'em they better hurry. By the way, I think the French got the message. I for one, however, am not buying their story. They knew exactly what they were doing, though I don't know why. Davidson out."

Davidson turned to look at Alex, whose gaze was focused on the instrument panel. Alex could feel the stare from Davidson. He looked at Davidson and said, "Hey don't look at me. I am just an innocent passenger here."

"Passenger, yes. Innocent, I'm not sure about," shot back the Colonel.

"Colonel, did you really think they were going to shoot us down? Shoot down an American military aircraft?"

"I am not sure," he replied as he checked their fuel status again. "I'm just not sure. Lots of tempers are still hot in this part of the world after Esfahan, even with the Accord in place. The EU has made it fairly apparent they are no longer our friends. One thing's for sure. You've worried someone enough for them to risk this stunt."

Alex considered this for a moment. Could it be that someone was trying to stop him? He didn't think this was likely. Only two people knew the contents of his briefing to the President and those were the President and Secretary of Defense. Even his friend Will was unaware of the final content of his briefing. No, it was more likely that the EU was flexing its military muscle in an attempt to send a signal to the region. The deployment of peacekeeping forces to the Mideast was the first overseas deployment of the new EU military. Word would eventually reach the media that an American plane had signaled Mayday after two unidentified planes staged an attack. The more Alex thought about this the more it made sense. The mock attack had been designed to show the weakness of America in this part of the world. If they could not protect their own plane, how they be expected to protect anyone else? Specifically, how could they protect Israel?

"You good for the tanking?" asked Davidson.

"Should be like riding a bike, Colonel. She's not an Eagle, but she's a good plane," Alex said patting the top of the instrument panel.

The F/A-18s of Patriot Six, along with Patriot Four, took up escort positions alongside the Gulfstream. The MV-22 tanker had deployed the refueling probe. Alex eased the Gulfstream into refueling position behind the tanker. With their fuel tanks topped off, Alex disengaged from the tanker. Patriot Six and Four also replenished their fuel supply. They had expended a great deal of fuel in their flight, mostly supersonic, in responding to the Mayday. After tanking, they resumed their escort positions flanking the Gulfstream. GasHound 21 also fell into formation behind the Gulfstream. The Hornets would provide escort for the remainder of the flight until they were within twenty-five miles of Israeli airspace. As they approached the end of their flight, Colonel Davidson radioed Captain Beckham.

"Captain, next time you're in D.C., give me a call. The tab is on me."

"Roger that, Colonel. Hope they pay you Air Force boys well. I have an appetite." Captain Beckham dipped his starboard wing toward the Gulfstream as a farewell gesture and then adjusted his course to return to the *George Washington*.

BEN-GURION INTERNATIONAL AIRPORT

TEL AVIV

10:08 p.m.

Alex was making final adjustments to the flaps as the Gulfstream approached the runway of Ben-Gurion International Airport. He guided the aircraft down to the runway for a perfect landing. He received instructions from the tower for taxiing and maneuvered the aircraft to the designated spot on the tarmac. As the plane came to rest, Alex looked over at Colonel Davidson and said, "Colonel, I must say it has been quite an unusual flight. It's been a pleasure flying with you."

Davidson extended his right hand, which Alex shook, and replied, "You too, Alex. You handled yourself real well back there. Lot of guys might have frozen up. You can be my co-pilot any day. I'm not sure what you are here for but good luck with the rest of your mission. Next time you're at Andrews, look me up. I owe you a dinner."

"Thanks, Colonel. I'll take you up on that offer. I hope the arm heals well. Tell Ivey thanks for the drive and I hope his head is ok."

Before exiting the cockpit Alex looked out of the window and noticed a familiar figure waiting beside a limousine and two ambulances. It was Colonel Goldman. The two had formed a close bond during the recent peace talks. Jet lag was normally the traveler's enemy, but Alex was not tired. The adrenaline from their adventure and the freshness of the night air revived Alex as he made his way down the steps of the Gulfstream to greet his friend.

"Welcome to Israel, my friend," said Goldman as he shook Alex's hand. "I heard about your flight. I trust you were not harmed."

"Colonel, good to see you again. It's good to be back in Israel. We had a little adventure but everyone is ok," he said looking at the ambulance Ivey was being loaded into. Colonel Davidson had radioed ahead for a medical team for his co-pilot. Davidson himself was being tended to by the medics before he climbed into the second ambulance, which sped off into the night.

"You have been to Israel before?" inquired a surprised Goldman as they made their way to the limo.

"Yes, when I was a youth. My church came over for a tour of the Holy Land. It was a moving experience to see the birthplace of Judaism and Christianity," Alex said as they climbed into the limo.

Alex observed that security was much tighter than what he encountered in Geneva as they left Ben-Gurion International Airport. The four escorting vehicles, two ahead of and two behind the limo, each carried four heavily armed men.

"You are a man of faith then? You believe the Messiah has come?" inquired Goldman who was sitting opposite Alex in the limo.

"Yes, I am. I am a Christian, but I'm not the best example. I have a lot to improve on," Alex acknowledged. Anticipating the next question he added, "And yes, I believe the Messiah has come and will come again as He promised."

"Alex, may I ask you a question regarding an aspect of your beliefs?"

"Certainly, Colonel. You and I can discuss anything, you know that," Alex said drawing on the relationship he and the Colonel had developed during the peace conference. Mostly it was centered upon their common experience as soldiers and their love of flying.

"Do you believe my people crucified Christ?"

Alex was not taken back entirely by the question. He knew there was a history of persecution of the Jews for this very reason. The people who often tried to blame the Jews for the crucifixion of Christ often overlooked one salient point. At that time in history, the land of Israel was occupied by the Roman Empire. Only Roman authorities had the power to order someone crucified. And it was Romans who had crucified Christ.

"No, Colonel, I do not. I would say it was me who crucified Him," Alex replied emphatically.

"How is that, Alex?" Goldman replied very surprised.

"I believe that Christ died for my sins and would have done so if I were the only person on earth. I know many have persecuted your people for His crucifixion, but they were wrong to do so."

"I am glad to hear that, Alex. We have dealt with this as a people since His crucifixion."

"Colonel, if I may be so bold, may I ask you the same question? Do you believe the Messiah has come?"

"I am not sure, Alex. As a young boy I was taught He has not come. I have read the Torah and the Bible in search of the answer. There are many in Israel today who are looking for a sign of His coming. That is why the Accord and the prospect of rebuilding the Temple have spread like wildfire. Many believe it is a sign."

"Many in the States do as well," Alex noted. "Do you?"

"I am just not sure. It's hard for me to believe that someone would die for me just because I am a...what is the term Christians use?"

"A sinner?" Alex replied with a sincere face. He could tell Goldman had been wrestling with this issue and was looking for answers. They were the same answers that all mankind was looking for. Many just did not know where to look.

"Yes. A sinner. For now though, I prefer to put my faith in the IDF. That I can see and feel."

"I understand, Colonel. It is a difficult concept to accept, but think of it this way. You're prepared to sacrifice your life for Israel? For people you do not know? Many of whom have not served in the military?"

"Yes I am. That is part of my professional oath as a soldier, Alex."

"So, many people who may not deserve the benefits of your service actually benefit from your sacrifice as a soldier?"

"Yes," Goldman acknowledged slowly.

"And there is nothing you expect in return from them?"

"Nothing. It is my duty."

"Then, is it hard to believe one Man would do the same for mankind? Like you, make the ultimate sacrifice of one's life for people who do not deserve it so they can have a better future. Except in the case of Christ, He offers us eternal life."

"That is an interesting analogy, Alex. I've never looked at it that way. You have given me much to think on regarding this. Now tell me," Goldman inquired as he shifted the subject. "What are your impressions of the Accord so far?"

"Colonel, I, along with the rest of the world, am astonished by the Accord. No one would have ever envisioned Israel at peace with her neighbors; especially in light of what happened in Iran. What is the mood here in Israel?" Alex inquired.

"There is much joy in the land. So far all is well," noted Goldman with a degree of skepticism in his voice.

"You sound doubtful of the long term prospects. You still think it was a mistake for Israel to sign the Accord?"

"Alex, I am a military man. Not a politician. I have been trained to be aware of my enemies. My duty is to defend Israel," replied Goldman. "I will do so in peace or war. Our leaders have made a decision that is supposed to be in the best interests of Israel. It is my duty to ensure that decision is enforced." Alex noted the way Goldman's eyes narrowed as he made his comments. He could tell Goldman was skeptical of the Accord. But like any good soldier he was obeying his orders.

Goldman was a good enough soldier not to ask why Alex was there to see Weissman. Alex had hoped the reason for his visit would not come up. He did not want to have to put off his friend. Prior to his departure, President Sullivan had conveyed that he was to disclose the information only to Weissman and his Cabinet.

The two men continued to discuss the Accord. Eventually, the topic turned to flying, which was the topic they discussed the remainder of their trip to the American Embassy, where Alex would be staying. His meeting with Weissman was not until the next morning.

At 9:00 a.m. Alex's escort arrived at the embassy to take him to the Knesset and his meeting with Weissman. Israeli security for foreign diplomats remained unparalleled in spite of the Accord. The security forces took pride in the fact that no foreign diplomat had ever been assassinated while in their care. They were not about to begin with Alex. The streets of Jerusalem were decorated with signs of the Accord. Symbols of doves and olive branches were hanging from signs on buildings and buses. Alex noticed cars were adorned with magnetic stickers in the form of doves and olive branches. Even the ubiquitous T-shirt vendors had found their way to the Holy City. One thing was certainly thriving in Israel: capitalism. Someone had seen a way to make money off the event and had capitalized on it.

The drive proved to be uneventful. The armored limousine passed through a security gate that led to the underground entrance of the Knesset. This was the entrance used by the members of government. Alex noted the heavily armed soldiers at this entrance. This did not really surprise him. In matters of national security, there was trust and then there was prudence. The Israeli government was an adherent to the later.

Even though he arrived with an Israeli escort, Alex had to pass through security before being granted access to the interior of the building. He thought the security in Geneva had been comprehensive but even that did not compare to this. There were multiple layers of security. The usual metal detectors and German Shepherds were present, but the Israelis had added bio scans that included verification of Alex's fingerprints and retinas. Next, his bag was checked. A very thorough pat down was part of the final check. The guards, he noted, were very adept in this process.

His laptop computer was opened and plugged in to verify it actually was a computer. Satisfied he was not carrying explosives or any firearms, the guards finally allowed him admittance to the interior. Two armed guards and a man dressed in a dark suit greeted him and escorted him to Prime Minister Weissman's office. Alex had no doubt that the man in the suit was a member of Shabak—Israel's internal security service. He also was under no illusion that the guards had standing orders to shoot if he attempted any activity deemed suspicious. Not wanting to test his theory he followed the Shabak man as he made his way through the halls of the Knesset. No one spoke as they made their way to Weissman's office.

Coming to the end of one of the hallways they stopped at a set of double doors. The Shabak man reached into his jacket pocket and produced a small card. He inserted it into a slot to the right of the doors. Underneath the slot was a keypad on which he entered his password. Next, he placed his right thumb on the electronic eye. A green light blinked twice on the panel and the doors opened. Alex and the Shabak man passed through while the guards returned to their post. They walked down another hall and stopped at the third door on their right. His escort knocked on the door and opened it. He looked at Alex and gestured for him to enter. He closed the door behind Alex as they entered Weissman's office. The Shabak man took his position by the door.

Entering the office, Alex saw the Prime Minister seated behind his desk. The smallness of the office was not what Alex had anticipated. Not quite the size of the Oval Office, the room did not have the richness of decorations found there. Behind the mahogany desk to the left was the flag of Israel. There were various pictures of Weissman and his family on the desk and wall, along with photos of Weissman and other world leaders. Alex observed that one of the more prominent pictures was that of Weissman, Jallud, and Gerhard signing the Accord. A humidor full of Cuban cigars was on a table behind his desk.

Goldman was seated across the desk from Weissman. Weissman and Goldman were involved in a conversation that ended as Alex entered the office. "Good to see you again, Alex," Weissman said rising from his seat as he came forward to greet Alex. "Welcome to Israel. I heard about your flight. I trust you are well. You, of course, know *General* Goldman. The General was just leaving."

"Thank you, Mr. Prime Minister," Alex said as he shook hands with both men.

"Congratulations on the promotion, General. It is well deserved," Alex said as he gave Goldman a surprised look. "I trust I did not interrupt. I can wait."

"Thank you, Alex. I was just leaving. Mr. Prime Minister," Goldman said as he left the office.

"I have to be honest, Alex," Weissman said returning to his seat while motioning Alex to sit. "When your President called, I must admit I was very skeptical. However, one can never be too sure of anything in this world anymore. Now, what is this pressing matter that brings you all the way to Jerusalem?" Weissman asked as he reached for a cigar.

"Sir, I do not mean to be rude, but I thought I would be addressing the entire Cabinet?" Alex asked as he opened his laptop.

Weissman eyed Alex while he lit his cigar before responding. "I did consider that possibility. However, I feel it would be best if I reviewed your material first. Let's see what you have before we go further. Shall we?"

Alex did not like the way the meeting was going. Nonetheless he opened his laptop and began. To Weissman's credit, he paid close attention and asked many questions during the presentation. It took Alex about ninety minutes to review all of the information including the video of Gerhard and Al-Saim. He concluded the presentation by saying, "Mr. Prime Minister, I believe that Israel is in grave danger as a result of the Accord. With compliments from the President, we respectfully recommend that you increase your military readiness."

Weissman reclined in his leather chair and scratched his head as he thought. "Alex, this is an astounding hypothesis. Do you have any intelligence to verify any of your conclusions? Do you have a time frame for this attack?"

Alex looked at the Prime Minister. His stomach began to sink as he could see where Weissman was going with his questions. "No, sir. Unfortunately this is all a theory, which is what we hope it remains."

"I want you to understand I appreciate your concern, Alex. However, I don't see how I can bring this to the Cabinet. There is too much at stake if this was to leak out, and it would. The members of the Peace Movement Party in the Cabinet have their contacts in the media. Our media works like yours. We wouldn't be finished discussing your information before it was on *CNN* or *Al-Jazeera*. I can see the headlines now…Israel and U.S. accuse European Union and Islamic states of conspiracy. World opinion would persecute us. The Accord is still in its infancy. Already, we have seen unheard of cooperation among the Palestinians in Gaza. They are dispensing justice among their own people. Palestinians stopping Palestinians from attacking Israelis. Unprecedented!"

"Yes, I saw that report—" Alex began but he was interrupted as Weissman continued his oration, waving his cigar as if it were a magic wand.

"Homicide bombings have ceased for all practical purposes. I never would have dreamed this possible. The dedication ceremony for the Temple is in two days. Alex, I'm sorry. I can't allow you to present this to the Cabinet or anyone else without hard, verifiable facts. There is just too much at stake. With respect to your President, I am asking you not to discuss this with anyone. You are of course welcome to stay and observe the dedication ceremonies. It would be a good cover story for your trip," Weissman said as he rose from his chair and walked over to Alex.

Alex was disappointed but there were not many options available. He was being seen by the Prime Minister of a free and independent nation. Was it not his right to determine what was presented to his government? Alex closed his laptop and began to gather his papers. "Mr. Prime Minister, I understand your position. If I were in your shoes, I would probably do the same thing. Thank you for your time today."

"Don't take it so hard, Alex," Weissman said as he walked Alex to the door shaking his hand. "I am sorry you flew such a long distance for such a short meeting. You have Israel's best interest at heart my friend. I sleep well knowing we have a friend in you and your President. Please give him my regards. Mr. Sheinberg will escort you back," he said as he gestured for the Shabak man. *So he did have a name after all*, Alex noted.

"I will do that, Mr. Prime Minister. Again, thank you for your time today."

AMERICAN EMBASSY

TEL AVIV

1:21 p.m.

"No, Mr. President. He didn't buy it," Alex said as he spoke into the video phone. "The Prime Minister is bent on making the Accord work. Heck, I really can't blame him either. How would you respond if you were in his shoes?"

"Well, Alex, there isn't much more we can do at this point," Sullivan replied seeing the disappointment in Alex's face. "We can't force him to do anything. Besides, there is a strong possibility he is right. You could be just chasing rabbits on this."

"Yes, sir, you both may be right. Mr. President, I would like to remain in Israel for a couple more days. The Temple dedication is tomorrow. I would like to see first-hand the reaction of the man on the street. You don't get to see history made every day."

"Very well. Don't get yourself into trouble. And don't start an international incident. That's an order!" Sullivan said half joking but was also serious.

"I understand, sir. I will keep my nose out of trouble." Alex pressed the off button disconnecting the phone hookup. He had one other option he wanted to explore but, it too, was not a guarantee. He left the private office he had been using and went to the Ambassador's secretary. "I need one of the Embassy's vehicles."

Amir Air Base

4:35 p.m.

Israel is a small country not much larger than New Jersey, so it did not take Alex more than two hours to make the drive to Amir. Israeli military bases differed somewhat from their American counterparts. It was not uncommon for an American base to be located astride a main highway. Not so in Israel. Their bases, in particular the air bases, were located away from major highways or roads where possible for security purposes. Such was the case with Amir. Alex was glad he did not have car trouble. It would have been a long walk through the Negev desert.

He slowed his speed as he approached the gatehouse. A soldier waived him to a stop at the gate.

"Credentials please," demanded the corporal.

Alex noticed four other men armed with standard M-16 automatic weapons. A guard dog was being led around his car while another soldier inspected the underside and trunk of his car. No one had asked for permission to conduct the searches. Security cameras were also present. His face was no doubt being photographed, as was the license plate of his car. These would be checked and verified against Israel's security database. If they were as efficient as their reputation was for security, they would have a match on him and the car. Thirty yards past the gatehouse were two concrete bunkers. Each bristled with Negev light machine guns. These guarded the entrance to the main gate of the base.

"Mr. Stanton, what is your business here today?" asked the sergeant in charge of the detail.

"I have an appointment with General Goldman. He is expecting me," Alex said with his best poker face. The sergeant eyed Alex and then turned to the private in the guard shack. "Verify the appointment."

Alex could feel his heart beating. In spite of the coolness of the day he was beginning to sweat. He was counting on Goldman wanting to see him. If he did not, he would have a lot of questions to answer. The sergeant was called over to the guard shack. Alex could see him take the phone and begin talking. He looked over in Alex's direction and then hung up the phone.

"Mr. Stanton, please step out of the car, sir," ordered the sergeant, who was pokerfaced as well. "Search him."

As he stepped out of the car and the soldiers began their search, Alex was thinking of how he was going to explain this to not only the Prime Minister, but also President Sullivan. Sullivan had said no international incidents, and now he was going to be arrested for attempting an unauthorized entry to an Israeli air base. Two Hummers pulled along side Alex's car. Atop these vehicles were .50 caliber machine guns aimed right at his head.

"Please step in, sir. We do not allow civilians to drive on the base. We'll park your car in our security area," said the sergeant as he opened the door of the vehicle. "It will be here *if* you return." Alex was sure he was going to the brig. Realizing his options were now limited, Alex climbed into the front passenger seat of the Hummer. Two soldiers, both armed with Uzis, were in the back seat of the Hummer. They were taking no chances. The main gate opened as the driver quickly accelerated the vehicle. The driver stopped in front of a desert-camouflaged two-story building. The sergeant exited the vehicle, came around to Alex's door, and opened it for him. Escorted by the other soldiers, the two of them walked to the door of the building and entered.

"Is this the man at the security gate?" asked the officer who met them just inside the doorway. He was flanked by four soldiers brandishing weapons.

"Yes, sir," acknowledged the sergeant.

"Well done, Sergeant. He is under my authority now. You're dismissed." The sergeant and his men turned and left the building. The officer pointed to a desk against the wall. "Mr. Stanton, please have a seat over at that desk."

With that the officer disappeared behind a set of double doors. He returned a few moments later with a familiar figure leading the way.

"Is this the man, sir?" the officer asked Goldman.

"Yes. Welcome to Amir Air Base, Alex," said General Goldman as he walked over and greeted him. "That will be all, Captain. Compliments to you and your men." He motioned to Alex. "Come with me." They passed through the double doors and moved down a hallway. Taking a flight of stairs they came to the second floor and finally the General's office. Closing the door behind them, the General stopped and turned to Alex.

"Alex, you have a lot of nerve trying that stunt. You were very fortunate I was here today. Do you realize where you would be right now had I not been here? I ought to throw you in the brig myself. Do you understand the political consequences that would have occurred? Now what would make you take such a stupid risk?"

"You are right, General," Alex said not surprised at the General's demeanor. He deserved everything the General was saying. "It was a stupid stunt and I am grateful you were able to see me. General, may I ask you a candid question?"

"Yes, Alex, go ahead."

"Were you in favor of the Accord?"

"No I was not. You know that," Goldman said as he moved to the seat behind his desk. He motioned for Alex to have a seat.

"Sir, may I ask why not?"

"Israel is placing its security in the hands of non-Israelis. With all due respect, I include your country in that category. I don't expect you to understand my concerns though."

"No, General, I think I do understand. Perhaps for different reasons, but I understand. I think Israel is more at risk today than she was prior to the Accord. If you have an hour I would like to explain what I mean."

"Well, you must be convinced of something to have pulled this stunt." The General lifted his phone and gave an order they were not to be disturbed short of war. "Now, what do you have, Alex?" He didn't have to add it better be good. His voice said it all.

After Alex concluded his presentation, Goldman, who had remained silent during the presentation, looked inquisitively at Alex and asked, "How sure are you of this?"

"Honestly, General? It is just a theory. But the circumstantial evidence suggests there is a distinct possibility of this happening. Gerhard and Al-Saim were in the same hotel on the same date, Muslims overwhelmingly voted for Gerhard in the election, and suddenly this Accord falls in Israel's lap. European troops are manning observation posts in the Golan Heights and Sinai. And now we are seeing Palestinians exacting justice on their own people when fighting Israelis. And to top it all off, they are allowing the Temple to be rebuilt alongside the Dome of the Rock. It just all seems too good to be true. Separately, they mean nothing. Put them together and I believe something is there," Alex concluded.

General Goldman sat for a moment considering his options. "Add what happened to your flight over the Med and you may be on to something. This may come as surprise to you, but I am a student of eschatology or what I think Christians call End-Time prophecy. A lot of this falls in line with some of those theories. Problem is we can't prove any of it. Are you familiar with this?"

"Yes, sir, there are some similarities."

"Does this surprise you?"

Indeed, Alex was surprised to learn the General was a student of a discipline such as eschatology. But perhaps it made sense. The General was charged with defending Israel. Would it be so shocking for a military man to explore all possible avenues of intelligence no matter how unconventional the source?

"I will be honest, sir. I am a little surprised, but also relieved. General, are there any unusual military movements on the part of the Alliance?" inquired Alex.

Goldman pressed a button on the keyboard of his computer. "There has been the anticipated shifting of Alliance forces as the EU peacekeepers have been taking their place in Sinai and around the Golan Heights. The Syrians have begun the withdrawal of their armor from Golan. Three armored and two infantry divisions have not yet withdrawn. The Egyptians are repositioning their forces away from Gaza, though several divisions remain along the border. They are behind schedule somewhat but no one is complaining in our government. They are attributing it to incompetence on the part of the Alliance. Pretty arrogant if you ask me. A combined EU and Jordanian force has taken position on the Jordanian border. All is occurring as prescribed in the Accord."

"Disposition of Israeli forces?" Alex asked as he moved to look at the computer.

"We have completed the withdrawal of our forces as called for. Most will be on leave to celebrate the Temple dedication. The General Staff, including myself, will be in attendance at the ceremonies. Only skeletal crews will be manning defensive positions. Israeli defense will be almost naked," Goldman acknowledged.

"Is there anything else, General? Anything at all that might be considered unusual?" Alex persisted.

Goldman continued to scroll down on the page. He came to a section titled 'Order of Ceremonies' for the Temple dedication.

"One of our squadrons is scheduled to participate in the flyover at the Temple dedication. There are four squadrons participating from the Islamic Alliance. One each from Syria, Egypt, Jordan, and Iran. Nothing else."

Alex stood up and rubbed the back of his neck. What was he missing? "Are there any other IAF squadrons flying tomorrow?" he asked excitedly as he leaned on Goldman's desk.

"No. None other than the one scheduled for the Temple dedication. All forces have been ordered to stand down on both sides to avoid any misunderstandings."

"What is the order of the flights?" Alex asked.

"I see where you're going with this," Goldman noted as his mind grasped the threat. A quick glance of the orders confirmed his fear. "We are scheduled to flyover first. The Alliance planes will be on our six."

"That's right, sir. Are you thinking what I am thinking, General?"

"Yes, I am. Eighty-five Alliance planes will be over Israeli territory and free to strike after shooting down our squadron. If they have rehearsed the strike correctly they could inflict a crippling first blow. Such a strike could tip the balance of power in their favor in the event of war. It could be the Six-Day War all over except in reverse. We have always relied on command of the air to compensate for our inferiority in numbers on the ground."

"And now, if I am reading this map correctly, your armor has withdrawn from their positions in the Golan and Sinai," Alex noted reviewing the map.

"And with the observation posts occupied by EU forces on the dedication day, we are blind in these areas as well," Goldman finished. "Combine that with the stand-down in our forces and we will be wide open for an attack."

"General, is there any way to warn the other squadrons without arousing suspicion?"

Goldman thought for a moment before responding. "I can place calls to three of the other commanders. I trust these men with my life. I am not sure if it would be wise to contact the others. I'll also contact my brother. He's in command of an armored brigade that was stationed in the Golan Heights area. Keep in mind, Alex, a lot of people, even in the military, are in favor of the Accord. Too much activity or suspicion and we could be arrested. The political climate is still volatile. Some in my country would consider these actions treasonous. Sentiment still burns among our enemies for revenge for our raid on Iran's facilities. I don't care what is written on paper. Anything unusual could cause the Alliance to withdraw from the Accord and blame us for its failure. We are operating on a theory with no facts to support us."

"I understand, General. Both our necks are on the line. Officially I am not supposed to be here. I would hate to think what my President would say or do if he knew."

"Your President may not be able to help you. In the current climate of my country you would be arrested as a spy, or worse. Supporters of the Accord would rail against your presence as American attempts to undue the Accord. You would not be deported in the spirit of the Accord. Israeli justice can be most effective," Goldman gravely noted.

Goldman picked up the phone on his desk and began to make the calls. Two hours later he hung up the phone.

"They are willing to help. They're quietly placing their squadrons on alert status. One will be conducting 'navigational training' over the Mediterranean but will be fifteen minutes flying time from Jerusalem. The other two will have their planes ready for takeoff on a two-minute notice. AAA defenses will be manned more heavily. Your Hawkeye aircraft aboard *George Washington* are currently providing on-going intelligence updates on any Alliance movement. We've done all we can do. Now we wait and pray that we are wrong."

"Amen, General, Amen," said Alex.

THE NEW DAY

TEMPLE DEDICATION CEREMONY

TEMPLE MOUNT, JERUSALEM

January 8ᵗʰ

9:00 a.m.

The Accord had been in place for two weeks. The culmination of the celebrations would be in the dedication of the groundbreaking of the Jewish Temple. In spite of the Accord, security was very evident around the Temple Mount. The IDF had been charged with security. Nothing was being left to chance in the dedication of the Temple. This was understandable in light of the history of the Temple Mount. A sanitized area of three hundred meters had been declared around the Temple Mount itself.

Even though security was tight, there was joy everywhere in Israel at the prospect of once again having the Temple in which to worship. Though Israel was not an overtly religious nation, there was long-standing sentiment to reconstruct the Temple. It was felt by many that it would be the symbol that would unify Israel and Jews around the world.

However, it was the political ramifications of the construction of the Temple that mattered most. With the Temple being built on land that had been in dispute for thousands of years, it conveyed to every Israeli that their Islamic neighbors had finally accepted the sovereignty of the Jewish state. How else could one explain the willingness of the Alliance in sharing the third holiest site in all of Islam? Indeed it was this acceptance that had been the cornerstone of the Accord. What Israel, for all of its military excellence, could not wrest from the Arabs on the battlefield, it had accomplished at the negotiating table. The resulting cessation of hostilities that resulted from the Accord Weissman and the others had negotiated had been well worth the recognition of Palestinian rule in Gaza and selected parts of the West Bank. It was one of those rare moments in history when every side felt as if they had the better end of the deal.

The Rabbis had taken their places, as had the sole representative from the Islamic Alliance, at the Triple Gate located on the Southern Wall of the Temple Mount. Weissman, along with the Cabinet, members of the Knesset, and General Staff were present. As part of Israel's continuity of government plan, the Minister of Public Security had remained at Defense Ministry headquarters. Everyone else who was a leader in Israel's government, both at the local and national level, was present. It was a day none could be seen to miss, though one member of the General Staff was not present: General Goldman. For the first time in his military career he had disobeyed an order. Weissman was markedly upset Goldman was not present and had sent an aide to contact the General and remind him his presence was not optional.

An invitation had been extended to Gerhard to represent the European Union but he had declined. His reason for declining appeared to be a sound one. This was a moment for Israel and her neighbors to share; not outsiders. He expressed his sentiment that he was fortunate to have played a small role in the overall process, but he had only been a mediator. No one thought it strange the EU was not represented. Other Arab officials, including The Waqf, had also chosen not to participate for personal matters that were understandable in light of what was taking place.

In spite of the Accord it was hard for some of the faithful to accept the fact they would be sharing the Temple Mount with Jews. All the Alliance had asked for was a military tribute to the fallen comrades on both sides. It seemed a reasonable request and was granted without question. It had been decided to have one squadron of planes each from Israel, Egypt, Syria, Jordan, and Iran conduct a fly-over after the official groundbreaking. Aside from that sole request there had been little debate as to how the actual dedication ceremony would take place.

The order of ceremonies was fairly straightforward. There would be an opening statement by Weissman followed by the Islamic Alliance. Then the Levitical Rabbis would bless the ground and offer a prayer on behalf of all involved. Weissman would then make some concluding remarks, after which a symbolic number of bricks from the Triple Gate would be removed to signify the opening of the Temple Mount to both Jew and Arab and the start of construction of the Temple. It was estimated construction would not take more than a year. Next to last on the order of ceremonies was the flyover. Lastly, Weissman would lead the Israeli delegation to the Dome of the Rock for a tour conducted by the Waqf who were to join them after the ceremony. It would symbolize the close of one era and the beginning of a new one.

USS KENNEDY

MAYPORT

11:00 p.m.

Captain Spivey was in the CDC. It was a good thing the room was air conditioned for his temper had reached the boiling point. It had been weeks since the new software package was to have been installed. Right now nothing pertaining to the ship's combat systems was operational. He had had enough. Sanchez had seen the Captain's temper before and he was seeing it now in an even greater display. Not only was his face beet red, but the veins in his neck were popping out. That was never a good sign. He did not envy the consultants from Applied Technologies. It was apparent they had not experienced this type of dressing down too often in the corporate world. The Captain had been going on for ten minutes and was just getting warmed up.

"...and if you cannot get this thing working within the week, you are ripping it out and re-installing the old package. At least it worked. In case you haven't realized it this is a United States Navy combat ship. With that worthless program of yours, we couldn't fight off a rowboat of duckhunters! Do I make myself clear, gentlemen!"

The consultants could only look at the floor during their dressing down. The Captain was right and they knew it.

"And another thing," Spivey said as he headed for the door, "don't even think about charging the Navy overtime for this. The taxpayer isn't responsible for your incompetence!"

The consultants humbled "yes, sirs" fell on the door as it slammed shut. They looked at each other and Sanchez, who broke out in laughter at their predicament. "Welcome to the Navy, boys!" Sanchez said. "Welcome to the Navy."

"Is he always like this?" asked one of the berated consultants.

"Only when people screw things up, and I would say you've screwed it up pretty good. You boys better call your HQ and make this thing happen, or else it sounds like you are out of a job."

The Purple Line, established after the Six Day War, was the demarcation line separating Israel and Syria. Israel had constructed eleven observation posts along this line after the Yom Kippur War. From these vantage points the Israelis could almost see Damascus. One element of the Accord called for the joint manning of these posts with EU forces. All parties would be able to monitor the activity on either side of the ridge. It had been agreed that each side would provide four men for each site.

The morning watch was preparing to stand down. The Israeli soldiers were looking forward to returning to their homes to watch the Temple dedication on television or attending the ceremony. The Alliance soldiers were scheduled to depart as well. With their departure, this would leave only EU forces manning the observation posts. As the shift came to an end, the French lieutenant in charge of the EU force slowly reached for a trunk that had recently been brought to the post. Not wanting to appear suspicious, he waited for the Israeli soldiers to enter the barracks as they prepared to shower. He quickly gathered his detachment along with the Alliance troops. As he was opening the trunk, one of the Israeli soldiers, forgetting his radio, had returned. The lieutenant looked up with surprise on his face. His expression said it all: he had been caught.

"What do you have there my friend?" asked the Israeli soldier not sure if he should reach for his pistol.

"I must admit you have caught me at a most unfortunate moment," Lt. La Pierre coolly replied. "If you will allow me?"

He slowly withdrew his hand from the trunk. His face broke out into a grin.

"I thought it would be most appropriate if we could toast the beginning of a new era," he said holding up two bottles of champagne. He glanced at his watch. "I know it is early, but after all, today is a special day in history."

The face of the Israeli soldier just beamed. "Let me get my friends."

As he disappeared into the barracks, the lieutenant pulled out another bottle from the trunk and opened it as well. He poured four glasses from the first bottle and eight from the second bottle. He handed each of his men and the Alliance soldiers a glass from the second bottle. The four Israeli soldiers returned. He handed each of them a glass that was poured from the first bottle.

"Please allow me," he said as he made the toast. "*A notre sante*, to our health and to the Accord. And may we return home to the women who love us."

Everyone raised their glasses in salute and drank. As the lieutenant prepared to pour another round, the sergeant in charge of the Israeli troops suddenly doubled over in pain. Within seconds the other Israeli soldiers doubled over and collapsed as well. They convulsed for a moment as the poison quickly made its way through their system. Within two minutes they were dead.

"Signal the other posts," ordered the lieutenant. "It's time for the morning check-in. By now everyone should have drunk to their health," he said with a laugh.

At each observation post along the Purple Line the same scene had been repeated. Israel was now blind to what was happening on the Syrian side of the Purple Line.

JACKSONVILLE, FLORIDA

2:00 a.m.

It was two o'clock in the morning. His alarm had awoken him an hour ago. In spite of his excitement and anticipation of the mission, Abukar had managed to fall asleep with ease. Now, fully awake, he began the final preparation for the task at hand. He took one final look around the house. No identification had been left behind. Not that it would matter. Abukar knew he would not be coming back home; at least not to this home. But he did not want to provide the police with any information should they trace the home to him.

Abukar and his brothers had loaded the *Mayport Majesty* earlier in the evening. The house they had rented along the St. John's River had a covered boathouse. It had provided the perfect cover in which to load the packages of high explosives. They had brought these out to the boat in coolers. It was all designed to give the appearance of making ready for a fishing trip. If any of their neighbors were nosy, they would assume they were loading up on beer and other beverages. To keep up the appearance of a couple of guys getting ready for a marathon trip of fishing, they had also placed fishing rods and related equipment on board. Fishing licenses were on board in the cabin in the unlikely event they were stopped by a game warden or the Coast Guard. Nothing had been left to chance.

His brothers had already departed for their part of the mission. They were camping in Huguenot Memorial Park which was across the river from the naval base. Abukar left the house. Walking across the dew covered grass he breathed a deep sigh of satisfaction. All was going according to plan. In less than three hours it would all be over and his part in the War of Liberation would be completed. He walked along the dock of the boat slip. After readying the boat for departure, he started the engines. His ears were rewarded with the rumble of the 350 horsepower inboard motor. He put the throttle in reverse and backed the *Mayport Majesty* into the river. He allowed the current of the river to take the boat for just a moment to help clear the dock before pushing the throttle forward. Checking his compass, he adjusted his course northward.

The darkness of the night was pierced by the lights from houses and buildings along the banks of the river. Still, visibility was very low. The overcast skies did not help. Abukar had planned for such a contingency, however. He slipped on a pair of recently purchased night vision goggles and the darkness turned to an eerie green.

Jacksonville is a city that is divided by the St. John's River. Seven bridges provide access to the north and south sides of the northeast Florida city. At one time he and his brothers had contemplated attacking the bridges, but decided against that. No, they had wanted bigger fish he reminded himself.

As he approached the city, the lights of the Jacksonville skyline were reflecting off the water. Passing under the Acosta Bridge he approached the Main Street Bridge, which was a drawbridge. Fortunately, his boat was small enough that he did not need to signal the bridge master to raise the span. Car lights could be seen crossing the bridge as they were leaving the downtown area. No doubt young adults heading home after a night of debauchery in the local bars.

After clearing the city he lifted his radio. He slipped on the headset. The odds of anyone being able to hear, much less understand, his pending conversation were remote at best. But he knew sounds carried over water and he was leaving nothing to chance. He spoke into the microphone. "Are you there? How is the baby?"

Static crackled over his headset. "Yes, we are here. Our baby is sleeping soundly."

"I will flash my lights three times when I approach. Execute as planned."

Another hour passed and Abukar adjusted his course for the last time as he followed the course of the winding river. This time it was due east toward the Atlantic Ocean. He eased the throttle back for he was now approaching Naval Station Mayport, and he did not want to attract any undue attention. Ahead on his right he could see the *Kennedy*. Her massive hull was occupying C2; one of the two primary carrier piers at the naval base. Also present in the harbor were the seven ships of her battle group. It was unfortunate these were not to be attacked also. It would have been a crippling blow to the U.S. Navy. But he knew that more than one boat at this time of night might raise the suspicions of the naval base guards.

All was very tranquil and peaceful from what he could see. On his left he could see his brother's tents. To the casual observer they appeared to be typical campers that frequented the area. However, if one looked closer behind the tents they would see the 120mm mortars present that had been dug in and were now sighted on the runway. He reached down and switched the running lights on and off three times. A single light flashed back from the shore where his brothers waited. All was ready.

He was now directly parallel to the great carrier. He could make out men moving around on the deck and the dock. None appeared to pay his boat any attention. Why should they? His was just another boat that was leaving the St. John's River and heading out on a peaceful fishing trip as hundreds did on a weekly basis. He took one last look at the carrier and then over to where his brothers were. It was time. He eased the throttle forward, which was expected to help offset the current of the river as it met the Atlantic. Reaching the mouth of the river he pushed the throttle forward all the way. The boat lurched underneath him and he almost lost his balance. Fifty yards past the basin where the carrier was berthed he made a course correction for the last time. Turning the boat back around one hundred eighty degrees, he made a slight deviation in course. The new heading was now directly aimed at the stern of the *Kennedy*. The

Mayport Majesty was now traveling at forty knots. Her bow rode up as she crossed over her wake.

On the stern of the *Kennedy* Seaman Jose Sanchez was walking to stretch his legs after being in the CDC all week. His break was almost over. The coolness of the ocean breeze was reviving him. Glancing out toward the Atlantic, he also noticed the course change of the boat. *Some drunk fool at the helm*, he thought as he shook his head. He had seen enough weekend boaters to know a lot of drinking occurred on the water. Truth be told, he had practical experience himself at navigating while under the influence. At least twice he recalled. Whoever was driving the boat would realize soon enough he was heading the wrong way and quickly turn the boat back out to sea. He was making his way back to the door for his return to duty in the CDC when he paused and glanced out at the boat again. Something was different with this boater. The boat's course was not wavering as one might expect if the operator were drunk. It had straightened out and was on a direct heading toward the *Kennedy's* stern. This was no drunken fool at the helm. He knew something was wrong.

In the CDC, a young seaman suddenly sat up straight in his chair. A warning light was flashing on his console. "Ma'am!" exclaimed the excited seaman. "We have an unauthorized vessel in the Defensive Perimeter Area. Radar indicates she is headed this way at forty knots!" The Duty Officer, Ensign Trawick, instantly hit the General Quarters alarm.

Sanchez was running back to the door. This was no boat in distress or navigational error by some incompetent boater. The suddenness of the turn and course correction indicated one thing. This was an attack. Reaching the door he opened it and sounded the only alert he possibly could. He pulled the fire alarm switch located just inside the passageway.

Simultaneously, the General Quarters claxon sounded. Instantly the carrier began to teem with life as men stumbled out of their bunks heading to their emergency stations. Automatically, fire control doors began to swing shut as the carrier's automatic damage control system took over.

MAYPORT MAJESTY

4:02 a.m.

Abukar's eyes were fixed solely on the stern of the steel, grey hull. His target was dead ahead. The stern of the carrier loomed larger and larger as he approached. Then a thought overcame him that he had not antici-pated. *Fear!* This was something he had not contemplated. He was not prepared to die at such a young age. He had grown accustomed to the good life he had been enjoying. Images of his life flashed through his mind. Thirty yards away from the *Kennedy* he locked the steering wheel of his boat into place confident she would not miss. His next action was not one he had ever contemplated taking. He jumped over the side into the dark waters of the ocean.

USS KENNEDY

CDC

4:03 a.m.

"Engage sea whiz now!" exclaimed the Duty Officer. In the excitement she forgot one crucial update.

"Ma'am, she's not working on automatic...the software is down," said the seaman with fear in his voice.

"*Manual control! Now! Fire at will, fire at will!*"

MAYPORT MAJESTY

4:05 a.m.

Abukar surfaced in time to see explosions occurring around his boat as the Phalanx Gatling gun was being fired; but it was too late. The *Mayport Majesty* was veering to the right but she was going to hit. She impacted against the starboard side of the *Kennedy*'s stern. It was not a direct hit but the damage caused was enough. The stern of the *Kennedy* erupted with a violent explosion that lit up the night sky. Flaming debris landed on the adjacent pier causing auxiliary fires to break out. For a moment he was silhouetted against the ocean as the fire's glow brightened on the pier. Fearful he would be seen, he dove under the water and frantically began to swim.

USS Kennedy

4:06 a.m.

The *Kennedy* shook violently from the force of the blast. In Engineering, men were scrambling to stop the flooding. The main concern was in the area of the hull where the propeller shafts were. A huge section of the hull had been ripped open by the blast. The flooding was localized, however, thanks in part to the watertight doors that had automatically closed. Nonetheless, the *Kennedy* was badly wounded. Her boilers were intact, but there was not much left for them to drive. The starboard propellers and rudders had been destroyed and would have to be completely replaced. Worse still, seventeen of her crew were dead from the impact of the explosion. As if this were not enough, other explosions were soon being heard around the naval base.

Huguenot Memorial Park, North Bank

Mayport, Florida

4:07 a.m.

Abukar's brothers had seen the explosion. That was their signal. They knew they had perhaps fifteen to thirty minutes before the Americans responded and they were making the most of their opportunity. They already had laid out forty rounds of shells for each of the two 120mm mortars. The mortars were situated in two firing holes they had dug earlier in the evening. The activity of digging was not atypical for a camping trip. If anyone had approached them they would explain the holes were for the fires they would build later that night in which to cook their food. When darkness came they simply removed the mortars from their backpacks and assembled them.

They had already sighted the mortars on the runway of the air station. They loaded the first rounds and fired. The roar of the ocean concealed the *whoosh, whoosh,* of the departing shells. Within seconds, the mortar shells began exploding, cratering the runway. Six more rounds were aimed at the runway to insure it would be damaged enough to prevent its usage.

Satisfied they had damaged the runway they now shifted their fire to the other ships docked within the basin. They knew they would not be able to sink the ships but hoped to inflict the most damage possible.

Each brother had targeted a different ship. A geyser of water sprayed the deck of the *Boone* as the first round went wide. A quick adjustment of the settings resulted in a direct hit on the *Boone*. Now that he had the range dialed in, Mummar loaded and reloaded the weapon as fast as he could. His brother, who had targeted the *Roosevelt*, was also firing as fast as possible.

The exploding shells damaged the radar mast on *Boone*. *Roosevelt* was struck just aft of the rear superstructure, destroying the Phalanx gun system. They could see fires on the *Roosevelt* from their campsite.

Activity was picking up around the naval base as the personnel began to respond to the attack. Abukar's brothers were benefiting from the element of surprise, but that advantage was quickly passing. They now shifted the fire of their mortars and aimed indiscriminately hoping to create as much confusion and damage as they could.

Twenty-four minutes later they heard the approach of helicopters. Searchlights from the *Kennedy* and the other vessels were sweeping the ocean and coastline, as were the lights from the helicopters. They soon found their target.

Captain Sam Wheelhouse was scanning the shoreline using the FLIR system of his AH-64D helicopter. Movement around the campsite caught his attention. To his disbelief he saw the brothers firing their mortars.

"Home base from Defender One. Got'em! Suckers are at the camp-sites across from *Kennedy!*" Wheelhouse reported.

His wingman was maneuvering his helicopter into attack position.

The two brothers also saw the helicopters maneuvering into attack position. Scurrying for cover, they braced for the counterattack. One grabbed a Soviet made SA-7 Grail shoulder-fired surface-to-air missile and aimed for the helicopters. A flash of light erupted as the missile left its launcher. There was no time for evasive maneuvers.

A spectacular explosion occurred as the missile exploded against the engine of the helicopter. Wheelhouse watched in horror as fragments of his wingman's chopper fell into the river. Wheelhouse now swung his helicopter into an evasive maneuver that also enabled him to bring the 30mm machine gun on his helicopter to bear on the brother's location.

Before Mummar could reload the weapon, bullets from the 30mm machine gun on board Wheelhouse's helicopter sliced into his chest killing him instantly. His brother attempted to pick up the weapon, but he too was cut down by fire from the machine gun.

"Sir, it looks like that last shot took 'em down. I don't see anyone else," reported Lt. Al Sampson, his co-pilot. "I don't see any survivors from Smith's chopper either, Captain."

"Let's make sure we haven't missed anyone else. Nobody gets away with this trash. Swing her around for another look," ordered Wheelhouse.

Sampson adjusted the stick of the AH-64D and broke hover. He patrolled along the banks of both sides of the river looking for any signs of suspicious activity. Other helicopters had now joined the search that included the waters around the carrier and her attendant battle group. Utilizing their FLIR they were casting about in the darkness looking for survivors. Waterson soon spotted an individual in the waters leading to the naval base. His body's thermal energy stood out in stark contrast to the cold waters of the Atlantic. He was attempting to make his way to the shore but was having difficulty against the outgoing tide.

"Angel Flight, this is Defender One. We have one in the water at the mouth of the basin."

"Roger that, One. Moving to rescue," acknowledged Captain Henry Black aboard Angel Flight. He spoke into his mike addressing the rescue divers on board. "Get ready to hit it. Looks like he's going under. Take extra caution. This nut may be armed," he ordered while maneuvering the HH-60 Seahawk into a hover above Abukar.

The two rescue divers gave the thumbs up and jumped into the water. They were going to attempt to save the life of the man who had just killed their comrades-in-arms. Swimming underwater, they approached Abukar from behind. He offered very little resistance. Fighting the currents had exhausted him. Coming up from behind him, one of the divers grabbed him around the chest and secured his arms behind his back. The other secured his feet. They pulled the rescue vest over him that had been dropped with them. After securing him in the vest they signaled he was ready for extraction. As he was being lifted out of the water, Abukar glanced to the location where his brothers' camp had been. Searchlights were still illuminating the campsite. Seeing no movement, Abukar knew his brothers had been killed. Alone now, he began to cry as the reality of his cowardice began to sink in. He had failed himself and his brothers. He vowed he would be tougher during the inevitable questioning.

9:33 a.m.

It began as a picture perfect day. Worshippers had gathered before first light for sunrise services at the Western Wall. The Al-Aqsa mosque was filled to capacity with the faithful as they prayed against the events that were transpiring below them. The morning dew had burned off under the sun that was now shining brightly in the eastern sky causing temperatures to rise above the average for the time of the year. The skies over Jerusalem were blue without a hint of clouds. Glistening in the bright sunshine was the golden casing of the Dome of the Rock. The beauty of the day contributed to the overall festive mood of the throng of people that had gathered for the Temple dedication.

Television crews were everywhere broadcasting worldwide what was potentially one of the greatest historic events in all of man's tenure on the planet.

The Sanhedrin, led by Rabbi Mier Barkley, had led the official proceedings by bestowing their blessing on the dedication of the new Temple. They represented the religious leaders of Israel and her connection with Israel's past. Prime Minister Weissman was now concluding his remarks, "Today, Israel takes the first step toward reconnecting with her past. I hereby dedicate this day as Temple Day." He then turned to the engineers waiting by the Triple Gate and motioned for them to proceed.

Small charges had been installed to loosen the stones in the gate. A chain had been attached to four small hooks that had been drilled into one of the stones. One of the engineers attached the chain to an awaiting bulldozer. Mounting the bulldozer, the driver signaled to his partner that all was ready. His partner lifted the handle of the plunger and thrust it down. Four small explosions detonated raising a cloud of dust from the stone as it was now loosened from its resting place of over one thousand years.

The engineer on the bulldozer engaged the throttle and the machine began to move forward placing tension on the chain. The stone was reluctant to move from its resting place. The engineer applied additional power and the stone began to acquiesce to the demands of the machine as horsepower overcame mortar.

A man dressed in traditional Arab clothing was moving easily in the crowd that had gathered to witness this historic day. His arms were tucked inside his white tunic to conceal the small transmitter he held within his hand. Al-Saim had handpicked him to perform this sacred task. He had been briefed as to exactly when to send the signal. He had memorized the order of events so as to best position himself in direct view of the Southern Wall. His smile grew as he heard the bulldozer's engine whine along with the roar of approval from the teeming crowd. The racket generated by the bulldozer would provide the perfect cover for any noise that might be heard from the resulting explosion. As the roar of the bulldozer's motor increased, he pressed the sole button on the transmitter and began to make his way away from the Temple Mount.

Within the tunnel located under Solomon's Stables on the southeastern side of the Temple Mount, the receivers attached to the explosive devices received the signal from the transmitter faithfully detonating the charges. The explosions had the desired results. The walls of the ancient structure were the weakest above the tunnel. The underlying support structure began to weaken and collapse with far reaching consequences.

Outside of the Temple Mount, the bulldozer had finally wrested the stone from its ancient resting place. Doves were released in celebration of the moment as the crowds offered their roar of approval.

As the engineer began to power down the bulldozer, a slow rumbling began to be heard even above the applause of the crowd. At first, the multitude gathered around the Temple Mount thought that an earthquake was striking the region. As they looked around they realized this was not the case. The sound was more focused and was emanating from the Temple Mount itself. Understandably, they were slow to appreciate what was happening.

Atop the Temple Mount, cracks began to appear in the floor of the Al-Aqsa Mosque. The ancient pillars supporting the Mosque started to collapse and with them the Mosque itself. The faithful gathered in the Mosque looked around in disbelief as they saw the cracks beginning to multiply. Since the Accord was signed, they had been there praying that this day would not come. The ornate decorations on the walls and ceiling began to fall injuring those present. Their screams were not those of pain, but of disbelief as they realized their prayers had been in vain. One chasm swallowed a worshipper as he began to run from the Mosque. Others fell into the growing fissure as they too tried to make their way out of the collapsing Mosque. The other two thousand worshippers not fortunate enough to escape were crushed as the ceiling crashed on top of them. For those that did make it out of the Mosque, their escape from danger was only temporary. Their foot speed was unable to outpace the growing fissures as the ground opened up underneath their feet causing them to fall to their death.

The fissures continued radiating away from the Mosque with increasing speed as more of the subterranean supports collapsed. As these gave way the paving stones of the Temple Mount began to fall and slide down Mount Moriah. The Gobiet Fountain located between the Mosque and the Dome ceased to flow as the water line shattered.

The cracks continued to make their way to the Dome itself. Though located on Mount Moriah, the resulting stress from the collapse of the southern part of the Temple Mount took its toll on the Dome. Onlookers saw the building begin to shake as stones fell from the ancient structure. The golden Dome, which had stood as the predominant structure in the Jerusalem skyline, began to splinter into pieces. Ornate stonework was falling from the Dome on the courtyard causing further injuries and loss of life to the crowds gathered there to pray. The interior columns of the ancient building were unable to withstand the stress being placed on them and buckled, bringing down the glittering golden Dome that for so long had represented all things Islamic in Jerusalem.

The throngs of people gathered around the Temple Mount were transfixed in disbelief at the spectacle unfolding before their eyes. Gripped with fear by the unfolding events, but yet paralyzed by the desire to see the conclusion, many were killed as the ancient walls of the Temple Mount crumbled and collapsed. It was a scene no one could have ever envisioned. With a crescendo of noise, what was left of the Al-Aqsa Mosque and the Temple Mount crashed to the ground and began to slide down Mount Moriah in a rising cloud of debris and dust. The Dome of the Rock was in ruins. The spire that crowned the top of the Dome could be seen lying at a forty-five degree angle. Only the northern wall of the Dome remained standing, but it too was near ruin.

In a matter of less than ten minutes, the third holiest site in Islam had been laid to ruin with all of the far-reaching, and as yet unimagined, consequences.

The Western Wall was not spared from destruction in spite of the prayers of the Rabbis gathered there. They had been praying for the day when the Temple would be rebuilt ever since Israel recaptured Jerusalem. And now, the very stones that many believed were part of the Second Temple came crashing down upon them along with the people gathered there.

Weissman, along with those present at the dedication site, was also overcome by the incredible events transpiring. They were slowly coming to their senses and taking the first small steps away from the disaster unfolding before them. Even if they had run at the first sign of the pending disaster they would not have escaped. They were too close to the wall and were crushed under an avalanche of stone and debris as the Southern wall collapsed.

The dedication ceremony of the Temple was being televised around the world. The historic significance of this event had garnered the largest television audience for any event since 9/11. Now, viewers around the world were eyewitnesses to an unprecedented turn of events. What had been billed as the greatest event in the modern history of mankind was now turning into the greatest disaster.

The television announcers whose broadcast locations were closest to the Temple Mount were hurriedly running away from the site while encouraging their retreating camera crews to stay focused on the structure as it continued its collapse. Those that were closest to the Southern Wall were caught in the increasing tide of debris. As reporters and camera crews were overcome in the deluge of stone and debris, the television networks were forced to switch coverage from one camera to another. They soon realized that with their pool of reporters lost they would have to share those that survived. It was quickly agreed that all network affiliations would cease to be used while the signal was being shared. Ironically, *Al Jazeera* was the network able to field the most surviving reporters on the ground.

NAVAL STATION MAYPORT

JACKSONVILLE, FLORIDA

6:30 a.m.

The black table and chairs offset the white walls of the interrogation room. There was a pitcher of water with a stack of paper cups on the table. On the wall to the right of the door was a mirror. Abukar suspected it was a two-way mirror his interrogators were using to watch him. Along the same wall was a television monitor.

He was sitting in the room alone. All track of time had been lost as he had been unconscious from the time he had been rescued and taken aboard the helicopter. Neither his feet nor his hands were restrained. He suspected the restraints were not needed as there were armed guards likely posted outside of the door. He looked down to check his watch but found that it had been removed along with his original clothing. His attire was now an orange jumpsuit with the word PRISONER emblazoned in white on the back.

Two men entered the room and sat in the chairs opposite the table. Both were wearing navy colored suits with freshly pressed white shirts. Their ties were dark red. Abukar deduced they were from DNIS. Neither spoke to Abukar at first. They busied themselves reading the folders they each brought into the room. At last one began to speak.

"Mr. Fernandez. Or should I say, Mr. Abukar? You're in a deep load of trouble, son," the agent said with a heavy Southern accent.

Abukar's face remained impassive at the charge. He did not shift in his seat or even look in the man's direction.

"Looks like he has a hearing problem," said the second agent from DNIS. Abukar placed the accent as being from New York.

"Yeah, cold water can do that sometimes," replied his partner.

"Mr. Abukar, could you please tell us what you were doing swimming in the vicinity of a U.S. naval base? Kind of late for a midnight swim isn't it?"

Abukar continued to ignore their questions. *Mind over substance* he reminded himself. Within his mind he was constructing walls that symbolized his attempts to block out their questioning. The walls were also designed to keep the fear he was feeling from gaining a foothold in his mind.

"Still not gonna talk?" noted the first agent. He stood up, walked over to the door and pressed a button on the wall. "Ok, send him in."

The agent waited for a knock on the door. He opened it and a young seaman entered. It was one of the rescue divers. Abukar thought the man looked very familiar but he could not place his face. His mind was still groggy from the events of the evening.

"Is this the man?" asked the agent.

"Yes, sir."

"Please tell us where you know him from," inquired the agent.

"Sir, he works at the Quik-Mart just outside of the base."

Abukar's eyes dilated ever so slightly but enough for the agents to see. Clarity of thought now set in. The man was one of his regular customers. He was the infidel that was always talking about women.

"Well, Mr. Abukar. It looks like we know something about you after all. By the way, this is the man who saved your life tonight in the water. But how ironic this is. He may also be the man that ends your life by ID'ing you tonight."

The agent nodded to the seaman dismissing him.

"You see, Mr. Fernandez, or rather, Mr. Abukar," began the second agent, "we have been doing a little investigating since we plucked you out of the Atlantic. We pulled the phone records of the store where you worked. One very interesting phone call was received and one was made from the store. We were able to trace the call's origin. Because of your generous cooperation our agents are in the process of making a few additional arrests."

"I know nothing of what you speak. These are all lies. As an American citizen I demand my attorney," blurted Abukar.

"Mr. Abukar, there is just one small problem with your request for an attorney. That right applies to legitimate American citizens. Unfortunately, we cannot confirm any record of your birth in this country. Nor can we verify any attempt at legal immigration in our database. The way I see it, that makes you a non-citizen. Add to that an enemy combatant. As soon as you become a citizen, we will be glad to honor your request. Now, it appears that you have been very busy with your credit card," the second agent said as he held up a sheet of paper scanning it as he continued. "You seem to have a fondness for the water don't you? I'm referring to the purchase of a certain vessel registered as the *Mayport Majesty*. My, how very sentimental you are."

"And they said the Patriot Act would invade people's privacy," noted the first agent with disgust in his voice. He looked at Abukar who was becoming visibly shaken at this point.

"Only on the guilty," his partner said with satisfaction in his voice. His attention turned to Abukar.

"I know of no such things," spat Abukar. "All of this is based on lies. You lie tonight just as you lied about your country attacking my people. You will pay for this deceit."

"Lies? Come now, Mr. Abukar," the first agent said mockingly. "You would have us believe it is all a coincidence that a boat purchased by you was used in an attack on the *Kennedy?* And that you just happened to be taking a midnight swim right after the explosion?"

"Believe what you want," said Abukar.

"Oh, we don't have to believe. We have the whole thing on video. You see, Mr. Abukar, the waters you sailed through tonight are continuously monitored." The second agent walked to the wall and pressed the intercom. "Play the security video on our monitor."

Abukar's face went blank as the video began to play. Upon conclusion of the tape, the agent walked over to Abukar.

"Mr. Abukar, under the authority of the Patriot Act, you are under arrest for terrorist crimes committed against the people of the United States of America, and for the willful and wanton attack of United States government property. Specifically, Naval Station Mayport, USS *Kennedy*, USS *Roosevelt*, USS *Boone*. You are also charged with the murder of eighty-six civilians and members of the United States military in the aforementioned attacks. You're going away for a long, long time. Get him ready for transport to 'Gitmo," the first agent said to his partner.

AMIR AIR BASE

10:08 a.m.

Alex and Goldman had chosen to view the ceremony in the Command Center. Both were transfixed as they watched the unfolding events at the Temple Mount. The eyes of every man and woman were riveted to the main monitor in the Command Center. The mood of the room reminded Alex of the office at CFA when the World Trade Center was attacked. At first, no one in the Command Center spoke. Even the battle-tested veterans were stunned into momentary inaction by events of such magnitude. Conversation began as whispers until the initial shock of the moment wore off. Then the Command Center, as if coming out of a deep sleep, recovered with a flurry of activity. Alex looked at Goldman with a look of incredulity. Even he could not believe what was happening.

"Signal all units. Code Omega. My word, Alex. You were right," Goldman said as he gave the order to launch the Raptors and Ra'ams. They would be airborne is less than two minutes.

"It is YK2," Alex whispered barely audible but loud enough for Goldman to hear.

"We're going to be in for the fight of our lives. This war will determine our fate as a people. We are in greater peril now than at anytime in our history. I hope your President's word to Prime Minister Weissman remains. Israel will need America as an ally."

"General, there are not many things in life you can count on. But the word of President Sullivan is one of them. He will keep his commitment—I promise."

ISLAMIC ALLIANCE HEADQUARTERS

SYRIA

10:09 a.m.

General Abdul-Hassan was also watching the events occurring at the Temple Mount with mixed emotions. He understood the need to sacrifice the Temple Mount from a tactical point of view, but emotionally he was in turmoil. However, like a well-trained soldier, and more importantly, a man in the Islamic world, he did not shed the tears he wanted to. He knew his emotions, like those of his men, would best be channeled into fighting his enemies. Lifting his command phone and with a voice barely containing his emotions he exclaimed, "Jihad! Repeat, Jihad!"

2000 FEET ABOVE THE TEMPLE MOUNT

10:12 a.m.

As called for in the order of services, the four squadrons of planes were approaching the Temple Mount. The flyover was timed to occur five minutes after the dedication ceremony had ended. They were approaching from the northeast and would conduct their flyover on a northeast by southwest axis. The Israeli Phoenix squadron consisting of twelve F-16I Sufas was the lead squadron. Five hundred feet behind them were the Egyptian 63rd and Jordanian 51st squadrons each flying twenty EU-made Rafale C fighters, along with the Syrian 3rd squadron of MiG-23s and the 28th Iranian squadron of Sukhoi Su-34s.

The lead pilot of the Egyptian 63rd squadron, Captain Ahmed Mummar, heard the command "Jihad" crackle over his headset as did the other pilots. Each pilot had already identified and selected their target as instructed in their briefing. Captain Mummar switched on his targeting radar and immediately received the "lock" tone on his chosen prey. He selected a Magic 2 air-to-air missile from the inventory of missiles and pressed fire. Upon leaving its mounting rail, the missile ignited and its infrared targeting system locked onto the exhaust of the lead Israeli F-16I. With a little under five hundred feet to cover, the missile rapidly closed on the Sufa and scored a direct hit destroying the unsuspecting plane. He had already adjusted his radar and locked onto the next plane. He pressed the firing button releasing another missile that quickly found its target destroying another Sufa.

He was pleased to see other missiles streak by and destroy all but two of the remaining Israeli planes. Realizing they were under attack, the pilots of these two planes ignited their afterburners and broke formation peeling away at a steep angle. Four members of his squadron set off in pursuit.

With the initial objective of the destruction of the Phoenix squadron accomplished, the Syrian and Iranian squadrons altered their course and headed for the air bases in the Tel-Aviv area. Armed with air-to-ground missiles, their mission was to disable the runways thereby preventing the Israeli squadrons based there from taking off.

The Alliance knew that command of the air would be essential for any chance of success against Israel. They were attempting to emulate Israel's success in the Six-Day War when Israeli aircraft dismembered the air forces of Egypt, Syria, and Jordan on the first day of the conflict. To this end it had been decided all available squadrons of combat aircraft would be committed in the initial strikes. Jallud was confident in this approach, as the European Union had deployed an additional four squadrons on Egyptian and Syrian airfields. These were the trump card for the Alliance. The EU planes would protect Alliance bases from any Israeli planes that might become airborne, freeing Alliance planes to engage the Israelis.

Sixteen additional Alliance squadrons were already taking off from airfields in Syria and the Sinai. Their intended targets were Israel's twelve main air bases. An additional ten squadrons were detailed to strike ground targets including the vital command and control facilities. One primary command and control target was the Knesset. Attempting an attack on Israel's seat of government had been contemplated in the Yom Kippur War, but was ultimately decided against as it would be seen as an escalation of the war. Having struggled against Israel's demonstrated proficiency in combat, the Egyptian generals of the time were uncertain they would be able to protect their own government buildings in the certain Israeli counterattack. Plus, there was the potential counterattack from Israel's rumored, though unsubstantiated, nuclear weapons if the war went badly for Israel.

Now, buoyed by the presence of EU forces, this strategic target had been included in the overall battle plan. The counterbalance of EU nuclear weapons was calculated to keep the war conventional.

MYSTIC THREE, E-2D HAWKEYE

10:14 a.m.

Mystic Three had been airborne for five hours and was nearing the end of its patrol. It had been detailed to maintain radar surveillance over Israel and her neighbors. The APS-145 radar mounted above the aircraft was scanning a radius of over two hundred miles when the electronic signals from the transmitter made contact with multiple objects where none should have been.

"Sir," reported Specialist Thompson, "I have multiple radar contacts emanating from Syria, Egypt, and Jordan! Climbing to altitude." A minute later Thompson reported. "They're on inbound courses for Israel. Contacts are increasing in number. Now detecting twenty-eight contacts becoming airborne in Israel."

First Lieutenant Doug Taylor, who was the Combat Information Center Officer on Mystic Three, looked at the data now being displayed on his radar screen. "This is incredible. Captain, we have what appears to be a massive air attack being launched on Israel. Three hundred plus contacts and rising!"

"Notify *GW* now!" Captain Seimens ordered. "Be sure they are awake in CDC. Are we transmitting to IDF headquarters?"

"Yes, sir. Data link shows green for both," acknowledged Taylor. "They're seeing what we're seeing but it may be too late."

AMIR AIR BASE

10:17 a.m.

Amir was the newest of the three National Command Centers in Israel. The Command Center was buried forty meters below the surface in a hardened structure. As part of Israel's continuity of government plan it was designed to withstand all means of attack, including nuclear. A previous defense review had indicated that the two existing Command Centers were not structurally able to withstand the latest bunker-buster class of weapons. These weapons were capable of penetrating the earth and reinforced concrete and steel of which those Command Centers were constructed.

Amir was designed to remedy those deficiencies. It was rumored that Amir's Command Center had been incased in an updated version of Choblam armor up to twenty-five feet thick in places. Though classified, Israeli scientists had allegedly cracked the composition of the legendary armor improving its effectiveness by twenty percent. The engineers who constructed the Command Center testified it would withstand a direct hit from any known conventional weapon currently in existence or in development. It was even rumored to be able to withstand the blast from a one-megaton warhead. Theoretically it was bombproof.

The Command Center was modest in size but was equipped with state-of-the-art communication and electronic data processing equipment. Data links with Israel's commanders provided real-time information on the disposition of their forces. Looking forward from Goldman's office was the main display that was flanked by two additional displays on either side. Each monitor displayed various pieces of key information such as weather, deployment of naval and land forces, etc. Every piece of intelligence Goldman needed to command was available for display on the monitors. Today those monitors were presenting unsettling information.

The officer supervising the Air Threat desk felt his heart race as the radar screen he was monitoring darkened with the contacts detected by Mystic Three. He lifted the red phone that dialed straight to the General's command desk.

"What do you have?" Goldman said snatching the phone off the cradle.

"Sir, signal from the *George Washington*. They are detecting five hundred plus contacts inbound from Syria and Egypt. Tracks now on the main screen, sir."

The officer had transferred the radar contacts to the main tactical display. Goldman rose from his chair in disbelief as he saw the tracks on the huge tactical overlay. He was not pleased with the information he saw. The Alliance squadrons were already crossing into Israeli airspace. The display showed five Israeli squadrons airborne. His two squadrons, one from Tel-Nof that was returning from its training mission over the Med, one from Lod Air Base, and one from Hatzerim Air Base. Goldman gave the order to intercept. The odds were not good. One hundred thirty-five Israeli planes versus over five hundred for the Islamic Alliance. He knew Israeli pilots were the best trained in the Mideast, if not the world, but against odds of three-to-one it would take every bit of their training and some luck. Protection of the air bases would be crucial. But with the planes engaging their opposite numbers, only the base air defenses would provide any cover for now if, and it was a huge if, the men had made it to their stations.

"YK2, Alex. What is that?"

"What? I'm…I'm sorry, General," Alex said transfixed on the monitors. "YK2. Yom Kippur Two. It is a simulation scenario recreating the events of the '73 war with multiple variations."

"Did it include this scenario?" Goldman asked.

"A version of it. Yes, sir, it did."

"The results?"

"Without U.S. intervention or Israel resorting to nuclear weapons," Alex paused for a moment before he replied with a hushed tone, "Israel lost."

USS George Washington

Eastern Med

10:17 a.m.

The activity in the CDC resembled that of a well-rehearsed dance. Each officer and enlisted man had been trained repeatedly in various scenarios ranging from a routine search and rescue mission to that of all out nuclear war. When the reports of the Alliance air strikes on Israel began to come in from Mystic Three, there was the expected increase in the pace of activity, but nothing close to panic or disbelief. Each man and woman was performing his or her job as trained.

Receiving the information while on the bridge, Alvarez ordered battle stations and the ready five to be launched. He also ordered additional assets to be prepared for launch in expectation of receiving orders from Washington. He then headed to the CDC. Six thousand men and women aboard the *GW* were moving into action to comply with the Admiral's orders.

"Alright, what do we have?" he asked his XO, Dwight Fontana, as he entered the CDC.

"Admiral, initial reports have five hundred and thirty aircraft attacking Israel. Israelis have one hundred thirty-five in the air. All ships report battle stations as ordered. Patriot and Wildcat are all airborne. The ready five, Bulldog Three, is being launched now." A total of twenty-six F/A-18 Super Hornets were now flying CAP.

"Ambushed. Those suckers ambushed 'em," he spoke as he addressed those in the CDC. "Alert CAG, I want more assets in the air. No need to tell you to keep a sharp eye out. Now is not the time to be cautious. Report any contacts no matter how incidental they may appear. This ship could be all that stands between Israel's survival or destruction. What are the Europeans doing? I thought they were there to keep this kind of thing from happening."

He had no sooner uttered those words when another report, this one more urgent than the previous one, was received in the CDC. His XO was talking on the headset with *Mystic One*, the second E-2D patrolling to the west of the *GW*. "Admiral, Mystic One reports eighty bogeys bearing our direction on course three-three-zero. Coming from Europe, sir."

"Is this part of their scheduled deployment?" Alvarez demanded anxiously.

"No, sir," noted Fontana. "And no IFF signal either."

"That may be our answer regarding our European friends," Alvarez commented.

"What do you want to bet they're not part of a tour group?" Fontana commented to no one in particular.

Alvarez suppressed a grin. His XO's sense of humor was dry at best. It seemed the more intense the situation the more it manifested itself. He noted a few of the crew had heard the comment and were attempting not to grin. This was a good sign thought Alvarez. He knew some officers that would have blown an unsuspecting crewman out of the water for this. Alvarez held a different viewpoint. He allowed this type of comment if it helped break the stress of the moment and did not impact the performance of the crew. His men knew and appreciated this.

"Updated report, Admiral. Mystic now detecting thirty additional bogeys on two-two-zero coming from the south, sir," advised Fontana.

Alvarez eyed the tactical display now being relayed from Mystic One. The symbols on the monitor indicated planes were approaching from Egypt, south of *George Washington*, and the northwest from Europe. The

E-2D Hawkeye's patrol station was two hundred miles due west of the *GW.* The symbols displayed indicated the inbound targets were potentially hostile planes.

The display showed additional tracks beginning to originate from the planes. That could only mean one thing: missile attack. Mystic One had detected a cruise missile attack being launched from EU and Alliance aircraft.

"Let's look sharp. Signal all units. Missile attack. Splash the bandits. Weapons free," Alvarez ordered. "Get Knighthawk and Bulldog squadrons up as soon as possible."

The inbound tracks on the display screen were flickering on and off causing Alvarez concern. A normal attack by cruise missiles was cause for concern, but the Aegis battle management system had a high chance of defeating the attack due to the ability to track the incoming missiles. With the detection problems they were encountering it led Alvarez to one conclusion. The missiles must have stealth capability.

"What cruise do they have in their inventory with stealth characteristics?"

"Sir, that would have to be the SCALP EG. It's a French designed missile capable of GPS guidance with fire and forget capability. They recently deployed it. Nasty sucker. Worse than the Exocet."

"I never did like the French," Alvarez quipped returning his attention to the tactical display.

2000 FEET ABOVE THE TEMPLE MOUNT

10:20 a.m.

Captain Mummar now changed course to his primary target—the Knesset. He and his wingman were streaking toward Israel's center of government at an altitude of five hundred feet. His altitude was so low it felt like he was skimming the treetops. Upon dispatching the Israeli planes, he had swung his plane around Jerusalem for a better angle of attack on the Knesset. His plane had been outfitted with four air-to-ground missiles in anticipation of this strike. So far they were not encountering any resistance. From the lack of response it appeared they had achieved complete strategic surprise. His attack on the Knesset had been rehearsed countless times in the simulator. Every conceivable scenario had been flown through that wonderful machine. Long the sole purvue of the Western and Israeli Air Forces, the Alliance had acquired them three years ago and they had been put to good use.

Following his landmarks the Knesset loomed in his sight. He selected the AS-30L air-to-ground missile and pressed the release button on the joystick. The missiles left their hard points and followed the laser targeting system to the illuminated target. Missiles from his wingman's plane were also bearing down on the heart of Israel's government. The Knesset was engulfed in an immense fireball as eight missiles struck home. *A perfect shot*, he thought to himself. Mummar banked his aircraft right and prepared to make a strafing run on any survivors. Over his headset he could hear the reports of his fellow pilots as they were making their attack runs.

Other pilots were attacking the underground National Military Command Center that had been constructed beneath the Defense Ministry, the Kirya, in Tel-Aviv. The "Bor," as the facility was known, was an essential target. Israel's ability to coordinate a counterattack would be severely diminished with the destruction of the Knesset and the Bor. He could not believe the good fortune they were enjoying in attacking Israel's command and control facilities. Other planes had been detailed to strike the Command Center at Nevatim. From the initial reports the attack on this facility was successful as well.

On the ground, suicide bombers were charging the gates of the airfield at Nevatim in addition to the other airfields in Israel. There had not been a shortage of volunteers for these missions. It was not likely they would be able to penetrate the base defenses. Their primary task was to create panic and confusion on the bases in coordination with the air strikes. Additional commando units were assailing radio, television, and phone links to aid in crippling Israeli communications.

As he began to make his strafing run on the Knesset, an alert became audible over his headset and quickly brought his attention back to the cockpit. The alert indicated he was being tracked by another plane. The radar indicated it was approaching from his six. In the excitement of the strike, and hearing the other reports, he had committed the one cardinal sin of a pilot: he had allowed an enemy plane to approach undetected from his rear and obtain radar lock.

Lt. David Greene was in the F-15I Ra'am that was closing on Mummar. He had radar lock and depressed the fire button releasing an AIM-9 Sidewinder air-to-air missile. Mummar's plane erupted in a brilliant flash as the Sidewinder found its mark. Greene's wingman dispatched Mummar's wingman with a similar shot as the skies above Jerusalem became the scene of the first major aerial engagement of the war. The Hammers squadron, which was on a navigational exercise over the Med, had arrived over the battlefield and was now engaging the Alliance pilots. The commander of the squadron was glad he listened to his old friend's warning.

The Hammers squadron was beginning to gain a temporary advantage in the air. This was due in part to the support being received from Mystic Three. The benefit of the information being received from the Hawkeye was proving to be invaluable. The Israeli pilots had received course and altitude of the Alliance planes. With this information, Mystic Three had directed them on an approach that offered the least chance of detection. Approaching at tree top level, they popped up to one thousand feet. Utilizing the fire and forget capabilities of the F-15I's fire control system, multiple AIM-120 missiles had been fired temporarily clearing the Alliance planes from the skies over Jerusalem. However, this was not before the command and control facilities of Israel had been destroyed.

The attack on these facilities had been devastating—more devastating than initially realized. In the opening moments of the war, the Knesset, along with the Israeli Defense Ministry, and two command centers had been eliminated as functioning elements of Israel's command structure. Radio and television stations, along with telephone exchanges, had also been struck to further degrade Israel's ability to respond to the attack. Without these communication systems functioning, the mobilization alert was slowed. The resulting paralysis from such an attack would normally have been the decisive element in a war that would be over in less than twenty days. However, aware that such a 'bolt from the blue' strike could occur, Israel, like the United States, had developed a continuity of government plan. Both countries had multiple layers of redundancy built into their COG plans in the event one or more layers of control were destroyed. Israel was fortunate to have adhered to this tactic. One command and control center had survived: Amir. With the loss of the civilian and senior military officials the burden of leadership now fell to one man: General Goldman.

The CDC tactical display continued to show the tracks of the inbound cruise missiles. At ninety miles, the Aegis Battle Management System would begin engaging the targets. Information supplied by Mystic One would extend the range of engagement, increasing the probability of interception. If Aegis were unsuccessful, the Phalanx systems aboard each ship would be the last line of defense. Alvarez hoped it would not come down to that. The sheer size of the *George Washington* would enable her to receive multiple hits and continue operations. This size was both a blessing and a curse. Her ninety thousand tons would enable her to withstand hits that would disable or even sink the smaller carriers of the EU, or any other adversary. However, the tradeoff for this protection was the loss of maneuverability. She was nimble for a ship of one hundred thousand tons but not as that of a fifty thousand ton ship.

Alvarez knew that all watertight doors had been secured but that was not his main concern. His thoughts kept drifting to the flight deck and the consequences of a lucky strike hitting during launch and recovery. In the hanger deck planes were being readied for combat. The fuel and ammo load out of those planes was more deadly than the warheads carried by the cruise missiles—provided they were not nuclear.

The strategy of the EU's attack was straightforward. Attempt to overwhelm the carrier strike group's defenses with a massed missile attack in anticipation that some of the missiles would find their target. It was a classic battle of attrition that the Japanese initially employed through the Kamikaze attacks on American carriers in World War Two. The Soviets had adopted these tactics as their primary strategy of engaging U.S. carriers in the event of hostilities during the Cold War. Aegis had been developed to counter just such a concerted attack. Now, the scenario was being played out for real.

As former allies, the EU knew the strengths and weaknesses of the strike group. Alvarez considered this as he and his officers racked their brains to see what possible defensive tactic had been overlooked.

"Sir, what if *GW* is not the primary target?" inquired Fontana. Puzzled at first over the question, Alvarez's palms became clammy with the realization of his answer.

"Contact both Mystics. Tell them to shut down all emissions now!"

he ordered. "They're the first targets. Their goal is to blind us and then hit us," he said to Fontana.

"Pretty smart move on their part. Tough having former allies as enemies," replied Fontana.

The main tactical display went blank for a second as both Mystics powered down their radars. The radar data from *Vella Gulf* replaced the display.

"We're going to have to rely on radar from the Hornets. Get me Mystic One and Three. Who would have ever envisioned the Hornets in a AEW role?" he said to Fontana.

"Captain, I've lost contact with Mystic One," reported the seaman at the communication desk.

On board Mystic One, the Radar Officer realized they were the target of at least some of the missiles. He had moved to shut down the EM emissions but was too late. Two of the missiles exploded in close proximity to the Hawkeye, blowing it into fragments. The remainder of the missiles continued on their track toward the *GW.*

As the SCALP EGs approached to within ninety miles of the *George Washington*, the first of many SM-2 missiles erupted from the multipurpose launchers of the cruiser *Vella Gulf* as her Aegis Battle Management System automatically responded to the incoming threats. SM-2s from her sister ship, *Mobile Bay*, were also being launched.

Soon, both ships were shrouded by smoke as missile after missile was loaded and fired even though they were cruising at flank speed. Controlled entirely by computer, no single human could have reacted with the speed and objectivity of Aegis. One by one the incoming missiles were destroyed in systematic fashion as one hundred missiles were shot down. As good as Aegis was, though, it was not invincible. Six SCALP EGs slipped through the protective missile shield and continued to the *GW* battle group.

"Admiral, six vampires headed our way," said Fontana.

"Sound impact. Hard to port. Fire decoys." Alvarez was vainly hoping he could deflect the angle of impact and minimize the damage the starboard side was about to receive. At three thousand meters, the tracking radar of the Phalanx CIWS detected the missiles and locked on to the targets. Even with automatic reload, the gun's ammo supply of three thousand rounds was quickly expended. Two of the missiles were quickly destroyed, but three of the remaining missiles struck the *GW* almost simultaneously sending shudders through the great ship as the two thousand pound warheads detonated. One missile missed the *GW* entirely but impacted on the *Stout*, an *Arleigh Burke*-class guided missile destroyer.

Three explosions erupted on the aft starboard side of the *GW* sending huge fireballs into the sky. The hanger deck doors had been closed but one of the missiles directly impacted on the door of hanger number three, the aft most hanger on the starboard side. The resulting damage was overwhelming. Number three elevator was almost blown off of its mountings. Twisted and warped metal remnants of the elevator were all that remained. The remnants were hanging from the side of the carrier and dragging in the waters of the Mediterranean.

Inside the hanger, fires from the explosion ignited fuel and ammo from the planes of Knighthawk squadron that were being readied for launch, causing secondary explosions. The aircraft and men inside were all lost. Fortunately, the massive internal blast doors had been closed effectively creating a firewall within the hanger preventing the fires from spreading. The hanger's fire suppression system further contained the fires.

The second missile struck just below the flight deck on the portside of the damaged hanger, destroying the Sea Sparrow missile launcher and Phalanx gun system. Combined with the damage from the first missile, a massive hole was torn in the flight deck. Pieces of twisted metal arched skyward as the force of the blasts pealed the three-inch thick metal flight deck away. The remaining missile struck under the island, just above the water line, inflicting the most serious damage upon the great ship. The hole created by the blast extended below the water line allowing the cold waters of the Mediterranean to enter. The *George Washington* began to take on water. Had the ship not been secured for battle the damage could have been much worse.

"Damage control parties, report all damage," ordered Fontana over the ship's intercom. It was five minutes before the first reports began to filter in. By all accounts, the *George Washington* had been dealt a serious, possibly fatal, blow.

"Admiral, we have reports of hull breach amidships. We're taking on water. Damage control reports hatches secure and flooding is contained to local decks at this time. Aft starboard Phalanx and Sea Sparrow destroyed. No hope for repair. It keeps getting worse. Serious damage to elevator three and adjacent hanger. Crews are working to contain the fire to that area. Initial casualty report estimated at two hundred dead. Eighteen were pilots. Another one hundred plus injured. Fourteen were pilots. Flight deck is reporting the arrestor wires are useless. The blast severed all the wires and destroyed the arrestor housing. No way to repair them. Just as well. The flight deck has a hole the size of the Grand Canyon. Useless."

An ensign turned to report to Alvarez. "Incoming message, sir. *Stout* is reporting massive damage. She is sinking, sir. Going down by the bow."

As quickly as it began, the attack was over. Alvarez hung his head and rubbed the back of his neck. The others who heard the news eyed the Admiral. Their ship had been wounded and wounded badly. The sudden loss of their comrades struck each member of the crew.

"Receiving transmission from *Mobile Bay*, Admiral. She has pictures of us," Fontana noted, breaking the silence after a moment.

"Let's see'em," ordered Alvarez.

One of the monitors in CDC flickered as the image from *Mobile Bay* was received. Alvarez was primarily interested in the hole in his ship. The picture showed the hull breach was about fifteen feet long and ten feet high. How far below the waterline was a guess. Fire continued to belch from the aft part of the ship as crews worked to contain the fire from spreading.

"Hit us pretty good, sir," Fontana observed.

"Damage to the reactor?" asked a worried Alvarez.

"Engineering reports the reactor is secure. No damage to that area of the ship. At least we still have power. That's something," Fontana commented.

"How many planes did we lose?"

"Admiral, Air Boss is reporting we lost pretty much every bird aft of the island. Total count lost is thirty-seven. Almost half the wing."

"Is there any good news?" asked Alvarez as he pondered on the status of his ship.

"The Lightnings survived," Fontana noted referring to the F-35C Lightning II V/STOL aircraft. "*Wasp* is reporting no damage to anyone over there."

"Yes, but without the ability to recover our birds, we're out of business."

Without the ability to recover her aircraft, the *GW* had just become the most expensive parking lot in the world. *At least she could still launch so that was something* thought Alvarez. He considered his sole remaining option.

"Contact IDF HQ for permission to land our planes. Tell them they're going to have some company. Whatever we have left, let's get'em up. Inform the pilots," Alvarez ordered. "It looks like we may be in bed with the Israelis on this thing."

The tactical data from Mystic Three was now being displayed with the passing of the attack. On another monitor, Mystic Two could be seen taxiing to cat one in preparation for launch along with two F/A-18F Super Hornets.

Fontana looked at Alvarez. "We were fortunate on that round, but we're going to have to find a way to protect the Hawkeyes."

"Sir, I'm not able to establish contact with IDF headquarters. Lost them right after the attack," interrupted Thompson.

"Anything wrong with our equipment?" Alvarez asked with growing frustration.

"No, sir, but I think I know why we lost contact. Sat recon just now coming online."

"Let's see it," Alvarez ordered as he leaned in to see the monitor.

There was no mistake about what the pictures showed. The images showed smoke plumes rising from where the Knesset and Bor used to be.

"Cut off the head and the body withers," Alvarez said to no one aloud. "Can we contact Amir?"

"Attempting to, sir. Will advise when contact is re-established."

"Admiral, not meaning to eavesdrop but if I may, sir," it was Radar Specialist Tomlinson.

"Go ahead, son, if you have an idea," Alvarez said with a reassuring nod of his head.

"Sir, EU people know the frequencies our radars operate on. Best thing we can do is modulate 'em, sir. Heck, we could even shut the radar down and turn it back on intermittently. Mystic would reacquire the radar tracks but their missiles would theoretically lose their initial lock. Might buy us some time."

Alvarez listened intently as the specialist explained his theory in greater detail. Fontana, who held a master's degree in electrical engineering, concurred with the theory. Alvarez ordered it to happen.

"Have we confirmed where the planes come from?" inquired Alvarez now turning his attention to potentially larger issues.

"EU bases in France and Germany and El Minya in Egypt, sir," Fontana advised.

"Put me through to CFFC. I want to know our options before we expand what looks like World War Four," ordered Alvarez. "Who dreamed up this nightmare?" he asked Fontana.

USS ENTERPRISE

PERSIAN GULF

11:30 a.m.

O'Brien was stretched out on the bunk in his cabin. The bunk barely contained his six foot one inch frame. He had been asleep perhaps three hours when the phone rang disturbing his pleasant dream of landing a mess of trout. O'Brien was looking forward to his next leave. He had a three-week trip lined up that would have him hiking and fishing through the Grand Canyon. Most importantly, he would be alone. No responsibilities and no phones awakening him in the morning. No alarms demanding his attention. Though with the situation in the Middle East he knew that it would be a while before he took that vacation. He rolled over, switched on the light by his bunk, and answered the nagging sentry before it had a chance to ring again.

"O'Brien," he spoke into the phone as he rubbed the sleep out of his eyes silently cursing Alexander Graham Bell for his wonderful, yet irritating, invention.

"Admiral, better get down here fast. It's hit the fan. We have a shooting war and we are in the middle of it."

"On my way," O'Brien said, now fully awake, as he returned the phone to its cradle. Within minutes he was dressed and in the CDC. A quick glance of the main tactical display told him what he needed to know. Air plots were recording the movement of Alliance planes into Israeli space. The plot also showed incoming tracks toward *Enterprise* and her strike group emanating from Iranian airspace. These were identified as Exocet anti-ship missiles. Additional tracks from Iranian territory were streaking from the northern Persian Gulf on course for the Arabian Peninsula. Outbound SM-2 missiles from the *Enterprise* strike group were now tracking on intercept courses as the cruisers *Gettysburg* and *Philippine Sea* responded to the attacks.

"Morn'n Admiral," McLaskey said as O'Brien calmly entered the CDC. One of the men brought him a cup of coffee for which he was grateful. "Iranians have launched a two-pronged air and missile attack. Our Hornets have dispatched the two *Hudongs*. Tried to fire their Exocets but we beat'em to the punch. Iranians have launched an additional missile attack from the vicinity of Deyyer on their southwest coast. Our cruisers are responding. We also have reports of suicide boats heading our way. The ready five has already been launched as per your orders in the event of attack. The Saudis and other Gulf states are on alert. Good thing, too, as it appears the Iranians are aiming for the refineries. If they can take out Ras Tanura and Al Jubayl it'll put a hurt on the world economy for a long time."

The two refineries McLaskey was referring to were located on Saudi Arabia's eastern shore of the Gulf. They are two of the largest refineries in the world. The loss of, or any serious damage to, these refineries would be a major blow to the world economy.

"Assets for JUST SRTIKE are preparing for takeoff per your orders in the event of an attack. Commander CENTCOM has confirmed the strike. We also have reports of three tankers under attack in the Straights. No confirmed sightings of who hit them but a first year analyst at DNIS should be able to figure that one out."

"Sub attack," O'Brien responded.

"Yes, sir. Latest intel has four of their *Kilo* class subs deployed in the eastern Gulf. Iranians have promised to shut the Straights in the event of war. Looks like they are attempting to make good on it. Captains of the other tankers in the Gulf are screaming for protection. Tankers outside of the Gulf are turning around."

"What the devil happened?" O'Brien asked sipping his coffee as he digested the enormity of the unfolding events.

"You're not gonna believe it, Admiral. As the Israelis were dedicating the Temple Mount the whole thing collapsed. We have the video for replay if you want to see. Whole Islamic world is exploding. It's Jihad. But here's the kicker. EU and Alliance forces hit *GW.* She was hit pretty hard. Can't land her birds. *Stout* was lost."

"Casualties?" O'Brien asked.

"Over seven hundred so far," McLaskey solemnly replied.

"Disposition of Iraqi forces?" O'Brien said as he absorbed the news of the casualties.

"They've gone on alert as has everyone else in the region. No reports of strikes in Iraq as of now. They have three squadrons in the air all operating inside their airspace. Iranian planes are playing cat and mouse with'em right now. Appears they're focusing their attention on the Saudis and us for now."

"Get the additional assets airborne. We're gonna try to protect the Saudis and others best we can. Contact their headquarters. I want to coordinate our CAP activities. Now is not the time for a friendly fire incident. We have to take out their missile bases. Launch JUST STRIKE."

O'Brien was stunned by the news of the attack on the *GW.* He had anticipated that hostilities would break out at some point after the Israeli raid on Iran's nuclear facilities, but he never foresaw this scenario.

WHITE HOUSE

WASHINGTON, D.C.

4:40 a.m.

Tom O'Hara was hurriedly making his way to the First Family's living quarters. Though he was known to the Secret Service agents on duty, he still had to show the proper identification before clearing the Secret Service checkpoints. He knew and understood their professionalism but blast it was slowing him down.

"Come on, hurry up. The President needs to be awakened," he anxiously told the Secret Service agent who was performing the security check. They had also been watching the events unfolding in the Middle East.

Satisfied after the check of O'Hara's credentials, the senior agent said, "Come with me please, sir."

The senior Secret Service agent on duty accompanied O'Hara as he knocked on the door to the President's bedroom. He felt sure the President and First lady were asleep, but he still respected the family's privacy. Hearing no reply he slowly opened the door, walked over to the king sized bed, and gently shook the President's left shoulder. Tom reached for the light on the nightstand and turned the dimmer on low, faintly illuminating the room.

"Tom, what? What are you doing here?" asked a groggy Sullivan while reaching for his glasses on the nightstand.

"Mr. President. I hate to wake you, sir. But Israel is under attack."

Sullivan, hearing the word attack, now became fully awake and sat up in bed. "Israel? Attacked? By who?"

"Reports are suggesting the Islamic Alliance, sir. Possibly assisted by EU forces. There is more, sir."

"More? What else could there be?"

"Mr. President, the *George Washington* has been attacked. Initial report indicates she has been severely damaged but is still maneuverable. The *Stout*, one of *Washington's* escorts, was sunk. Over three hundred reported dead. *Enterprise* has also been hit. Reports indicate EU and Alliance forces hit our ships. There was also an attempted attack on the carriers at Norfolk, but the terrorists were stopped before they could inflict damage. We also have confirmed an attack on the *Kennedy* at Mayport. Casualties there are unknown at this time."

"*Kennedy*, Norfolk? How?" asked a stunned Sullivan who felt as if he had been punched in the gut.

"Witnesses report yachts were used to ram the *Kennedy*. She is not sunk, but her steering is damaged. At Norfolk, six attempted the same thing. Apparently, the one that attacked the *Kennedy* did so ahead of schedule. The *Kennedy's* Duty Officer signaled a Delta Red warning. Gave the folks at Norfolk enough of a head's up. They blasted all six out of the water before they could get near the carriers."

"Is there anything else?"

"Yes, Mr. President, there is. We have received unconfirmed reports that one or more of the Saudi refineries have been attacked by the Iranians as well," O'Hara concluded with a calm but hushed voice.

"Unbelievable," said an incredulous Sullivan. The weight of the office had been heavy before but now he felt as if the universe had come crashing down on his shoulders.

"Wake Defense, State, and DNIS if they haven't been already. I want a meeting in thirty minutes. Move the terror alert level to Red. This could just be the beginning."

"Yes, sir, Mr. President," acknowledged O'Hara as he left the room. Another detachment of Secret Service agents was taking up positions along the hallway. As he was departing he saw Sullivan lean over to his wife who had begun to stir. Her reaction to the news was predictable.

She gave him a quick hug as he slid out of bed. Leaning back on her pillows, First Lady Kelly Sullivan switched on the television in the room as her husband began to ready himself for the task that was before him.

The newscaster on *Fox* was trying to keep up with the unfolding events. "Remarkable, unprecedented events are rocking the Middle East and America this morning…" O'Hara could hear the concern in the broadcaster's voice as the door closed behind him.

12TH MISSILE BRIGADE, SYRIAN
WESTERN SYRIAN DESERT
11:49 a.m.

Thirty SCUD transporters had been deployed in this remote part of the desert. The crews of the trucks had already elevated the launchers and programmed the guidance package of the SCUD-D missiles. This latest version of the Soviet weapon had been improved in both payload and guidance. The new inertial navigation system allowed for the missiles to achieve a ninety percent chance of landing within forty meters of the target.

The commander of the 12th Missile Brigade gave the order to launch and then disperse. One by one the missiles left the erectors in a blinding light. Their targets were specific: government buildings in Tel-Aviv and Jerusalem. Three other SCUD brigades had targeted IDF bases. As soon as the missile departed, the erector was lowered and the crews scrambled to their transports. Within five minutes each transporter had left the area on a different course to avoid a possible counterstrike. It would not come today though: the IAF was pre-occupied with their brothers in the air.

RAS TANURA REFINERY
SAUDI ARABIA
11:52 a.m.

Air raid sirens were sounding throughout the massive refining complex. The men manning the anti-aircraft defenses were on edge in anticipation of the pending attack. Three men were huddled around the radar console in the control room. The screen was filled with tracks of the incoming missiles from Iran.

"Launch the missiles!" ordered the senior commander. Beads of perspiration were rolling down his forehead in spite of the air conditioning in the room. He turned and shouted to the refinery technicians, "Shut off the oil flow and divert it to the overflow fields." The refineries had been designed with these overflow fields in the event of an emergency. The techs quickly pressed the emergency cutoff buttons diverting the oil in the pipelines to the emergency dump fields.

As the oil was being diverted, the Patriot-PAC 3 missiles were leaving their launch canisters in a flurry of smoke and noise in an effort to meet the assailants. A hail of missiles were engaging the invaders, but their efforts were overcome by the incoming missiles as they penetrated the defensive measures of the refinery. Massive explosions were now being seen and heard around the facility as the SCUD missiles were tearing into the pipes that carried the precious black liquid from the refinery to the tankers. Some struck the tankers that were loading their cargo at the terminal adding to the fury of the fires that were leaping toward the sky. Others struck the massive holding tanks creating explosions that were heard a hundred miles away. Black smoke was beginning to cover the area as the oil burned. For those who had survived Desert Storm, it was all too eerily reminiscent of Saddam's attempt to destroy the Kuwaiti oil wells. Ras Tanura, for all practical purposes, was destroyed.

Saudi Arabia had lost one of her primary refineries and the world oil market was quickly reeling with the news. The Iranians had made good on their promise to shut down Saudi Arabia's oil fields.

14TH ARMORED BRIGADE

GOLAN HEIGHTS

12:25 p.m.

Colonel Julian Goldman leaned forward on his Merkava IV tank's turret and took stock of the situation. His brigade, though not at full strength, was now deployed along the road west of El Al on the southern end of the Golan Heights. He had moved his tanks into position during the night. Camouflage netting covered each tank. He didn't know if they had been spotted during their move. It was hard to mask the movement of forty-five Merkava tanks.

This was an historic area for Israeli forces. The Syrians had penetrated as far south as El Al during the Yom Kippur War before being halted by another generation of tankers of the 7th Armored Brigade.

He had watched the Temple dedication and subsequent catastrophic events via satellite link on the monitor in his tank, as had the rest of his men in their tanks. Their reaction was not unanticipated. Chatter filled the radio immediately after the attack. Goldman ordered his men to clear the radio so they could hear his orders with clarity. He also wanted radio silence to avoid giving away their position to the Syrians.

"Colonel, radar contacts approaching from the northeast. Incoming bandits, sir," reported Lt. Abramoff who was in charge of his AAA detachment.

Goldman turned his gaze in the direction of the incoming planes. He made out their silhouettes as MiG-21s. The MiG-21 was not a modern aircraft compared to the inventory of the IAF. But in a ground support role it was still a deadly aircraft when armed with air-to-surface missiles.

No doubt the Syrians anticipated catching his unit by surprise. However, thanks to the warning from his brother, General Goldman, he had quietly readied his men. They had done their fair share of complaining as most soldiers did when pulled away from leave and their families. But, as Goldman had explained, neither of these would matter if Israel were overrun. There would be no homes to which they could return. The complaining quickly subsided and turned into steeled resolve with the destruction of the Temple Mount and subsequent attack on Israel.

The AAA unit of his brigade performed brilliantly. The Stinger surface-to-air missiles brought down ten of the twenty-four MiGs. It apparently was enough to discourage the MiGs from returning for a while. He knew they would not stay away long. Except on the next run they would return with more aircraft. The attack from the Syrians had been costly though as evidenced by the seven Merkavas and four M113 APCs that were now ablaze. He realized it would have been much worse without the warning provided by his brother.

He was looking through his binoculars across the border when he spotted a rising cloud of dust. As he adjusted his view he recognized the silhouettes as those of French-made Syrian LeClerc tanks. Now he knew why the MiGs had not returned. They did not want to chance hitting their own tanks in the close quarters of the upcoming battle.

Adhering to the principle learned through many battles, that the tank that fired first had the greater chance of survival, he ordered his tanks to fire upon target acquisition. His gunner locked in on the lead Syrian tank. The range was three thousand meters.

He felt his tank shudder as fire erupted from the 120mm gun. The other tanks of his brigade began to fire as well. Through his binoculars he saw the lead LeClerc's turret lift off the hull as the HEAT armor piercing shell from his tank's gun struck home. Fire and explosions ensued as the ammunition and fuel aboard the doomed tank ignited. He tried not to think about the four men who had just died a painful death. The best he could hope for the Syrian crew was that death had taken them quickly. He didn't dwell on the prospects of being burned to death inside, what, one would think, should be the protective armor of steel. He harbored no illusions about the safety of his tank. Anything made by the hand of man could be destroyed.

He did take comfort in knowing that the Merkava had been designed with the protection of the crew as a priority. Every possible safety and protective feature had been incorporated into the design of the tank. It was considered by many armor experts to be one of the safest tanks in service. However, as evidenced by the destroyed Merkavas he knew no tank was indestructible.

His gunner fired again with the same results to another Syrian tank. Suddenly, the tank on his left flank was engulfed in a furry of fire and smoke as it was struck by a Syrian round. Two men managed to escape the blazing wreck.

Knowing that movement was the surest way to increase their chances of survival he ordered his driver to move to the next prepared position as he saw additional Syrian tanks emerging past the burning hulks of their comrade's tanks. Goldman estimated he was facing at least two divisions of enemy tanks. That meant at least three hundred tanks versus his forty-five. In addition, he knew Alliance air support would be returning soon. More importantly, he wondered where his air support was. He adjusted the frequency on his radio.

"Base, this is Tiger Brigade. We have engaged Syrian tanks at El Al. Encountering at least two, possibly three, divisions of tanks with air support. We are executing Operation Gideon."

"Alex, who would have ever believed? Son, were you ever right. What kind of response is the IDF providing?" asked Sullivan as he watched the broadcast still being reported from the Temple Mount. The news services were describing a brief air battle that had just occurred. There was spectacular footage of two Israeli planes as they crashed into surrounding buildings. They were also beginning to report on what sounded like artillery shells exploding in the vicinity. No doubt, the battle for Jerusalem was taking place. The morning newspapers were still on his desk as were several from overseas. All were running headlines that were so similar it was as if they had been written according to a script. *The New York Times* was representative of them all as its headline read: "Treachery over Accord: Temple Mount Destroyed." The implications were obviously directed at Israel.

"Mr. President, I am in the Command Center at Amir. The mood here is pretty tense. Fortunately five squadrons were on alert. From what I am gathering they are responsible for blunting the initial attack. You saw what happened at the Temple Mount. Israel's government has been wiped out. I am not sure who is in command now, but General Goldman is acting on his own initiative until it can be determined if there are any survivors of the government. Mr. President, I heard about the *George Washington*. How bad was it?"

"She was hit pretty hard. We lost the *Stout*. Not as bad as it could have been though. Good thing someone listened to you or else those squadrons might not have been airborne. I have ordered the 2nd Fleet to the Mediterranean. The *GW* strike group, if able, is being ordered to assist. Alex, she was hit by EU forces operating with the Alliance. Looks like our former allies are no longer. That's not all. Our carriers at Mayport and Norfolk were also targeted. *Kennedy* is damaged but Norfolk was spared. Apparently the terrorists struck the *Kennedy* early giving time to warn Norfolk. I have placed a call to Gerhard. Time for a little heart-to-heart talk. Alex, stay in touch and keep your head down. May God have mercy on us."

Alex slowly hung up the phone as the impact of the President's statement rung home. He gathered his senses and moved to inform Goldman of the attack at Mayport and Norfolk along with the *GW*. The magnitude of the implications was beyond comprehension. European Union and Alliance forces were now joined together in a war against Israel and the United States. It had all been a set up. It had all been too good to believe and now the dream was turning into a nightmare. The Accord was shaping up to be the greatest hoax played upon a country since the Trojan Horse.

The Raptors and Ra'ams were returning to refuel and rearm. Their foray into the surprise war had been most successful. For the loss of four Ra'ams, they had accounted for forty-five enemy planes. The ground crews were waiting for their planes as the pilots taxied to the concrete revetments. Over time, the ground crews had grown accustomed to referring to the planes as their own. After all, they maintained it and were up in the late hours of the night repairing any damage or system. They spent more time with the planes than the pilots did. The pilots were merely the drivers.

An American would find the scene strangely resembled that of a pit stop during a NASCAR race. As the planes came to a stop, the crews swarmed over them looking for damage. If they found none, they moved to their area of specialization. Some checked the hydraulics while others rearmed the plane with new missiles. One serviced the most critical system aboard: the pilot. An energy drink and high carbohydrate bar were given to him. The average person didn't realize the physical exertion required to fly modern combat aircraft. G forces, up to nine times gravity, combined with the stress of combat, often left the most physically fit pilot exhausted. That was precisely the reason Israel had two pilots for each plane.

The whole process of turning the plane around required less than twelve minutes. As the last service ladder was being removed from the Raptors and Ra'ams, the pilots began to taxi to the runway. Clearance for takeoff was obtained from the tower. Approximately eleven minutes, twenty-seven seconds had elapsed and the runway at Amir was clear of planes again as they departed in search of their foe once more.

General Goldman was reviewing the latest reports of the battle in the Command Center. Communications within Israel had been severely impacted by the Alliance attacks. Only now was Goldman able to piece together what was happening. The results were not encouraging. Of Israel's twelve air bases, four had been destroyed while the remainder had incurred either moderate, or severe damage. The destroyed bases were Ramon, Hatzor, Ramat-David, and Sde-Dov. The damaged bases, including Beer-Sheeva, Tel-Nof, and Palmahim, were reporting they could be operational again in twelve hours if given sufficient air cover. That was the challenge before Goldman. How to protect the air bases?

Burning wrecks of F-15Is and F-16Is now littered these bases. Those planes that were fortunate enough to be in reinforced concrete revetments had been spared most of the attack. The support infrastructure of the bases absorbed the greatest part of the damage inflicted.

Amir had also been struck during the Alliance's initial attacks. Fortunately, the anti-aircraft defenses of the base were on full alert and had exacted a toll on the attackers. The burnt-out frames of ten Alliance planes two miles outside of the perimeter were testimony to the accuracy of the anti-aircraft defenses. However, several of Amir's support buildings and hangers had been destroyed during the raid. Worse, thirty-five casualties were being tended to at the base medical facilities. There were twelve that had gone on to the afterlife.

The Alliance Air Force had achieved a tactical, but not strategic, advantage. They had not been able to repeat the Israeli success of the Six-Day War. The IAF had been dealt a serious, but not fatal blow. They would live to fight another day.

The concern over the loss of the air bases and aircraft was alleviated by the fact that the majority of the pilots had survived. Most had been granted leave to celebrate the Temple dedication and had been with their families. They were beginning to make their way to their bases with the realization their nation's life was at stake. Israel's air assets were now under extreme pressure. Command of the air had been the decisive element in the '67 and '73 wars. Goldman wondered whether they would be able to repeat that success.

Islamic Alliance Headquarters

5:00 p.m.

The situation on the ground was providing the same frustrating results as the air campaign. Seven armored and six infantry divisions from

Syria had crossed into northern Israel and were now flanking the Golan Heights in a pincer move. From the north, two armored and one mechanized infantry divisions were entering Israel via Lebanon down the coast road toward Nahayria. One armored division was making for Hatzor. Two infantry divisions were moving to occupy the ridge in the Golan Heights overlooking Israel. Artillery units were taking position to provide fire support for the invasion. The remainder of the divisions, of which three were armored and equipped with EU-made Leclerc tanks, were advancing toward El Al south of the Golan Heights near the Syrian/Israeli/Jordanian border. If a breakthrough could be made in this area, they would be able to enter Galilee and link up with the force coming in from Lebanon.

However, the latter divisions were encountering resistance from an armored brigade which intelligence had not reported to be there the day before. It was subsequently identified as the 14th Armored, which was last reported as not up to full strength. Nonetheless, the blunting of the initial thrust by the Israeli armored unit suggested otherwise.

South of Lake Tiberias, formerly known as the Sea of Galilee, around Tawfiq, a Jordanian armored and infantry brigade were moving to seal off the Golan Heights and block Israeli reinforcements coming to the aid of the 14th Armored Brigade.

On the southern front along the Israeli/Sinai border, two Israeli armored brigades were acting as a brake on the advances of Egyptian forces in that sector. These Israeli forces were being overcome, though with casualties unanticipated by the Alliance and a corresponding delay in the advance. Again, the Israelis were where they should not have been.

The same frustrations were repeated in the air assault. But it was here that Jallud's forces should have enjoyed greater success. The initial air strikes against the IDF command and control facilities were successful. The IAF airfields were attacked resulting in over one hundred seventy-five planes destroyed on the ground in addition to several of the airfields destroyed or heavily damaged. That in itself was a remarkable achievement. But, the IAF had managed to put five squadrons of planes in the air just as the battle began. One of these squadrons was equipped with the Raptor. The casualties inflicted by the planes of these squadrons, in particular the Raptors, were all out of proportion to their numbers. The Alliance had started the war with over eleven hundred planes available for combat. But by the end of the second day, two hundred eighty-five Alliance planes would be downed by the IAF; one hundred and six by the Raptors alone. This rate of loss could not be sustained by the Alliance and Jallud knew this. At least not without reinforcements.

And this was where the strategic goal had not been accomplished. Expediency had been implemented in forfeit of the strategic goal. Most of the available aircraft were deployed, as it was easier to ready them for the attack. However, it had been impossible to deploy every division in the first wave. Either Israeli intelligence or American satellites would have detected that level of activity.

For that reason, it had been decided to employ what the Russians called a cold start attack. Basically, it meant those units that were in position would launch the attack with the expectation the defender would be caught unprepared. It was felt the impact of such a strike would deliver an overwhelming blow to the Israelis, rendering them unable to respond and allowing the Alliance time to complete their mobilization. This was what Jallud had counted on and was what his Russian and German advisors had promised him would lead to success. However, the strategy had failed to achieve the desired results. Jallud knew his forces were now in for a fight.

It was no secret that the Alliance had units near Israeli borders. Under normal circumstances the border areas had been some of the most heavily manned in history. After the raid on Esfahan, these forces had been increased even further. Under the terms of the Accord these were to be gradually withdrawn but they had not yet been. Fortunately, the Israelis had allowed leave for the majority of their armed forces to celebrate the Temple dedication. Units were supposed to be manned with only skeleton crews. Jallud knew the Alliance would not have been able to launch the attack if this had not been the case. The imbalance of forces favored the Alliance; at least on paper. But yet the Israelis had again been ready for war. Not all of their forces were mobilized, but enough were there to blunt the initial attack. How?

WHITE HOUSE SITUATION ROOM

January 10th

7:00 a.m.

"Mr. President, Israel is starting this war with practically nothing in their favor," reported General Don Peterson, Chairman of the Joint Chiefs of Staff. "Satellite recon shows Alliance forces have made significant incursions into Israeli territory as evidenced on the map. The bad news is that not all Alliance forces have been deployed yet. Taking a page from the Russian playbook, they employed a cold start strategy. In other words, only those forces immediately deployable were utilized in the attack. This amounted to half of their armored forces. However, they were able to deploy almost all of their aircraft as reported by *George Washington*. The Alliance was most efficient in their opening attacks. From what we have been able to ascertain, all command and control facilities were destroyed, save Amir. Their civilian government has ceased to exist. Of the twelve air bases four have been destroyed while the remainder took significant damage. We are unable to determine the number of aircraft lost. Israeli forces are counterattacking but in isolated pockets based on reports."

"General, what is the order of battle for Israel compared to the Alliance?" asked Sullivan.

"Mr. President," the Chairman began, as he turned to a different page in his briefing papers. "If you will turn your attention to page six, current orders of battle for Israeli and Alliance forces are presented there. In summary, Alliance tanks number 9,210 where Israel deploys 3,930. In the air, Alliance forces have 1,490 planes compared to 485 Israeli. Numbers for the Alliance include EU forces deployed to the region."

Peterson continued his briefing for those present regarding the status of U.S. forces available for deployment in addition to updates from the battlefield in the Middle East. Already the world's economy was reacting to the news of the attack on the Saudi oil refineries. The initial reports indicated production capacity would be curtailed for at least six weeks under optimal conditions. All bets were off for repair if hostilities continued. It was conservatively estimated that the price of oil was going to increase at least three fold.

Sullivan was now faced with the double prospect of a military and economic war. He was confident about winning one; the other was in doubt.

As the General was fielding questions from those gathered, the President's phone signaled. "Mr. President, Mr. Gerhard for you," said Jeannette Brown. The Chairman dismissed his assistant and moved to his seat at the conference table.

"Thank you, Jeanette. Patch him through," Sullivan said as he waited for the call to be transferred to his phone. He was furious at Gerhard. He had contacted Gerhard immediately upon learning of the initial attacks. That was four hours ago.

"Good morning, President Sullivan," began Gerhard. "I am so glad you called. There is much we have to discuss. I apologize for the delay in returning your call. In case you were not aware, events in the Middle East have demanded my immediate attention. You are fortunate to not have to deal with this matter. I am afraid there has been a terrible betrayal of the Accord by Israel. I must admit, I myself am at a loss as to this misunderstanding."

Betrayal? Misunderstanding? Sullivan could hardly believe what he had just heard. Gerhard had completely ignored the attack on the *George Washington* and the loss of the *Stout*. Updated reports just handed to him by Clairmont were now placing fatalities at over eight hundred.

"President Gerhard, your forces were supposed to be there guaranteeing the peace. How can you explain what is happening not only there, but with the attack on our carrier, *George Washington?* Was the loss of one of her escorts also a misunderstanding?" Sullivan's voice was remarkably masking his true emotions. He continued to press his point with Gerhard. "That terrible misunderstanding, as you call it, has resulted in many Israeli and over eight hundred American casualties. From accounts I am receiving, your forces appear to have deliberately attacked our carrier. How you can characterize that as anything but a betrayal is beyond me. Or is that a misunderstanding *also?*"

"President Sullivan, our forces received information indicating they were the target of an attack from your carrier's air wing. Their actions, regrettably tragic, were purely an act of self-defense. This most unfortunate incident is a result of what I believe our generals call the fog of war. But that is not the important issue before us. Now that hostilities have occurred as a result of Israel's wanton destruction of the Temple Mount and willful violation of the Accord, surely you cannot expect the Islamic Alliance to just do nothing? As the one responsible for the Accord, I am ordering all non-European forces to be removed from the area. The presence of such forces will complicate my already difficult task of restoring the peace as evidenced by the mistaken attack on your carrier."

Gerhard continued as he ignored Sullivan's accusations. "I have declared the Mediterranean, Persian Gulf, and Red Sea closed to all foreign air and sea traffic. All non-European forces are required to leave within the next six hours. They will be given safe passage out of the area. We do not want to have any additional misunderstandings that could broaden the conflict. I assure you, Mr. President, I am taking the necessary steps to restore the peace. American presence will only further complicate the situation."

Sullivan had by now placed the call on speaker so that the others in the Situation Room could hear. The faces of his staff were pensive as they listened to the conversation. He had heard enough and now unloaded on Gerhard.

"Mr. President, with all due respect. What you have just told me is the greatest amount of bovine scatology that I have ever heard. Your forces were there to keep the peace. From the intelligence I have seen, they have done nothing to stop the attacks on Israel. In fact, it appears they are aiding in the assault. As to who started this mess? Well, that doesn't even deserve a response. My strong suggestion is for you to contact your commanders and have them enforce the Accord. If you cannot keep the peace, we can, and we will. I also want to assure you that no additional harm best occur to, as you have termed them, foreign forces. The consequences would be most unfortunate. Further, we will not have our right to free navigation of the seas or air dictated by anyone. I am not going to sit idly by and watch Israel be annihilated. *Do I make myself clear, Mr. President?*" Sullivan emphatically concluded.

"Mr. President, I would question the intelligence you have received in light of your country's past experience with Iraq. Nonetheless, you have made your intentions very clear, I am sorry to say. I had hoped for greater responsibility and foresight on your part, Mr. President. It is unfortunate you have chosen to respond this way. From your tenor it is apparent our conversation is concluded. Good day to you."

Sullivan sat stunned for a moment as the line went dead. He picked up the phone and slammed it down to its cradle. The force of the impact cracked the unit. At this point he did not care. He looked at those seated around the table. Their frustration with the prior conversation showed. They were also shocked, but pleased, at Sullivan's response. He was known to be a passionate man on issues he cared about, but he had never displayed his emotions so forcefully. But then, he had never talked to such a deceitful person. No one moved for a few moments as they collected their thoughts. Only the hum of the luminescent lights overhead could be heard.

"Mr. President," it was Clairmont who spoke first breaking the tension that hung in the Situation Room. "Sir, if I may?"

"Go ahead, Mr. Secretary," Sullivan said gruffly.

"Mr. President, that was a declaration of war against not only the United States, but against Israel. He has left us little room in our response." The others nodded their heads in agreement.

"James, you're right. The United States has been on the sidelines long enough in this state of affairs. We are about to play hardball. I hope Gerhard is familiar with basketball, because we are going to put on what is known as the full court press. Israel is going to receive everything we can help her with. At the same time, we will neutralize the EU's ability to interfere with the war. We are going to keep this thing conventional unless Gerhard wants to escalate it, and I do not believe he does. Does anyone have a different slant? I need to hear it now if you do before we go forward with this."

There was a general round of agreement from everyone that the course of action was correct. The only suggestion, and this came from of all people, Secretary Stanfield, was to call for an immediate ceasefire and for all sides to return to their respective borders. As she noted, it would be an attempt to play the diplomatic card to disarm the doves in Congress. Sullivan agreed this should be incorporated into the response.

"Tom, call the House and Senate leadership. I want both parties in on this one. This is one case where politics best stop at the border and remain there. I don't want to see even one toe from either party in the Atlantic. I want to address Congress and the country ASAP."

"I'll get our best folks started on the speech," Tom said as he was hurriedly writing down the President's orders.

"Let's see if we can get the networks on message. I know they are clamoring for an interview on this. Get what's his name from NBC as part of an exclusive interview panel. Let's see if we can get him on our side for a change. And no leaks unless I authorize them. I don't want to see what we're doing in the *Times* before we do it. I don't want a hatchet job on Israel from our press either."

"Yes, Mr. President. He will be an excellent choice," Tom said making his notes.

"Madame Secretary, release a press statement calling for a ceasefire in two hours. Mr. Secretary," Sullivan said to Clairmont, "authorize DEFCON-1. Let's get our people moving!"

BATTLEZONE

USS SHANKSVILLE
ATLANTIC OCEAN
January 10th
11:33 a.m.

The *Shanksville* Expeditionary Strike Group (SEGS) was steaming one hundred miles west of the Azores Islands. Located one thousand miles west of Portugal these islands are strategically located in the Atlantic Ocean. Due to their location they have served as the central refueling center for American military aircraft deploying to the Mediterranean and Middle East theaters of combat.

It was access to Lajes Field on the island of Terceira that had proved the difference in the 1973 Yom Kippur War. American C-5 and C-141 transports were able to refuel at this base en route to resupplying Israel. The Israelis urgently needed the tanks and equipment they carried. So urgent was the need, that as the tanks were unloaded, they were driven straight to the battlefield. With the collapse of NATO, the availability of this base was in question. Would the EU allow use of the base in the event of future hostilities in the Middle East? Potentially, the only base available to American aircraft for refueling was now Gibraltar, but access to it was also subject to EU approval. With hostilities occurring between EU and American forces, there was no doubt access to either of these bases would come only one way.

"Admiral, we have flash traffic from Commander Fleet Forces Command," reported XO Alan Bowden.

"Let's have it," ordered Admiral David Yi.

"Sir, EU and Alliance forces have launched a surprise attack on Israel.

Initial reports indicate heavy Israeli air loses. *George Washington* reports she has come under attack from EU and Alliance forces in the Med. She is heavily damaged. Her runway is out. *Stout* was lost. *Enterprise* has come under attack as well. Second Fleet has been ordered to the Med. SEGS is ordered to secure Lajes Field on Terceira by 1600 hours Thursday and make ready for air operations. Establish and maintain air and naval superiority in and around Azores. DEFCON-1 is authorized. Looks like we are at war, sir," Bowden concluded as he handed Yi the message.

Disbelief was on the face of every man on the bridge of the *Shanksville*. The impact of the message regarding the *GW* and *Stout* stunned the men on the bridge. Each knew it took a lot of damage to disable a *Nimitz* class carrier. The only sound present for a moment was the hum from the ship's engines. Yi took the message from his XO and read it again. It was inconceivable what he had just been told.

"So we are," he said. Yi did not hesitate on his next actions. "Acknowledge message to CFFC. Assemble the department heads at 1200 hours. Change course for Terceira. Increase speed to twenty-five knots. So much for peace in the Mideast."

2ND FLEET HEADQUARTERS

REAGAN CARRIER STRIKE GROUP

NORFOLK, VIRGINIA

10:30 a.m.

The four *Nimitz* class carriers were tied up to their berthing piers along with their attendant escorts. Their steel grey hulls were silhouetted against the grey morning sky as a light rain began to fall. Sailors would have proudly called such a line up 'Murderers Row' during World War Two. The air wings assigned to these carriers boasted over three hundred seventy-five combat aircraft. The planes would join the carriers once they were deployed at sea. The remainder of the crews were making their way up the gangplanks in preparation for departure, as last-minute provisions were being loaded. Lines were being cast to the tugboats that were waiting to guide the massive carriers and their escorts to the Atlantic Ocean in preparation for their deployment.

Within three hours, forty thousand men and women, thirty-four ships and submarines of the *Reagan* CSG were transiting to the Atlantic and from there to the Mediterranean.

Park had chosen the location for its obviousness. The streets of the business sector of Pyongyang were filled with office workers hurriedly making their way back to work after lunch. Very few cast a glance, much less a second look, at the window table of the upscale restaurant. It was not uncommon for the workers to see the elite members of the government frequenting such establishments. However, what was uncommon were the members of the lunch party who were dining together.

"War is imminent due to this foolishness," noted Shin Jong Pil. "The American response is understandable. They have been very sensitive to even the slightest threat to their homeland since September 11, much as we would be."

"See Park, there are many who feel as we do in the military. They know this course is suicide," Lee Koo said attempting to encourage Park.

"How far are they willing to sacrifice?" asked Park, still unsure of this meeting. "Will they lay down their lives for this cause? The American carriers and stealth aircraft are deploying; no doubt as the vanguard of a first strike. The South is mobilizing, as are we. We must ask under what circumstances would we find ourselves if our missile had not detonated in the Pacific. What if their defense could not intercept our missile?"

"The same circumstances we do now. We must end this foolish pursuit of nuclear weapons. It is a dagger we hold on our own throat," Pil remarked in a voice barely above a whisper.

"The Leader will never agree to that. He is bent on increasing the inventory and further pursuing this course," Koo reminded those at the table.

"Then there must be a change," Park said in a hushed voice. He lifted his cup of tea to his lips and took a sip as his eyes searched those at the table. Adrenaline surged through his body at the realization of his statement.

The table fell silent as each man contemplated what had just been vocalized. The others had been thinking this but were afraid to voice their fears. Trust was something that did not come easily in North Korea. It was possible one of the occupants of the table was a spy who had infiltrated their ranks. The only reason Park spoke was that he knew his life was going to end after the next meeting of the People's government. Each man nodded his head in silent agreement. The conversation quickly accelerated now that each man's thoughts were known.

"How much support can be relied upon?" Park asked.

"Eight in the Cabinet and four on the General Staff. But two are key. Security and logistics," advised Pil.

"Who will lead?" Park asked somewhat hesitantly.

"It has to be you. You are trusted," Pil whispered.

Park had considered this a possibility. He was hoping it would not be him. He had no desire for leadership, but he understood that without him this opportunity might pass.

"Very well," Park acquiesced. "Begin to make the necessary arrangements. We must move swiftly before the situation deteriorates further."

The men at the table nodded in agreement and proceeded to finish their meal.

USS SHANKSVILLE

3:01 p.m.

Colonel Eric "Buzz" Waterson was in his quarters finishing the details for his Marines' assault on Lajes. He slipped off his reading glasses and rubbed his eyes. There were two things he hated in the world: paperwork and doctors. As a career Marine he had learned to deal with both. He now had even more reasons to dislike doctors. He had just turned forty before the deployment and the mandatory eye exam revealed the change in his vision. He hated getting old. More importantly, he hated wearing glasses in front of his men. Never mind that he could out bench press any man on board as that new Marine sergeant found out on the night of his birthday celebration. To him the glasses conveyed a sign of weakness. Too much ribbing the 'Old Man' had led him to challenge anyone to prove otherwise.

The crew, or as much of it that could, had gathered in the hanger deck of the *Shanksville* to wish him a belated surprise Happy Birthday after their deployment. After blowing out the candles on the cake, Admiral Yi led the men in singing Happy Birthday to the 'Old Man.' When the singing was concluded Waterson took the mike to address the men. He remembered his words. "I may be forty, but I guarantee I can whip anybody's tail on the bench," he boasted to the cheers and catcalls of the crew. With a ship full of young testosterone-laden men someone was bound to take him up on the offer. Those that knew Waterson laughed at the young sergeant who had raised his hand in acceptance of the challenge. What the sergeant did not know was that Waterson had made the same boast on his birthday for the past five years and had won each time.

The young sergeant was George Alton Ivey. He was fresh out of East Wheeling High School in Lansing, Michigan, when he joined the Marine Corps four years ago. He had been the starting linebacker and quarterback on the football team and led the Beavers to their first state title. With such athletic skills he could have attended any Big Ten school on a football scholarship. But Ivey had lost his oldest brother in the 9/11 attacks on the World Trade Center while he was in the 7th grade. The loss of his brother impacted him severely. His brother had served in the Marines and then later became the first in his family to graduate from college. In doing so, he had become young Alton's role mode. And that role model had been forcibly taken away on that fateful day.

One of his brother's favorite sayings was "not in my backyard." It was a sports analogy meaning that the opposing team didn't stand a chance of winning when playing at your home field or gym. And now, terrorists had come into his backyard and had won a victory. Young Alton promised himself he would do something about that. That promise led him to focus on the future. While other classmates were out goofing around town, he would remain home and do two things: study and work out. So when he joined the Marine Corps he was already in peak physical and mental condition. His hard work and focus quickly led to him being promoted to sergeant. Never one to back down from a challenge, Sergeant Alton Ivey had won the strong man contest in his squad and in doing so a healthy respect from his men. Now he was to challenge the Commander of the MEU.

The contest began with both men easily lifting one hundred fifty pounds. To find out who the real man was, the weight on each successive round was increased by fifty pounds. At four hundred fifty pounds, Ivey could not move the bar off of his chest. Two fellow Marines helped him lift the weights back to the rack as the crew howled in disappointment at Ivey's inability to best the Old Man.

But the contest was not over yet. Waterson would have to lift the weight in order to win. As he sat on the bench he sprinkled some talc powder on his sweating hands. The humidity in the hangar was not helping the situation. He reclined on the bench, placed his hands on the bar and closed his eyes. He began to breath deeply and then, with the force of a five-inch gun being fired, he lifted the bar off the rack. Holding it for a second to steady his balance, he lowered the bar to his chest and began to raise it to the cheers of the crew until his arms were locked. He then lowered the weight again and raised it one more time before returning it to the rack.

He stood up, turned to Ivey, and said with a grin, "Not bad for an Old Man, eh, Sergeant?" The crew erupted in applause for the Old Man who had again lived up to his reputation in the eyes of another group of Marines. He and Ivey shook hands before the humbled Marine returned to his seat. As Waterson watched Ivey return to his seat he knew he had a squad leader he could rely on.

USS TEXAS

BAY OF BISCAY

EASTERN ATLANTIC

3:12 p.m.

The *Texas*, second unit of the *Virginia* class attack submarine, was patrolling forty miles off the western coast of the EU province of France. She had been alerted to monitor the transit of any of the EU's SSBNs should they decide to leave their base at Île Longue off the Brittany coast of France. The patrol had not produced any contacts so far.

"Reckon they are sitting this one out, Captain?" asked the XO, Sam Petrovski.

"Don't know, Sam. I sure hope they are. The deployment of their boomers would not be a positive sign," replied Captain Dan Kominski as he took a drink of coffee.

"I remember Ivan used to do this when tensions heated up during the Cold War. Now the Chinese have adopted the tactic," Petrovski said referring to increasing reports of Chinese boomers taking station off the east coast of Taiwan.

"Yeah. Ain't it great how much we can learn from each other. Nothing like sixteen nuclear-armed missiles parked off your doorstep. Heck of a way to send a message," noted Kominski.

"Well, when you only want to send the best," Petrovski wryly noted.

"Conn, sonar. Think we have something, Captain."

"On my way, Chief. Sam, you have the conn," Kominski ordered as he made his way toward the sonar room.

Kominski quickly made his way to the sonar room. When he arrived he saw the operators staring at the main display and pressing their headsets to their ears in an effort to better hear. The sonar room was one of the quietest places on board the *Texas*, but even the slightest bit of noise could cause an operator to misread the signals he was hearing. Green tracks were arcing down the video monitor as the *Texas*'s external sensors relayed information to the sonar room. He did not have to ask what was happening. He knew his men would tell him when they were ready.

"That's who it is, Chief. Bet my next check on it," noted Sonar Specialist Eric Jenkins as he adjusted a dial on the sensor panel.

"Very good, son. I agree. Besides, I would hate to take your money again," Chief Petty Officer Lemont Jones fired back. He slipped off his headset and stepped over to the Captain.

"Sir, we have an outbound boomer from their pen at Île Longue. Screws indicate it's *Le Vigilant*. Her course is currently two-zero-zero and speed is twenty knots. Going somewhere in a hurry."

"She could be transiting to take up launch position," Kominski noted as he placed his hand on his chin pondering out loud.

"Yes, sir. The Bay is a nice safe place for her. Lots of potential cover if needed and it puts the whole Mideast in range. So far, though, no sign of escorts," the Chief observed.

"They are out there somewhere, Chief. Keep your ears clean. We don't want to be taken by surprise. Good pickup on the boomer. Keep me posted," Kominski ordered as he returned to the conn.

"Aye, Captain," Jones said. He turned back to his men. "Alright, you heard the Captain. If you ain't listening you're swimming home." The men quickly returned to their duties.

USS Shanksville

4:45 p.m.

Yi was conducting the briefing for his officers. He did not have to emphasize the importance of this mission.

"As you can see from the map, Lajes Field is located on the northeast side of the island. The runways are capable of handling the largest air-craft in the U.S. inventory including the B-1 and B-52 bombers. Latest intelligence reports that EU forces are deploying their Mediterranean fleet to shut the Straits of Gibraltar. In addition, EU is deploying air assets to Spain and Portugal to reinforce the block. *GW* and *Wasp* are the only assets we currently have deployed in the Med. As you have seen from the intel reports, *GW* is out of action for now. We are surging *Reagan* CSG to reinforce *GW* and assist in defending Israel. Colonel Waterson will now brief us on the amphibious part of the operation. Colonel," Yi said as he turned the meeting over to Waterson.

Waterson rose from his seat and began to cover the amphibious aspects of what was now known as OPERATION STRADDLE. Marine Harrier VTOL aircraft from the *Shanksville* would establish local air superiority. Amphibious forces would then be launched in a two-pronged assault. The initial assault would be vertical. Marines would be airlifted to a position one mile from the airfield by the twenty CH-46 Sea Knight and CH-53 Sea Stallion helicopters aboard *Shanksville*. From there, they would move to secure the airfield. They would be supported with close-in fire from six AH-1W Super Cobra attack helicopters. The horizontal assault would be delivered by the forty AAV-P7A1 amphibious assault craft carried in the cavernous landing bay of the *Shanksville*. If all went according to plan, seventeen hundred Marines would be ashore and in control of the airfield in less than two hours. Enemy forces would be neutralized and a defensive perimeter established in preparation for reinforcements from CONUS. He returned to his seat as Yi stood to conclude the meeting.

"H-hour is at 1930 hours. Any questions?" he asked as he looked at his officers. The expression on their faces told him there were none. "Gentlemen, control of the Azores and establishment of air superiority is going to be crucial to our success in this war. Lajes will be the base we deploy assets from to break through into the Med. Lajes is going to become a very important piece of real estate. Good luck to us all and Godspeed."

The debate was intense between the Conservative, Labour, and Europe First Parties. The members had been discussing England's role in the Union since the attack on the Temple Mount. In fact, England's role in the EU was an on-going debate that had never really ended after Parliament narrowly voted to join the EU. The young war in the Middle East was only furthering that debate.

"Was this what we agreed to when we joined the bloody Union? Treachery? Deceit? Lies? *And now murder?*" Sean McGregor, leader of the Conservative Party asked as members of his party echoed their vociferous support.

The last question was in reference to the recent discovery of the slain body of Malcolm Cunningham in a Paris hotel. He had disappeared after the Council voted to sever ties with the United States. His body had been found in a compromising position with a prostitute, also murdered, further incensing the Conservative Leader. He had received a call from Cunningham after the vote was taken on Operation Rosh. He could tell Cunningham was concerned about the meeting but wanted to meet in person to discuss it upon his return to London. McGregor recalled he had pressed him for details, but Cunningham would not discuss it on the phone. All he would say was that it was of the utmost importance. Unfortunately, he never returned.

An investigation into his whereabouts had proved futile until the shocking details of his untimely death appeared in the media. When the story broke, McGregor immediately suspected foul play but was unable to offer any evidence to support his departed friend.

The media had had a field day with the story, plastering the photos of the stricken Cunningham on the front page. He held up a copy of the headlines in *Le Monde* and *The Guardian* as a reminder to those in the room. His party jeered at the headline: "Conservative: Not So."

"The very words make me sick to my stomach. To think that our colleague was murdered. And now his reputation is being smeared across the continent in this most distasteful fashion. I knew him. You knew him. You know he led his life above reproach. Each of us knows he would never stoop to this kind of debauchery as have some in this room."

That statement drew another chorus of yeas from his party's members. Even some members of the Labour party echoed their agreement. The Europe First members merely sat with their arms folded. Their coalition with Labour was hanging in the balance. But there was little they could do to stop the combative Conservative. It was clear McGregor was in command of the room and was pressing his advantage. Worse, Labour members were listening and beginning to agree with him.

"Look 'round this room," McGregor continued. His Scottish accent becoming more pronounced as the tempo and tenor of his speech increased. "Each of you. Need I remind you that at one time we found ourselves as Israel is today. Attacked and alone. Until, as Mr. Churchill called her, the Great Republic joined us in our crusade against Hitlerism. And now, we learn that EU forces have conspired to launch an unprovoked attack on an aircraft carrier of the Great Republic as she was steaming off the coast of Israel. And some in this body say we do nothing. That we ought not lift a hand to right this wrong. I say the ghost of Chamberlain still walks amongst this body. We have talked enough. I call for a vote. Do you stand with England or the Union?"

USS Shanksville

7:30 p.m.

The flight deck of the *Shanksville* was filled to capacity with the first wave of CH-46 Sea Knight and CH-53 Sea Stallion helicopters. Marines laden with their backpacks were struggling to embark in preparation for takeoff and assault on the island. The whirling blades of the choppers were whipping the rain from the squall. When it hit a man's face it felt like small ice picks digging into the skin. Spray from the waves crashing over the deck only added to the misery of those on the flight deck.

Colonel Waterson was preparing to board his helicopter when he noticed a seaman running in his direction. The whir of the helicopter's engines, coupled with the wind, was creating an almost unbearable noise.

"Colonel, Admiral needs to see you on the bridge ASAP," shouted the seaman as he struggled to make himself heard above the storm and helicopters.

"What the devil for?" exclaimed Waterson.

"Don't know, sir. Admiral just said he needs to see you ASAP."

Waterson followed the seaman back to the island and made his way to the bridge from there.

"Admiral, what's the problem?" he asked as he entered the bridge. Water began to puddle at his feet as it dripped off his poncho.

"Colonel, something you need to see. We have a problem at Lajes." He was holding several pictures, which he gave to Waterson. They were satellite photos of the island and close-ups of the airfield.

"We just received these a few minutes ago," Yi noted. "As you can see there are twelve Tornado fighter bombers plus three transports. Three of the planes were caught taking off as they were on the runway. This photo," as he handed it to Waterson, "shows a company of men taking up positions around the airfield. Looks like they brought portable SAMs also. SIGINT indicates more are headed this way, but we have caught a break due to the weather. Right now this weather front is between Lajes and Europe. Our weather folks say it is expected to increase to a strong gale in the next two hours. Nothing is expected to be flying in or out of Europe for the next 48 hours."

"Reinforcing the island," observed Waterson.

"Looks like they figured this would be a strategic chokehold," concurred Yi. "The weather is buying us some time."

"The Tornadoes will make it difficult for my Harriers and choppers if they are flying," Waterson said as he studied the pictures. "Looks like we're going to have to change our approach and come in from the west side of the island in light of these developments. So much for the easy mission."

"Sorry a wrench got thrown in the works, Colonel," said Yi. "If we had our Aegis cruiser I would push us closer. Right now we have the element of surprise on our side. No one expects an attack in this weather; plus they don't know we're out here. You have thirty-six hours to secure the island."

"Thirty-six hours? Ok. We've done more in less. I need to inform my pilots. Wish us luck, Admiral," Waterson said as he saluted.

"Semper Fi, Colonel," Yi said as Waterson began his way back to the flight deck. There, he boarded his Sea Stallion helicopter that had been outfitted as a flying command post. He reviewed his map to verify the new insertion coordinates.

He lifted the command phone and signaled the rest of the pilots of the change. "Ok, let's go," he said to his pilot as he returned the phone to its stored position. "Take us in nice and low. We don't want to wake up the neighborhood."

From the bridge, Admiral Yi watched as the first Sea King slowly rolled forward, and then lifted from the pitching deck disappearing into the night. The remaining helicopters followed. In twenty minutes the deck was cleared. The only sound heard on the flight deck was the wind and rain lashing the *Shanksville*. With the change in weather it was decided the assault craft would not be deployed. The main assault would now be conducted by the helicopters.

They were skimming about fifty feet above the ocean as they approached Lajes. The ride in was a rough one as promised. The helicopter was encountering severe turbulence that buffeted the machine. Several of the men in his helicopter were suffering the effects of airsickness. Through his night vision goggles Waterson could see the island looming closer. His pilot was approaching from the northwest. The plan was to touch down three miles from the airfield. The power generation station was located on the route they would take to the airfield. His men would secure the power station and knock out power to the search radar.

From what he could see, there was no activity in the landing zone. He picked up his command phone, "Raider One to Raiders. LZ is clear. Look sharp!" Waterson gave the thumbs up to his pilot as he made his approach. The pilot set the Sea Stallion down in a grassy field and kept the rotors turning. Waterson and his men quickly exited the helicopter and formed a defensive perimeter. Waterson looked to the northwest. Through his night vision goggles he could see the other helicopters beginning to make their approach. One by one the Sea Stallions and Sea Knights landed in the LZ depositing more of the assault force to the island. Within fifteen minutes, two hundred Marines were on the ground and preparing to move to the primary objective. The rain and wind had increased in intensity.

Waterson spoke into his portable command phone. "All squad leaders. Execute plan Alpha-Zeta."

This called for the force to split into two groups. The plan was to approach the airfield in a pincer move creating the illusion the assaulting force was larger than it actually was. The primary objective was to secure the airfield in operational condition. The second group, Raider Two, began to move out as did his group. Waterson radioed the *Shanksville* to confirm their landing. "Raider One to, Umpire, Raider One to, Umpire. Raiders have kicked off."

"Confirmed, Raider One. Defense in a three twelve prevent. Repeat, defense in a three twelve prevent. Umpire out."

The reply from the *Shanksville* indicated their presence had not been detected for the moment. But he was not confident that would last. The three twelve defense prevent notation meant that three of the twelve Tornados were still airborne. They were most likely on an AEW mission but one could not discount the possibility they would discover the *Shanksville* and her group. The prevent part meant that the EU troops previously seen disembarking had taken up defensive positions around the airfield. They were not expanding their defensive perimeter beyond that strategic target for the moment. At least Waterman's force had not been detected—yet. The noise from the helicopters was somewhat masked by the howling winds, but the distinctive sound of helicopter blades beating the air could not have been lost on the homes the pilots had flown over on the egress path. And those homes had phones.

He could not worry about that now. He directed his mind to the mission at hand as his forces began to move out.

London, England

8:32 p.m.

The vote was close but a majority chose England. Enough Labour votes switched their support to the Conservatives at the last minute giving McGregor the victory he had been seeking. The Europe First members fumed at the betrayal by their Labour allies, but there was precious little they could do to stop the unfolding dilemma. The Queen was immediately informed. She asked that a coalition government be formed and a Prime Minister elected by Parliament. The Conservative Leader was pleased to announce to the Queen that such a vote had already occurred and that he, Sir Sean McGregor, had been elected to fill the post.

McGregor moved swiftly in his first few minutes as Prime Minister. He first announced that England was withdrawing support and membership from the European Union and was willing to uphold its former obligations under NATO. Next, he issued a stinging indictment of Gerhard. The repercussions of this startling change in England's political landscape had a profound impact across the continent. Within the hour, secret contacts from Estonia, Latvia, Lithuania, Poland, The Czech Republic, and Malta all signaled their willingness to withdraw from the Union if England led.

8:34 p.m.

The six-wheeled Fuchs recon truck was negotiating the rain swept road along the northwest coast of Terceira. They had been detailed to reconnoiter the island. As they were rounding the curve they saw what appeared to be the blades of a helicopter as the lightning flashed. The driver stopped the vehicle and said to his partner, "Did you see what I think I did?"

"Yes, I think so. Wait here and let's be sure."

They waited for five minutes. "Looks like we must have been seeing things," the driver said as he pressed the gas pedal. The truck was pulling forward when another helicopter roared across the road fifty feet in front of them. The bold white letters were unmistakable: U.S. Marines. The driver slammed on the brakes causing the vehicle to skid before coming to a halt. He reached for the radio. "Base from Recon One. Reporting visual confirmation of helicopters leaving the island. American Marines are here."

The wind and rain were coming down harder now, slowing the Marines' progress. It had taken Waterson and his men longer to cover the final two miles than planned as a result. The earpiece in his head-set crackled with static, "Raider One, this is Umpire. Game has been called on account of weather. Repeat, game has been called on account of weather. Umpire out."

He knew the weather was deteriorating on the island. But what Waterson did not know was that the *Shanksville* was now enshrouded by gale force winds and rain. Since their departure the weather had deteriorated to a nine on the Beaufort Scale, meaning the *Shanksville* and all aboard were taking a pounding from the weather. She was being buffeted by winds of forty-six mph and waves approaching thirty-two feet. The helicopters had barely been able to return to the *Shanksville*. One returning chopper had crashed on the flight deck as the *Shanksville* was tossed about by the violent weather.

The chance of launching any additional reinforcements was impossible for now. Whatever chances the mission had now rested upon Waterson and his men. "Umpire, this is Raider One. Confirmed," he replied. "Raider Two, game called on account of weather. Game is up to us. Repeat, game is up to us."

"Raider One, this is Raider Two. Confirm game status. We have secured the power station. Ready to turn the lights out on the party."

"Confirm Two, One out." At least there was some good news Waterson noted.

Waterson had split Raider One into two groups. If all could be coordinated with Raider Two, the airfield would be assaulted from three axes of attack. His men had finally crested the mountain overlooking Lajes. The mortar squad was taking up position to provide fire support for the main assault. With the power relay station in their control it would soon be time to turn out the lights.

From his vantage point, Waterson had an unobstructed view of Lajes. The runway was bathed in an eerie incandescent light. Lights were on in the control tower and some of the hangers. Off to the right, not more than a mile away, lay the town of Praia Da Vitoria. All appeared tranquil in the island's largest town. The citizens were apparently unaware of the pending battle. Through his binoculars he could see a few lights on. No doubt the late night party crowd of tourists. Terceira boasted a thriving tourist business. They were going to be in for a surprise if they were not too drunk to react to the sounds of battle. He was positive their travel agent had not promised them ringside seats to a battle zone.

Ivey tapped him on the shoulder and leaned in close to his ear to make himself heard over the winds. "Take a look, Colonel. Three birds on the ground and the rest in hangers." Waterson switched his view back to the airfield. Ivey was right. Three Tornadoes were on the runway. The tie downs on the planes were the only things keeping them from blowing away. Why they had not rolled them into the hangers was beyond him. That was good. At least they were no longer airborne. Even the all-weather capability of the Tornado had to respect the fearsome power of Mother Nature.

"Where do you think their men are, Sergeant?" Waterson inquired to Ivey.

Ivey thought for a moment. "If I were them, sir, I would be behind and between the hangers. Dark over there and gives them a good place to hide."

"I agree. Pass the word, Sergeant. We are doing Flanker One. Let's move'em out."

"Raider One to, Raiders. Snap the ball. Repeat, snap the ball. Execute Flanker One," Ivey ordered to the men. Next he signaled Raider Two. "Raider two, cut power now."

Lajes was plunged into instant darkness, as was the local town, when Waterson's men cut the power. The light from the incandescent lights was now replaced by the green of their night vision goggles.

Waterson and his men began to move from their positions. They were sloshing their way through ankle deep water as they approached the level grounds of the airfield. They were perhaps three hundred yards from the airfield when the first mortar rounds began to explode around them throwing up dirt and water.

"Incoming! Take cover!" Waterson ordered as he flung himself to the saturated ground seeking the cover of terra firma. Over his headset he could hear cries for medics as four of his men were injured by the EU mortar rounds. The benefit of surprise had been forfeited. The EU forces had somehow detected their arrival on the island. Perhaps one of the Tornadoes had discovered the *Shanksville* and her task force.

"Mortar squad, lay down covering fire," Waterson ordered.

Within seconds, he saw flashes of explosions as the outgoing rounds detonated at the suspected EU locations. The mortar rounds from the EU forces stopped for a moment. No doubt they were moving their location. Waterson was not going to be at his current location when they repositioned themselves.

"Raiders, let's go," he yelled into his mike as he lifted himself from the soggy ground. "Fire and cover!" One half of his men began laying down suppressing fire as the other half advanced. They continued this pattern until they were within one hundred yards of their objective. Using a small rise as protection, Waterson scanned the airfield with his binoculars and saw what he was looking for. The EU mortar team was situated behind a small storage building on the opposite side of the runway. Mortar rounds now began to detonate behind and to the left of Waterson and his men. Their aim was being impacted by the wind. Where was the spotter? Then it struck him. They were receiving their coordinates from the control tower. It was the obvious choice, as it was the only building providing a clear view of the area.

"Raider One to mortar teams. Enemy sited behind third building from the end of the runway." His men were the best and they were about to prove it once more. They had been deployed to Afghanistan during the hunt for bin Laden. The experience gained in the mountainous regions of Afghanistan with its swirling winds was now being realized.

The EU forces were failing to compensate for the wind. However, his men were making the adjustment. The first rounds landed wide, but the next barrage was on target. Waterson watched the explosions cover the EU position. When the smoke cleared he saw the slumped bodies.

"Ivey, we need to take that tower," Waterson said gesturing to the control tower. "That's where they're coordinating their attack from."

Ivey turned and pointed to seven of his men. "Up here, now." The men quickly gathered around him.

"We gotta take that tower to shut'em down. We're gonna blitz'em. Any questions?"

The men shook their heads. Their faces told the story. Seeing their fellow soldiers wounded in the earlier mortar attack had refocused their minds to eliminating their opposite numbers.

"Alright Marines, let's move out!" Ivey ordered.

OVAL OFFICE

8:15 p.m.

Sullivan was working the phones with key congressional leaders to ensure their continued support of the very young war. He had the television muted. The *Fox News Alert* icon flashed catching his attention. The scene dissolved to a picture of 10 Downing Street. A convoy of black cars was pulling into the scene. Sir Sean McGregor exited from one of them. The caption read: Newly-Elected Prime Minister of England.

"Ted, hang on one second," Sullivan said to the Senate Majority Leader as he turned the volume up.

Reporters were swarming around McGregor peppering him with questions.

"Sir McGregor, can you confirm you have formed a provisional government?" shouted the reporter from the *BBC*. "Are there are other countries willing to renounce their membership in the EU?"

"It is true that I have been elected Prime Minister and have formed a government at the Queen's request. The deceit and treachery that has been perpetrated by President Gerhard cannot be condoned by freedom-loving peoples. To this end, England is re-joining the North Atlantic Treaty Organization. In accordance with the by-laws of that treaty, we stand ready to aid the United States in this unprovoked act of war by the European Union."

"What about the other countries, Mr. Prime Minister? Who are they and do they stand with England? Are they rejoining NATO?" one of the reporters asked as he pressed for details.

"There have been some discussions with other members of the EU, but I am not prepared to comment any further at this point. Now, gentlemen, if you will excuse me. There is much to be done."

With those comments, the Prime Minister entered 10 Downing Street leaving a flabbergasted press corps to digest his comments.

"Ted, did you see McGregor's press conference?"

"Yes, Mr. President. Quite a turn of events I would say. Looks like Gerhard's dream of a united Europe is beginning to unravel."

"It may come undone even more when they realize the cost of their actions."

"Speaking of actions, Mr. President, how is the progress of releasing oil from the Strategic Petroleum Reserve? My constituents are flooding my office with complaints of price gauging. The price of gas is over eight dollars a gallon. In my hometown there are reports of fights breaking out among people waiting to fill up their cars."

"I signed authorization to release oil from the Reserve upon the outbreak of hostilities. It will be about two weeks before we see an impact in the market place. That should stabilize the market and keep those fights down. With the Saudi refineries down for at least three months we are going to have to husband our resources. Incidentally, the Saudis, Kuwaitis, and the Gulf States have secretly invited us to provide military assistance to protect against further aggression from the Iranians and who knows else who. They are making a limited number of airfields and ports available for our use."

"Yes we are, Mr. President. That is good news regarding the Saudis. Never should have asked us to leave in the first place. What did they say about our assisting Israel?"

"The King summed it up with one sentence. A man can have more than one friend."

"Implied meaning is that we can only use the bases to protect the Kingdom?" confirmed the Majority Leader.

"Something like that. Still, it is significant they are allowing us to use their bases at all. Ted, I've gotta run unless there is anything else," Sullivan said not wanting to cut the conversation short. Sometimes even members of one's own party would turn on you if they felt their ego had been bruised. Political infighting was the last thing Sullivan could afford at this point.

"Don't worry, Mr. President. I will keep the troops in line. You can count on the full support of the Senate and the House. I have been in touch with the Speaker and the House is on board."

"Thanks, Ted. Keep up the good work. Your shot at this seat is coming up one day. The people will remember your leadership during this time."

"Thank you, Mr. President. That means a lot. Let's hope that will be in seven years. Call me if I can help."

BERLIN

10:58 p.m.

Gerhard was also monitoring the progress of the war from his office in Berlin when he saw the special news bulletin on the television. Gerhard glared at the monitor that was tuned to EU-4. His attention became riveted to the screen when he saw McGregor standing in front of a group of reporters in front of 10 Downing Street. He knew what he was about to hear. The Majority Leader of the EU had informed him of the vote in Parliament. Still, he wanted to see the interview. Turning up the volume, Gerhard sat upright in his chair as he listened to the press conference.

"No! Traitors!" he exclaimed, startling his aides who came running into his office along with six security guards with weapons drawn, not sure what had caused the outburst from Gerhard. He moved to the front of his desk and began to pace while rubbing the back of his neck.

"Stupid Englanders. I knew they could not be relied upon. They have consistently attempted to undermine my attempts at unification of our great continent. And now they are leading others to their destruction." Under his breath he whispered wistfully, "If only we had finished them in nineteen forty."

His coffee cup was on his desk. With frustration mounting, he reached down and grabbed the cup as one would a baseball. In a fit of rage he hurled it against the far wall. The porcelain cup shattered upon impact spilling the contents of the cup. The brown liquid began to run down the wall and pooled on the floor.

His aides were unsure what to do. Rarely had they seen him display his anger in such a manner. Their leader's demeanor was usually one that resembled the eye of a storm. Now they were witnessing the storm that surrounded that eye. Gerhard caught himself. He walked back to his desk and stood behind it. Remaining standing, he closed his eyes and began to breath deeply. Clasping his hands together in front of him, he lifted his arms over his head while continuing the deep breathing. He continued to repeat this motion. His aides, unsure what to do, merely stood and watched. After five minutes of this, Gerhard's face began to relax, as did his entire body. Frustration was now channeled into positive thoughts. His mind began to focus once more on the immediate problem.

Opening his eyes he asked, "Status of their armed forces?"

"Sir, last reports showed their forces deployed as follows." His military aide placed a map on Gerhard's desk. The aide noted a British carrier task force, *Illustrious,* was off the coast of Portugal in route to Gibraltar. Two squadrons of Tornadoes were at Gibraltar and one was at Malta.

"We are detecting increased air activity along the Polish and Czech borders. Royal Air Force has also increased its activity. So far, no penetration of EU airspace at this time. Disposition of British nuclear forces unknown at this time."

"Intentions?"

"Sir, unknown at this time. All contact has been cut off. If they are serious about honoring the NATO agreement we will be unable to reinforce the Alliance. We may even be required to withdraw our forces from the Mideast."

"There will be no withdrawal! I will handle America and NATO," Gerhard said emphatically.

SUPREME PEOPLE'S ASSEMBLY MEETING
PYONGYANG, NORTH KOREA
January 11th
8:00 a.m.

Park arrived at the People's Great Hall via his chauffer-driven car. It was one of the perks he enjoyed as a member of the Leadership Council. A stern-faced guard wielding an AK-47 opened his door. Exiting the vehicle, he straightened his jacket and smoothed out any wrinkles before proceeding up the steps.

The irony of the name of the building was not lost on him. Though it was named for the people, none of North Korea's citizens, other than the powerful elite, would ever see the inside of the elaborate building. The presence of the security guards, at least a battalion strong and heavily armed, would ensure that only the invited would have access to the building.

He presented his credentials at the initial security checkpoint. Despite being a member of the Leadership Council, he still had to pass through security. Paranoia was rampant throughout the government due to the Leader's insecurity. Having satisfied the guards he was merely carrying documents for the meeting, he was allowed to enter the main section of the building.

Pictures of the Leader adorned the walls of the hall that led to the Cabinet Room where the members of the Supreme People's Assembly were meeting. The sound of his shoes on the marble floor was the only noise disturbing the hallway. Security guards were present every thirty feet. Their posture was so stiff, that if one were not sure, they could be mistaken for wax figures. Two stood in front of the ornate oak doors at the end of the hallway that opened to the Cabinet Room.

Without speaking they opened the doors for him as he approached. Once inside the room he proceeded to greet the other members that were present. He bowed before each one in the customary greeting. Looking into the eyes of each one, he was searching for confirmation or acknowledgement of their willingness to join in the *coup d'état* that would hopefully unfold in the next hour. Each face was impassive. Park now began to wonder if the plan had fallen through. Was the whole thing a sham designed to expose traitors to the Leader?

A gong rang twice signaling the Leader's pending entrance. Each man moved to his representative seat at the oak table. The civilian members of the Cabinet were arrayed on the left side of the table with the military on the right side. Each was seated according to their rank or Cabinet importance. Park was seated eighteenth out of twenty.

Two oak doors opened on the far side of the room to reveal the Leader. His face was void of emotion as he entered the room. All rose and bowed in honor of the exalted Leader who moved to the head of the table as aides pulled his chair for him. Bowing to the assembled ministers he took his seat. The Cabinet returned to their seats.

The usual business of the state was begun with each minister reporting on their respective department. The first to speak was General Sun-Jing, The Chief of the General Staff, who rose to his feet for his report.

"Members of the People's government. Our glorious armed forces, under the enlightened leadership of his Excellency, have delivered a message to the imperialists. They now know we have the ability to deliver our power. America and the South cower in the shadow of our light. With the war in the Middle East their resources are overstretched. Their economy is reeling due to the discontinuation of oil from the Middle East. Our spies in their government tell us the opposition party is discussing impeachment. With these distractions the Americans will not be able to send reinforcements when we invade the South. They do not have the stomach for another land war in Asia after their failure in Vietnam."

Park was stunned by the words he was hearing. This was delusional insanity. He had seen the reports of American carriers and stealth aircraft deploying to the Western Pacific in obvious preparation for a counterstrike. The fact it had not already occurred is what escaped Park. The South Koreans were mobilizing. War was imminent if events continued to progress. His heart began to race as he rose to his feet. As he stood, the members of the Cabinet shifted their attention to him. Such a display of disrespect in the Cabinet Room was unprecedented. It usually resulted in death for anyone foolish enough to attempt what Park was doing.

"Gentlemen, I wish to speak. With due respect to His Excellency," Park said as he bowed in the direction of the Leader. "His Excellency is leading our country down a course of destruction. As our people starve, he plans to divert our resources into a war with the Americans and our brothers in the South. American forces are deploying for a counterstrike. The South is preparing for war. You have seen the reports. The General is choosing to overlook this salient point." His voice was now strong and steady. He then uttered what no one ever thought would be spoken. "This is national suicide. I call for the immediate removal of the Leader and the formation of a new government."

Park's eyes met the Leader's as he concluded his statement. Perhaps stunned by such a blatant challenge to the Leader, the Cabinet did not initially respond. He could feel his heart beating in his chest as he maintained his feet.

The Leader sat for a moment. His face remained impassive. Then slowly he began to smile. He laughed a little at first and then began to boisterously laugh out loud. As he did, he motioned to the guards in the room to come forward. Obediently the eight men came and stood before the Leader awaiting his command.

"Arrest the traitor," the Leader said this time no longer smiling. His eyes glared at Park.

Park shot a glance at the First Vice Chairman of the National Defense Commission who rose to his feet. "Yes. It is time to arrest the traitor," Kim Rhee acknowledged. He motioned for the guards who moved to surround the Leader.

Four members of the General Staff made an attempt to defend the Leader. Drawing their weapons was their second mistake. They managed to get off two shots in Park's direction, one of which struck him in the arm knocking him to the floor. The guard's reactions were swift as the four men were shot before they could fire additional rounds. The Leader turned to the General in disbelief.

"You! You have betrayed the people. This treachery will not go unpunished." Turning to the Cabinet he continued. "Have the rest of you no honor as these who are dead? Your families will pay for your deceit!"

"No, sir. It is you who has betrayed our people. Remove him," Park ordered now standing again. One of the guards was tending to his arm. "We do this for the people. I announce a new coalition to lead. Those who join me, please stand."

All but three members stood. These three men were placed under arrest along with the Leader. Park watched as the guards began to remove the men. They had almost reached the door when the Leader, along with the three Cabinet members, lunged away from the guards. The Leader managed to take the rifle away from one of the guards and turned to fire on Park and the remainder of the treacherous Cabinet. As he did shots were again exchanged. When the smoke and noise subsided, two additional members of the Cabinet lay dead in their chairs; one was Shin Jong Pil. More importantly though, four bodies were crumpled by the door in a pool of blood. Streaks of blood ran down the door from where they had attempted to escape their fate before being cut down by return fire.

First Vice Chairman Rhee was still standing with his pistol aimed in the direction of the fallen body of the Leader. He slowly walked over to where the body lay on the floor, still training his weapon on the Leader as if he expected him to be moving. He would not have discounted that as the Leader had survived several previous attempts on his life. But there would not be a second chance for the Leader or the others that lay dead around him.

Rhee nudged the bodies with his foot. Seeing no movement he reached down to check for a pulse on each man. Finding none, he stood and looked in Park's direction and nodded. He motioned for the guards to remove the bodies from the room.

Park moved to the head of the table when they cleared the room. Carrying his chair with him, he kicked the chair of the now disposed Leader away. After placing his chair at the head of the table he walked over to the wall where the painting of the Leader hung. He took the picture down and looked at it for a moment. Then he tore it out of the frame. He wanted all vestiges of the Leader removed from the room before he began. Now, moving to his chair he bowed before all and sat down. Not quite sure what to do, the members of the Cabinet bowed in return and took their seats.

Park addressed the bewildered members. "I do not seek this chair for my glory. I seek to represent our people. We must signal to the Americans the change in our government. We do not wish for war. Only for them to respect our right of autonomy. Surely they will understand that."

USS ENTERPRISE

8:15 p.m.

"Admiral, CENTCOM has issued new tasking orders," McLaskey said as he handed O'Brien the orders. It read:

> 2015 JAN 11
> >>FLASH TRAFFIC<<
> FROM: CMDR CENTCOM
> TO: CMDR USS ENTERPRISE
> CLAS-EYES ONLY-PRIORITY ALPHA
> SUBJECT: OPERATION ANVIL HAMMER

ENSURE SURVIVAL OF ENTERPRISE STRIKE GROUP

NEUTRALIZE ENEMY AIR AND NAVAL FORCES PERSIAN GULF/
IRAN THEATER

SECURE CONTROL OF STRAIGHTS OF HORMUZ, OPERATION
CHOKEHOLD

SUPPORT SAUDI AND LOCAL ALLIED GOVERNMENTS.
AUTHORIZATION FOR SECURING OILFIELDS BY AMPHIB
FORCES APPROVED IN EVENT OF GVT COLLAPSE

The remainder of the order confirmed strike times. It was to be a massive coordinated counterattack on Alliance and EU forces in the theater. This would mark a significant change in policy in the Middle East, for it was the first time American armed forces would be fighting side by side with Israeli forces. It was apparent that Washington was throwing full support to Israel.

"Looks like we're going to finish what the Israelis started. JUST STRIKE has been replaced by ANVIL HAMMER. Surviving Iranian nuclear facilities are being hit by B-2s after we secure control of the air. Well, we have the EU to thank for this. Let's be reviewing our strike plan," O'Brien said to the men of his command. "By the time we get finished there won't be much left of Iran's air and naval forces. Better keep the coffee coming. We're going to be busy for the next couple of days."

LAJES AIRFIELD

AZORES

January 12th

3:32 a.m.

On the southern end of the airfield, Lt. Gordon and his men were encountering strong machine gun and mortar fire. The EU forces had barricaded themselves in the hangers and service buildings. Waterson reminded him their orders were to preserve the airfield for their use. But, as Gordon noted, one had to have the airfield first.

"Sgt. Jones, flank attack on that hanger. Time for some urban renewal," Gordon ordered.

Lt. Gordon's forces continued their attack in coordination with the main body of Marines under Waterson. On the mountainside of the airfield, Sgt. Ivey's assault force was making their way between two of the hangers. They were perhaps thirty yards from the entrance to the control tower with Ivey on point. He was edging his way along the side of the hanger in a crouched position. At the end of the building he stopped and held up a raised fist signaling his men to stop.

Two EU soldiers were guarding the entrance to the tower. They were barricaded behind sandbags. Ivey raised his M-16, took aim, and fired. The first soldier crumpled to the ground. He trained his sights on the second soldier and fired, but not before a downdraft of wind slammed him into the hanger wall. His shot went wild missing the soldier, who by now was reacting to the death of his comrade. The soldier ducked behind the sandbags and made his way to the door of the control tower. Flinging it open, he jumped inside the safety of the reinforced concrete walls of the tower as rounds from Ivey's second salvo struck the door.

Ivey muttered a silent curse at both his failure and the wind. "Come on, we're going in," he signaled to his men. He and his men sloshed through the standing water as they sprinted to the tower. Ivey was first to the tower and scaled the sandbag barricade easily. He tried the door and found it had been secured.

"Johnson, C4," Ivey ordered as he stood to the other side of the door.

Johnson reached into his satchel and pulled out a C4 package. Ripping the back off the explosive package he slapped it on the door and yelled, "Fire in the hole!"

Ivey and his men rushed in with weapons at the ready after the door was blown clear. On the floor was the body of the first soldier Ivey shot. He had somehow managed to crawl into the control tower before dying. To his right was the elevator used by the staff to access the control room of the tower. Further down the hall were the stairs. Ironically, the emergency lights were in operation.

"Raider One, Ivey. We're in. Proceeding to the control room," he signaled to Waterson.

"Confirmed, Ivey. Keep your head down," replied Waterson.

Ivey led his men down the hallway to the stairs. He turned the handle on the stairway door and slowly opened it. He was surprised it was not locked or barricaded...or booby-trapped. The lights were off in the staircase. Glass on the floor indicated it was not by accident. Entering cautiously, they began to work their way up the stairs. On the fifth staircase, Ivey noticed a sign on a door that read: Control Room - Authorized Access Only. He reckoned the M-16 he was holding would be his authorization.

"Johnson, C4 on the door. Everybody else ready on flashbangs," ordered Ivey.

As Ivey and his men stood clear, Johnson applied the explosive. When the door blew, flashbang grenades were thrown in to stun anyone not already dazed by the C4 explosion. Not all of the EU troops were affected and they opened fire on Ivey's men. An intense exchange of gunfire quickly resulted in the surrender of the EU troops in the tower. Seven bodies lay on the floor. Two were Ivey's men. Ivey himself had been struck in his left arm, though he did not feel it immediately.

"Who is in command?" Ivey asked as his men were tying the hands of the surviving EU soldiers. The EU soldiers just stood with their eyes focused ahead.

"Hey, Sarge, maybe they don't speak English," said Johnson.

Ivey considered this a possibility but not likely. English was the common language of the EU. Ivey saw the eyes of one of the EU men dart to another and then back again. Walking over to the survivors, he looked square in their eyes and again asked who was in command. The tone of his voice indicated his desire to know the answer. The M-16 he was cradling added to his argument.

One of the soldiers spoke up. Gesturing with his head to one of the bodies on the floor he said, "That was our commander. I am the Executive Officer. Major Mangose."

Ivey spoke into his mike, "Raider One, Ivey. Tower is secure. XO is in custody. The commander is dead."

"Tell him to order his men to surrender or more will be killed," came Waterson's voice over Ivey's headset.

"You heard the man, Major. You are ordered to surrender," Ivey said as he trained his M-16 at the man. "Order your forces to surrender or they will be going home in body bags."

"Terms of surrender?" asked Mangose.

"Terms? You will not be killed is the best I can offer at this time. I've seen too many of my buddies killed. Understand?" he said as he leaned in close to Mangose. Ivey was a good three inches taller and fifty pounds heavier than the man. Fear registered in the eyes of the EU officer. He was not ready to die and his eyes told the story.

"I will agree to your terms. I need the radio to contact my men." He gestured to a bag on the console.

"No tricks, Major. My men are not in a good mood if you follow me," Ivey gestured at his troops.

"I understand. There will be no tricks."

One of Ivey's men brought the radio over and held the mike for the Major. "This is Major Mangose. I order you to cease firing and surrender. Repeat, you are ordered to cease firing and surrender. Assemble by the control tower."

It took a few minutes for all of the EU forces to receive the order. As they did, the firefights ceased as the EU units began to surrender and make their way to the control tower.

Waterson was receiving reports from his units that the EU forces were surrendering. "Umpire, this is Raider One. Touchdown. Repeat Touchdown. All is secure. We have casualties that need immediate evac. Get those birds airborne. Weather here is clearing," he said. The battle had been short but fierce. The EU defenders had put up a gallant fight before surrendering. "Better get those reinforcements here ASAP."

"Confirmed, Raider One," acknowledged Admiral Yi aboard the *Shanksville*. "Reinforcements already deploying. Semper Fi, Raider One. Umpire out."

Waterson looked around at the smoldering airframes of the destroyed Tornados as he crossed the runway on his way to the control tower. The waves were crashing against the island's shore. He had not noticed them until now. The light of the sun was casting a red hue on the morning clouds. Looking up he saw an American flag being unfurled atop the control tower. In the distance he could hear the *thump, thump, thump* of approaching helicopters. The rest of the 22nd MEU was being deployed to the island. The engineers would have a lot of debris to remove from the airfield before the fighters and bombers arrived. However, the airfield at Lajes, while damaged, was secured.

AMIR AIR BASE

5:32 a.m.

While the situation on Lajes was improving it continued to deteriorate in Israel. The air assault by the Islamic Alliance was unrelenting. So far they were holding their own with the Israeli Air Force. More importantly they were matching the IAF sortie rate preventing Israel from achieving the air superiority for which their armed forces so desperately depended. With Israel's command facilities destroyed, Goldman was struggling to coordinate their defense.

"General," a worried staff officer reported as he handed Goldman a summary of the battle, "we are receiving reports that EU forces have joined in the attack. Our pilots have visually confirmed the EU insignia on planes engaged in the Golan Heights and Southern front."

"So much for their peacekeeping role," Goldman wryly noted as he reviewed the report. Looking at Alex he said, "If we are unable to stop them with conventional weapons, I am prepared to order the use of tactical nukes on strategic targets both in the Alliance and their treacherous allies in Europe."

Though he was shocked to hear that, Alex understood what Goldman was telling him. Goldman was running on very little sleep and lots of coffee. He appeared to be in command of his faculties though one never knew how stress and exhaustion would impact a man. Alex was careful how he phrased his reply.

"I understand, General. I respectfully caution you, though, on their use..." Alex began but he was cut off by Goldman.

"Don't lecture me on tactics, Alex!" Goldman snapped. "You are here only as a courtesy to your President."

"Sir, I don't mean to lecture. I am pointing out options. It is what I do for President Sullivan. I apologize if I have overstepped my welcome here, General," Alex countered, hoping his reply wasn't perceived as a counterattack by Goldman. He knew the man was feeling the pressure of events.

"You haven't, Alex," Goldman acknowledged as he rubbed the back of his neck. It was tight from the stress he was under. "Go ahead with what you were going to say," Goldman said pouring another cup of coffee.

"We don't know for sure if the Alliance possesses their own nuclear weapons or not. Plus, it's possible that EU forces would go nuclear if you launched a first strike. It would be opening Pandora's box. General, think about this," Alex said leaning on the General's desk. "They know we're planning a counterattack. EU participation must mean one thing. Desperation on the part of the Alliance. The Alliance is unable to win without their support."

"Kicking in their reserves?" acknowledged Goldman.

"Precisely, sir."

"That may be, Alex. But understand this. I will not allow Israel to be destroyed as a nation or a people. We have suffered too long and too many times when we should have fought back. Europe and America did nothing when Hitler began his barbaric treatment of my people in the thirties. All the warnings were there, yet no one lifted a finger in the western democracies to stop him. Hitler almost killed my entire family in his death camps and probably would have had the war not ended when it did. My grandparents survived Auschwitz. Each member of my family has sworn an oath that we will not allow that to happen again. At least one member in each generation of my family has fought and died for Israel. I do not expect you to understand."

Alex could see the pain and determination in the man. He was intent on seeing that promise through. It was not exhaustion driving the man, but the basic instinct of survival. Alex was not sure he wouldn't feel the same way. He recalled the anger and indignation he felt on 9/11. He had resolved that day to do whatever he could to prevent another such occurrence.

"Are you familiar with the story of Sampson?" Goldman continued.

Somewhat surprised by this reference to the Biblical character, Alex nodded his head wondering what the significance of the example was.

"From the Old Testament?" he asked.

"Yes, the same. The story tells us that after the Philistines had captured Sampson, he was summoned to entertain them. As he was standing between two pillars, he told the small boy who was holding his hand, 'Let me feel the pillars on which the house rests, that I may lean on them.' As he did, he prayed to Jehovah for strength that he might pull the pillars down on which the house rested. Jehovah answered his prayer. When he began to pull he shouted, 'Let me die with the Philistines.' Over three thousand died that day as a result of Sampson's action."

"The Sampson Option?" Alex asked in a stunned whisper now fully understanding Goldman's reference to the Old Testament account. "Is that how Israel feels? How you feel, sir?"

The Sampson Option was long rumored to be Israel's nuclear option. He now knew Goldman was serious and was fully prepared to order the use of nuclear weapons. He was prepared to eliminate the enemies of Israel once and for all and Alex could not blame him. Goldman did not verbally answer. He did not have too. The stoic expression on his face spoke for him.

"General, I understand your position. The President assures me reinforcements are on the way. In twenty-four hours our assets will be in position for their initial strike. Carrier groups will be within striking range within four days. If we had landing rights anywhere in the region we could bring airpower to bear sooner. I implore you, General, give the President that time. It is not time for the Sampson Option. Not yet."

"Twenty-four hours for the first strike. Four days for the carriers. That is a long time. We have already lost Jerusalem, the Golan Heights, and Bethlehem. I will wait. But understand this," Goldman said as he indicated on the map, "if Alliance forces enter the Tel Aviv defensive zone, I will order the use of our nuclear forces. This is the heart of Israel and will be defended at all costs."

Seeing the General's resolve, Alex merely nodded his head in understanding. He had pressed Goldman for more than what he should have considering the stress the man was under. In fact, Goldman had given more than Alex thought he would. It was clear Goldman was relying on American support and was giving as much time as he could for U.S. forces to respond. But he had no doubt Goldman would defend Israel as promised. A staff officer hurriedly ran up to Goldman with the latest intelligence update. Goldman managed a small smile. It was the first time he had done so in days.

"Alex, some good news. We have received word American forces have captured the airfield at Lajes in the Azores. Now they will have to break the EU blockade around Gibraltar."

"Four carrier strike groups with support from Lajes will be hard to be beat, General," Alex offered. At least he hoped they would be. Reports continued to be received that more EU forces were being deployed to the Gibraltar chokepoint.

OVAL OFFICE

7:16 a.m.

"You're sure of this?" asked an anxious Sullivan as he read the note handed to him by Stanfield who had just entered the Oval Office. If it were true it might possibly alleviate the prospect of a two-front war.

"Yes, Mr. President," acknowledged Stanfield as she took her seat in front of Sullivan's desk. "I have spoken with Prime Minister Park within the past hour. He informs me The Leader is dead. Here is a picture of the Leader on the floor of their Cabinet Room. It looks pretty gruesome. Park has formed a provisional government and informs me he will be issuing a formal apology within the next three hours. He recognizes the need for his country to join the family of nations."

"Disposition of their armed forces? Are they standing down?" asked Clairmont who had joined them via conference call.

"He indicated they were initiating a phased stand-down. There is the matter of national pride he has to contend with," noted Stanfield. "Plus, there is some house cleaning he's having to do to get his people in place in the army."

"Mr. President, if that is the case we could redeploy one or two of the carriers to the Gulf," advised Clairmont. "Recommend we keep one close by just in case. It could be our version of a phased withdrawal. I am sure *Enterprise* would appreciate the additional assets."

"Stanfield, what do you think?" inquired Sullivan.

"I agree with the Secretary, Mr. President. That would send the appropriate signal to the Koreans. It would legitimize Park as Prime Minister."

"Throw him a bone, eh?" Sullivan noted.

"Exactly, Mr. President. It would send the right message," Stanfield concurred.

"This would be a significant improvement in the world situation," noted Sullivan with a note of optimism in his voice. "If Park is legit and honors what he has communicated to Stanfield, redeploy the carriers to the Mideast. That will help our Israeli friends."

The apology did come within the next two hours as promised. More importantly, North Korea began to withdraw their forces ten miles from the DMZ. The number of airborne aircraft was reduced by half. Satisfied with these developments, Sullivan gave the order to redeploy *Truman* and *Eisenhower* to the Persian Gulf.

AMIR AIR BASE

9:18 a.m.

Goldman was conferring with his staff on the progress of the battle. They were huddled around a map of the battlefield in his office, which had a glass front wall that overlooked the Command Center. Alex was seated at the conference table as a courtesy from Goldman. But in reality, he had nowhere else to go.

A buzz on the speaker phone interrupted their discussion. "General, sorry to bother you, sir. The President of the United States wishes to confer with you." Goldman shot a glance at Alex that told him to stay seated.

"Ok, Lieutenant, patch us through."

"General, President Sullivan. I'm going to dispense with the pleasantries and get to the point. I am sure you've seen the news regarding England and the other six countries splitting with the EU. The newly elected Prime Minister has contacted me. He has reaffirmed England's membership in NATO and is preparing to honor the terms of the treaty. How much support we can count on I do not know."

"Yes, Mr. President. We saw that. That is a significant development. Perhaps the continent is not as united as we were led to believe," Goldman noted.

"Perhaps not. Now, for something that will impact you directly. At 0200 hours your time, OPERATION ANVIL HAMMER will be launched. It is a counterstrike aimed at Alliance Air Force and command facilities. Simultaneously, the *George Washington* and *Enterprise* strike groups will attack Egyptian and Iranian facilities. That should give you some breathing room until the carrier groups arrive."

"That should level the playing field, Mr. President," Goldman said with a sparkle in his eye. He looked directly at Alex with a grin on his face. "Your assistance is greatly appreciated and is overwhelming, Mr. President. You are a man of your word and a friend of Israel. You realize, of course, the world reaction to this?"

"I'm not interested in world opinion. I am more concerned about preventing an old ally from being overrun. Besides, I hate to see someone sucker punched."

"Mr. President, I must excuse myself. We have much to prepare to take advantage of our newfound fortune. We will speak again after the attack. Meanwhile, we will continue our defense."

"Good luck, General," Sullivan said as he ended the conversation.

Alex looked at Goldman. The man looked as if half the weight of the world had been lifted from his shoulders. Goldman lifted his command phone. "Lieutenant, please contact the senior officers at our bases."

"Right away, sir," came his hurried reply.

"General, we have received this intelligence update from EU headquarters," the aide reported as he handed Jallud the transmission.

"The Americans have taken Lajes airfield in the Azores. No doubt that will be their staging base for their thrust into the Mediterranean. In addition, North Korea has undergone regime change. The new leader is signaling peace toward the Americans. They are standing down their forces from the DMZ. That has freed up their carrier group in the Pacific. Two American carrier groups are now approaching. One in the Atlantic with four carriers and one entering the Indian Ocean with two carriers. Five hundred aircraft," Jallud read aloud with a hint of concern and frustration in his voice. He knew the firepower of a single carrier group could be devastating; but to multiply that by six was enough to shift the balance of power over to the Israelis.

If Israeli pilots were not the best trained in the world it would have to be the Americans. Not only did they have the resources to continually train their pilots but they had an edge few of his pilots or those of the EU did: combat experience. Unfortunately, the combat experience of the American pilots was gained in the Second Iraqi War and Afghanistan, plus other operations conducted in the name of democracy in the crusade against his people. He hated the Americans for their wealth and arrogance. He hated them for what they did in Iraq and Afghanistan. Mostly he hated the Americans because they were accustomed to winning. So accustomed to winning they did not have a concept of defeat. It was time to change that.

He needed to talk with Gerhard. Their window of opportunity was waning. He wanted his assurance the Americans would be kept out of the war zone. Reaching for his command phone he spoke to his aide, "Our European friends are failing us. We may have to make other arrangements. Put me through to Gerhard."

Ground crews were swarming around the twenty B-52Hs parked along the tarmac. They were hurriedly completing their task of arming a mix of twenty AGM-86C and AGM-86D conventional cruise missiles on board the enormous planes. The refueling trucks had already topped off the massive fuel tanks of the B-52Hs and departed. Once airborne the B-52Hs would rendezvous with KC-10 Extender tankers and refuel again for their long journey.

All of the aircrews boarding the B-52Hs were far younger than their planes. In fact, the life of the venerable B-52 had been extended in ways never envisioned by its original designers in the fifties. The surviving H models had been converted to carry the Conventional Air Launched Cruise Missile in the 1980s. GPS was married to the cruise missile in the nineties. This update to the cruise missile, coupled with the extraordinary combat radius of the B-52H, offered U.S. military planners an option not available to any of the combatants in the war—a long range stand-off launch platform.

The plan called for the B-52Hs to launch their missiles while over the Indian Ocean. The pilots had received their final briefings. In another hour, the first B-52H would lumber down the runway, climb to altitude, bank left, and proceed to the designated launch point.

Colonel Goldman's brigade had been savagely attacked the day before, reducing his effective strength by another ten tanks. He was attempting a delaying action against Alliance armor as his unit conducted their withdrawal from the Golan Heights area. His goal was to delay the onrush of Alliance tanks to allow time for Israel's forces to mobilize. His brigade, or at least what was left of it, was proceeding on the road to El Al when two squadrons of MiG-27s roared over the brigade from the south. The air-to-ground rockets and strafing from the MiGs took their toll on his tanks. Eight more Merkavas were destroyed by the attack. One erupted in a spectacular explosion that separated the turret from the hull of the tank. Fortunately for Goldman and all of the tankers, they were unable to hear the screams of the doomed crewmen as fire engulfed the remainder of the tank.

His AAA units had been unable to provide an effective defense due to the surprise of the attack. He scanned the horizon for the Israeli Air Force. All he saw were the contrails of the MiGs as they were banking for another run.

The surviving tanks were laying a smoke screen in an effort to camouflage their positions. The AAA units, now alert to the attack, were locking onto the MiGs and were engaging them.

"Leader to units, execute wheelhouse." Goldman had ordered his brigade to, what the Americans used to call, "circle the wagons." The dust cloud generated by the churning treads, combined with the smoke dischargers, was obscuring the MiG pilot's visibility. Without a clear target the MiGs fired into the dust cloud anticipating they would hit something. Goldman could hear the screaming jets approach and the inevitable explosions as their ordinance detonated. He was comforted somewhat by the sound of his AAA units firing. As his tank emerged from the cover of the smoke and dust he saw two MiGs falling to the earth in flames, victims of the AAA fire. However, his brigade had lost an additional four tanks in the attack. There were now only fifteen left.

"Leader to base. Encountering substantial enemy air activity in sector twelve. Twenty-two additional tanks destroyed. Where in the world is our bloody Air Force?" he asked sternly.

"Base to Leader. Confirm air activity in your sector. You are ordered to establish a defensive position at coordinates Y36, J62. Enemy forces must not be allowed to penetrate this line."

Goldman could hardly believe the orders he had just received. How was he supposed to fend off air and armored attacks without air support and only fifteen tanks? His men had been without sleep now for almost three straight days. The stress of battle, combined with the lack of sleep, was taking a toll even on Goldman. "Base, who is in command now?" he asked tersely.

"Leader, that is a need-to-know basis."

Goldman slammed his hand down on the turret. Only a desk-bound clerk would have the temerity to give that answer.

"Base, this is Leader. If a man is being ordered to die, he has a right to speak to his commander. Now who is in command?!" he emphatically requested.

"General Goldman," came the reply.

"Base, this is his brother. Is he available?" Goldman said as he signaled his driver to continue their movement. There was a pause of several minutes before he received a reply.

"This is General Goldman," came the resolute, but tired voice over his headset.

"General, Colonel Goldman, sir. What is happening? Things are pretty tight up here. The Syrians just shot up my unit pretty good. I am surrounded and running low on everything. Where is our Air Force?"

"They are coming, Colonel. Have you been monitoring the reports?"

"Yes, General, I have. They are not encouraging." The Colonel had indeed been monitoring the reports. Israeli forces were being systematically worn down. With each passing hour, Alliance forces were penetrating deeper into Israeli territory. Jerusalem had been encircled. Reports were being received that the flag of the Islamic Alliance was flying over the grounds of the destroyed Temple Mount. For the first time in Israel's recent history, panic was beginning to grip the population. Goldman himself was beginning to have doubts as to Israel's ability to survive short of employing her nuclear weapons.

"We have been promised assistance from the Americans," General Goldman offered.

"Well, it had better get here fast or there will be nothing left to save. If I do not speak to you again brother, I want you to know I love you and I am proud of you," the Colonel said as tears formed in his eyes.

In the sanctity of his office where no one could see, the General's eyes also misted. "Good luck to you, brother. I love you as well. Our parents would have been proud of you."

LAJES AIR FORCE BASE

AZORES

January 12th

11:16 a.m.

Activity on Lajes escalated quickly as the 22nd Marine Expeditionary Unit had fully secured the island. The wounded troops had already been airlifted back to the *Shanksville*. Arriving first were Engineer units. They surveyed the cratered runway and immediately began making repairs. They soon had Lajes' runways sufficiently repaired and ready to receive aircraft. Recon units were patrolling the island to guard against the possibility of EU commandos being landed. Intel reports were being received that EU forces were preparing to counterattack. In the control tower, air traffic controllers from the *Shanksville* were directing the influx of planes as reinforcements began to pour in from the United States.

Upon receiving notification that Lajes was secure and operational, four squadrons of F-15E Eagles, a squadron each of F-22C Raptors, KC-10 Extenders and P-3 Orions (anti-submarine warfare planes) and two E-3B AWACS immediately scrambled for Lajes. One thousand additional Marines were immediately being airlifted to reinforce the 22nd MEU. Another thousand were scheduled to deploy to the island in two days.

In two days, the *Reagan* CSG would be passing the Azores in route to the eastern Med to reinforce the beleaguered Israeli Air Force. But before they could accomplish this, control of the Straits of Gibraltar and Mediterranean would have to be secured. DNIS had been intercepting increased transmissions among EU air and naval forces. The traffic confirmed they were marshalling their forces in and around Gibraltar in an effort to prevent U.S. forces from entering the Med.

Waterson was in the control room monitoring the on-going communications. He had taken great pride in the accomplishment of his men. The sign that hung from the control tower summed it up: "Welcome to Lajes. Under New Management: 22nd MEU."

His men had fashioned the sign from tablecloths they found in the officers' mess. They had sought his permission to hang the banner. Looking into the tired, but jubilant eyes of his young Marines, who had just hours before faced death and the loss of their comrades, he had only one reply: "Ooh-rah!"

USS RONALD REAGAN

WESTERN ATLANTIC OCEAN

11:32 a.m.

Admiral LuAnn Kingston had selected the *Reagan* to be her flagship. Her strike group of four *Nimitz* class carriers, *Reagan, Lincoln, Roosevelt,* and *Nimitz*, had finally cleared the confining waters of Hampton Roads and was now proceeding at flank speed toward the Mediterranean. Within the hour the first elements of the air wings would be joining the carriers.

In her spacious Admiral's quarters, she sipped on her coffee as she read the tactical update received from the National Military Command Center. Rank did have its privileges and entitled her the extra space on board, though room was limited even on the massive carrier. On her desk, pictures of her family reminded her how much she missed them and the sacrifices they had made to support her career. She had told her husband this would be her final year of service. They were going to retire to their home in Hawaii. They had met there some thirty years ago at a surf meet on the North Shore of Oahu. They had purchased a condo on Oahu and kept it as a second home, but now planned to make it their permanent residence with her retirement.

On the bulkhead were two framed letters. One was from her dad and the other was from then President George W. Bush, congratulating her on her promotion to Admiral. The letter from her dad was one he had written to her when she was born. In the letter he told her how much he loved her and how proud he was of her even though she couldn't talk or walk at the time. The last paragraph was especially touching to her and had been the cause of her drive in life.

> *And sweetie, I want you to remember this. Never let anyone tell you that you cannot do something just because you are a girl. You are my little girl and always will be, and my little girl can do anything she wants when she puts her mind to it…*
> Love, Dad

She had not disappointed her dad. Her drive helped her make history by being the first woman to command an aircraft carrier. In fact, her career had seen many firsts. Always an aviation enthusiast, she had learned to fly at the age of fifteen. She decided upon a career in the Navy with a goal of flying F-14s. After graduating first in her class from Annapolis she began her flying career at Pensacola. Her flight instructors quickly recognized her prowess in the cockpit. She knew she was entering what had previously been the sole domain of a man's world. She quickly mastered the T-38 trainer. After proving her aviation skills on various planes she was selected to participate in the F-14 Tomcat program. Consistently downing her male counterparts, she garnered the eye of her superiors and the begrudging respect of her male counterparts. Her flying skills earned her the right to participate in the Navy's Top Gun program where she continued her dominance in the sky becoming the first woman to win the coveted title of Top Gun.

When al-Qaeda struck on 9/11, she led one of the first sorties from the *Enterprise* against al-Qaeda training camps in Afghanistan. She continued to enjoy success and was eventually promoted to flag rank. It was not uncommon for a woman to make flag rank. But it was her assignment to command the *Reagan* Carrier Strike Group of the 2nd Fleet in America's response to this latest war in the Mideast that garnered the attention of the nation. It was the first such command for a woman.

The phone on her desk buzzed for her attention. "Yes," she said answering its call.

"Admiral, satellite recon shows no change in disposition of EU forces in the Med. They remain inside the straits, east of Gibraltar."

"Waiting for us, Captain?" she asked.

"Or scared to come out and play, Admiral."

"Either way, we are going to find out soon enough. Our orders remain, Captain. Proceed to the Eastern Med and execute OPERATION JUST CAUSE in support of Israel. The President has made our intentions clear and we are going to carry out his orders."

ANVIL HAMMER

WHITE HOUSE
January 13th
1:50 p.m.

An apprehensive Sullivan contacted the Chairman of the Joint Chiefs. "General, Israeli forces are getting it handed to them. What is the status of ANVIL HAMMER?"

"Mr. President, in about five minutes our assets will be in position. Poor devils won't know what hit them, sir. This will give the Israelis some breathing room until the fleet arrives."

"Very good, General. Keep me informed on the outcome. I think our little fireworks display will send a message that you don't screw around with the United States or our friends."

"Is that a reference to anyone, Mr. President?" the General asked with a wolf's grin.

"I'm going to answer that with my favorite press conference answer: no comment," Sullivan replied with a grin that equaled that of the General's as he switched off the monitor.

BLACKKNIGHT SQUADRON
INDIAN OCEAN
1:40 a.m.

"Colonel, approaching launch point," reported the navigator of the lead B-52H.

"Affirmative. Blackknights prepare for launch," ordered Colonel Walter Josephson.

The B-52Hs of the Blackknights were nearing their launch position. Target data for the twenty cruise missiles aboard each B-52H was confirmed one last time. Upon launch, the missiles would be guided to their targets by GPS. The target destination: Alliance airfields and command facilities.

USS Santa Fe

1:52 a.m.

The *Los Angeles* class submarine *Santa Fe* was sliding through the murky waters of the Indian Ocean.

"Chief of the Boat, make your depth one hundred feet and hover. Weapons release has been authorized. Slow to five knots."

"Aye, aye, Captain. Making my depth one hundred feet and hovering. Slowing to five knots."

"Sonar, Conn. Contacts?" inquired Captain Martin Gunn.

"Conn, Sonar. Showing all clear."

"Very well. Weapons, Conn. Confirm target data and warhead. Make sure we don't pop a nuke out by mistake," Gunn ordered.

"Conn, Weapons. Target data and warhead confirmed. Load is conventional though they deserve a nuke, Captain."

Gunn privately agreed with his weapons officer but they were not in charge of policy. "Weapons, Conn. Acknowledged."

The crew was making final preparations for launch of her twelve cruise missiles as the *Santa Fe* came to launch depth. These were targeted on Syrian airfields and command facilities.

U.S. military leaders had conferred and agreed with their Israeli counterparts that Alliance forces based in Syria were posing the greater threat to Israel and would be targeted first.

"We are at launch depth, Captain. Holding hover," confirmed the Chief of the Boat.

Blackknight Squadron

2:00 a.m.

"Knight One to Round Table, launch weapons. Say again, launch weapons and execute evasive maneuvers," ordered Josephson.

The exhaust of four hundred cruise missiles pierced the darkness of the night sky as they left the internal launch bays of the B-52Hs. Josephson immediately banked his B-52H to a heading due south and out of the range of any potential fighters that might choose to intercept them. He then banked left again and adjusted his course back to Guam.

USS Santa Fe

2:00 a.m.

Thirty thousand feet below, the waters of the Indian Ocean foamed in anger as an additional twelve cruise missiles were ejected from the launch tubes of the *Santa Fe*. At twenty feet above sea level, their engines ignited, casting an eerie glow upon the Indian Ocean.

Upon launch, Gunn ordered the *Santa Fe* to dive to three hundred feet as she sped away from the launch position in the unlikely event a counterstrike was launched.

USS Enterprise

Persian Gulf

2:00 a.m.

Simultaneously sixty-four cruise missiles were leaving the launch tubes from the *Gettysburg* and *Philippine Sea* on outbound courses for Iranian airfields and surface-to-surface missile launchers. F/A-18D Super Hornets and F-35C Lightnings were shooting off the catapults of the *Enterprise* in route to their intended targets.

Alliance Air Base Shayrat

Syria

5:15 a.m.

Three hours later the cruise missiles, aided by GPS, found their intended targets. At two of the airbases the missiles arrived as squadrons were on the flight line being prepped for takeoff. The results at Shayrat air base were representative of what happened with the impact of the cruise missile attack. Fully loaded with fuel and munitions the twenty MiG-27s presented a rich target. The first missile detonated in the nearby hanger resulting in a chain reaction along the flight line. One by one, explosions engulfed the MiG-27s. Ground crews were scrambling for cover as missiles, heated by the fires of the burning MiGs, screamed from their launch rails. Missiles that were stored in the hangers were exploding in an expanding inferno. Other cruise missiles released bomb caplets that peppered the runway with explosives turning it into a scene that resembled the face of the moon, rendering the runway useless. In less than three minutes it was over. The air base at Shayrat was enshrouded in smoke and fire and was out of action.

Similar scenes were repeated at airbases around Syria, Iran, and Egypt. The SAM batteries guarding the bases did manage to bring down a number of the missiles, but the tracks of the GPS equipped cruise missiles enabled the majority to approach their targets from angles where the defenses were the weakest. As the smoke and fires were clearing from the airbases, it was apparent the advantage the Alliance had enjoyed in the air was now negated.

Alliance HQ

5:22 a.m.

This salient fact was not lost on Jallud. His own headquarters had been savaged in the attack. He was thankful his command post was buried deep enough that it was not directly impacted by the missiles; at least not yet. The facilities above ground did not fare as well. One of these was the power generator. When it was struck, the lights and computers in his control room went dark until the auxiliary power kicked in. It had been unnerving to be in total darkness so far below the ground, if even for only a few minutes. Jallud had thoughts that this was what death must be like.

His base commanders, at least the ones who were able to do so, were beginning to report. They were all describing severe damage to their bases. The runways had been rendered useless at all but four of the air bases. Hangers, fuel, and ammunition supplies were either damaged or on fire at all of the bases. Communication and control facilities were marginal at best. Jallud quickly signaled all pilots to land on roads if they were unable to do so at their bases. They were to strafe traffic to clear the roads if necessary. He could afford civilian casualties. What he could not afford was the loss of the planes and their pilots. They were so close to victory, but now it appeared to be slipping away much as a mirage in the desert. What was starving their win? It appeared the Israelis had again been given a respite. Was their God intervening for them again?

Many had discounted, even scoffed, at the notion of religion being a part of war. But Jallud was a student of Israeli history. More times than not, the Israelis were victorious when they should have been defeated. He had read the Old Testament and the accounts of Israel as they were conquering their enemies. The Old Testament recorded that Jehovah had intervened on behalf of Israel to give them victory numerous times.

Inside his heart he knew Jehovah must have been with Israel since they came to be a nation again in 1948. Nothing else could explain how a foe that was surrounded and outnumbered by odds of three-to-one had consistently defeated his Arab brothers. He would never publicly acknowledge this though, for to do so would be blasphemy and the end of his life.

It was time to release his reserves. Before the Americans could launch a second strike and cripple what was left of the Alliance Air Force.

BATTLE OF THE MEDITERRANEAN
STRAITS OF GIBRALTAR
January 15th
2:18 a.m.

The opening salvo was fired by F-117 Nighthawks operating from Lajes and British Tornadoes operating from Gibraltar. Their primary mission was to neutralize the EU early warning stations at Rota and Lisbon. The plan was to wedge open an air corridor through the Straits and force the EU to rely upon airfields either in France or Libya. The stealth characteristics of the F-117, although known to the EU defenders, still enabled them to penetrate EU airspace over Portugal and Spain. Two of the F-117s were tasked to disable the radars in Morocco to assist in clearing the path to the Med. The AGM-88 anti-radar missiles dispatched the radar facilities with marked efficiency. With mission accomplished the Nighthawks returned to Lajes safely. The Tornadoes unfortunately met their demise in their missions. It was just as well as EU forces had counter-attacked the legendary base destroying its airfield.

Following the Nighthawks were cruise missiles launched from the *Reagan* CSG and from B-1Bs based at Dyess AFB in Texas. Their missiles were targeted at the EU airfields in Portugal and Spain. Both of the preemptive strikes against the airfields and radar stations were successful. Closely following these strikes were F-22C Raptors and F-35C Lightnings. Their unique stealth abilities enabled the Raptors and

Lightnings to engage the Rafales and Mirages of the EU Air Force with near impunity. The EU simply had no answer to the near invisibility of the Raptors and Lightnings. Thus, these planes were in the vanguard of the American attack.

The primary airborne target for one flight of Raptors was the EU AWACS operating over Spain. Its radar was providing an electronic eye around a two hundred mile radius over the battlefield. A pair of Raptors was able to close upon the AWACS practically undetected. Upon target acquisition, four long-range AIM-120D missiles were launched from the lead Raptor with striking results. The AWACS exploded in a ball of fire. The wingman similarly dispatched its escorts.

With the demise of their AWACS, the Mirages and Rafale fighters of the EU were practically blind to the battlefield, except for their on-board radar. Unfortunately, like the radar aboard the now destroyed AWACS, it was unable to detect the Raptors.

With their electronic dominance of the skies, the Americans quickly established air superiority over the Straits. On the American side, the E-3B Sentry AWACS provided excellent targeting for the Raptors and Lightnings. As targets were acquired, their location was fed to the awaiting Raptors. The fire-and-forget capability of the Raptors enabled them to launch their AIM-120D missiles well outside the radar range of the surviving EU aircraft. The Mirages and Rafale fighters were savagely mauled by the Americans and forced to withdraw.

The EU Air Force could not overcome both the devastating impact the cruise missile attacks had on their bases in Spain and Portugal and the loss of their AWACS. Without air cover the air bases were wide open to further attack from the American carrier group. The initial cruise missile strikes by the Americans were followed up by strikes from F-15Es based in Lajes and F/A-18Es operating from the *Reagan* CSG. After these attacks, EU forces simply did not have the logistical support they needed to have a reasonable chance at engaging the Americans on a prolonged basis. The loss of the forward bases in Spain and Portugal forced the surviving EU planes to begin to withdraw from the combat area. The survivors were now reluctant to engage the U.S. aircraft and began to withdraw to bases in France.

Stripped of their land-based air cover, the naval forces deployed also began to withdraw but not until after they were struck. These forces were organized around the aircraft carrier *Principe de Asturias*. The carrier was Spain's major commitment to the EU navy. At just under eighteen thousand tons, she was about one-quarter the size of a *Nimitz* carrier. P-3 Orions operating from Lajes and F/A-18Es from the *Reagan* CSG launched multiple Harpoon salvos against the *Principe de Asturias* and her battle group. Six Harpoons struck her within seconds of each other quickly sending her to the bottom of the Mediterranean. All but one of her escorts were sunk or damaged.

The western gateway to the Mediterranean had been cleared.

USS RONALD REAGAN

5:30 a.m.

Admiral Kingston and her staff were reviewing battle damage assessments. The satellite images showed the damaged bases and cratered runways. The initial conclusions indicated the *Reagan* CSG and aircraft from Lajes had delivered a devastating riposte to the EU forces in the vicinity of the Straits.

"Admiral, EU forces are withdrawing from the Straits. It looks like they are quitting the battle in this part of the Med. Intel indicates they are regrouping in the Tyrrhenian Sea. Smack in the middle of Sardinia, Sicily, and the Italian mainland. Looks like they are going to make their stand there. The intel boys are calling it the witches cauldron."

"They are?" noted the Admiral with a slight grin on her face.

"Yes, ma'm," said Captain Smith.

"Good as name as any. It just might be that. We will be surrounded by unfriendly forces on all points if Alliance forces join the fray. What intel do we have on the intentions of the Alliance in this part of the Med?"

"Admiral, we are presuming they will adopt a hostile posture based on what happened to the *GW.*"

"That is what I figure as well. If I were the EU commander, I would be redeploying my forces in the same manner in light of their losses. They must realize that this thing could escalate into a full-fledged war beyond this theater. They just might need those planes in that event. Best to save your air assets for later. *De Gaulle* will be protected by those air bases," she said scanning the satellite images. "They are almost daring us to run the gauntlet. Remember what Halsey's motto was, Captain?"

"Whatever we do, we do fast?" replied Smith. He knew the Admiral was a fan of Halsey and he had made it a point to learn as much as he could about the famous World War Two Admiral.

"Precisely, Captain. Maintain course and speed. We have an engagement to keep."

IT'S ELEMENTARY, MY DEAR WATSON

AMIR AIR BASE

January 17th

11:45 p.m.

Alex was reviewing footage of the collapse of the Temple Mount. It was still inconceivable to him that the Temple Mount had collapsed as a result of opening the Triple Gate. All Israeli television stations remained off the air as they had been targeted in the initial Alliance attacks. One advantage of being in the Command Center was access to all commercial satellite feeds. Another benefit was access to video from the many security cameras that were located throughout Jerusalem. On another monitor he was watching video feeds from the major networks via satellite.

The major networks, including the *BBC* and *Al-Jazeera* were replaying video of the collapse of the Temple Mount and subsequent attack. The talk shows were enjoying unprecedented ratings as viewers were transfixed by the events of the Temple Mount and resulting war. The availability of satellite feeds, coupled with videophones, was enabling the networks to provide real time imagery of the war. The talking heads were voicing every conceivable, though predictable, explanation for the Temple collapse and consequent war. Alex did not have to be a public relations expert to know the impact the collapse of the Temple Mount was having, not only throughout the Islamic world, but the world itself. Most of the talking heads were clearly laying blame for the collapse of the Temple Mount on Israel's attempt to open the Triple Gate. None were focusing on what appeared to be a planned attack on Israel.

But Alex was more interested in the video that preceded the attack and ensuing collapse. A technician had shown him how to replay the video feeds from the networks and security cameras. The current footage he was reviewing was one that panned around the Temple Mount area. This was the shot most of the networks had used for their broadcast on the morning of the dedication. Everything looked fairly routine to him. Nothing out of the ordinary appeared that he could detect on the tape. But then, Alex wasn't sure what it was he was looking for.

The next tapes were those of Weissman's speech dedicating the opening of the Temple to all Israelis. Again nothing Alex could see caused any suspicion. He had been at this for close to five hours and his eyes were getting bleary. There was one tape from a security camera he had yet to review. Inserting the tape into the slot he decided this would be the last one he reviewed before taking a break.

The tape played across the monitor showing the throngs of people that were gathered for the ceremony. The camera was panning from left to right across the crowd. Alex was about to press the stop button when something on the screen caught his eye. He almost missed it as it was in the lower right corner of the monitor. This was not where the human eye instinctively went to when watching a monitor. The eye tended to focus on the middle of the screen.

All of the people were standing and paying close attention to the speech by Weissman except for one individual who appeared to be attempting to stand by himself. At least as much as one could in a crowd. He was trying to blend in with the crowd but still remain apart from it. Alex noticed him reach into his tunic and then begin to make his way through the crowd away from the Temple Mount. Thirty seconds later a dust cloud filled the screen. The only thing that could have caused that was the collapse of the Temple Mount. *Coincidence?* Alex thought. Or was his mind just tired and seeing things? He stood up and walked around in order to get his blood flowing again and clear his head. After stretching his arms and legs, he took a drink of the Coke he had been nursing for the past three hours.

Instead of sitting down, he stood before the console and cued the tape again. This time he replayed it in slow motion. His mind was now fully alert as the adrenaline, along with the caffeine, began to flow. He pulled the tape of Weissman's speech and subsequent collapse of the Temple Mount from one of the networks to run on another monitor. As he did, he synchronized the time sequence on both the security tape and the network tape so they rolled at the same time. It was apparent what the tapes revealed. Stunned, he sat in his chair unable to believe the images on the monitors. There was no doubt about what he had seen. But how could he prove it? Moreover, would anyone believe it?

He picked up the phone and dialed a familiar number. The voice on the other end was genuinely surprised at who the caller was.

"Alex, is that you? Where in the world are you?"

"Yeah, Will, it's me. Never mind where I am. You wouldn't believe it if I told you. Look, I need some information about seismological occurrences in the Jerusalem area. Specifically the Temple Mount. And, Will, no questions."

"You're kidding, right? Seismological data? Only the biggest disaster in the world and you are looking for earthquakes!"

"No, Will, I'm serious as a train wreck which is pretty much what we have now."

"Ok, give me a few minutes."

"I'll call you back in an hour…that ok?"

"Good enough. Stay low, buddy," Will said as he hung up the phone and began to make some calls.

THE CAULDRON

USS RONALD REAGAN

January 18ᵗʰ

11:55 p.m.

The pilots of the Fighting Vigilantes and Stingers squadrons were receiving their final mission review in the ready room. The twenty-four men seated in the room were listening intently to the mission orders from their commanding officer.

"Men, we have been tasked with the prime assignment. Our target: the main EU battle fleet and that means *Charles de Gaulle.*"

The room was immediately filled with comments announcing the final resting place of the *de Gaulle.* Most indicated it would be the infernal regions of the underworld. Commander Mitchell "MP" Thomas ignored the outburst and continued the briefing. In fact, he would have been concerned if the outburst had not occurred.

"Our mission is pretty straightforward. Utilizing the stealth characteristics of the Lightnings, we will avoid EU radar and CAP where possible. We will proceed to these coordinates and harpoon that baby. Questions?"

Lt. Tom "Steeler" Pitt spoke up. "Cutting it kind of close there aren't we, skipper? I mean launching from seventy miles. They can spit on us that close."

"What's wrong, Steeler?" countered Thomas. "Afraid the French won't like your aftershave? Word is your last date certainly didn't!"

"Something like that, sir," replied the humbled pilot as his fellow pilots broke out in laughter.

"Now, if no one else has anything else to add," Thomas observed.

The rest of the men were quiet and making final notes. "Gentlemen, man your planes and good hunting."

Alex continued to review the tape until the time had passed. He anxiously made the call. "Will, what do you have for me?"

"You might be on to something there, Sherlock," Will began. "A slight seismic tremor was recorded at 9:59 local time."

Alex did a quick calculation and checked the time on the tape when the Temple Mount collapsed. It was a perfect correlation. The seismic occurrence happened and then thirty seconds later the Temple Mount began to collapse. The chance of a coincidence was practically nil.

"One more fact for you," Will continued. "I asked my contact to ascertain the cause and epicenter. The epicenter was directly below the Temple Mount. Estimated depth was one hundred feet. It did not follow a normal earthquake pattern. The cause was man-made."

"Thanks, Will. I appreciate the fast turn around. You thinking what I'm thinking?"

"It appears to say one thing for sure. The Israelis may not have been responsible for the collapse of the Temple Mount. If we are thinking the same thing this could be huge!"

"Yes, it could. I'm going to put something together on this and I would like you to review it. I'll also need an ID of someone on a tape. This will take a few minutes to put together so keep the line open. And remember, not a word of this to anyone. If we are wrong on this..." Alex's voice trailed off underscoring the gravity of the situation.

"I understand, friend. You don't have to hit me over the head with a brick."

Alex hung up the phone leaving his friend in a curious state of mind. Next, he secured the technician's help in editing the two tapes. He didn't want to involve anyone else in this but he didn't have a choice. This was her area of expertise and he didn't have time for a crash course in video compilation. It took almost two hours to make the final edits but Alex was pleased with the end result. More importantly, he was pleased she had not asked any questions about the images on the tapes. She merely looked at him with inquisitive eyes when the final tape was played for his review. He knew he had to be sure on this. The technician encrypted the video for secure transmission. Upon pressing the enable feature, the video was uploaded to Will's workstation at DNIS.

"Pretty fascinating stuff, Alex," Will observed. It had been two hours since he had received the video from Alex. "Called in a favor with a buddy in photo imagery. Don't worry, though. It's someone who can keep their mouth shut. We have a positive ID on your friend in the video. The man in the video is Omar Bandakar. He is a player in the terrorist world. Last intelligence update had him working with al-Qaeda. He was their primary hit man. Not someone you would want to meet in a dark alley."

"Looks like he found a new employer," Alex observed wryly.

"Yes, it does. Now here is where it gets interesting. On a hunch, I checked the previous video you sent me from the hotel. Give you two guesses who was at the hotel with Al-Saim and the first one doesn't count."

"Bandakar," Alex noted.

"Bingo! Bandakar was with him in Berlin when they met with Gerhard. The security tape at the hotel had a clear shot of his face. A little slack in their security considering his area of expertise. Find him and Al-Saim is not far away."

Will continued, "So, here is what we have. Al-Saim's hit man is at the Temple Mount. He reaches into his tunic, splits the scene and thirty seconds later, after a man-made seismic occurrence, the Temple Mount collapses. Conclusion?"

"Elementary, my dear, Watson. The Alliance took down the Temple Mount and pinned it on the Israelis. The world, in particular the Islamic world, is incensed and the last Jihad is on. And the EU is in bed with'em on this."

"Why would anyone do this knowing the ramifications?" Will asked.

"Why would anyone fly planes into the World Trade Center knowing the ramifications?" Alex countered.

"Incredible," was all Will could say.

"Will, thanks for your help. Not a word," Alex cautioned him.

"You got it, buddy. Stay out of trouble," Will said, ending the transmission.

Alex considered his next move. He had the tape edited to include the Berlin hotel video thereby establishing a link between the two. This new information needed to be shared with the world, but it could not be seen coming from Israeli or American intelligence sources. Most of the media would quickly dismiss the information as political spin.

He went to Goldman's office. He knew the General was busy but the interruption was necessary. "General, I need ten minutes of your time."

Goldman was reviewing updates from the battlefield as his aide stood by. From the look on his face Alex could tell things were not going well in spite of OPERATION ANVIL HAMMER. Goldman gave him an annoyed look that said *don't bother me.*

"Sir, it *is* urgent," Alex said forcefully but respectfully. The officer from the communication section that accompanied Alex to the office nodded his head in agreement.

"OK, give us ten minutes, Colonel," Goldman said to his XO as the staff exited the General's office.

"Yes, sir. I will come running with any changes," the Colonel said as he returned to the main part of the Command Center. He eyed Alex warily wondering what was the information this American had that was so important, that it could interrupt battlefield reports.

As Alex entered the office Goldman eyed him and said tersely, "This better be worth it, Alex."

Alex nodded and quickly opened his laptop. He knew the General was feeling the stress of the campaign and it was beginning to show. The video actually took nine minutes to play and explain. As Alex concluded, Goldman starred at the laptop in disbelief. "This is more conclusive than the hotel video you showed me previously. Where did you get this?"

"A little investigative work with the kind assistance of your communications section and DNIS."

"No one is going to believe this, Alex. I am not sure I do," Goldman offered. "They will say we fabricated the tape as a propaganda move."

"Precisely, sir. That is why I suggest we bypass the major news networks and go straight to the Internet. Once there, the others cannot ignore the story. The power of the New Media is remarkable. We will have instantaneous worldwide coverage without the slant of the Old Media. I will need to involve the President for this part."

"Why?" inquired Goldman.

"There are contacts we can leak the information to. Reliable contacts that understand how to keep a source confidential."

"Very well, make the necessary arrangements," Goldman ordered.

14TH ARMORED BRIGADE

GOLAN HEIGHTS

4:43 a.m.

Alliance forces had completed the encirclement of Bethlehem and were preparing their move to Tel-Aviv. In the north, Syrian armor from Lebanon had penetrated to Haifa and was preparing to bypass that city. On the Southern Front, it was not much better as Alliance forces were nearing Beersheba.

The 14th Armored found itself encircled and cutoff from its supply lines. Goldman had attempted to withdraw south of Lake Tiberias but found his way blocked by Alliance armor. However, his remaining nine tanks had caused considerable confusion all out of proportion to their numbers. He had withdrawn his unit from the main roads choosing to engage his enemy in a game of cat and mouse. So intent on advancing to Israel was the Syrian command, they had chosen to ignore his beleaguered unit. The change in tactics enabled him to harass Alliance supply lines emanating from Syria, thereby acting as a brake on their advance.

It was nighttime and his tanks had just destroyed a supply column of forty trucks and APCs. Their burning hulks now littered the road. He withdrew his tanks in time before Alliance reinforcements arrived.

But now he had to face the reality of his tactical situation. His tanks were low on both fuel and ammo. His men were exhausted. They had been fighting practically non-stop for four days. He knew they would not be able to extract themselves from their current situation. He made his decision and gathered his tank commanders around for his orders.

"Men, as you know, our situation is grave. It will not improve with Alliance forces still in command of the air. Israel needs you more than she needs our tanks. We are going to attempt to make our way back to our homeland and regroup."

"Colonel, how are we going to do that?" asked Lt. Goldstein. "My tank has one round left and four liters of petrol."

Another commander spoke up, "Sir, my tank is in the same shape."

"I realize this. Here is what we're going to do. We are going to transfer our remaining ammo and fuel to five tanks. We will fight our way to Lake Tiberias, commandeer boats, and return to Israeli territory. Once across the lake, we will rejoin our brothers and continue the fight."

"Colonel, with due respect, what are our chances?" asked Lt. Goldstein.

"Better than we have now," Goldman replied firmly. "To remain here is a waste of our experience. My plan gives us a chance to live and fight for Israel another day. Start the transfer of fuel and ammo. Disable the tanks we leave behind."

IN THE CAULDRON

S teeler was maintaining an altitude of one hundred feet above sea level. The other eleven planes of his squadron were in formation. Each was armed with four AGM-64 Harpoon anti-ship missiles. Three additional squadrons were making their approach from separate courses to avoid detection. Between the four squadrons, one hundred ninety-two Harpoons were targeted on the *de Gaulle* battle group. The mission planners anticipated some of the missiles would be shot down by the shipboard defenses.

De Gaulle, along with her escorts, boasted some of the most formidable defenses ever included on a sailing vessel. Many naval experts considered them comparable to the Aegis battle management system. It was quite possible that all the Harpoons would be required to score at least a couple of hits on the EU carrier.

For this reason, an E/A-18G Growler ECM aircraft was assigned to each squadron. Its mission would be radar suppression. The two HARM missiles on board would be targeted on any radar energy emanating from *de Gaulle* or her escorts.

Steeler checked his instrument panel. The LCD was displaying the position of his aircraft relative to *de Gaulle*. The signal he was receiving was from the E-2D Hawkeye that was tracking *de Gaulle* as well as the other air and sea traffic in this part of the Med. There was not much of the latter though, as the majority of civilian traffic had wisely cleared the air and sea lanes once hostilities erupted, leaving the Med to the combatants.

His radar was showing ten Rafales of *de Gaulle's* air wing on Combat Air Patrol, but they apparently had not detected his squadron. Plus, they were probably preoccupied with the squadrons that had been detailed to attack any CAP assets. The Growler, in conjunction with the stealthy characteristics of the F-35C Lightnings, had done an excellent job in neutralizing the radar of the *de Gaulle* battle group.

Steeler activated another button on the LCD, this time bringing up the weapons load out. Four Harpoons and two AIM-120C missiles were displayed. He selected the Harpoons and fed in the targeting data. Each pilot had received a specific target. He had been detailed to attack *de Gaulle.*

"All right, gentlemen. It's show time. Let's show these amateurs what the U.S. Navy is all about. In the words of the Great Communicator, 'Now there we go again.' Lock and load!" his squadron commander ordered.

Keeping peace through strength Steeler thought as he pressed the fire button four times, releasing his Harpoons. Outside of his cockpit he saw the Harpoons streak away from his plane. In the darkness, the trails of other Harpoons could be seen leaving the squadron. He executed the pre-arranged evasive maneuver that would take him to the rendezvous with the tankers. The radars on board the French E-2C would soon detect the incoming missiles now that the Growler was withdrawing with them. At a launch distance of sixty miles it was almost a moot point. The defenses would not have much time to react.

Skimming at sea level, the Harpoons were detected by *de Gaulle's* Hawkeye twenty miles out. Warnings were quickly transmitted to the command center on board *de Gaulle.* Morganeau's reaction was similar to that of Alvarez's when the *GW* was the target. In almost repetitive fashion as when the *GW* was attacked, *de Gaulle's* escorts began launching their Pomona SAMs, which began their hunt for the incoming intruders. One by one they tracked down the Harpoons. As advertised, the defenses of the battle group were good. The SAMs shot down over sixty Harpoons, but those that survived pressed on to the ship they had been designated.

The close-in weapons on board the ships were now firing with some degree of effectiveness. The hail of bullets and Mistral SAMs brought down another fifteen Harpoons, but it was too little too late. The first Harpoon to strike impacted the stern of the *Cassard*, a French-built destroyer, destroying her engine room. A second struck amidships crippling the already injured vessel. Fires broke out and were soon out of control as the *Cassard* began listing to port. With the loss of her engines, she dropped out of formation.

As she did a gap opened in the defenses of the battle group, enabling more Harpoons to strike home. *Jean Bart*, *Cassard's* sister ship, erupted in a massive fireball as three Harpoons struck her. The impact broke her back, splitting her in to two pieces, which began to sink into the waters of the Mediterranean. *Surcouf* and *Aconit*, two of the newest frigates of the former French Navy, were each hit by a Harpoon damaging critical systems on both. That they did not absorb more hits was a tribute to their design, which incorporated stealth features in their construction. *Surcouf's* air search radar had been damaged while *Aconit's* aft missile launcher was destroyed.

On board *de Gaulle*, Captain Morganeau looked on with dismay as his escorts took hits. He had little time to worry about them though. Off the port beam, he saw incoming streaks of light bearing down on his ship. Within seconds, *de Gaulle* shuddered as four Harpoons struck the aft part of the vessel. It was hard to believe that a forty thousand ton vessel could shake so violently, but she did. He knew his ship had been damaged severely. And as most captains did, he took it personally as if he himself had been punched.

"Damage report!" he ordered.

He looked out of the bridge window, which surprisingly was still intact, at the flight deck. It was engulfed in smoke and flames, obscuring his vision. The landing lights were out on the forward part of the ship. It was just as well he could not see because the deck was warped from the explosions. The sole reason for *de Gaulle's* existence had been neutralized just as *George Washington's* had been in the opening moments of the war.

Below deck, men were struggling to their damage control stations through darkened passageways. Where hatches should have been they found twisted and charred metal. Additional explosions now racked *de Gaulle* as fuel and ammunition detonated from planes that were loaded in preparation for takeoff. The hanger deck was engulfed in flames in spite of the advanced fire suppression system.

Morganeau was fighting to maintain his balance. He checked one of the bridge instruments. It indicated the massive ship was beginning to list. Her speed had also dropped to six knots.

"Bridge, engineering. Reactor is damaged. I am taking it offline. We have two hours of emergency power remaining," reported the engineering officer.

That sealed it. His ship was as good as dead.

Looking around at the faces on the bridge, he saw disbelief where there had previously been an air of confidence when the first air strike was launched against the American carriers. "Who is left?" he asked.

"*Capitaine*, only *Courbet* is undamaged. *Surcouf* and *Aconit* are damaged but maneuverable. *Cassard* was last reported as sinking. *Jean Bart* has sunk."

He swore under his breath. "Cursed Americans. Curse their navy! This war is on their hands."

"*Capitaine*, the Americans will soon be launching a second strike. We must withdraw. Our flight deck is ruined. Are we going to sacrifice ourselves for the Jew and Arab? Best if they bleed each other to death with the Americans," his XO implored him.

Morganeau's mind went back in time when another Admiral was faced with a similar decision. Yamamoto had wisely withdrawn his ships from Midway after the Americans had sunk his four carriers. Now, deprived of air cover he had no choice but to make the same decision Yamamoto had made in 1942.

"Yes," he said wearily, "withdraw. Order *Courbet* to prepare a line to tow us out of the battle zone. Set course for Toulon. Best possible speed."

USS RONALD REAGAN

MEDITERRANEAN SEA

6:48 a.m.

"Admiral, we have satellite images now," announced the specialist.

"Let's see them," Kingston acknowledged as she took another drink of her coffee.

The main display in the CDC flickered for a moment and then stabilized. The images were instantly recognizable as ships even in the early morning light. If one were not sure they could have been mistaken for an American carrier group. Plumes of smoke were seen emanating from three of the ships.

"Can we enhance the image?" she asked.

The specialist adjusted a few controls. The images on the screen seemed to jump as the camera zoomed in. The clarity was so good from the satellite that the faces of the men scrambling to contain the damage on *de Gaulle's* flight deck were clearly recognizable.

"Looks like we hit her pretty good, Admiral. Four hits evident. Estimate her list at fifteen degrees," said Captain Smith. "If you look closely here," he indicated on the screen, "it appears she is under tow. Must have got her propulsion system."

"Check out the flight deck. No planes leaving there anytime soon. Not that many survived their attack on us to make it back," the XO noted. "Intel indicates the survivors made it to Sicily and other bases in Italy. Not much else in the air either other than some patrols. However, they are remaining close to their bases."

"Contact Alvarez on *GW*. Tell him he owes us one," Kingston said to Captain Smith.

"Intel indicates the rest of the Med is clear of traffic. Looks like the EU isn't going to sacrifice their navy for this fight," Smith observed. "The road is cleared, Admiral."

"Switching over to the defensive. Don't blame them. Planes and tanks are a lot easier to replace than ships. This may not be the last time we scrap with these folks either. I am sure they want as much of their fleet back home safe and sound as possible."

"Aren't we going to finish her off, Admiral?" inquired Smith.

"No, Captain. Orders were to disable or sink *de Gaulle*. With her disabled and the damage we inflicted on her battle group, Washington has not authorized a follow up strike."

"I hate it when wars become political," Smith said somewhat dejectedly.

"I agree. But remember, all wars are political, Captain. At least we won't have to put any more pilots at risk on this mission. Besides, the message has been sent. You don't screw around with the United States Navy," Kingston said with a satisfied look on her face. "Pour on the coal, Captain. We have an appointment to keep."

Gerhard's aides were briefing him on the turn of events on both the military and political battlefield. Things were not going well for the EU or the Alliance.

"Sir, several members of the Council have called," another of his aides noted. "They are concerned about the recent turn of events in the course of the war. The damage to *de Gaulle* and the loss of her escorts has them worried. Add to that England's defection and the potential impact this will have on the rest of the Union. Some have intimated a change in leadership may be needed if circumstances continue to unravel."

"They have, have they?" Gerhard noted with a smug shrug of his shoulders. "I will deal with them later. They forget that an omelet is not made without breaking some eggs."

His aides were puzzled over his last statement, but he did not have the time or inclination to explain it to them. Inwardly his frustration continued to mount but he had regained control over his emotions. He was boxing the frustration into a little corner of his mind that would be stored away and soon forgotten. He had to as the negative thoughts were clouding his thought process.

However, he was concerned that his plan for unifying the continent was unraveling due to the American support of Israel. Without their support, the Israelis would have been defeated by now. Now his reputation and that of the EU was on the line. It was time to exercise the authority of a superpower.

"Contact Strategic Command. It is time to end this. I am authorizing a nuclear strike on Israel. If we eliminate them, we eliminate the reason for this war. I had hoped to avoid having to use these weapons, but the Americans have forced my hand."

His aides were unsure what to do. The prospect of the war escalating to a nuclear one was something they had not anticipated given Gerhard's background.

"Herr Gerhard," one ventured to speak. "Surely there is another way. Neither Israel nor the U.S. will stand by idle if nuclear weapons are employed. Plus, use of nuclear weapons must be approved by the Council."

"The U.S. will not go nuclear over Israel. They want to be as rid of them as much as I do. We needn't worry about a retaliatory strike from the Israelis. They do not have a weapon that can threaten EU soil. I do not have time to debate the use of these weapons. Timing is everything in war. The Council will follow my leadership on this issue. *Now, carry out my orders!*"

The aides quickly moved to comply with his wishes.

Sullivan responded to the video Alex had prepared much as he did when CFA was the target of a hostile takeover. Alex had heard some rather colorful language from Sullivan during that time but nothing like he heard now. Sullivan was overwhelmed at the treachery and deceit the images revealed on the tape. He contacted O'Hara to make the necessary leaks.

"Alex, this is the hammer we have needed. I think I know best how to use this. We are going to find out how serious the new Prime Minister is."

"An excellent idea, Mr. President. It will enhance the credibility of the information."

The Prime Minister was as good as his word. Within the hour a news conference was being conducted from London. The video, coupled with the stinging oratory of McGregor was most persuasive. There was no doubting the sincerity or authenticity of the Prime Minister.

Simultaneous with McGregor's announcement was the release of the story on the Internet.

The headline on the website read: "Treachery and Deceit." Gerhard and Al-Saim's photos, along with photos of the destroyed Temple Mount, were juxtaposed underneath the headline to make the reference clear. A link to the video was provided. No mention of U.S. or Israeli intelligence was made. The story had the desired effect. Led by the New Media of the Internet and talk radio, the Old Media could not ignore the story and reluctantly began reporting on it. Images of Gerhard and Al-Saim at the hotel in Berlin, along with events at the Temple Mount, were soon being viewed around the world. AP and UPI were also carrying the storyline. It was too tantalizing a story to ignore.

14TH ARMORED BRIGADE

LAKE TIBERIAS

January 20th

3:55 a.m.

Daybreak was an hour away as Goldman's unit reached Lake Tiberias. Scanning the shore with his binoculars he spotted two boats. They appeared to be large enough for their purposes. He ordered six men to secure the boats while the remainder stayed with the two remaining tanks to give covering fire if needed. They were fortunate to have reached the Lake as the tanks were down to their last liter of petrol.

The boats were typical fishing boats. Fortunately, the owners had not risen from their sleep, but they soon would. Goldman's men quickly untied the boats and signaled all was ready. He gave the order to disable and abandon their tanks and make for the boats. Running, they quickly covered the mile to the boats. As they boarded, Goldman gave one last command: "You are now in the navy. Make for Israel and may Jehovah be with you!"

USS TEXAS

BAY OF BISCAY

3:19 a.m.

The *Texas* had been shadowing the EU boomer since detecting her off the French coast after her departure from Île Longue.

With the demise of the Soviet navy, many so-called defense experts had predicted the end of attack submarines such as the *Virginia* class. Expenditures on such weapons systems were a waste of money they argued. Yet, Kominski found himself again performing the very mission the 'experts' said was no longer needed.

"She is holding steady on course one eight zero. Speed five knots at one-five-zero feet. The exact profile a boat would show if preparing to launch, Captain," noted Petrovski.

"Maintain contact. She has been cruising like this for the past three hours." Kominski looked at his watch. He was working on four hours of sleep a day since they detected the EU boomer. That was almost ten days ago. The coffee he had been drinking was no longer providing the stimulant he needed. He knew he needed some sleep and very soon. He expected his men to be at their peak at all times, and he demanded even more from himself as their Captain. He checked his watch again.

"Sam, I am going to catch an hour of sleep," Kominski said. Pointing to the bow of the ship as if he could see the EU submarine, "If that sucker even hints at anything hostile…"

"I will come running with a cup of coffee," finished Petrovski. He knew his Captain was tired and was glad to see him finally realize this. An exhausted man of any rank was a potential liability on any ship; it was magnified even more when it was the Captain. "XO has the Conn," Kominski announced as he made his way out of the conning tower.

Kominski had no sooner climbed through the hatch when Petrovski called after him. He spun on his heels and rushed back to the conn.

"Sonar, say again," Petrovski ordered. Re-entering the conn, an anxious Kominski listened intently as Jones made his report.

"Conn, outer doors on the boomer are opening. Not the torpedo doors *but the missile doors!*"

"Sonar, this is the Captain. How many, Chief?" he asked as adrenaline was now doing what the caffeine had been unable to do.

"*Four, Captain. What are they thinking?*" reported an unbelieving Jones.

"Solution now!" he ordered. "Must be getting desperate to do this." What seemed like days passed before Petrovski reported.

"Solution ready, Captain. We are not going to let him shoot are we?"

"Flood tubes one through four," Kominski calmly ordered. "No, Sam. My orders are clear. If they open their doors we take him out. That has been communicated to the EU to be a hostile act. Guess they must be getting desperate."

"Tubes flooded, Captain. Boat is ready to fire," Petrovski reported.

"This is the Captain. Shoot tubes one through four. Say again, shoot one through four." He looked around the conn as the air pressure forced the torpedoes into the cold waters of the Atlantic. His eyes came to rest on an inscription on the forward bulkhead that epitomized his feelings. It read: "You don't mess with Texas."

"Conn, sonar! Four tracks in the water running clear." A second later Jones added, "Plus one additional track from *Le Vigilant. It's not a torpedo, Captain. Its course is vertical, repeat vertical!*"

Four MK 48 ADCAP heavy torpedoes left the bow of the *Texas* at fifty knots. *Le Vigilant* was one thousand feet dead ahead of the *Texas*. At soon as the torpedoes left the *Texas*, the sonar operators aboard *Le Vigilant* detected their launch.

"Conn, sonar, they've heard us. She is executing evasive maneuvers. Ejecting decoys. Speed increasing. No way she's going to outrun the fish." Two of the torpedoes went for the decoys ejected by *Le Vigilant* and exploded harmlessly away from the submarine.

"Two tracks remaining. Closing fast. Think we're going to get him, Captain!" exclaimed the Chief. The remaining two torpedoes had not been fooled as easily.

The hull of *Le Vigilant* was constructed of HY 130 compound steel. It enabled the submarine to withstand the pressure exerted by the ocean at depths of fourteen hundred feet. What it could not do was protect the submarine from both the ocean's pressure and that from the explosion of the two MK 48 warheads.

At three hundred feet below sea level, the MK 48 torpedoes detonated against the hull of the submarine. The overpressure ripped an opening in the hull causing the sub to implode on itself in a massive underwater explosion.

"Conn, sonar. Detecting massive hull popping. She's breaking up, sir. We got 'em," a relived Jones reported.

"Thank you, Chief. Helm, make course 270. Let's be a hole in the water. Sonar, conn. Keep your ears open for her escorts. They're out there somewhere."

GEORGE WASHINGTON

CDC

4:22 AM

"Admiral, receiving report from NORAD. Missile launch detected from Bay of Biscay," Lt. Donald Ellis manning the air threat monitor said with alarm in his voice. "Trajectory is Israel!"

"Some idiot has just taken us to the next level. Alert Amir. I hope their Arrow bases are intact," Alvarez ordered. "Are we sure we're not the intended target?"

"Can't say for sure, sir. Trajectory continues to show Israel as primary area of impact," Ellis reported. "But with six to ten MIRVs some could be tasked against us."

"Confidence?" Alvarez pressed the officer.

"Confidence is very high, Admiral," he replied emphatically.

"How are we on SAMs?" Alvarez now inquired.

"We have fifteen SM-3s for this. We should only need four if we catch the right intercept angle," Fontana advised.

"Let's be sure we do," Alvarez tersely said.

AMIR AIR BASE

4:23 a.m.

Goldman was moving quickly as reports were being received regarding the incoming missile. Alex had the good sense to stand out of the way for the moment. The actions or inactions taken in the next eight minutes could touch off the next world war.

"Missile defense reports ready, General. Target acquisition in eight minutes. *GW* reports standing ready for missile intercept. Estimated impact area is Tel-Aviv," noted the officer at the air threat desk.

"Alert *Leviathan* for immediate counterattack," Goldman ordered, thinking about his next decision. Contact was being established with one of Israel's three *Dolphin* class submarines armed with nuclear cruise missiles.

GEORGE WASHINGTON

4:27 a.m.

The Aerospatiale SLBM's trajectory had entered its descent stage. The missile contained six multiple re-entry vehicles each armed with a one hundred fifty kiloton warhead. It was not a large warhead compared to the larger thermonuclear warheads with yields in the megaton range. But it was large enough to effectively destroy the four largest cities in Israel: Jerusalem, Tel-Aviv, Haifa, and Rishon-LeZion, and with them almost one quarter of Israel's population.

"Missile entering terminal stage, Admiral. Intercept will be automatic," Fontana calmly noted.

The Aegis system aboard *Mobile Bay* was tracking the missile. Four SM-3 missiles departed from the launch tubes aboard the cruiser. Traveling at a speed of over Mach 3 and guided by the radar aboard *Mobile Bay*, the missiles quickly closed on their intended target.

All eyes were riveted to the main tactical display in the Command Center. Goldman's hands were clenched on the sides of his desk as he watched the incoming track of the missile and the tracks of the SM-3s launched by the Americans. The first two detonated behind the missile, but the third detonated in close enough proximity to destroy the missile and the EU's attempt at changing the fortune of the war. As the incoming missile track terminated all in the Command Center let out a collective yell of relief.

GEORGE WASHINGTON

4:28 a.m.

Simultaneously, the crewmembers in the CDC celebrated the interception of the missile. A potential disaster had been averted.

"Admiral, missile intercept successful," reported an exuberant Fontana extending his hand to the Admiral.

"Thank God for that. Signal Amir the good news. Tell *Mobile Bay* good shooting," said a relieved Alvarez as he pumped Fontana's hand.

BERLIN, EU

8:38 a.m.

Gerhard was in the middle of a breakfast reception when an aide came to his table. It was clear from the expectant look on his face that he was anticipating world breaking news from his aide. It indeed was world breaking, but not what he was anticipating. The aide whispered a summary of the developments in his ear. Inwardly, Gerhard was a raging volcano at hearing the news, but on the outside his demeanor did not show any sign of concern. He rose and excused himself from the breakfast with a quick apology to his guests.

His aide was filling in additional details of the news as they entered his office. One television was tuned to the *BBC* while the second was on *CNN*. He turned up the volume on the *BBC* broadcast. He stared in disbelief as the video was again playing across the 52-inch high definition screen. He quickly muted the *BBC* and turned up *CNN*. Having had almost a day to digest the video and its allegations, both networks were putting the same spin on the story: that while they couldn't confirm the origins of the video, they were now confirming its accuracy. The commentators were saying *reliable* news sources were attesting to the accuracy of the contents. Just the day before they were condemning the video as a ploy by Israel to shift the tide of public opinion. *Fickle journalists*, Gerhard thought. Nonetheless, the damage was done. No amount of spin was going to make this go away. He changed the channel to *Al-Jazeera*. They continued to report the story as nothing more than a U.S. and Israeli deception.

Not much different than he expected. That was the best he could hope for at this point. The downside was that *Al-Jazeera* was not available in the United States.

The news then turned to a summary of the war including video of *de Gaulle* and her battle group limping back to port.

"Is there an update from Strategic Command?" Gerhard demanded.

"Sir, that is the other development. I did not want to tell you at the breakfast. Strategic Command has reported our missile was intercepted as it entered its terminal stage. It apparently wasn't the Israelis that intercepted. Reports indicate it was the Americans."

"Initial polling data is indicating a shift in support for the Americans. There has even been a shift in support among some members of the Union itself. Herr Gerhard, that video has to be stopped, or at least we need to offer a stronger counter explanation," one aide noted.

"Pulling for the underdog now are they? The world loves a sucker," Gerhard noted as he began to formulate a way out of this debacle.

The cell phone of one of his aides rang who quickly answered the device. "This cannot be. Are you sure?" he asked with a distraught look as he met Gerhard's eyes. "Very well. Inform me if you have something else."

"What is it?" Gerhard asked as his aide closed the cell phone.

"Sir, Strategic Command is reporting they lost contact with *Le Vigilant* over three hours ago. She was one of our missile subs. Her escorting sub, the *Rubis*, was in the area and reported an underwater disturbance in the vicinity of *Le Vigilant* and then nothing. The sonar man aboard *Rubis* reported that the sounds resembled that of an explosion and then a hull imploding. She is still investigating."

"Impossible," Gerhard said as he fell into his chair. He sat for a moment before he spoke to his aides. The tide of battle was definitely shifting against the EU and Alliance. And more importantly, the court of world opinion was shifting as well. "First this rubbish regarding the Temple and now this."

"The American carriers will soon be within striking range," his military aide added.

"This cannot be happening to me," Gerhard said glaring at his staff. He thought for a moment more before he addressed his staff. "Not a word of this to anyone. Not even the Council. The people cannot be trusted to understand what I am attempting to accomplish."

Though the leadership in the EU viewed itself as the new format for progressive government, it was still nonetheless a bureaucracy. And within any bureaucracy there were competing forces at work for power. The EU was not exempt from such forces. The report regarding the loss of *Le Vigilant* had not been solely reported to Gerhard's office.

14TH ARMORED BRIGADE

LAKE TIBERIAS

5:43 a.m.

Morning light came slowly as the dawn broke. Overcast skies were preventing the sun from shining. A wind from the northwest was beginning to kick up causing whitecaps to form on the water. To add to the misery of the day a light rain was beginning to fall. Goldman was thankful for the inclement weather. Anything that helped obscure their presence on the water was a blessing he told his men. However, the weather was not as helpful as he had hoped. His men were halfway across the lake when an Alliance artillery unit spotted them.

"Who are they?" asked the Syrian commander as he looked through his binoculars.

"Their uniforms suggest IDF, sir. My estimate is they are from the 14th Armored. Recon units found several destroyed tanks near the east shore of the lake. Their markings were found on one. If this is them, they exacted a tremendous toll on our forces."

"Yes, they did. Lieutenant, what do you think about some target practice for the men?" asked the commander with a devilish grin.

"An excellent idea, sir."

"Order the guns deployed," said the commander.

The self-propelled 122mm artillery pieces pulled to the side of the road that skirted the south of the lake. The turrets housing the massive guns swung to face the water and targeted the two boats.

"All units report ready, sir."

"Fire!" shouted the commander in anticipation of gaining revenge on Goldman and his men.

Smoke erupted from six of the barrels as the first echelon opened fire. The six units of the second echelon then fired.

On board the two boats, the men reacted to the sound of the artillery as the blast echoed across the water.

"Incoming!" shouted Goldman.

The incoming shells sounded like jets approaching as they pierced the air. Enormous geysers of water erupted forty meters away from the boats.

The commander of the artillery unit swore as he looked through his binoculars. Two sitting ducks and his unit had missed wide.

"Tell the commanders their aim better improve," he said to his lieutenant.

"Yes, sir," replied his lieutenant as he signaled the artillery commanders to fire again.

On the boats, Goldman knew they were helpless. The only solution was to split up. He gave the order for the other boat to head north while his continued west. This presented his boat as the broadest, and hopefully, easiest target. Both boats were zigzagging now to cause the Syrian gunners added difficulty. The second round of shells missed again, but two rounds struck close enough to swamp the boat veering to the north by the waves they created.

The men spilled out into the frigid waters. Goldman turned to look at the other boat. He saw the heads of his men bobbing in the water. The wind had picked up, creating larger white caps. Some of the men had managed to grab hold of their overturned boat, but it was obvious they would not be able to right it under the present conditions. Goldman did not hesitate in his next decision. He swung his boat around in an attempt to rescue his men.

He knew the Syrians were being chastised for their failure to sink the boats. Perhaps that was the only thing that would save them. Every minute they delayed enabled them to pull another man into the boat. As the last man was being pulled in the boat, Goldman trained his binoculars on the Syrians' position. He saw the barrels elevating for a third, and most likely, final round. His boat was now stationary and presented an excellent target.

He was still looking through the binoculars when movement in the air caught his attention. Planes were coming in from the south. Goldman assumed they were Alliance as he had not seen the IAF since hostilities broke out. They appeared to be coming in for a staffing run. Had the commander called in for air support?

He soon had his answer. The planes swept in low and released their ordinance. The shoreline where the Syrian artillery was located erupted in a firestorm of explosions as bombs from the planes detonated. Goldman glanced up just in time to catch the markings on the planes as his men cheered. The white star was unmistakable: American F/A-18 Hornets.

"Where did they come from?" asked his sergeant.

"Don't know and don't care. As long as they are here," Goldman said as he slapped the sergeant on the back. The men in his boat were hugging each other as they cheered on the aircraft.

The Hornets returned again for another pass, finishing off the Syrians. All that remained of the artillery unit were twelve flaming hulks.

"Were those IAF?" asked the sergeant.

"No, they're American F-18s! Carrier based," exclaimed Goldman.

"Looks like we have a friend in this war after all," noted the sergeant.

"It also means we may be winning if American planes are flying strikes in our area," Goldman observed. "Israel and America versus Europe and the Alliance."

"I'll take that fight any day," one of his men said exuberantly. "Yanks have probably been itching to kick some European butt after Iraq anyway."

"Could be. I would have never thought it possible, though. Come on, let's get this thing moving. We have to get back to Israel and find some tanks before this thing is over," ordered Goldman. Though he was tired and freezing, he was smiling to himself. He now felt confident of victory.

The ever-growing presence of American air power from the *Reagan* Strike Group over the battlefield had swung the tide of battle in favor of Israel. Aircraft from the four *Nimitz* carriers, in addition to those of the *George Washington*, were exacting a toll on Jallud's forces. The accuracy of the precision-guided weapons against Arab armor, in particular at the Battle of Nazareth, had a telling impact on the battle.

Two armored divisions, Jallud's reserves, had been detailed to punch through the remaining Israeli defenses in this sector. If they were successful, the tide of battle could swing back to the Alliance. It had been reported that Israel had already committed their reserves. So far, America had not been able to resupply Israel as during the Yom Kippur War. However, Jallud's forces were not able to effectively deploy the full weight of their firepower due to the interdiction of the American F/A-18s and F-35s, plus IAF squadrons, now operating over the battlefield with growing impunity.

First, the Americans interdicted the supplies that had been reaching the Syrian tanks. In a battlefield as intense as the Northern Flank, the disruption in logistics was as important as destroying the tank itself. Jallud reminded himself of the quote by Irwin Rommel, the Desert Fox: "In armored warfare, half supplies are almost as bad as no supplies." The law of overstretch had finally caught up with the Alliance tanks.

In utilizing the cold start approach to war, the Alliance had failed to adequately supply their units for extended fighting. The plan had been to engage the few Israeli units they anticipated, defeat these, and drive deep into Israel before Israel could mobilize. Tel-Aviv was to have been captured by the fourth day of battle. But, by the fourth day of the battle they had not penetrated as far as Nazareth in the north and Beersheba in the south. Israeli forces had fought to the death, delaying the Alliance advance and buying time for the IDF to complete its mobilization. Now, under the weight of Israeli and American airpower Alliance forces began to wilt.

His forces had been abandoned by their European allies. The remaining EU planes had made for bases in Italy and southeastern Europe. So infuriated were Alliance forces at their former European allies, that they fired SAMs after the fleeing Europeans bringing down several of the planes. Gerhard had contacted Jallud and explained the reason for his forces withdrawal was the urgent need to reinforce the EU in anticipation of further American attacks.

In a vain hope, Jallud had contacted Moscow for assistance but there was no reply forthcoming. Perhaps the leaders in the Kremlin were content to see the Alliance destroyed by Israel. It was possible that a weakened Alliance played into Moscow's long-term strategy in the Middle East.

It was now obvious to Jallud that his forces would not be receiving any additional assistance. With dwindling supplies, destruction of his armored reserves, and the Americans and Israelis in command of the air, Jallud was left with one option.

His mind turned to the WMDs, specifically the chemical and biological weapons that had been ferreted away by Saddam's army as the Americans marched toward Baghdad in 2003. There was one nagging unknown that plagued Jallud, however. If he did use the WMDs, how massive would Israel's response be? Would it be a limited response or full-scale retaliation? His own intelligence estimated Israel possessed roughly three hundred nuclear weapons. If the Alliance released their WMDs on Tel-Aviv, which city, or cities, would Israel destroy? Damascus? Cairo? Tehran? Ten or twenty of those weapons would devastate every major city in the Arab world. That was a prospect he could not accept. He was not even confident in their ability to launch the attack against Israel in light of their complete command of the battlefield. No, it was a choice that looked tantalizing on paper, but in reality was a dagger at his people's throat. That left him with but one option.

THE END

AMIR AIR BASE
January 23rd
10:28 a.m.

"General, Alliance forces continue their withdrawal. We are preparing to encircle Damascus. We have almost completed the conquest of Jordan. Here, we are preparing to cross the Suez Canal tomorrow morning," the Major continued as he pointed toward the map.

The review continued as Goldman followed along on the map. The tactical situation showed Israeli forces in what military analysts describe as the exploitation phase of battle. Having routed their foe, the discussion now began to shift as to how far their gains should be consolidated. With each kilometer of territory, Israel gained more room for a defense in depth and an age-old dream. But, with the conquered territory came the Arab population. They would never accept Israeli rule after all that had transpired.

The United Nations had finally acted and was calling for a cessation of hostilities and a return to the pre-war borders. The Chinese delegation had been particularly vocal in the call for a ceasefire. There was even a veiled hint of intervention in the battle if the ceasefire was not accepted. Europe was conspicuously quiet on the issue. Goldman had already decided there would not be a return to the pre-war boundaries; especially not after their betrayal. Israel would never let her guard down again and entrust her security to anyone. Not even to the United States. Land would be the security buffer between her and her Arab neighbors.

This war had reinforced this position more than any other war in her history.

"General?" his aide said disturbing his train of thought.

"Yes," an exhausted Goldman replied.

"General, UN Ambassador Hezzikiah Cohn for you."

"What does the Ambassador want?" Goldman asked.

"Sir, he has an urgent message regarding a potential ceasefire offer from the Alliance."

Stunned by the news, Goldman simply said, "Put him through."

The Ambassador was indeed reporting an offer of a ceasefire, with a provision for a peace settlement, had been extended through the Chinese Ambassador on behalf of the Alliance. There was not much else the Alliance could do in light of their current military situation. Neither the EU nor Russia was willing to send reinforcements on their behalf.

A quick buzz went around the Command Center. A peace offering always generated a sense of excitement, much as the initial shots of a war. Alex was making his way back from the facilities. *War was no respecter of the human bladder* he noted. He overheard two soldiers discussing the offer as he passed them in the corridor. Hurriedly, he made his way to Goldman's office.

Alex knocked on Goldman's door. Goldman motioned him in. His face asked the obvious question.

"Yes, it is true," Goldman acknowledged. "It appears we have a legitimate offer from the Alliance to discuss a ceasefire. Possibly even a surrender."

"What are you going to do?" inquired Alex as he pulled a chair close to Goldman's desk and sat down. On his desk was another situation map detailing the disposition of Israeli and Alliance forces. Alex also noticed some additional lines drawn on the map that extended well beyond Israel's current area of control and those prior to the war.

"Now that the tide of battle has swung in our favor, I intend to totally annihilate them," Goldman said in a voice devoid of emotion. "I am going to rid Israel of her enemies once and for all. I intend to take all of the land promised to Abraham and restore the Promised Land."

"Is that what these new boundaries are?" Alex asked pointing to the map.

"Yes they are, Alex. The Promised Land. Greater Israel as some call it. The land promised to Abraham and our forefathers," Goldman confirmed defiantly.

Alex was stunned at the reply. This was not the same man he had met in Geneva. War had taken a toll on the man. What Goldman was proposing was beyond belief. Part of Alex understood Goldman's desire to finish off the Alliance. It had become apparent that outside of the United States, Israel was alone in the world. Strategically it was dangerous to have only one ally in the world, but Israel had no other options. Still, the intention of Goldman to restore all of the Promised Land to Israel astonished Alex.

The map indicated the new borders of Israel would extend from the Nile River almost to the southern border of Egypt, then turn northeast and extend on a straight line to where the borders of Iraq and Iran meet along the Persian Gulf. The northern border would be the Euphrates River. If Goldman carried through on this plan, Israel would occupy a significant part of the Middle East. It also meant she would come into possession of almost one-third of the world's proven oil reserves. This was something that no Muslim would stand for, nor would the world body of nations. In addition, Alex knew President Sullivan would not condone such a move as a large part of Saudi Arabia and Iraq would come under Israeli control.

In fact, Sullivan had been moving for Israel to end the war in an effort to restore peace in the region as soon as possible. Sullivan had already ordered the standing down of American forces over the battlefield now that Israel's destruction was no longer imminent. Planes from the *Reagan* CSG were now acting as a shield against any further interference from any outside parties. They were not actively participating in combat. There had to be something that could be done to foster a peace settlement without Goldman following through on his plan.

"General, if I may be bold," Alex began somewhat hesitantly.

"Go on, Alex. I have come to expect that from you."

"Now is the time to secure Israel's security but through another means."

"Another means? There is no other way," Goldman said sternly.

"With all due respect, General, yes there is. Israel's borders are secure now. As secure as they are going to be when surrounded by enemies. General, with the Temple Mount destroyed, but in your possession, additional conquest of territory will only further alienate the Alliance.

You have won much." Alex paused for a second before continuing. "Now it is time to give."

"Give!" Goldman exclaimed pounding his hand on his desk.

"Yes, General. Give." Alex waited a moment for the thought to sink in before proceeding. "What has the Alliance wanted the most?"

"Our destruction, of course."

"Yes, but there is something else."

Goldman thought for a moment before answering, not sure where Alex was trying to guide him. "A home for the Palestinians?"

"Yes, sir. This has been one of the obstacles to peace since 1948. You have what Israel has wanted. Jerusalem and now the Temple Mount. Your people will rebuild the Temple now. No one expects you to sacrifice that gain again. Jerusalem is recognized as your capital. Grant the Palestinians their own state and secure your peace."

"You are not serious. I could not ask our people to *give*, as you say, the Palestinians a home," Goldman almost spat the words at Alex. "Not after what the Alliance and the Europeans tried to do to us."

"Then you condemn your people to a life of terror and war, General. Think about it. The loss of the Temple Mount, coupled with the lost land, will fester like an open wound amongst the Alliance without them gaining something in return. Jallud needs a card he can play for his people in the court of world opinion. A moment like this will not come again in our lifetimes. You, Israel, would gain new respect in the world. This will help heal the wounds of war. You cannot afford not to do this," Alex implored the General.

Goldman was stung by the ferocity of Alex's words. He knew Alex was right but he did not want to admit it. Doing so would remind him that his enemies were people and not murdering butchers. He continued to mull over Alex's premise.

"Perhaps you are right, Alex. This may be the time to *give* as you say. Maybe we can afford to be magnanimous after all."

Observation Point Six (OP6)

Golan Heights

January 25th

11:02 a.m.

It was decided that the ceasefire talks would be conducted at Observation

Point Six just to the west of the Golan Heights. The Heights were again in Israeli hands after having routed both EU and Alliance forces from the strategic mountains. Each side would bring three representatives and arrive by helicopter. By now, the IAF and U.S. Navy had achieved total air supremacy over the battlefield. The danger of being shot down by the Alliance was minimal.

General Goldman, his XO, and Alex exited the Command Center. The fresh air was a welcome relief to the men. It had been almost three weeks since they had seen the outside world other than through a monitor. Their eyes watered in the brightness of the sun. Alex had wondered at one point if the next sun he saw would be that of a nuclear fireball. He breathed a sigh of relief it had not been.

They boarded a Humvee that drove them past a pair of Raptors that were being refueled for their next mission. *How ironic* Goldman thought as they drove past the Raptors toward the awaiting Blackhawk. *It was those planes that had fired the first salvos in the war. No,* Goldman reminded himself, *it was the Iranians that fired the first salvo by reactivating their nuclear weapons research.* And now, he was going to meet his Alliance counterpart and determine if resolution could be brought to this war.

Four Apache helicopters that served as escort flanked the Blackhawk. Overhead a squadron of Ra'ams and Raptors flew CAP in the unlikely event of an attack. Goldman was taking no chances in light of the past few weeks. As they flew over the battlefield, destroyed tanks and buildings were prevalent. Every few miles there would be a cluster of burnt-out tank hulls where a battle had occurred. The sheer number of destroyed tanks was a testimony to the intensity of the battle. It was estimated the armored forces of both sides had been reduced by three quarters.

The Blackhawk helicopter swooped in low over OP6, banked hard to the left, and circled the area before the pilot set the machine down. There was another helicopter already present. It bore the insignia of the Islamic Alliance.

A solitary tent had been erected for the negotiations. Above the tent, the Star of David fluttered in the moderate breeze. Goldman had insisted the Israeli flag be present. He wanted to convey a clear message that it was Israel who had been the victors.

Exiting the Blackhawk, Goldman and his party made their way to the tent. Entering through the open flaps, Alex saw three men seated across the sole table in the tent. Jallud, wearing a military uniform, was in the middle flanked by two aides. Conspicuously absent was a representative from the European Union. Jallud and his men rose and saluted as Goldman and Alex entered.

Jallud's face momentarily revealed his surprise at whom he was preparing to negotiate with. *It was one of life's ironies*, he thought. He laughed to himself, which seemed to erase some of the exhaustion from the failed war.

"I see that we meet again," Jallud offered, "except that fate seems to have been kinder to you, *General.*"

"So it would seem, *General*," Goldman replied as he returned Jallud's salute. Alex was struck by the fact that these two enemies, who just hours before were attempting to annihilate each other, were adhering to military courtesy. "Let us be seated. We have much to discuss."

For the next two hours, Goldman detailed the items of the ceasefire to Jallud, who had very little choice but to accept the terms. The document called for the immediate cessation of all hostilities between Israeli, Alliance, and EU forces. They also discussed the terms of POW transfers and other items related to the military aspect of the ceasefire. Then the conversation switched to the political aspects of the talks.

These provisions called for the continued recognition of Israel's right to exist by all Alliance members and Jerusalem as Israel's capital. It also provided for the acknowledgment of Israel's new borders as permanent with some minor provisions. Jallud inquired as to what these borders and provisions were.

"General Jallud, this final part is subject to the approval of the new Israeli government. But I think the terms will be as acceptable to them as they will be to you," Goldman noted.

Goldman glanced in Alex's direction as he pulled a separate document out, accompanied by maps, and passed copies to Jallud. It took Jallud a moment to read the document. Then he looked at the map. He re-read the document just to be sure. He was caught off guard by the words on the paper. He looked up at Goldman to confirm this was a serious offer. Goldman was nodding his head confirming the legitimacy of the offer. The new northern border of Israel included that part of Lebanon from Saida to within five miles of Damascus. From there the border turned south along the main road from Damascus to Amman. It continued its southerly path along the main road leading from Amman to Al 'Aqabah on the Gulf of Aqaba. On the southern border, Israel would again occupy the Sinai. Also on the map was an area that was colored a light yellow. Jallud focused his attention on this part of the map. The accompanying document called for the formation and recognition of a Palestinian state within part of the West Bank. For a moment, Jallud sat still staring at the map and the documents. Israel was going to control more territory that was formerly occupied by his brothers. They were going to control the Temple Mount. There was nothing he could do to prevent either of those events from occurring. As if a reminder were needed, the sound of helicopters could be heard in the distance. There was nothing about the offer he liked. But he realized this was perhaps the best possible offer he was going to receive. In fact, he was completely surprised at the offer of a Palestinian state. If this were a chess match he would be down to his last move before the opponent declared checkmate. There was but one move left. To retain some sense of his honor, and that of his people, he looked at Goldman and spoke.

"It would seem that both sides have gotten what was wanted all along. You have Jerusalem and security. No doubt you will begin construction of your Temple. The Palestinians will have a home. Perhaps we are not so far apart on some of these issues after all."

"Yes, it would appear so," Goldman replied surprised by Jallud's response to the terms of the ceasefire.

"Perhaps if we had talked more seriously in Geneva, we could have avoided the loss of so many of our brothers," Jallud continued.

"Yes, perhaps," Goldman very guardedly replied as he was quite taken by Jallud's candor.

"Maybe one day it might be possible for us to visit and share some Baklava and coffee. As neighbors."

"That would be welcome, General. Perhaps that day is not far off," Goldman agreed.

"Well, until that day, General. Mr. Stanton," Jallud said as he rose from his chair sensing the meeting was over. Jallud saluted and then offered his hand. All shook hands before Jallud and his party departed. Alex and Goldman followed them out of the tent and watched them board their helicopter. The blades of the Mi-8 were already rotating as the pilot brought the machine up to takeoff power.

As the Mi-8 began to slowly rise, the down draft from the rotors generated a small dust storm. The pilot hovered the helicopter for a moment and began to move the machine on a course back to Syria as four IDF Apaches formed up for an escort. Jallud's aides eyed him with curiosity as they began their way home. Jallud could feel their stares. His eyes met theirs.

"My brothers, this is not over. You have my word. This I swear."

Back at Observation Post Six, Alex and Goldman watched as the Mi-8 departed over the horizon. The dust from the departing helicopter had finally settled.

Alex turned to Goldman. "Well, you could knock me over with a feather. I would never have dreamed this was possible."

"Me either, Alex, me either. But as we have both read in the Bible, there are many miracles we cannot explain."

"That is true, General. We have certainly witnessed one here. I suppose you are going to be a very busy man reestablishing the government. Have you ever considered running for Prime Minister?"

"No. That is not for me. I will leave that to the politicians. Perhaps there is a future with people like Jallud. How will your President deal with Europe?"

"There are deep wounds there. A lot of fence mending will have to be done with Europe. I never dreamed we would have fought our former allies. But we fought the British in our past and they eventually turned out to be one of our strongest allies. Same with the Germans and Italians. It will be a struggle, but all things are possible. It will all turn on who the future leader of Europe becomes. Who knows? This may be the catalyst for a true peace that could be embraced by the world."

"Come along, Alex. We both have much to do," Goldman said as he gestured to the awaiting Blackhawk.

Brussels, EU
January 26th
11:03 a.m.

Gerhard had returned to his office in Brussels. He knew he was going to have to act swiftly and decisively to regain his momentum. After all, appearances were everything in politics. A meeting of the Council of Ten had been called to discuss their future options. One of the more preposterous rumors he had heard was the possible dissolution of the EU.

Before they were to meet, Gerhard was scheduled to make a short statement regarding the turn of fortune in the war. He knew there was going to be fallout from the EU's inability to be more effective against the Americans. The loss of the *Charles de Gaulle* to the Americans was the most difficult to accept. She had been the pride of the EU navy. Fortunately, he had been able to keep the sinking of *Le Vigilant* quiet for the moment.

The Council meeting began without the usual fanfare as Gerhard moved straight to the main issue regarding the turn of events in the war.

"Ladies and gentlemen, like you, I am disappointed at the turn of events in the Middle East. Our forces fought gallantly but were betrayed by the Alliance. As a result, we have had to withdraw as you have seen in the news accounts. I seriously weighed the option of either continuing the war or temporarily withdrawing. After much consideration, I chose the latter course. The Alliance forces did not fight as I anticipated or was promised. To continue the war would have meant employing our nuclear weapons, and I was not prepared to do that. I am still committed to finding a solution for peace in the Middle East."

The members of the Council sat and listened as Gerhard continued to explain his rationale for ending EU activities in the Middle East and the future course they would embark on in that area of the world. Upon concluding his statement he sat down.

"Herr Gerhard," said Gerabaldi, "the members of the Council also join you in expressing our concern for the unfortunate turn of events in the Middle East. However, there is one point that we are in disagreement with you."

"And what would that be, Gerabaldi?" asked Gerhard.

"The attempted employment of nuclear weapons against Israel and subsequent loss of our nuclear submarine *Le Vigilant*," Gerabaldi stated emphatically as he held up a copy of the report detailing the loss of *Le Vigilant*. He had already distributed copies of the report to the other members of the Council. "We were in favor of your actions in the Middle East. But, Herr Gerhard, you did not have the authority to authorize the use of these weapons without the approval of the Council."

Sensing the mood of the Council was shifting support to Gerabaldi, Gerhard knew he had to move fast.

"Signor Gerabaldi, I understand your concerns, but the course of events unfortunately did not afford me the luxury of consulting the Council in this matter. I had to make an executive decision regarding what was best for the EU. I make no apologies for my actions," Gerhard replied firmly but not in an overbearing sense. He did not want to give the appearance of chastising Gerabaldi as he was well respected among the Council.

"Herr Gerhard," Gerabaldi continued as he pressed his position, "if word of this action became public knowledge it would impugn the reputation of the EU even more than it already has been. Your actions have imperiled the Union…"

"My actions have imperiled the Union?" Gerhard interrupted feigning surprise and dismay at the accusation. He was now becoming frustrated with this line of questioning and moved to end it before Gerabaldi gained additional momentum. "I would offer that it was my actions that saved the EU. You will recall the previous unsuccessful attempts at unification. *My* leadership enabled us to achieve our long sought after goal. Have I imperiled the EU? I say no. But there is one who has caused us much damage. And that is Alex Stanton. I believe it was he who tipped off the Israelis of our impending attack. Remove his actions from recent events and we are successful in our efforts in the Middle East. We will deal with Mr. Stanton later. Meanwhile, I will contact my counterpart in the Alliance regarding our future mutual interests in the Middle East. Ladies and gentlemen, we should continue to discuss this and learn from our mistakes, but that is for a future time. Remember the EU motto: ein volk, ein continent, ein euro."

It was one of the oldest tactics in the book but it was nonetheless still a good defense. Place the blame for your failures on someone else. Stanton was the logical choice. Removing him from future equations would prevent the problems the EU encountered in Operation Rosh. It had worked time and time again in the past and Gerhard could see that it was working with the Council. Politics was all so simple to Gerhard. It was just the manipulation of people to believe your ideas were the right course of action. However, Gerabaldi was equal to the task before him and moved to speak.

"Herr Gerhard, your words are eloquent and persuasive as always. You are a gifted politician. But your actions in this matter have masked your words. As I was saying before you interrupted. Your actions have imperiled the Union and quite possibly could have unleashed a nuclear nightmare if *Le Vigilant*'s missiles had not been intercepted by the Americans. The Israelis would have retaliated, as quite possibly would have the Americans. How do we know one of those missiles was not targeted for their carrier battle group?"

"You are insane to try and stop me in this, Gerabaldi!" Gerhard exclaimed.

"No, it is you who are insane, Gerhard," Gerabaldi replied with a firm voice. "The Council has already decided. You are removed from your office effective immediately. You will stand trial for your actions in this matter."

"What? My actions? My dear, Gerabaldi, need I remind you and the Council that you were as involved with Operation Rosh as I? Do you think the people will stand for that once they learn of your acquiescence in this?" laughed Gerhard.

"They will only know of your actions my dear, Gerhard. We are seeing to that now. You will be placed under arrest and stand trial for war crimes." With that, Gerabaldi signaled for security to enter and remove Gerhard.

Gerhard looked at the Council as the security forces made their way toward him. Their faces, which had once hung on his every word, were now impassive toward him. He came to the conclusion that further words were futile. If the media was already being fed a stream of misinformation about his actions, then he knew he was through for now. *It was incredulous*, he thought to himself, *that one as gifted as he had been outfoxed by someone like Gerabaldi.*

CONCLUSION

OVAL OFFICE

January 30th

9:30 a.m.

"Welcome home, Alex," Sullivan said meeting Alex halfway across the room. He grasped Alex's hand and patted him on the back. "It's good to have you back."

"Thank you, Mr. President. It is good to be back," noted Alex. "Any more word on the fallout in Europe?"

"Still too early to tell. One thing we are sure of. Gerhard has made a lot of enemies as a result of the EU's actions in the war," acknowledged Sullivan. "A major split appears to be occurring within the EU. The rest of Eastern Europe is threatening to withdraw from the Union. Apparently they were unaware of Gerhard's plans involving Israel. There is discussion of those countries forming a confederation of nations along with England. Nothing definite though. It will be interesting to see if Gerabaldi can hold it together. Good move on their part to remove Gerhard, though I am not sure how innocent the EU Council really is."

"Do we know the whereabouts of Al-Saim?" Alex asked.

"Unfortunately, we have not seen or heard from him since the peace negotiations. He has disappeared for all practical purposes. Again," noted Sheffield.

"The world is certainly a different place now isn't it, Mr. President?" Alex commented to Sullivan.

"Yes it is, Alex. But at least it is one without a nuclear-armed Iran and North Korea. We have seen to that."

"Let's not overlook the damage done to Iran's overall military capability. Her air and naval assets have been seriously degraded as were key components of their military infrastructure," Clairmont added with a degree of pride.

"Status of the *GW?*" Sullivan asked Clairmont.

"She is returning to Norfolk after temporary repairs in Israel. *Reagan* will provide escort on the return trip," Clairmont noted. "As per your orders, the remainder of the battle group is remaining in the Mediterranean for a while. We are keeping our carriers in the Gulf to shore up the Saudis and the Gulf States. Replacement aircraft are in route to both carrier groups to bring them back up to full strength."

"The Middle East is quiet for now but I wouldn't expect it to remain that way," Sheffield continued the discussion. "Arab pride has been severely wounded. The loss of the Temple Mount will not sit for long. There have already been overtures to China for military assistance from some members of the Alliance. At least Saudi Arabia, Kuwait, and Iraq have remained intact. It is imperative we get Saudi and Kuwaiti oil production back up. The Strategic Petroleum Reserve has been drawn down by one fifth. We are vulnerable right now until the oil starts flowing again."

"The last thing we need is Chinese involvement in the Mideast," Alex said shaking his head. "We are fortunate regarding the Saudis and Kuwaitis. I am sure their petrodollars will be heavily invested in defensive upgrades. As far as Gerhard…well his actions won't sit well with the Fundamentalists. He has left Gerabaldi a lot of fence mending."

"Alex, did you ever discover who sent you the tape of Gerhard at the hotel?" Sullivan inquired.

"No, sir, nothing. It was a gift from heaven though. It got the ball rolling on our suspicion of the Accord," Alex humbly replied.

"Yes it did and with far reaching implications. The situation with Europe is a whole new ballgame," Sullivan said switching the topic back to Europe. "Gerhard initiated a change in the geo-political landscape with his actions, and I see no reason why the situation will change even with Gerabaldi now in charge. His moving the EU capital to Rome is certainly meant to be a signal of that change, but we will have to wait and see. Alex, I want you to prepare a thorough review on the EU. Its history, suggestions as to how to posture our foreign policy, etc. You may have been on to something with the eschatology angle. Include your observations from that perspective as well. I have a feeling this is not the last time we will have to deal with them."

"I will start on that right away, sir. You're really worried about Europe aren't you, Mr. President?"

"Yes I am, Alex. Without Europe we have no natural allies in the world. Imagine a block of enemies consisting of the EU, China, the Islamic Alliance, and possibly Russia. Not very inviting is it?"

"No, sir, it isn't," Alex quietly replied.

"Well, enough of that for now," Sullivan continued as he shifted the conversation. "Alex, we are all very proud of you. You did an outstanding job for us over in Israel."

The others in the Oval Office joined in the congratulations. After a few moments, Sullivan gestured for all to find a seat.

"I received a very complimentary call from General Goldman regarding your service to both of our countries during the war. Without your efforts, the true story of what happened to the Temple Mount would be buried right along with Israel. You exposed the treachery Gerhard almost succeeded with. Well done, Alex, well done," Sullivan said beaming with pride at his Special Assistant.

"Thank you, Mr. President. I am just glad I was able to earn my keep over there. I think I will be happy just to get back to my normal life." He looked around the room and noticed everyone was grinning as if they were the cat that had swallowed the canary.

"Alex, I am not so sure you will be able to do that. There is a pressing matter you need to attend to," President Sullivan said as he gestured to the door. Alex's stomach tightened for just a moment not sure what the pressing matter was.

Turning, Alex saw his wife entering and looking as gorgeous as ever. She was wearing the diamond necklace he had bought for her in Europe. He did not realize how long it had been since he last saw her. He walked over and kissed her.

As their lips parted she said, "The President has something for you, Alex."

Turning, Alex looked at Sullivan who had now returned to his desk and was conversing on the phone. "Yes, we are ready. Alex, would you and Michelle please join me over here?" he said as Sullivan moved to the front of his desk. Alex's face had questions all over it not sure of what was about to transpire.

"Ok, Madame Secretary," he said with a nod.

Stanfield moved to open the door. Alex immediately recognized the individual who entered the Oval Office. It was General Goldman whom Sullivan moved to greet.

"Thank you for coming, General," he said as the two shook hands. "We are honored to have you at the White House. I know your time is limited."

"The honor is mine, Mr. President," Goldman said with a slight bow toward Sullivan. He moved to Alex and embraced him with a hug and a kiss on the neck. "It is good to see you again old friend. This time it is under much happier circumstances."

"Yes, General, it is," Alex said somewhat surprised by the greeting.

"Alex, the General has something for you." President Sullivan indicated toward Goldman.

"Alex, my country and I are forever in your debt. Your actions helped turn the tide of public opinion against the treachery committed by Gerhard and the EU. Further, you alerted us to the possibility of an attack allowing us to have some of our forces on alert. Their availability during those first days of the war may have been what saved Israel. For this, my people are grateful to you. In a small token of our appreciation, I am awarding you the *Ot ha'araha*, the Chief of Staff Medal of Appreciation." Goldman opened the case he was holding revealing the medal. The right side of the case held the medal itself. It consisted of a round silver medal attached to a white ribbon with two blue stripes on the edges. The medal was stamped with the Star of David and had an olive branch and a sword rest on its left.

"This award is presented as an expression of appreciation for acts of superior importance that contribute directly or indirectly to the strengthening of the IDF, and that significantly benefits the security of Israel. It is the highest award my country can bestow upon a non-Israeli. Alex, on behalf of the people of Israel and our departed friend, Prime Minister Weissman," Goldman concluded as he handed Alex the medal and shook his hand. "He would have wanted you to have this. He liked you, Alex. He said you had chutzpah."

Overcome by the moment, Alex was almost speechless. "I am not quite sure what to say, General. Except that I am honored and humbled at the same time. I know we both wish the Prime Minister were here for this moment."

The others in the room moved to congratulate Alex and meet Goldman. As they were completing the official photos, an Air Force Colonel entered the room and walked to Secretary Clairmont. Clairmont read the note and quickly moved to Sullivan. Sullivan took the note as he slipped on his reading glasses. After reading the note he cleared his throat.

"This is unbelievable. Everyone, your attention please. I hate to break up our celebration, but I am afraid we have pressing matters to attend to. Castro died thirty minutes ago. Venezuelan officials are claiming Cuba as their twenty-fourth state."

All in the room were stunned by the news. Goldman quickly excused himself from the Oval Office to leave his American friends with their work. Sullivan bid Alex and his wife good-bye for the rest of the day.

As the Stantons departed the White House, they walked out into a world where a new world order had been established. One foe in the Middle East had been vanquished. But a potential one had arisen in Europe and another was on the horizon to the South.